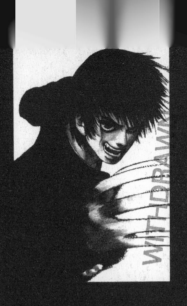

プロジェクトアームズ

PROJECT ARMS

The First Revelation: The Awakening

vol. 1

Project Arms
The First Revelation: The Awakening
vol. 1
Action Edition

This graphic novel contains PROJECT ARMS monthly
comics #1 through #5 in their entirety.

Created by Ryoji Minagawa and Kyoichi Nanatsuki

English Adaptation/Lance Caselman
Translator/Katy Bridges
Touch-up & Lettering/Bill Schuch
Cover and Graphics Design/Sean Lee
Editor/Andy Nakatani

Production Manager/ Nobi Watanabe
Managing Editor/Annette Roman
Editor in Chief/William Flanagan
Director of Licensing and Acquisitions/Rika Inouye
Vice President of Sales & Marketing/Liza Coppola
Sr. Vice President of Editorial/Hyoe Narita
Publisher/Seiji Horibuchi

Printed in Canada.

Published by VIZ, LLC
P.O. Box 77010
San Francisco, CA 94107

Action Edition
10 9 8 7 6 5 4 3 2

First printing, July 2003
Second printing, September 2003

CONTENTS

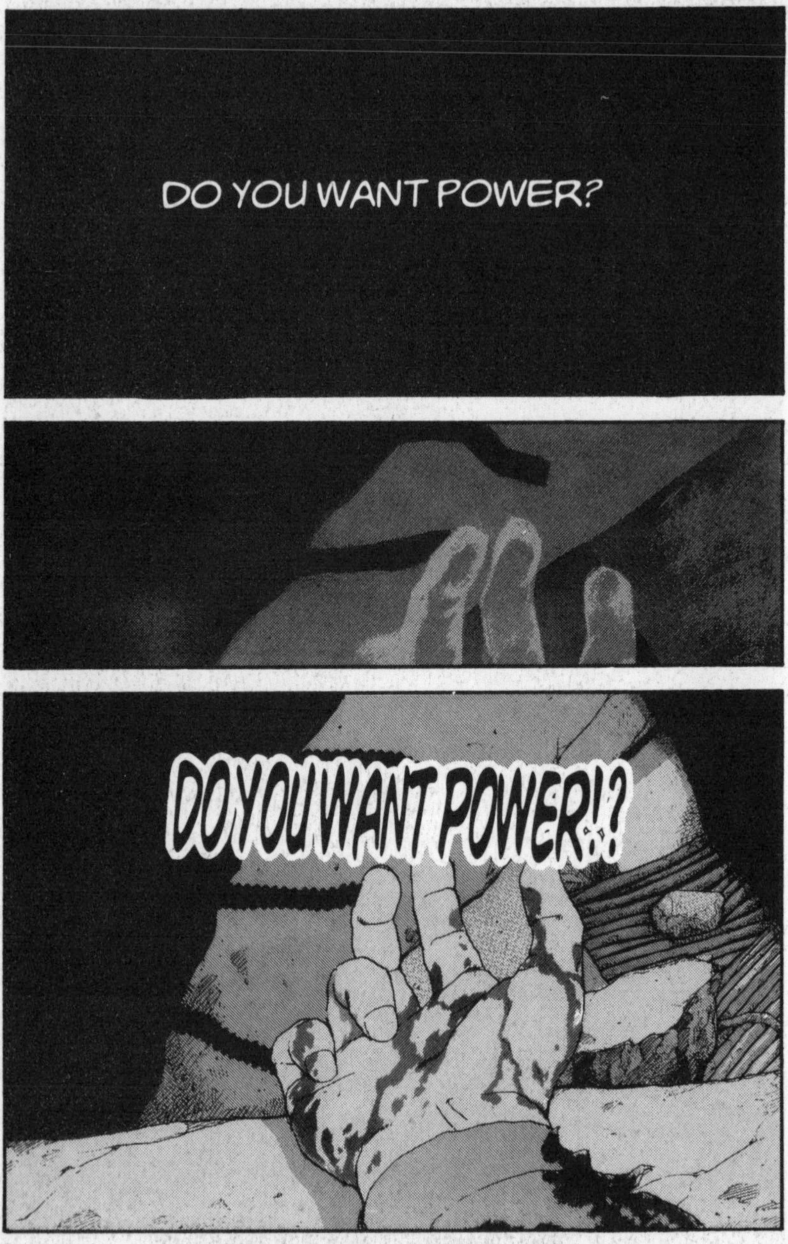
DO YOU WANT POWER?
DO YOU WANT POWER!?

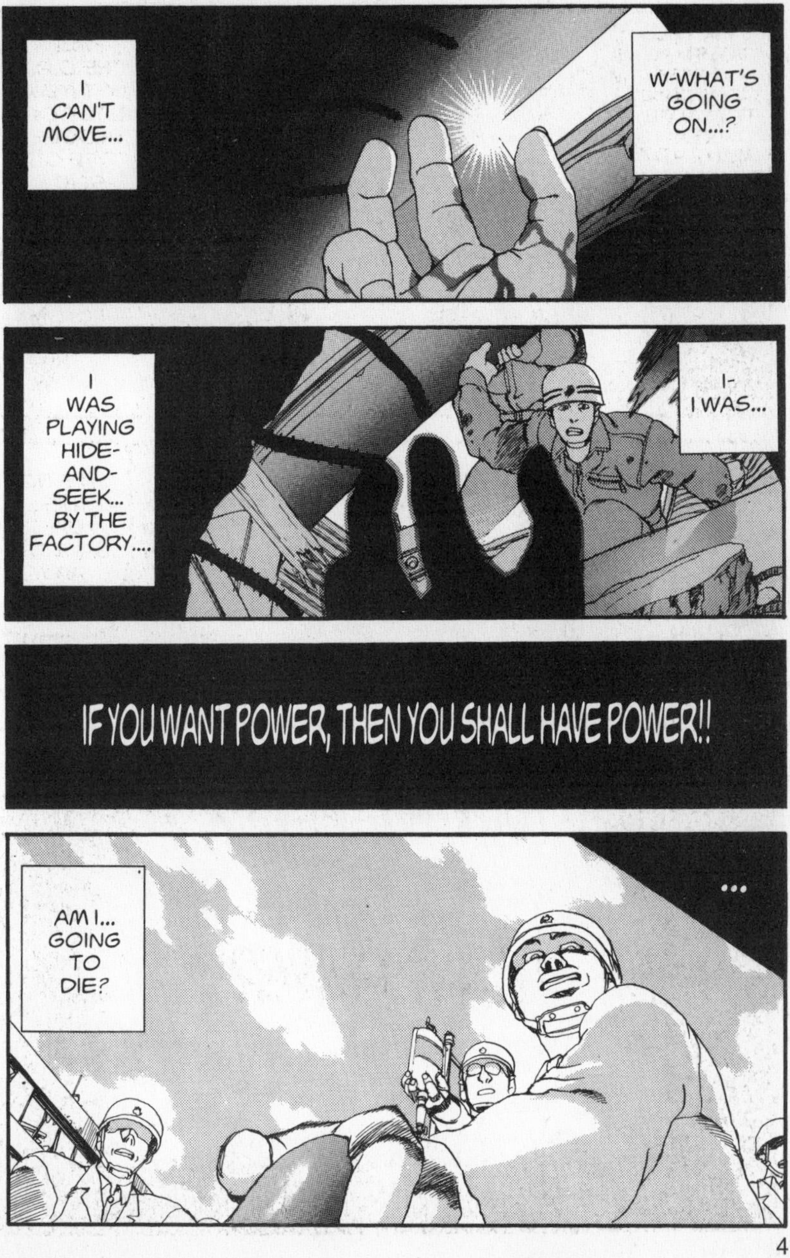
W-WHAT'S GOING ON...?
I CAN'T MOVE...
I- I WAS...
I WAS PLAYING HIDE-AND-SEEK... BY THE FACTORY....
IF YOU WANT POWER, THEN YOU SHALL HAVE POWER!!
...
AM I... GOING TO DIE?

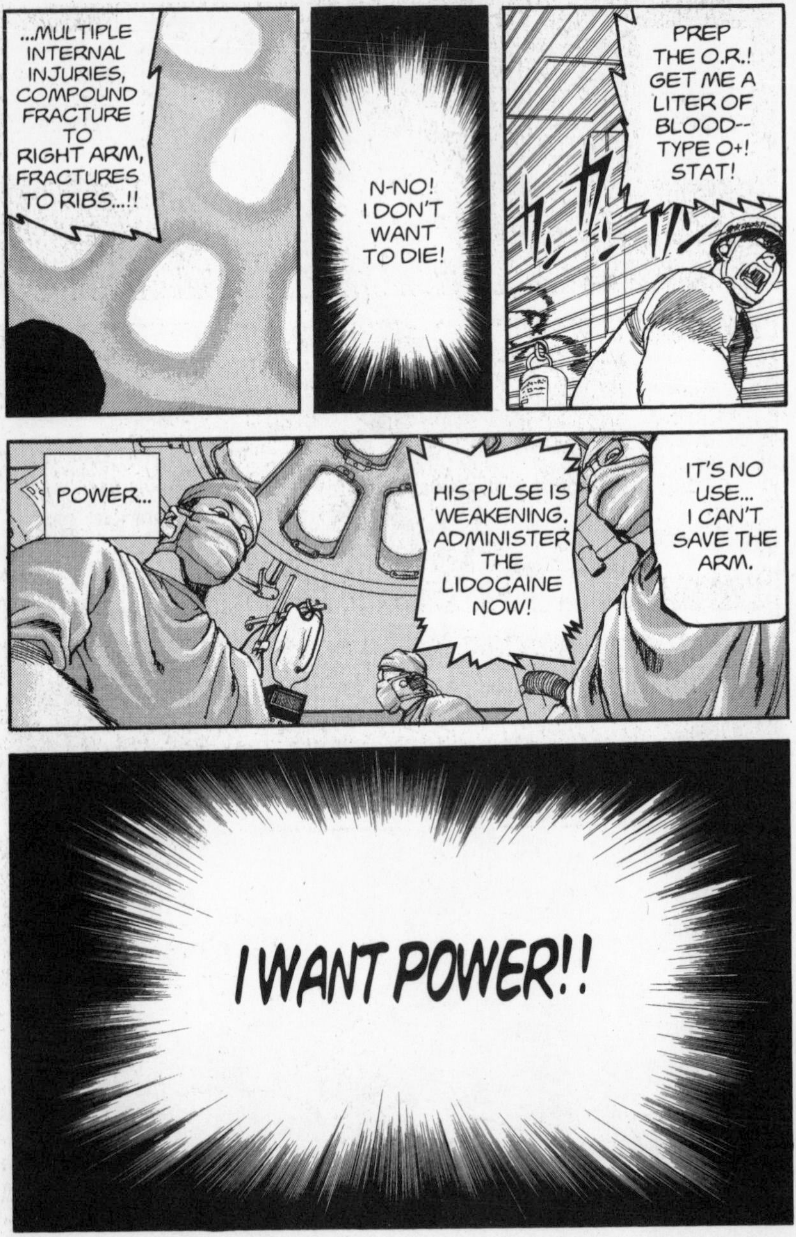
PREP THE O.R.! GET ME A LITER OF BLOOD-- TYPE O+! STAT!
N-NO! I DON'T WANT TO DIE!
...MULTIPLE INTERNAL INJURIES, COMPOUND FRACTURE TO RIGHT ARM, FRACTURES TO RIBS...!!
IT'S NO USE... I CAN'T SAVE THE ARM.
HIS PULSE IS WEAKENING. ADMINISTER THE LIDOCAINE NOW!
POWER...
I WANT POWER!!

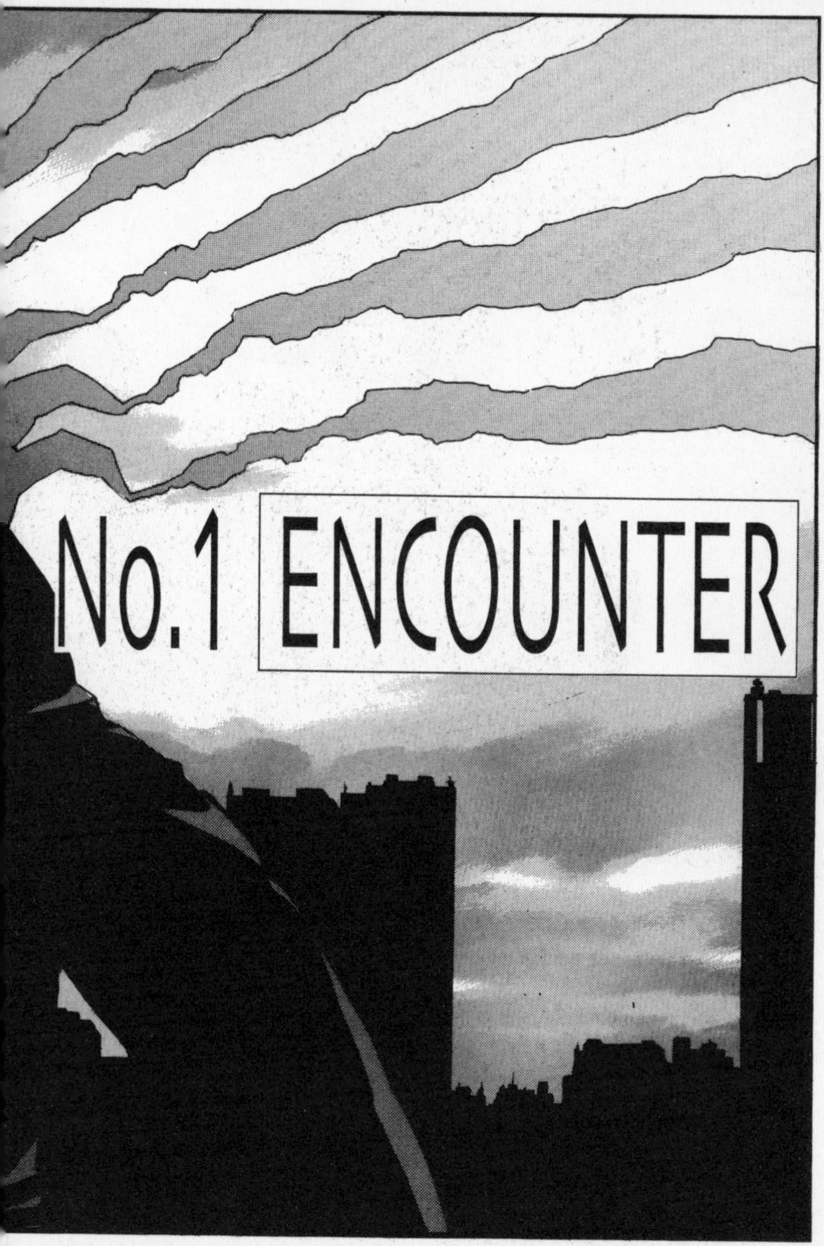
No.1 ENCOUNTER

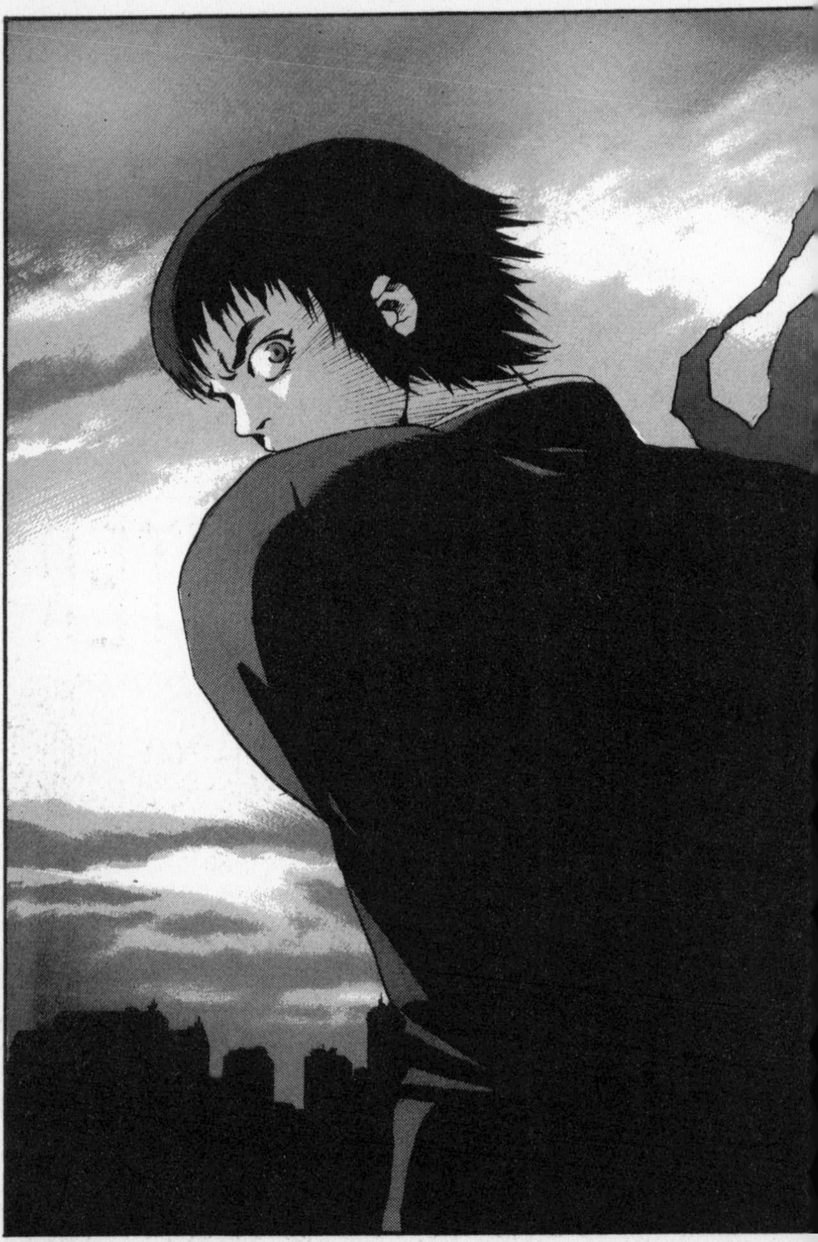

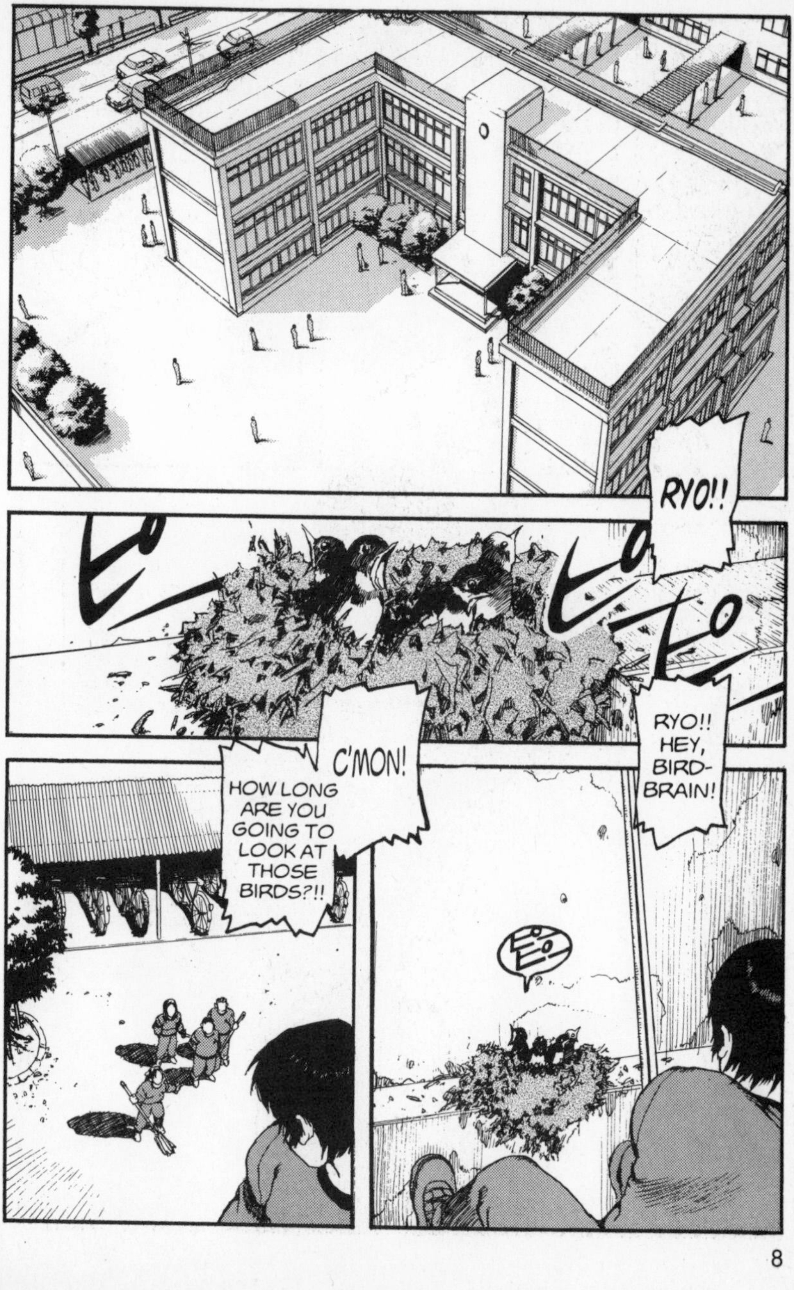
RYO!!
RYO!! HEY, BIRD-BRAIN!
C'MON! HOW LONG ARE YOU GOING TO LOOK AT THOSE BIRDS?!!

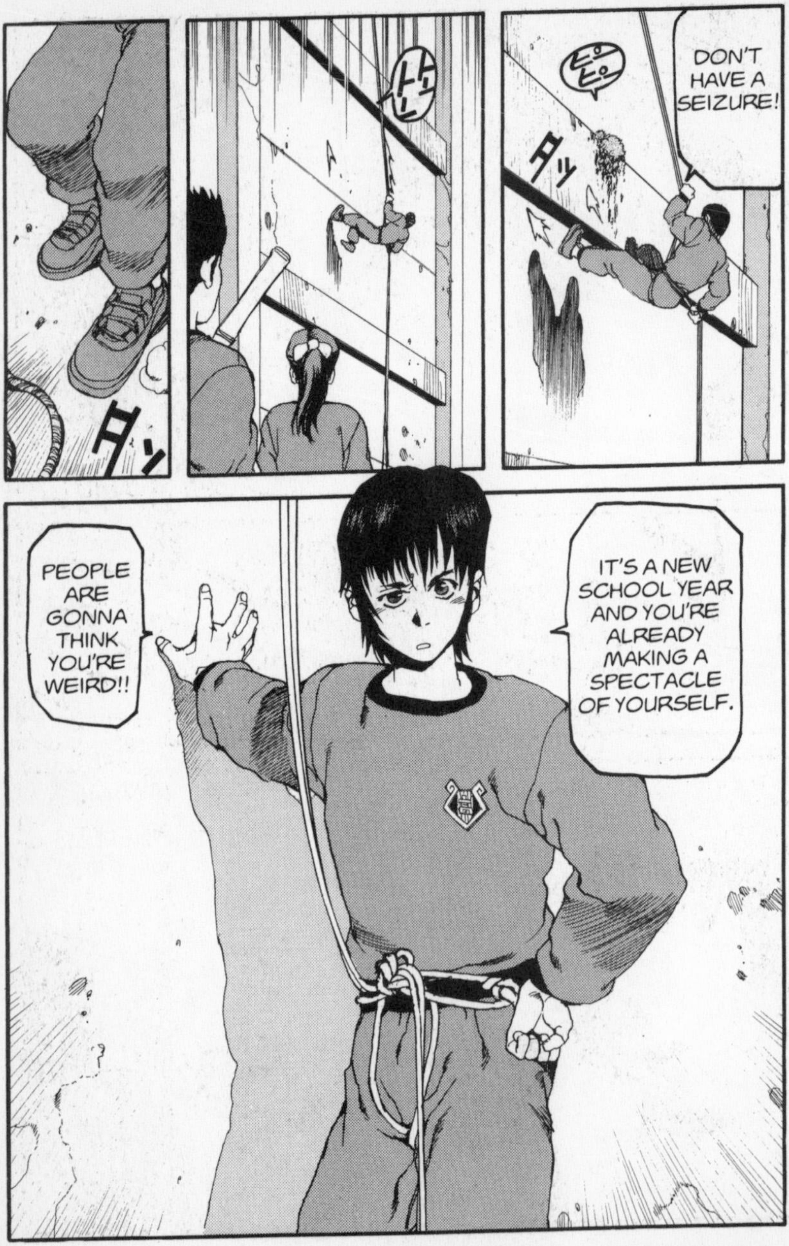
DON'T HAVE A SEIZURE!
ダッ
ダッ
IT'S A NEW SCHOOL YEAR AND YOU'RE ALREADY MAKING A SPECTACLE OF YOURSELF.
PEOPLE ARE GONNA THINK YOU'RE WEIRD!!

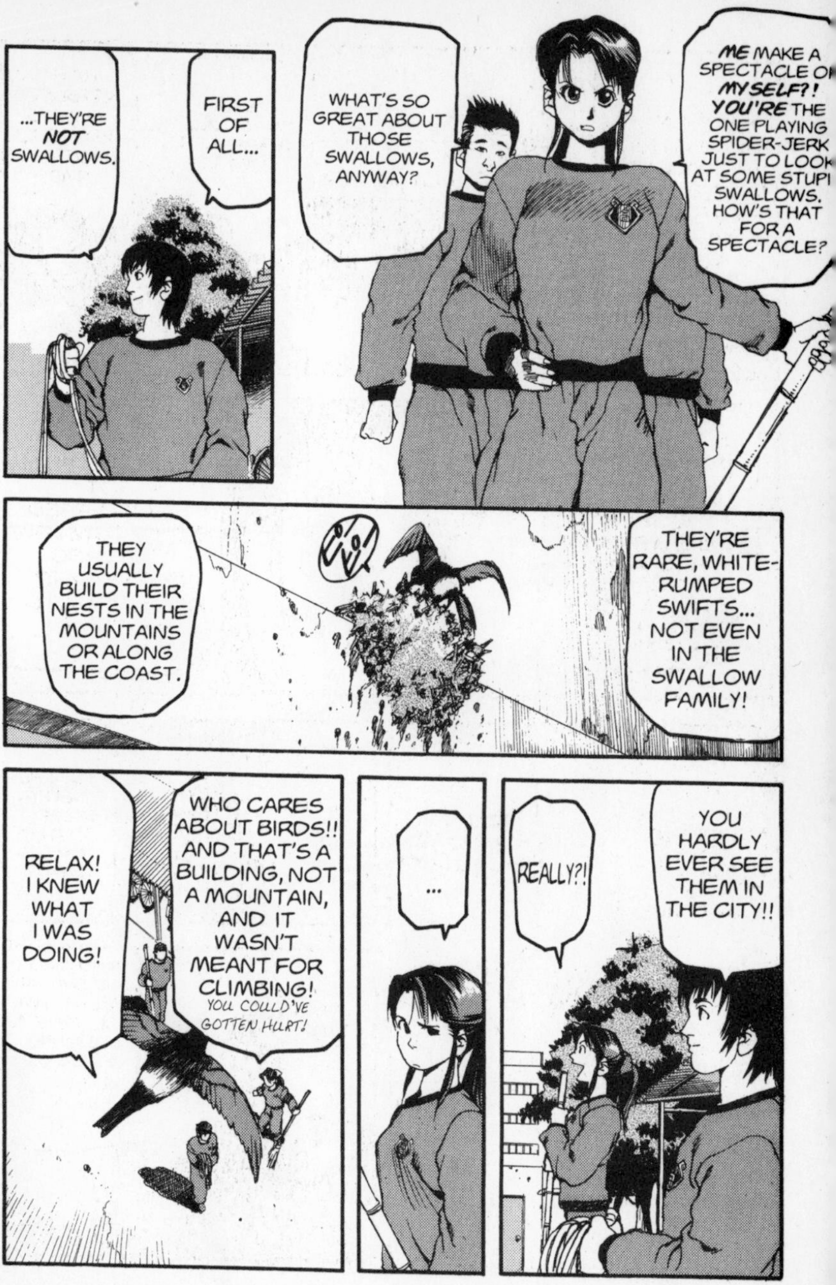
ME MAKE A SPECTACLE O MYSELF?! YOU'RE THE ONE PLAYING SPIDER-JERK JUST TO LOOK AT SOME STUPI SWALLOWS. HOW'S THAT FOR A SPECTACLE?
WHAT'S SO GREAT ABOUT THOSE SWALLOWS, ANYWAY?
FIRST OF ALL...
...THEY'RE NOT SWALLOWS.
THEY'RE RARE, WHITE-RUMPED SWIFTS... NOT EVEN IN THE SWALLOW FAMILY!
THEY USUALLY BUILD THEIR NESTS IN THE MOUNTAINS OR ALONG THE COAST.
YOU HARDLY EVER SEE THEM IN THE CITY!!
REALLY?!
...
WHO CARES ABOUT BIRDS!! AND THAT'S A BUILDING, NOT A MOUNTAIN, AND IT WASN'T MEANT FOR CLIMBING!
YOU COULD'VE GOTTEN HURT!
RELAX! I KNEW WHAT I WAS DOING!

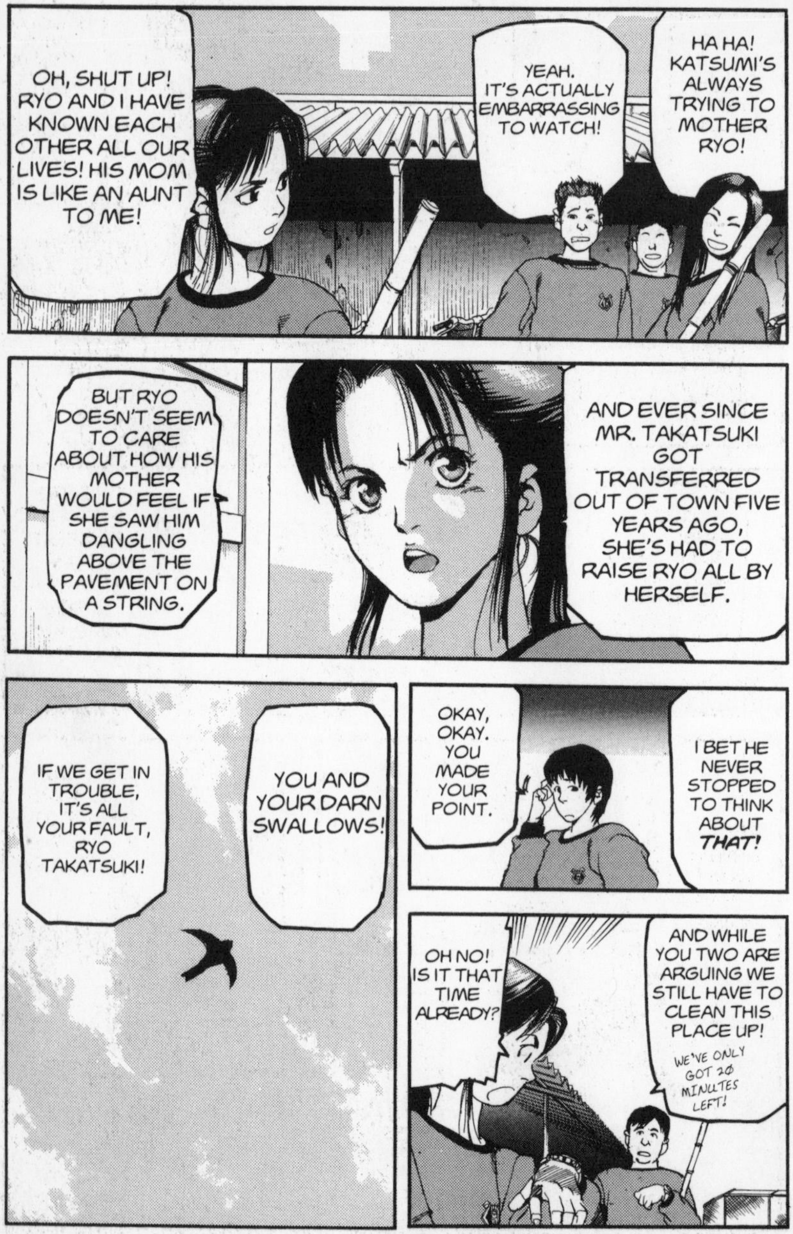
HA HA! KATSUMI'S ALWAYS TRYING TO MOTHER RYO!
YEAH. IT'S ACTUALLY EMBARRASSING TO WATCH!
OH, SHUT UP! RYO AND I HAVE KNOWN EACH OTHER ALL OUR LIVES! HIS MOM IS LIKE AN AUNT TO ME!
AND EVER SINCE MR. TAKATSUKI GOT TRANSFERRED OUT OF TOWN FIVE YEARS AGO, SHE'S HAD TO RAISE RYO ALL BY HERSELF.
BUT RYO DOESN'T SEEM TO CARE ABOUT HOW HIS MOTHER WOULD FEEL IF SHE SAW HIM DANGLING ABOVE THE PAVEMENT ON A STRING.
I BET HE NEVER STOPPED TO THINK ABOUT *THAT!*
OKAY, OKAY. YOU MADE YOUR POINT.
AND WHILE YOU TWO ARE ARGUING WE STILL HAVE TO CLEAN THIS PLACE UP!
WE'VE ONLY GOT 20 MINUTES LEFT!
OH NO! IS IT THAT TIME ALREADY?
YOU AND YOUR DARN SWALLOWS!
IF WE GET IN TROUBLE, IT'S ALL YOUR FAULT, RYO TAKATSUKI!

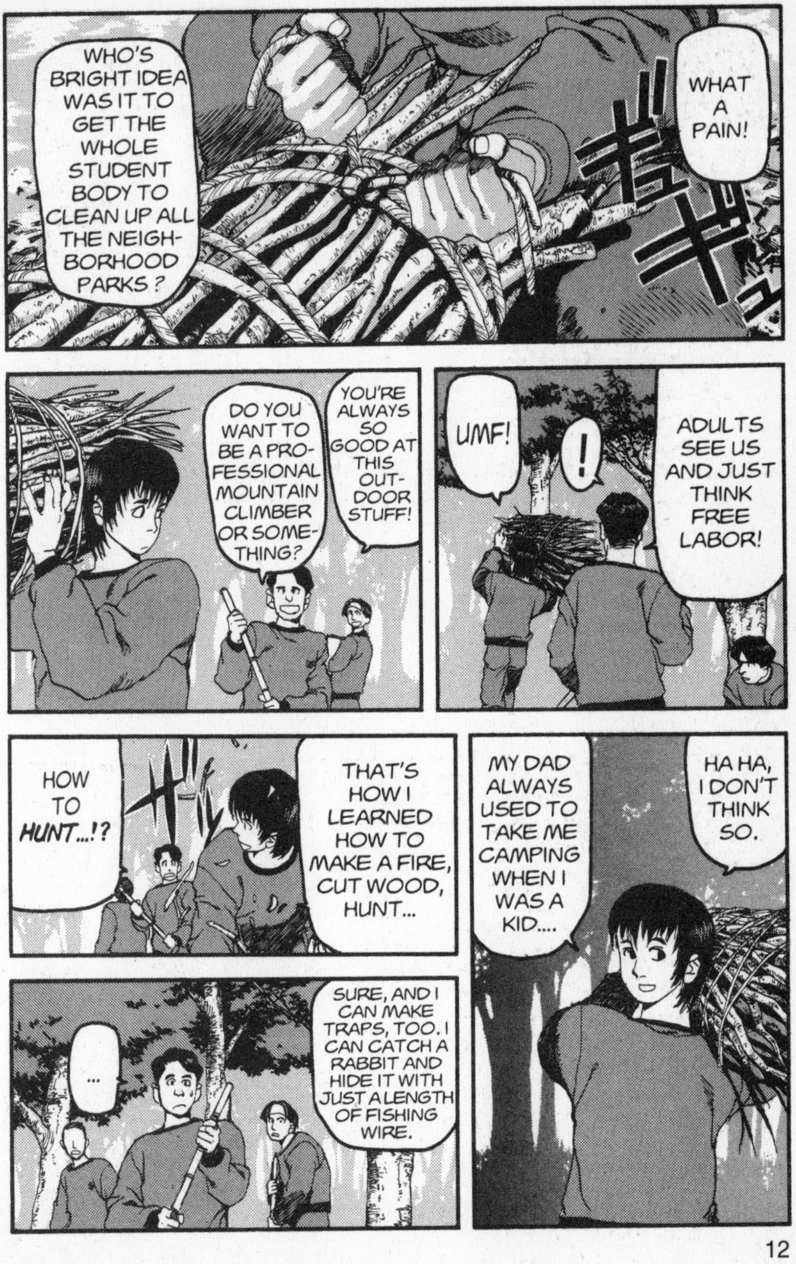
WHAT A PAIN!
WHO'S BRIGHT IDEA WAS IT TO GET THE WHOLE STUDENT BODY TO CLEAN UP ALL THE NEIGHBORHOOD PARKS ?
ADULTS SEE US AND JUST THINK FREE LABOR!
!
UMF!
YOU'RE ALWAYS SO GOOD AT THIS OUTDOOR STUFF!
DO YOU WANT TO BE A PROFESSIONAL MOUNTAIN CLIMBER OR SOMETHING?
HA HA, I DON'T THINK SO.
MY DAD ALWAYS USED TO TAKE ME CAMPING WHEN I WAS A KID....
THAT'S HOW I LEARNED HOW TO MAKE A FIRE, CUT WOOD, HUNT...
HOW TO *HUNT*...!?
SURE, AND I CAN MAKE TRAPS, TOO. I CAN CATCH A RABBIT AND HIDE IT WITH JUST A LENGTH OF FISHING WIRE.
...

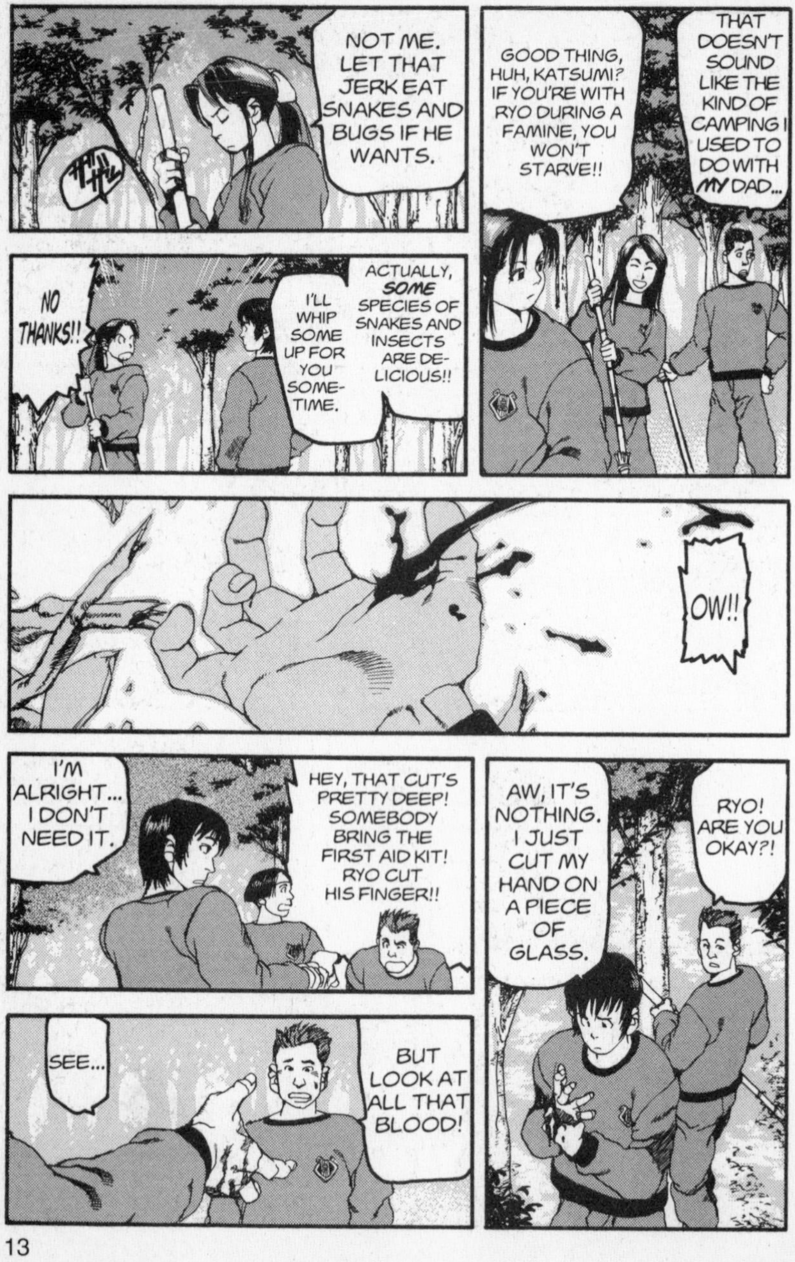
THAT DOESN'T SOUND LIKE THE KIND OF CAMPING I USED TO DO WITH *MY* DAD...
GOOD THING, HUH, KATSUMI? IF YOU'RE WITH RYO DURING A FAMINE, YOU WON'T STARVE!!
NOT ME. LET THAT JERK EAT SNAKES AND BUGS IF HE WANTS.
ACTUALLY, ***SOME*** SPECIES OF SNAKES AND INSECTS ARE DE-LICIOUS!!
I'LL WHIP SOME UP FOR YOU SOME-TIME.
NO THANKS!!
OW!!
RYO! ARE YOU OKAY?!
AW, IT'S NOTHING. I JUST CUT MY HAND ON A PIECE OF GLASS.
HEY, THAT CUT'S PRETTY DEEP! SOMEBODY BRING THE FIRST AID KIT! RYO CUT HIS FINGER!!
I'M ALRIGHT... I DON'T NEED IT.
BUT LOOK AT ALL THAT BLOOD!
SEE...

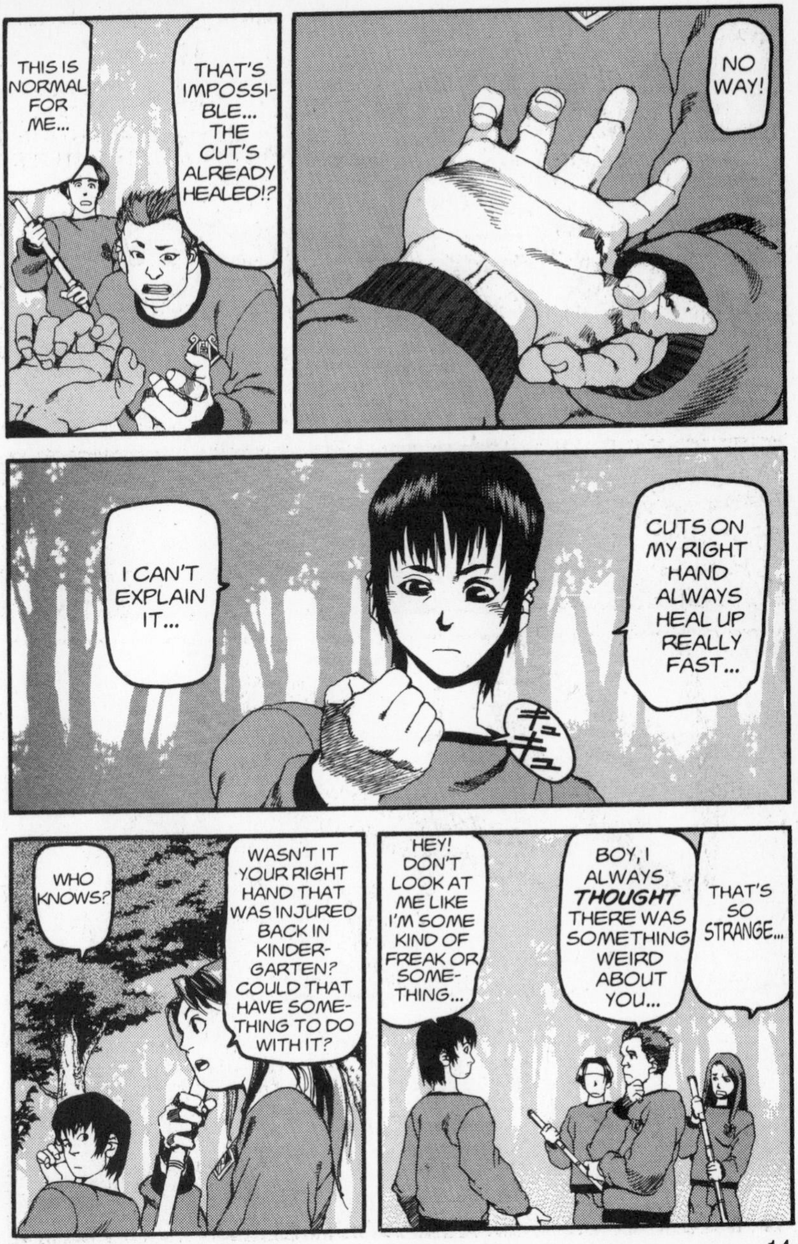
NO WAY!
THAT'S IMPOSSIBLE... THE CUT'S ALREADY HEALED!?
THIS IS NORMAL FOR ME...
CUTS ON MY RIGHT HAND ALWAYS HEAL UP REALLY FAST...
キュ キュ
I CAN'T EXPLAIN IT...
THAT'S SO STRANGE...
BOY, I ALWAYS ***THOUGHT*** THERE WAS SOMETHING WEIRD ABOUT YOU...
HEY! DON'T LOOK AT ME LIKE I'M SOME KIND OF FREAK OR SOMETHING...
WASN'T IT YOUR RIGHT HAND THAT WAS INJURED BACK IN KINDERGARTEN? COULD THAT HAVE SOMETHING TO DO WITH IT?
WHO KNOWS?

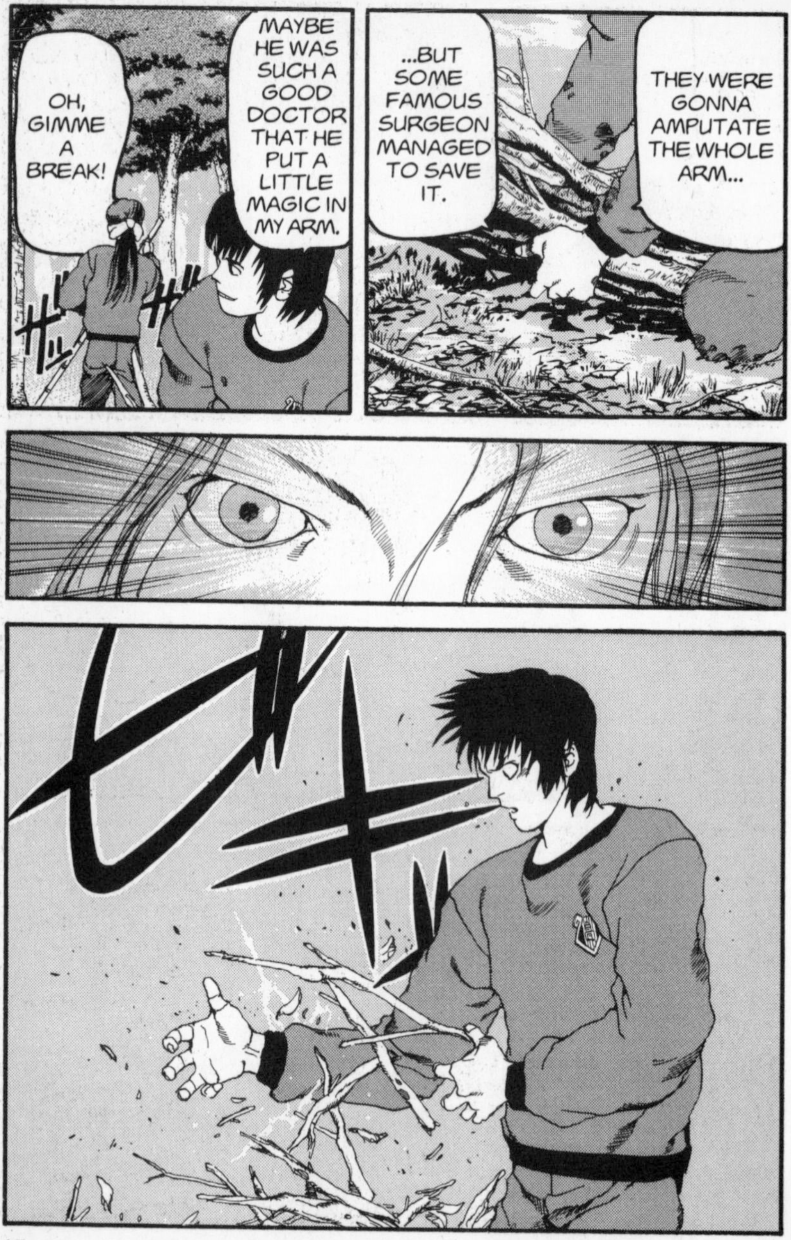
THEY WERE GONNA AMPUTATE THE WHOLE ARM...
...BUT SOME FAMOUS SURGEON MANAGED TO SAVE IT.
MAYBE HE WAS SUCH A GOOD DOCTOR THAT HE PUT A LITTLE MAGIC IN MY ARM.
OH, GIMME A BREAK!

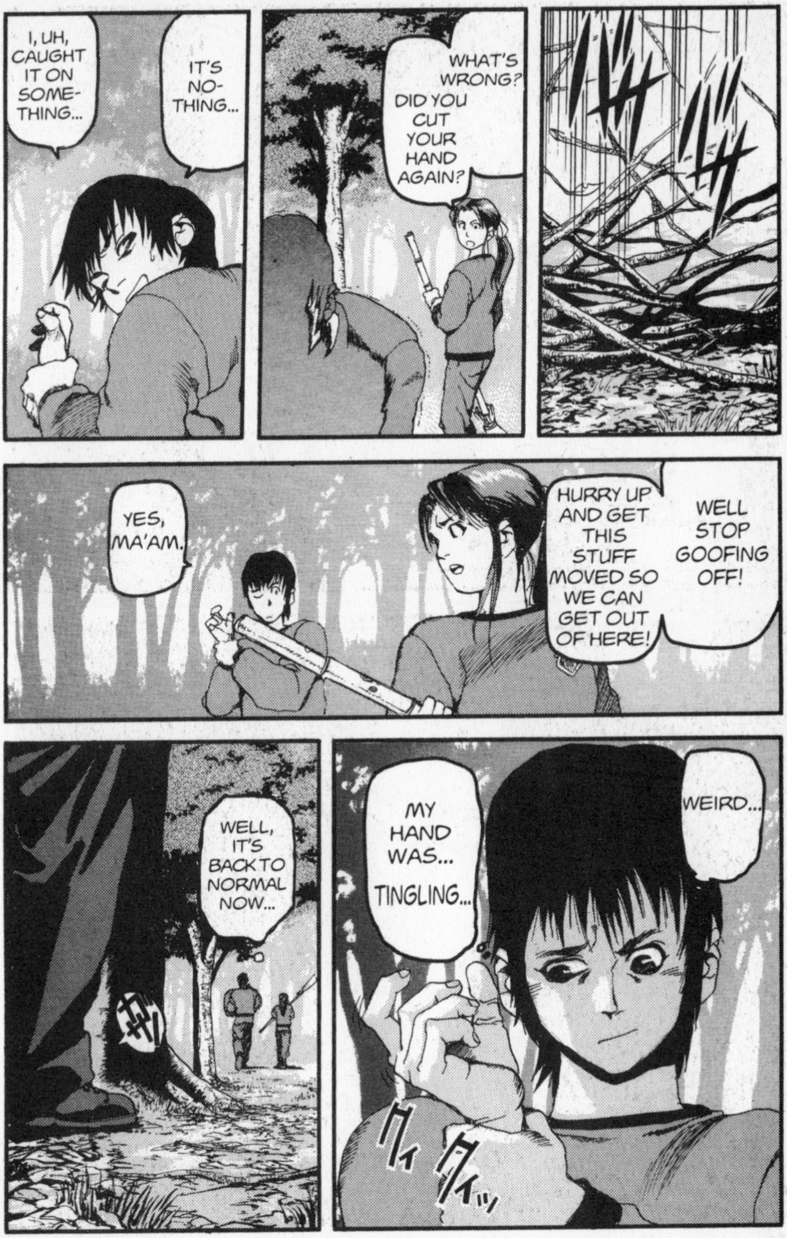
WHAT'S WRONG? DID YOU CUT YOUR HAND AGAIN?
IT'S NO-THING...
I, UH, CAUGHT IT ON SOME-THING...
WELL STOP GOOFING OFF!
HURRY UP AND GET THIS STUFF MOVED SO WE CAN GET OUT OF HERE!
YES, MA'AM.
WEIRD...
MY HAND WAS... TINGLING...
WELL, IT'S BACK TO NORMAL NOW...

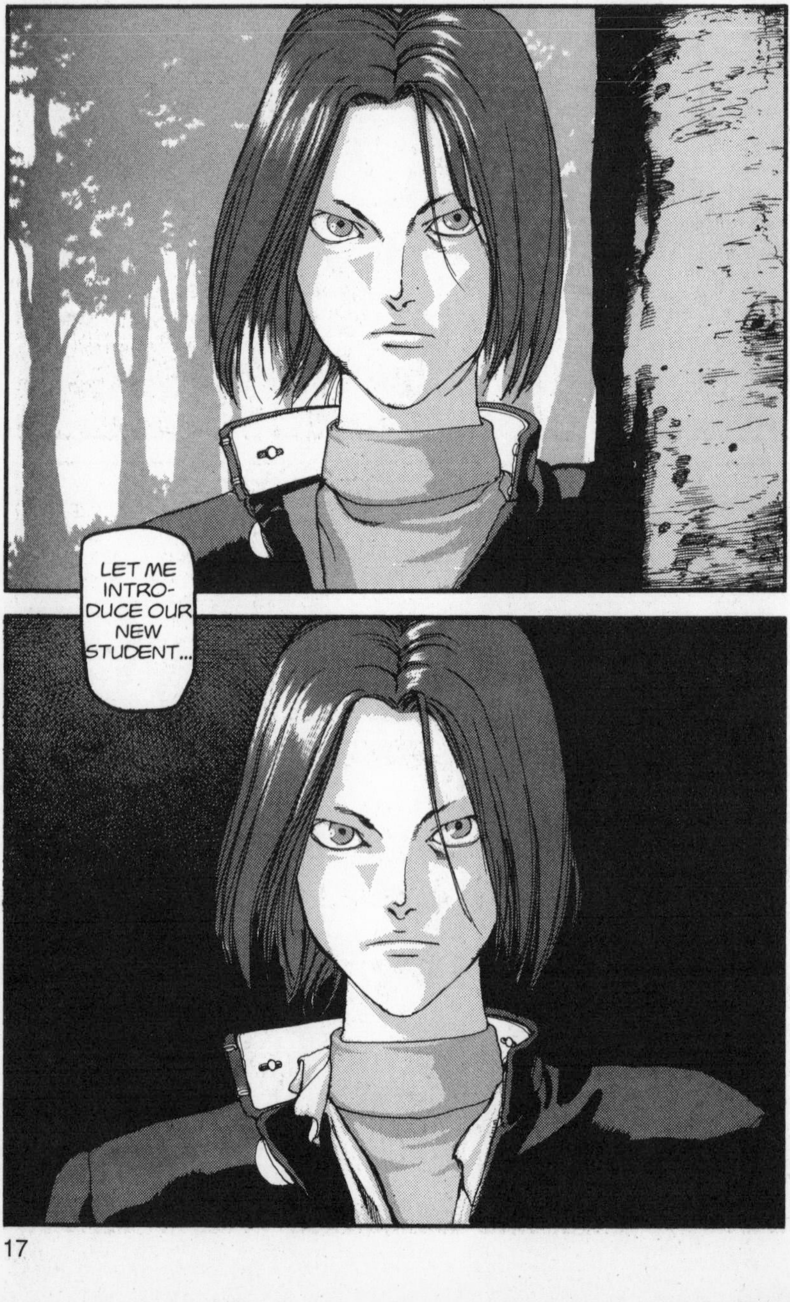
LET ME INTRO-DUCE OUR NEW STUDENT...

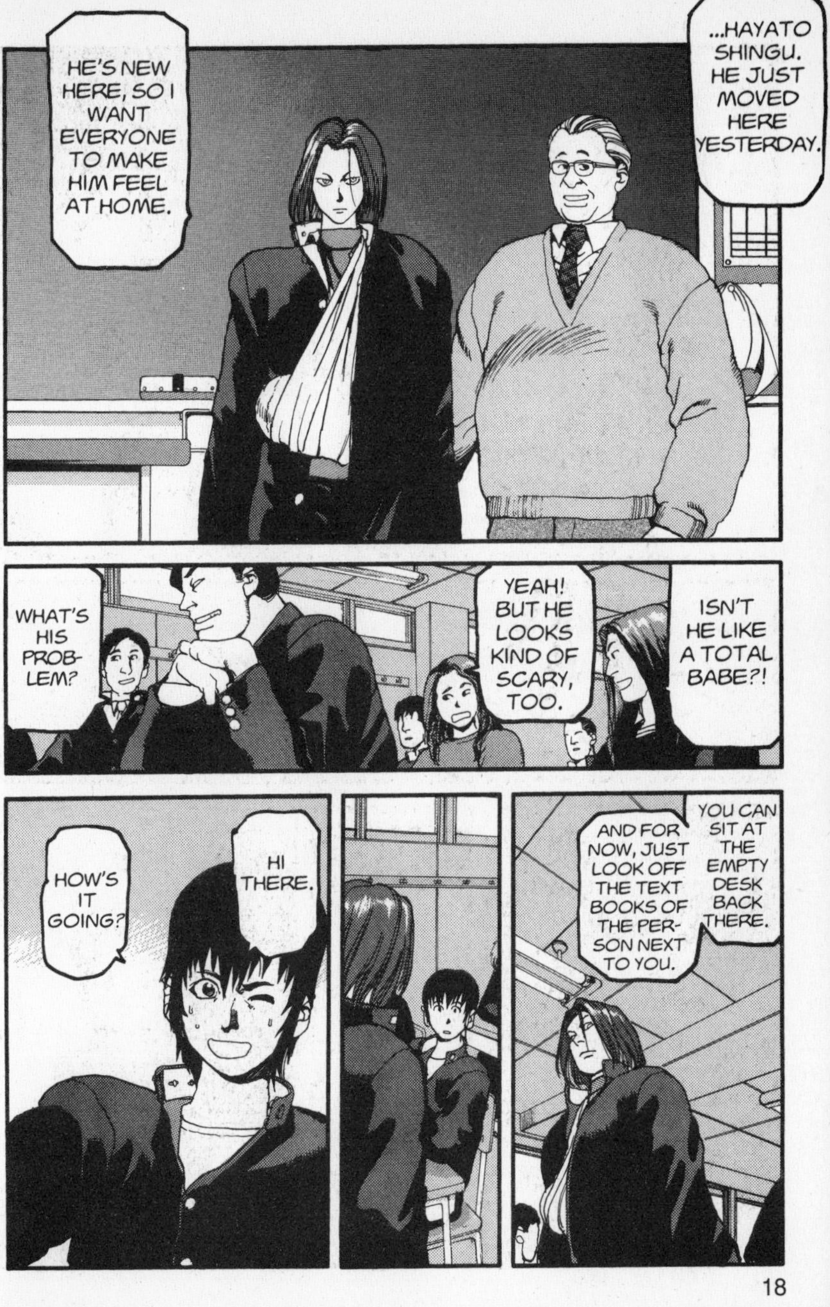
...HAYATO SHINGU. HE JUST MOVED HERE YESTERDAY.
HE'S NEW HERE, SO I WANT EVERYONE TO MAKE HIM FEEL AT HOME.
ISN'T HE LIKE A TOTAL BABE?!
YEAH! BUT HE LOOKS KIND OF SCARY, TOO.
WHAT'S HIS PROB-LEM?
YOU CAN SIT AT THE EMPTY DESK BACK THERE.
AND FOR NOW, JUST LOOK OFF THE TEXT BOOKS OF THE PER-SON NEXT TO YOU.
HI THERE.
HOW'S IT GOING?

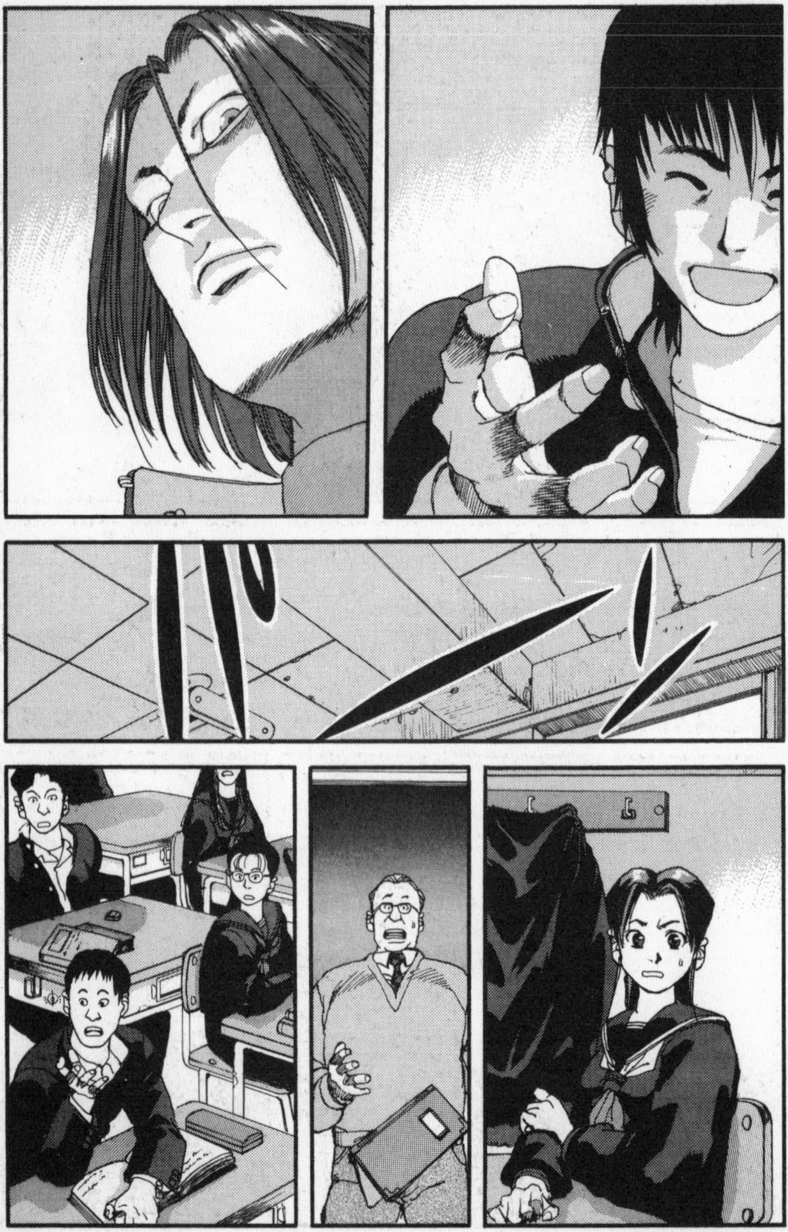

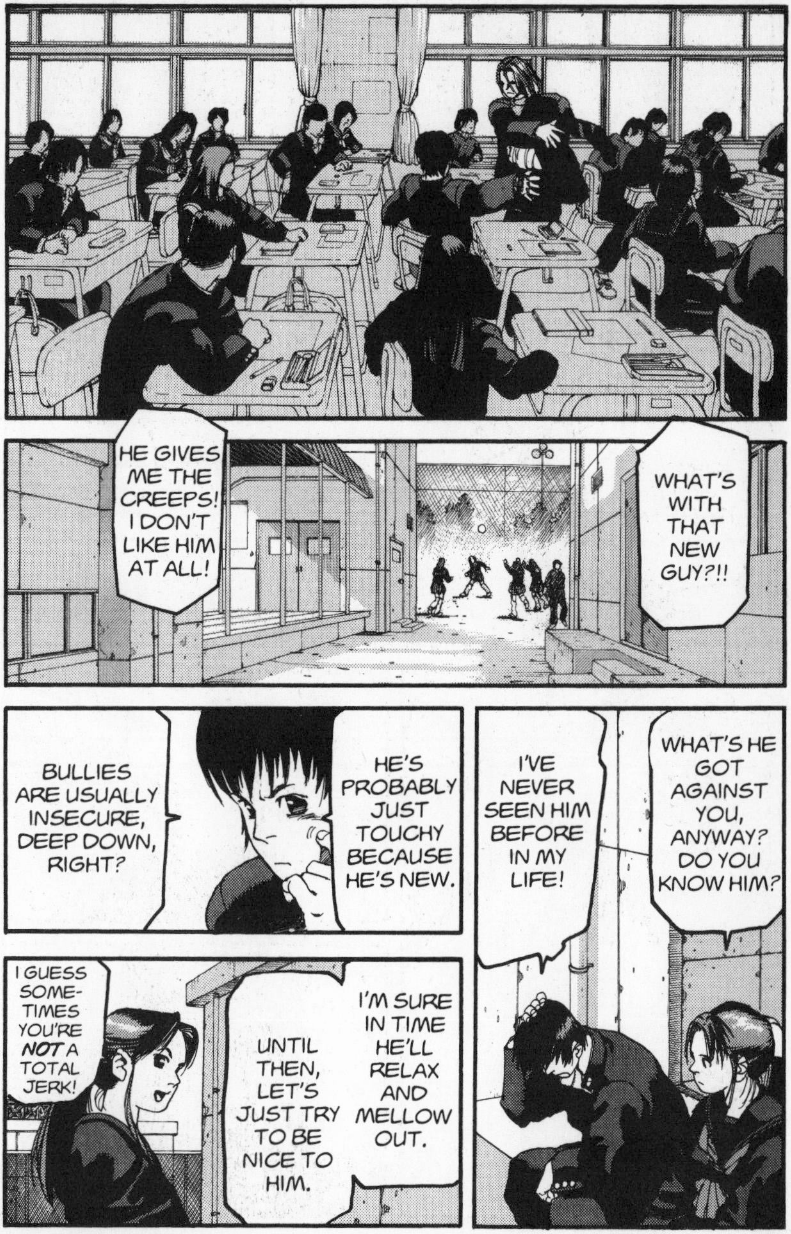
WHAT'S WITH THAT NEW GUY?!!
HE GIVES ME THE CREEPS! I DON'T LIKE HIM AT ALL!
WHAT'S HE GOT AGAINST YOU, ANYWAY? DO YOU KNOW HIM?
I'VE NEVER SEEN HIM BEFORE IN MY LIFE!
HE'S PROBABLY JUST TOUCHY BECAUSE HE'S NEW.
BULLIES ARE USUALLY INSECURE, DEEP DOWN, RIGHT?
I'M SURE IN TIME HE'LL RELAX AND MELLOW OUT.
UNTIL THEN, LET'S JUST TRY TO BE NICE TO HIM.
I GUESS SOME-TIMES YOU'RE ***NOT*** A TOTAL JERK!

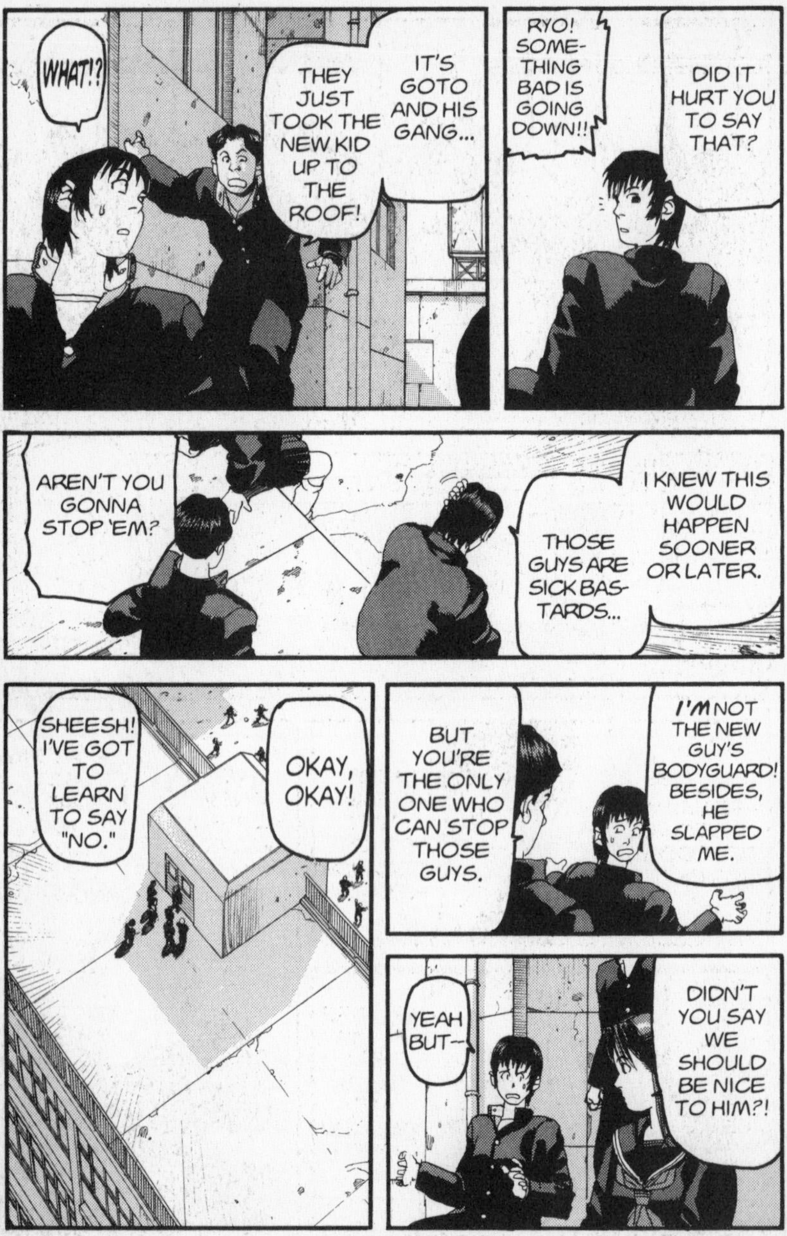
DID IT HURT YOU TO SAY THAT?
RYO! SOME-THING BAD IS GOING DOWN!!
IT'S GOTO AND HIS GANG...
THEY JUST TOOK THE NEW KID UP TO THE ROOF!
WHAT!?
I KNEW THIS WOULD HAPPEN SOONER OR LATER.
THOSE GUYS ARE SICK BAS-TARDS...
AREN'T YOU GONNA STOP 'EM?
I'M NOT THE NEW GUY'S BODYGUARD! BESIDES, HE SLAPPED ME.
BUT YOU'RE THE ONLY ONE WHO CAN STOP THOSE GUYS.
DIDN'T YOU SAY WE SHOULD BE NICE TO HIM?!
YEAH BUT--
OKAY, OKAY!
SHEESH! I'VE GOT TO LEARN TO SAY "NO."

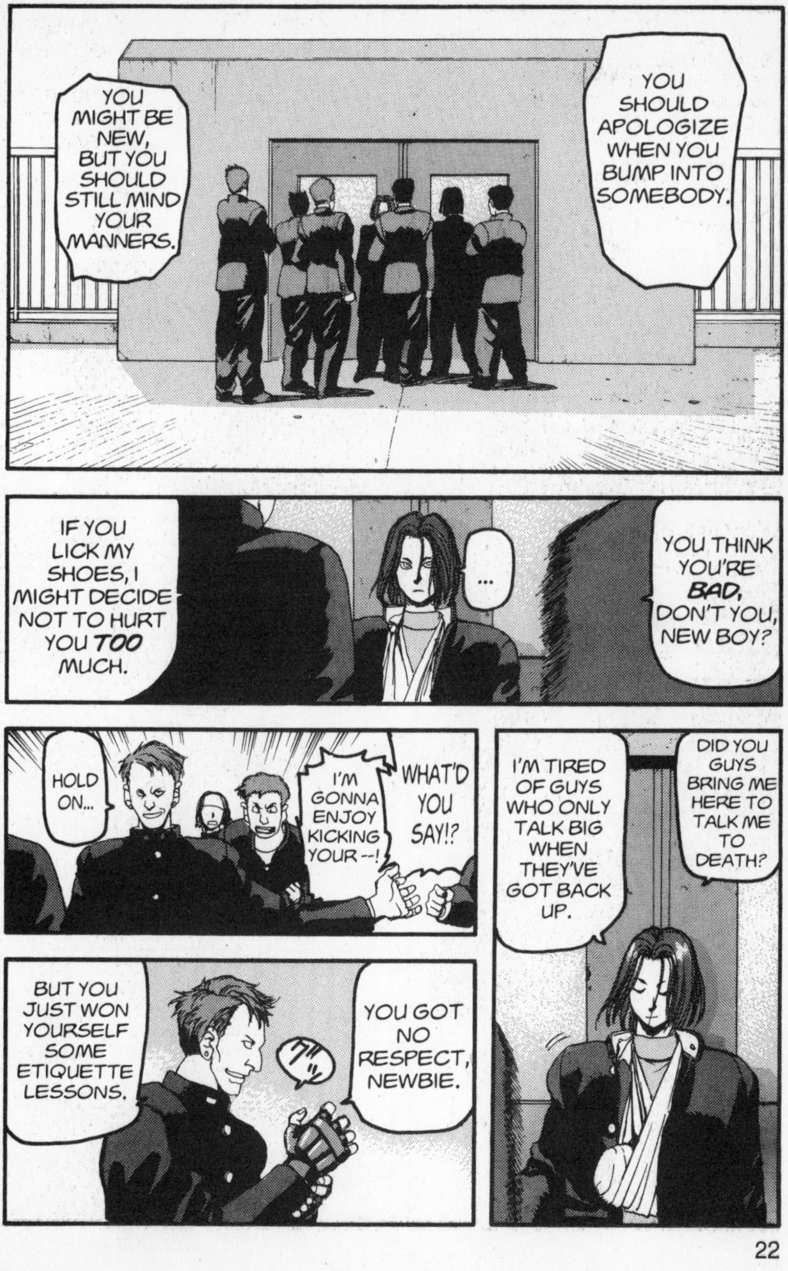
YOU SHOULD APOLOGIZE WHEN YOU BUMP INTO SOMEBODY.
YOU MIGHT BE NEW, BUT YOU SHOULD STILL MIND YOUR MANNERS.
YOU THINK YOU'RE *BAD,* DON'T YOU, NEW BOY?
...
IF YOU LICK MY SHOES, I MIGHT DECIDE NOT TO HURT YOU *TOO* MUCH.
DID YOU GUYS BRING ME HERE TO TALK ME TO DEATH?
I'M TIRED OF GUYS WHO ONLY TALK BIG WHEN THEY'VE GOT BACK UP.
WHAT'D YOU SAY!?
I'M GONNA ENJOY KICKING YOUR --!
HOLD ON...
YOU GOT NO RESPECT, NEWBIE.
BUT YOU JUST WON YOURSELF SOME ETIQUETTE LESSONS.

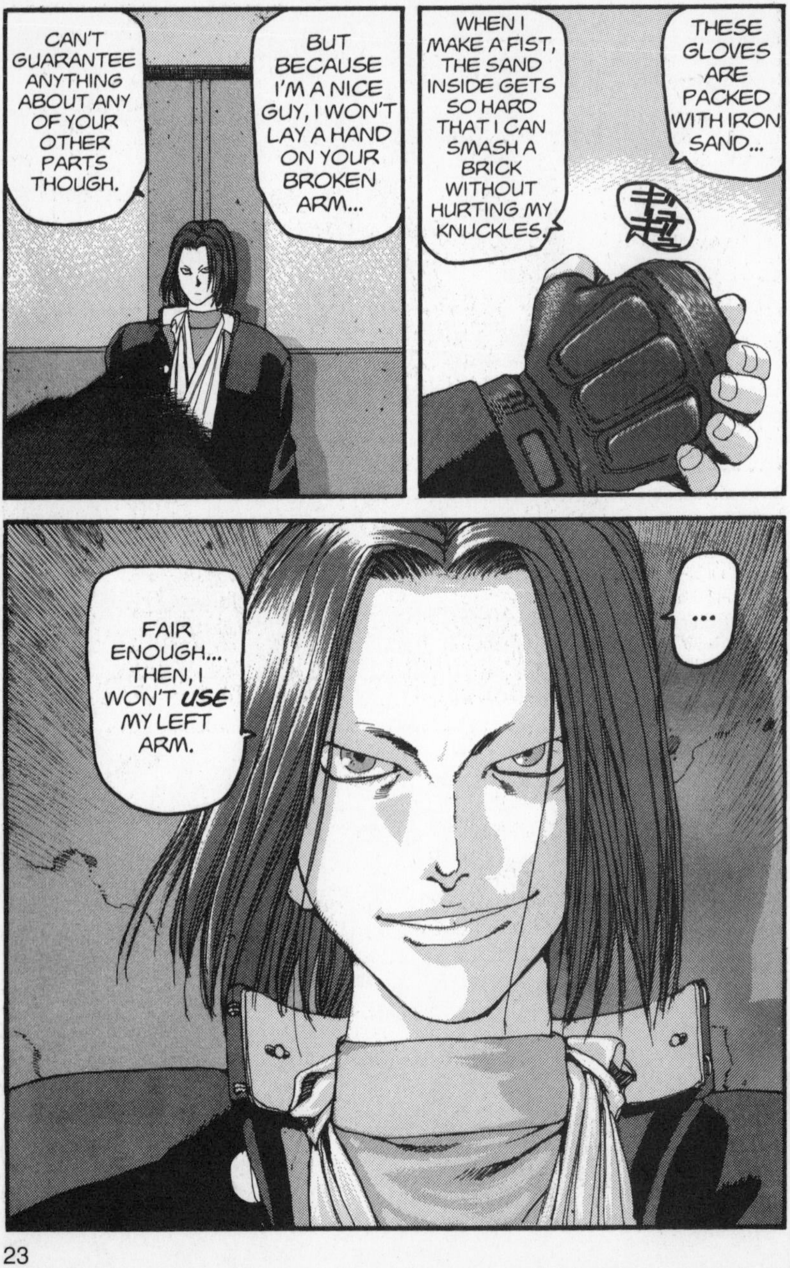
THESE GLOVES ARE PACKED WITH IRON SAND...
WHEN I MAKE A FIST, THE SAND INSIDE GETS SO HARD THAT I CAN SMASH A BRICK WITHOUT HURTING MY KNUCKLES.
BUT BECAUSE I'M A NICE GUY, I WON'T LAY A HAND ON YOUR BROKEN ARM...
CAN'T GUARANTEE ANYTHING ABOUT ANY OF YOUR OTHER PARTS THOUGH.
...
FAIR ENOUGH... THEN, I WON'T *USE* MY LEFT ARM.

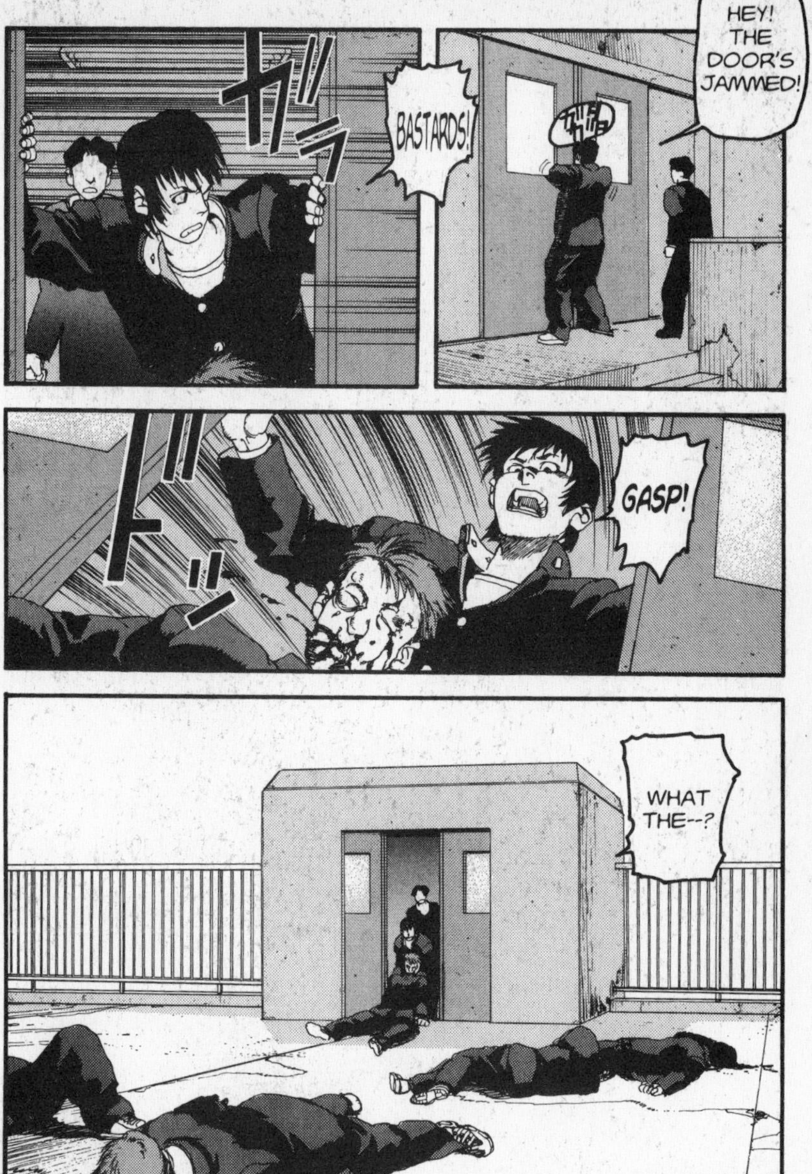
HEY! THE DOOR'S JAMMED!
BASTARDS!
GASP!
WHAT THE--?

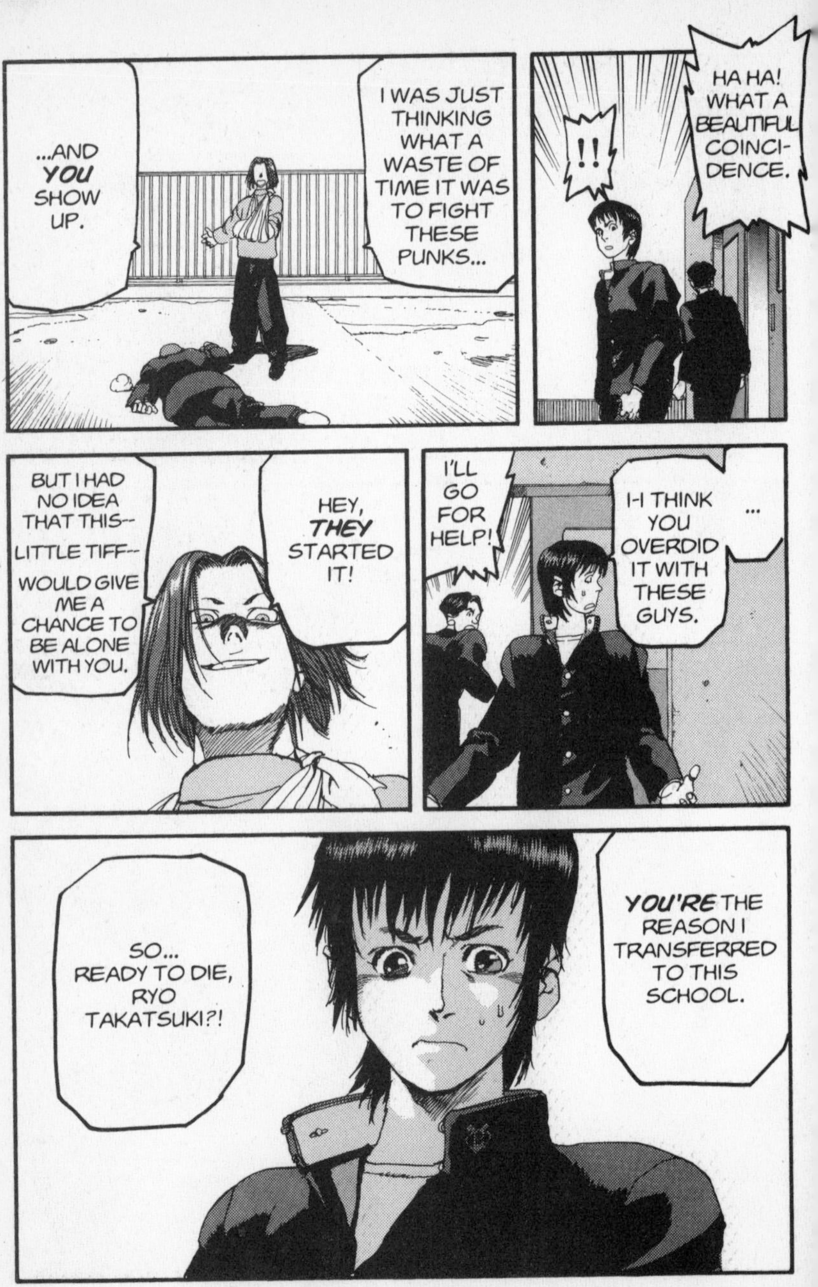
HA HA! WHAT A BEAUTIFUL COINCIDENCE.
!!
I WAS JUST THINKING WHAT A WASTE OF TIME IT WAS TO FIGHT THESE PUNKS...
...AND YOU SHOW UP.
...
I-I THINK YOU OVERDID IT WITH THESE GUYS.
I'LL GO FOR HELP!
HEY, THEY STARTED IT!
BUT I HAD NO IDEA THAT THIS-- LITTLE TIFF-- WOULD GIVE ME A CHANCE TO BE ALONE WITH YOU.
YOU'RE THE REASON I TRANSFERRED TO THIS SCHOOL.
SO... READY TO DIE, RYO TAKATSUKI?!

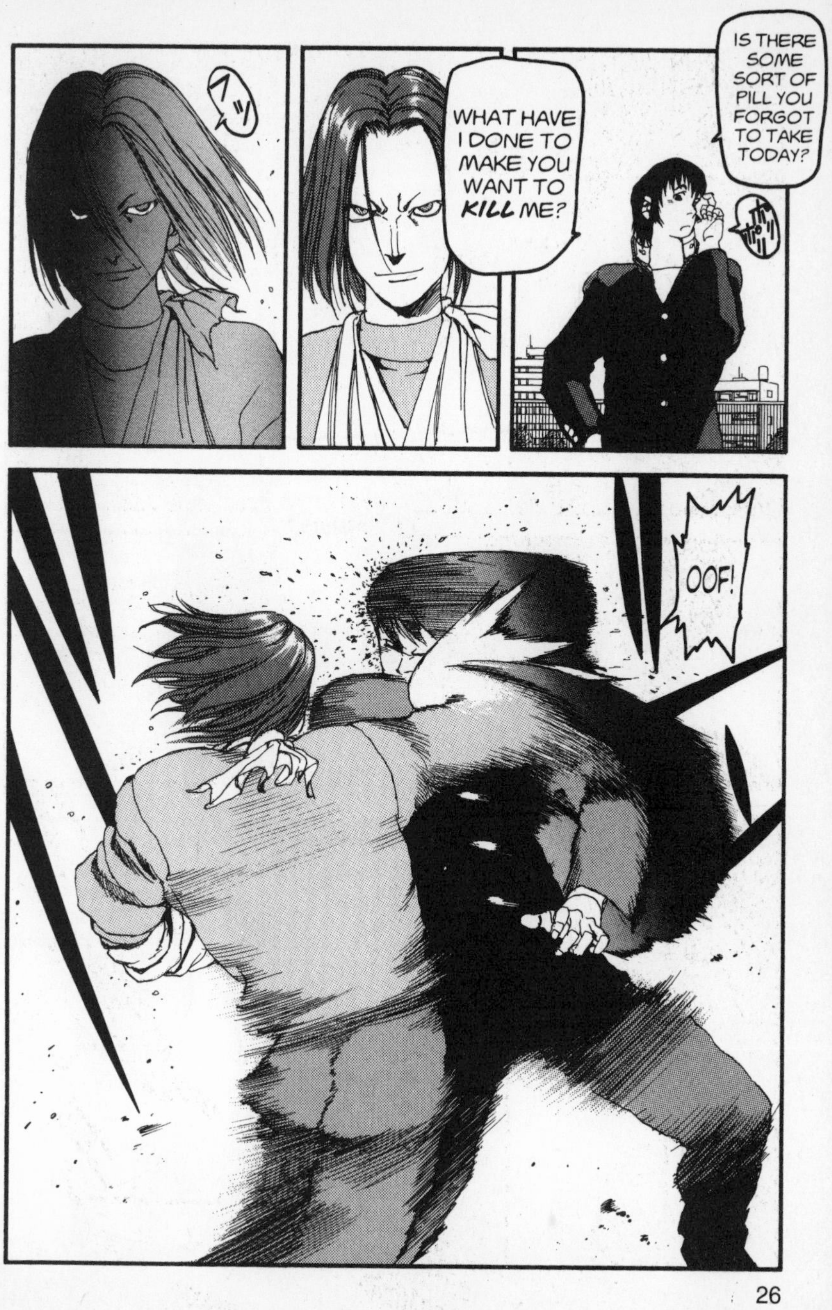
IS THERE SOME SORT OF PILL YOU FORGOT TO TAKE TODAY?
WHAT HAVE I DONE TO MAKE YOU WANT TO **KILL** ME?
フッ
OOF!

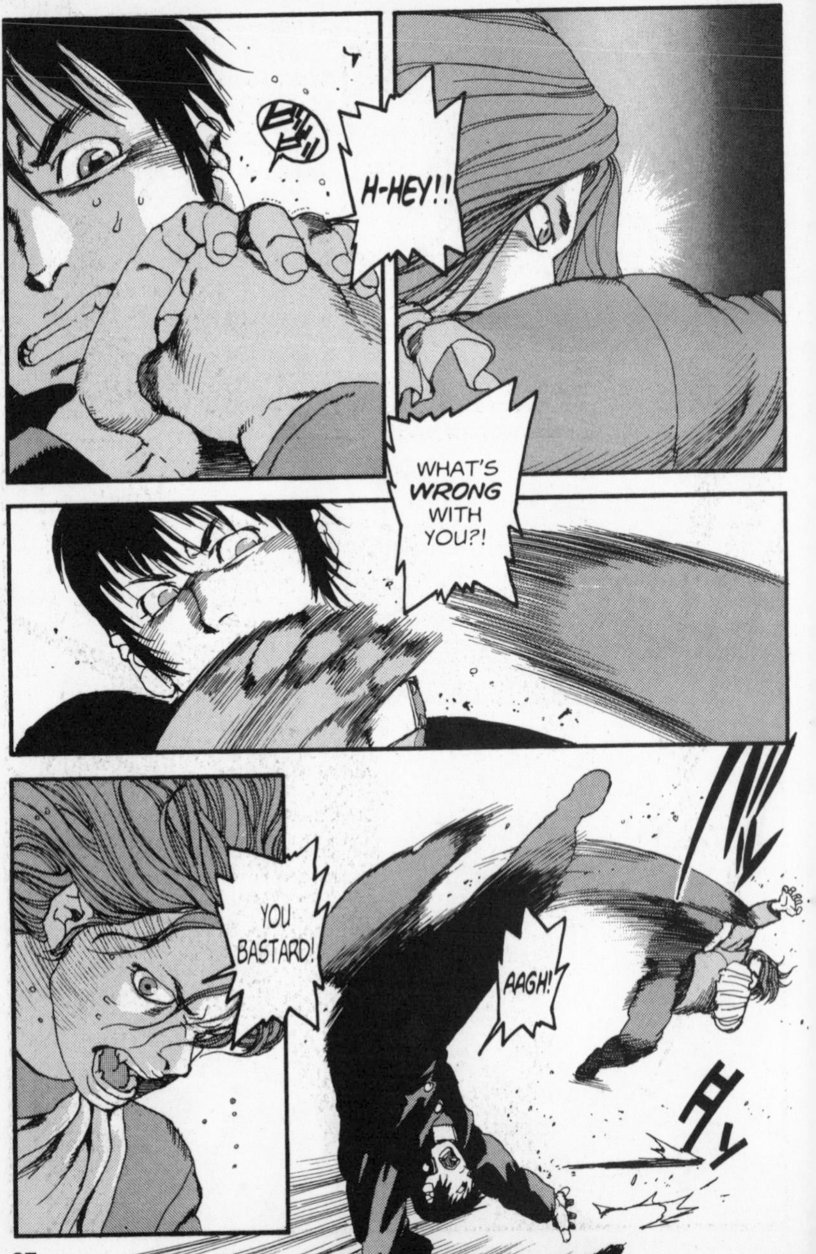
H-HEY!!
WHAT'S **WRONG** WITH YOU?!
AAGH!
YOU BASTARD!

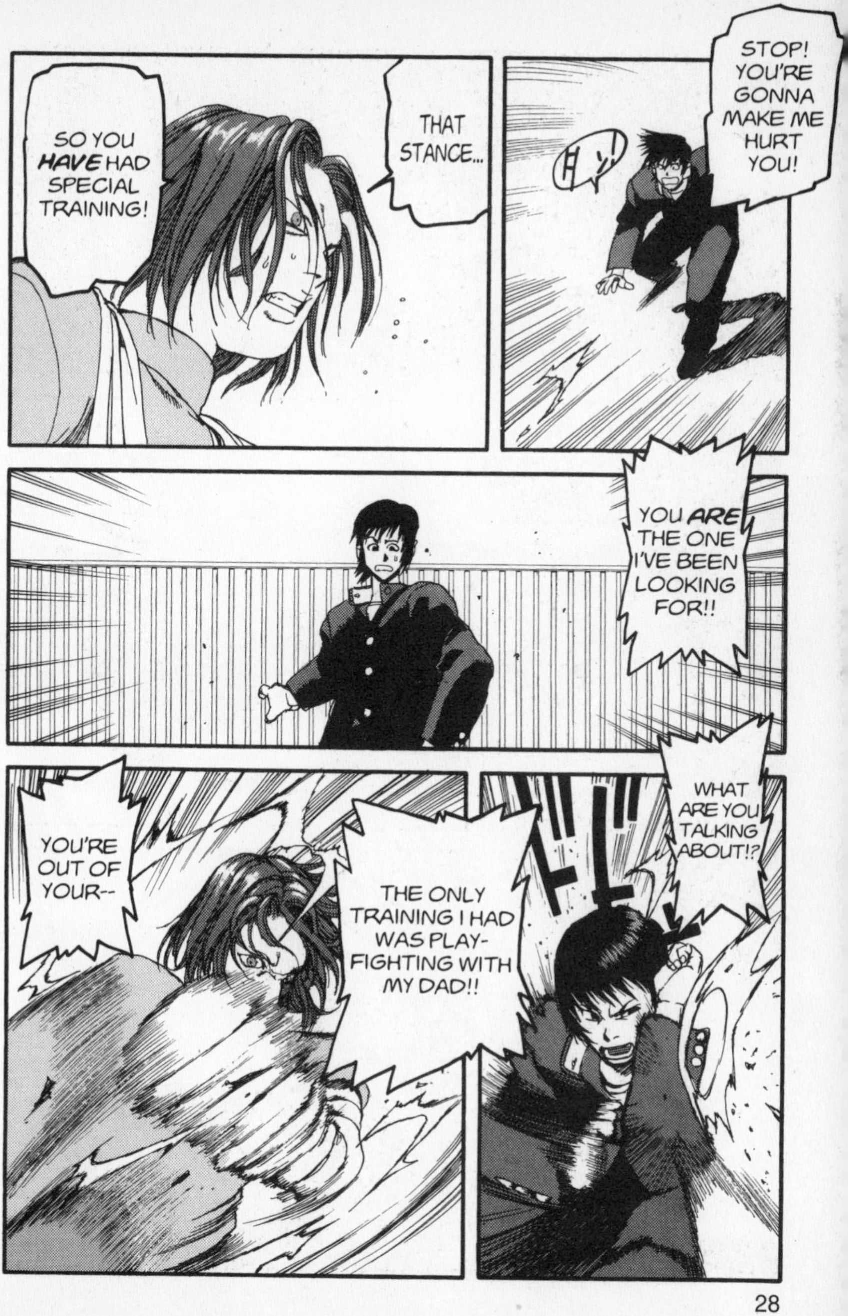
STOP! YOU'RE GONNA MAKE ME HURT YOU!
THAT STANCE...
SO YOU **HAVE** HAD SPECIAL TRAINING!
YOU **ARE** THE ONE I'VE BEEN LOOKING FOR!!
WHAT ARE YOU TALKING ABOUT!?
THE ONLY TRAINING I HAD WAS PLAY-FIGHTING WITH MY DAD!!
YOU'RE OUT OF YOUR--

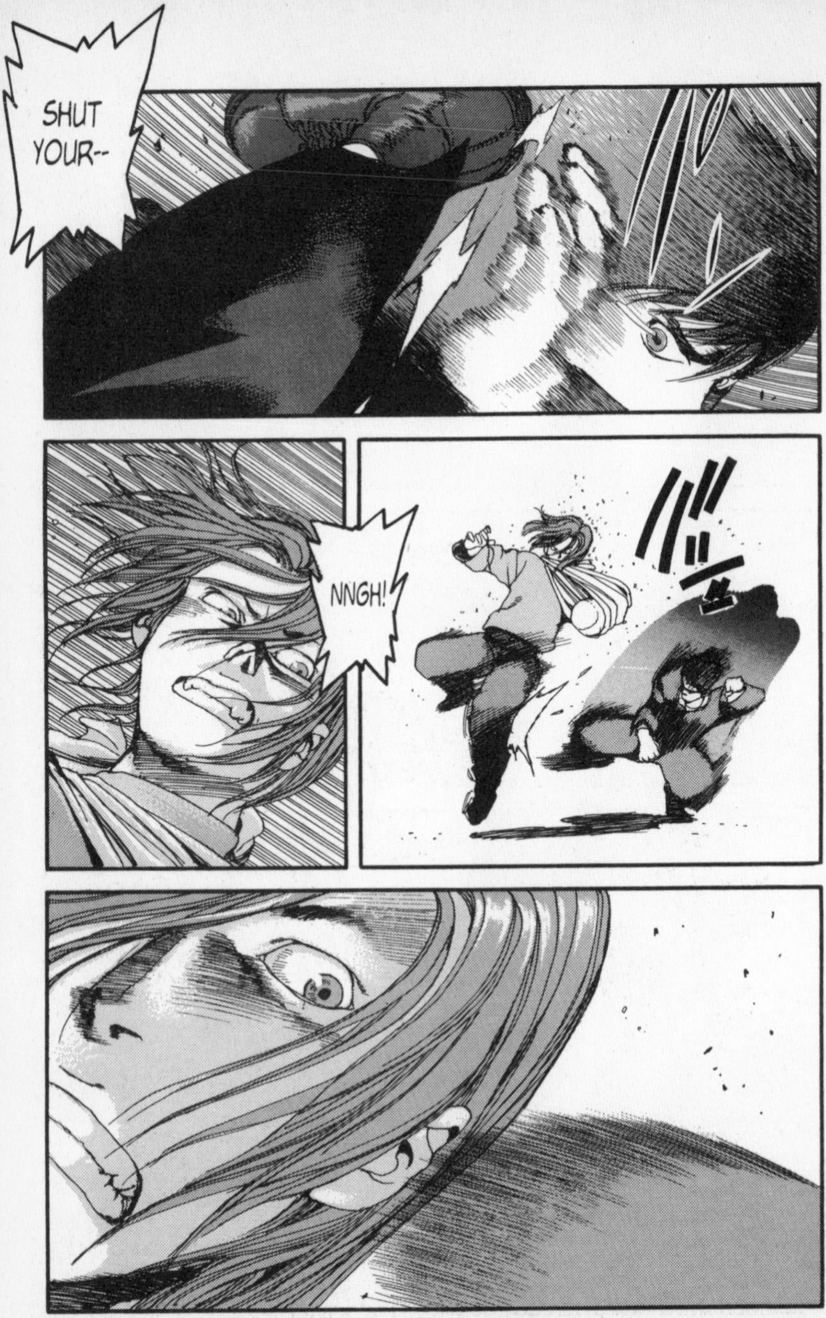
SHUT YOUR--
NNGH!

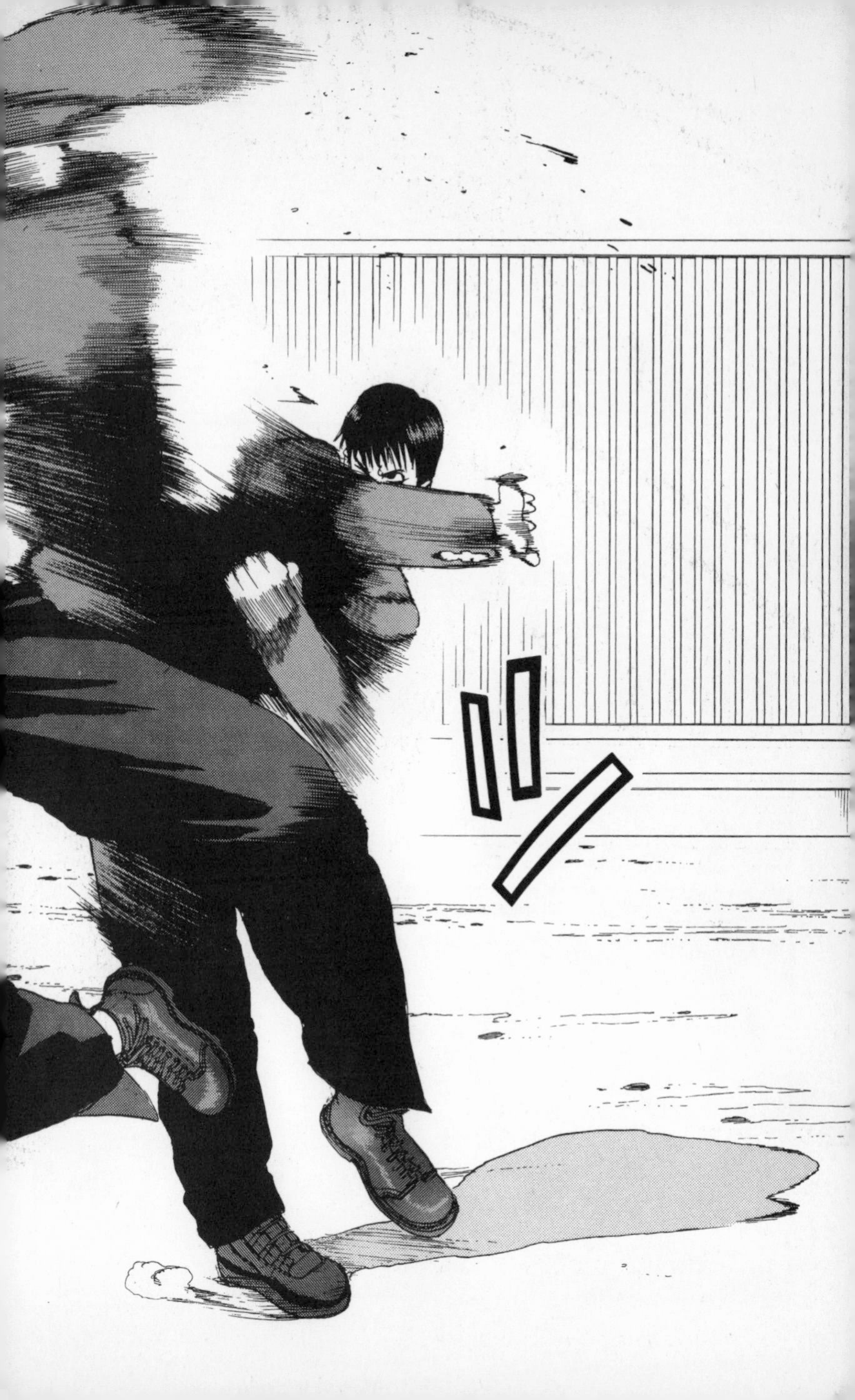

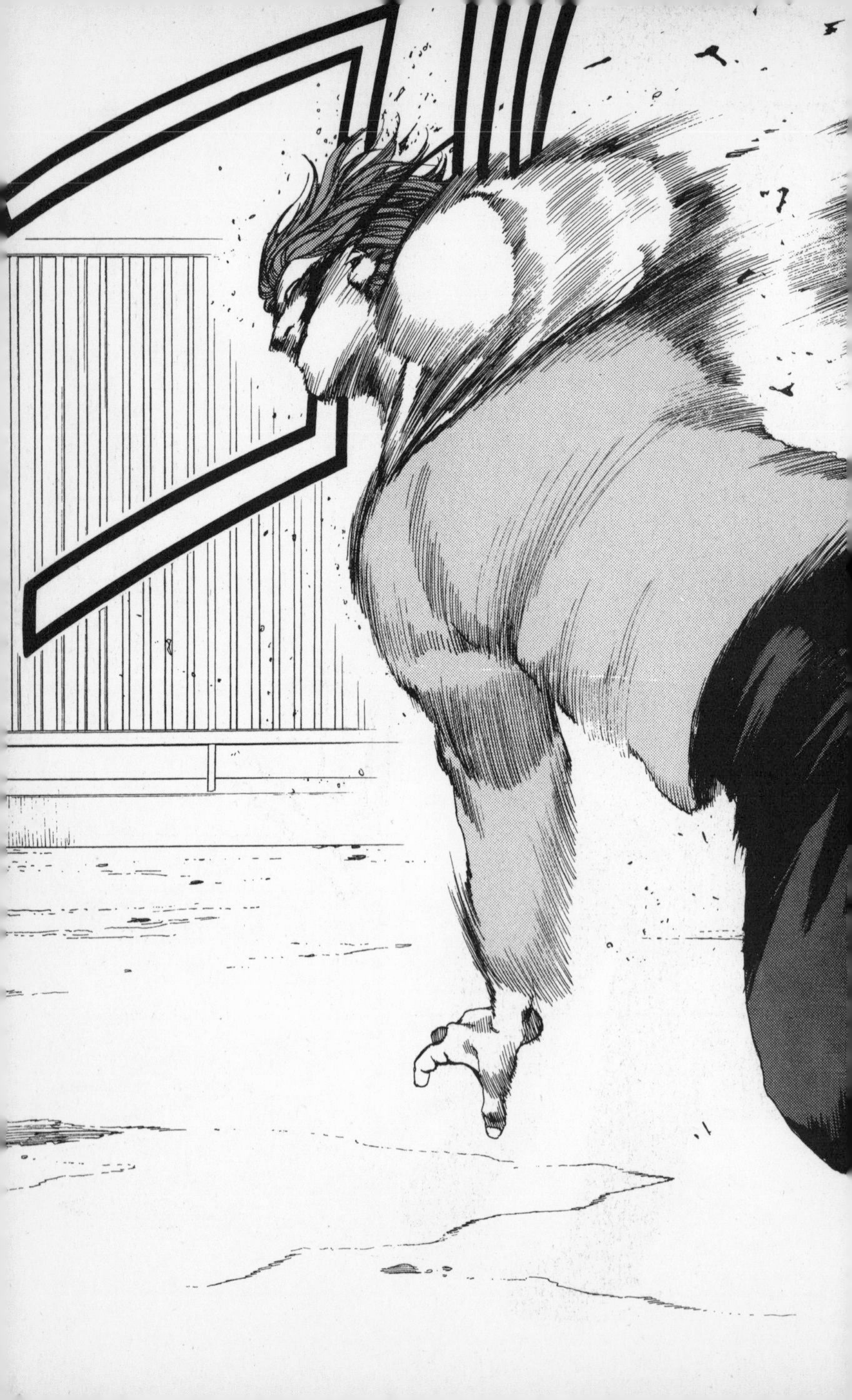

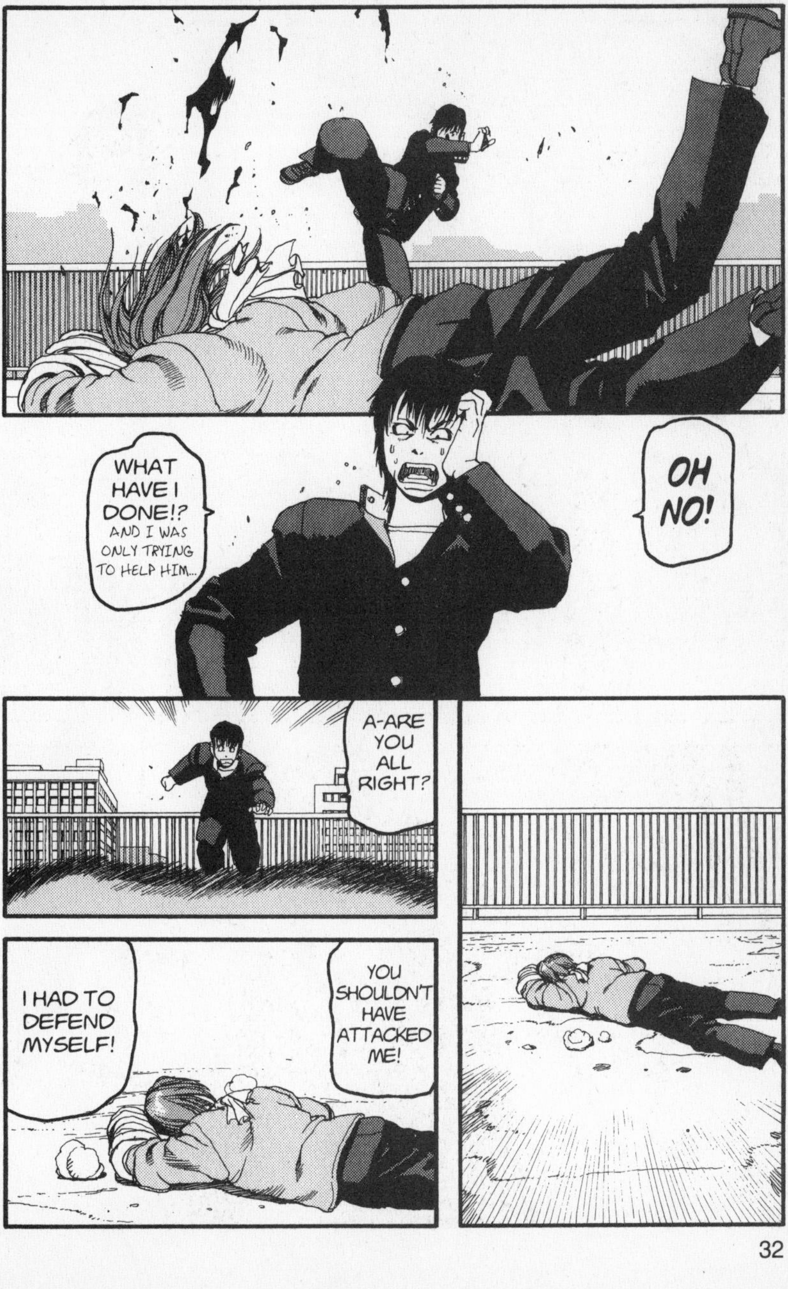
OH NO!
WHAT HAVE I DONE!? AND I WAS ONLY TRYING TO HELP HIM...
A-ARE YOU ALL RIGHT?
YOU SHOULDN'T HAVE ATTACKED ME!
I HAD TO DEFEND MYSELF!

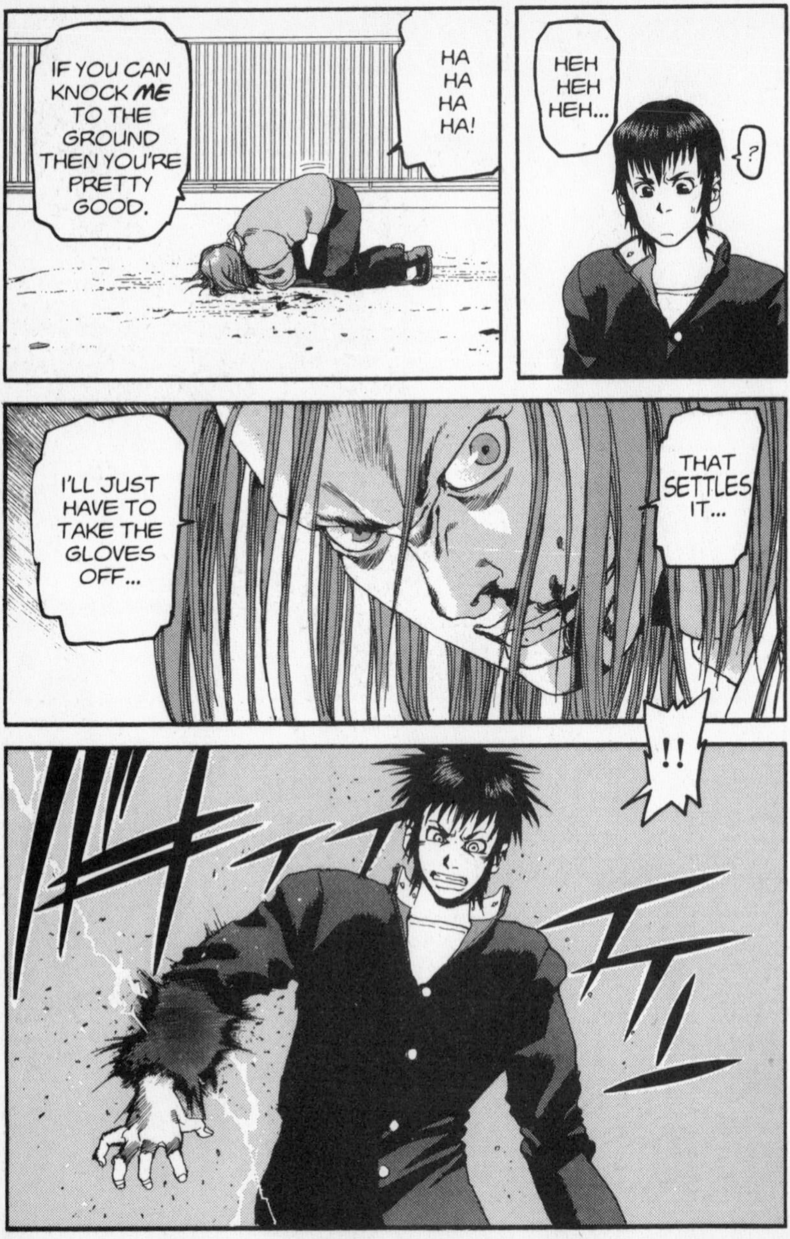
HEH HEH HEH...
?
HA HA HA HA!
IF YOU CAN KNOCK *ME* TO THE GROUND THEN YOU'RE PRETTY GOOD.
THAT SETTLES IT...
I'LL JUST HAVE TO TAKE THE GLOVES OFF...
!!

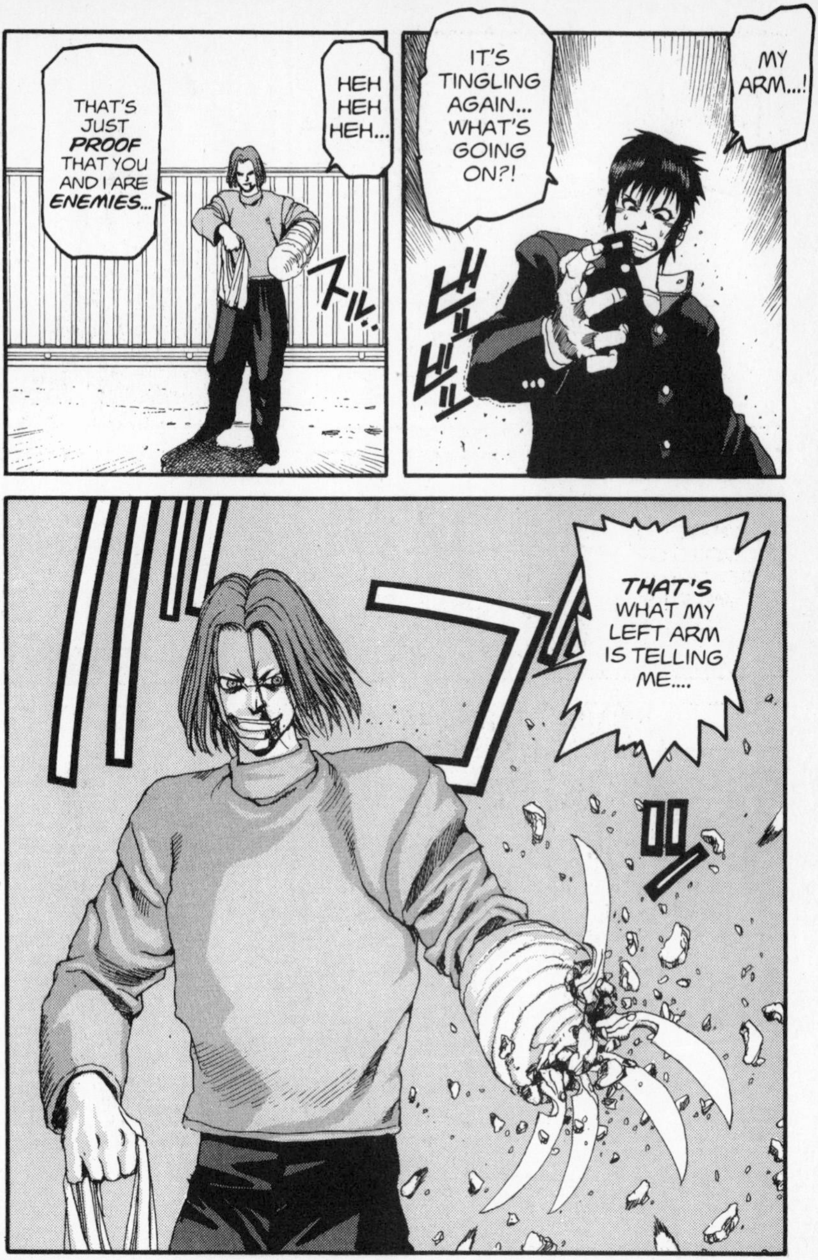
MY ARM...!
IT'S TINGLING AGAIN... WHAT'S GOING ON?!
ビッ ビッ
HEH HEH HEH...
THAT'S JUST **PROOF** THAT YOU AND I ARE **ENEMIES...**
スル..
THAT'S WHAT MY LEFT ARM IS TELLING ME....

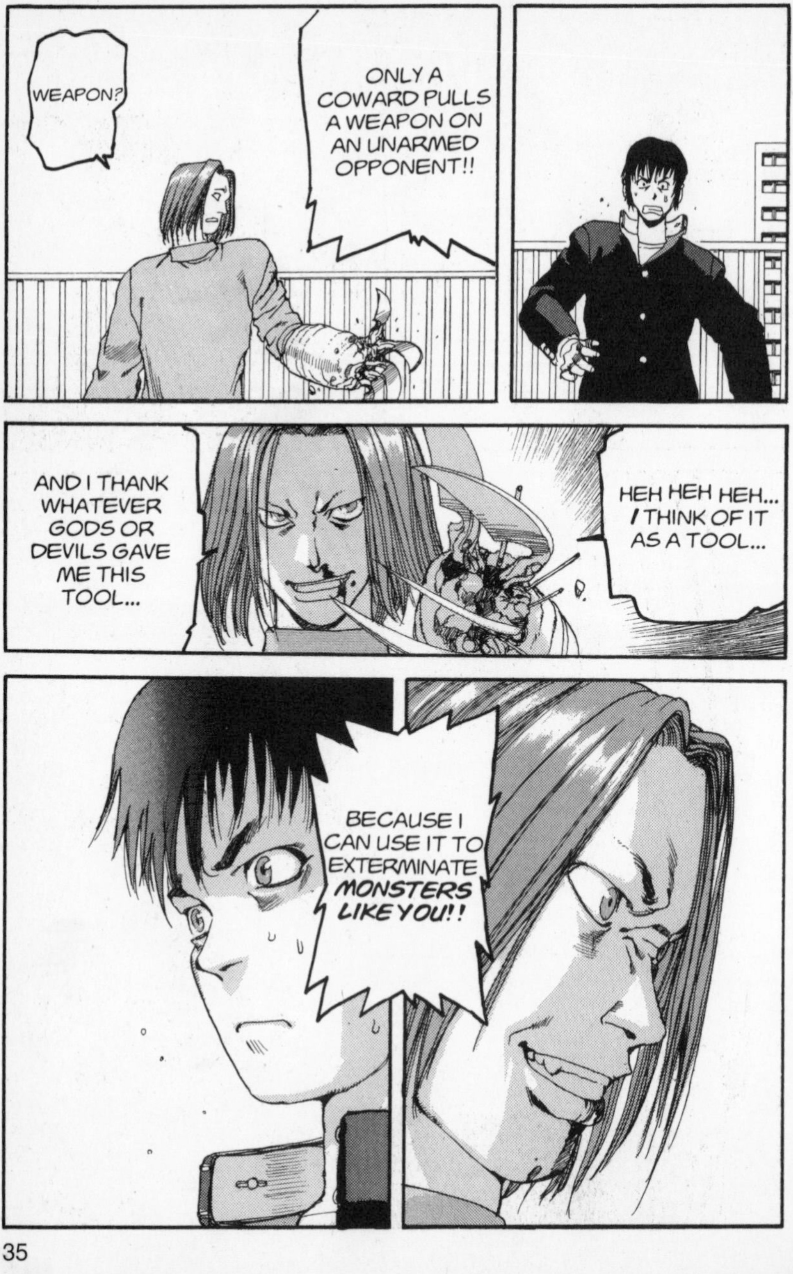
ONLY A COWARD PULLS A WEAPON ON AN UNARMED OPPONENT!!
WEAPON?
HEH HEH HEH... I THINK OF IT AS A TOOL...
AND I THANK WHATEVER GODS OR DEVILS GAVE ME THIS TOOL...
BECAUSE I CAN USE IT TO EXTERMINATE MONSTERS LIKE YOU!!

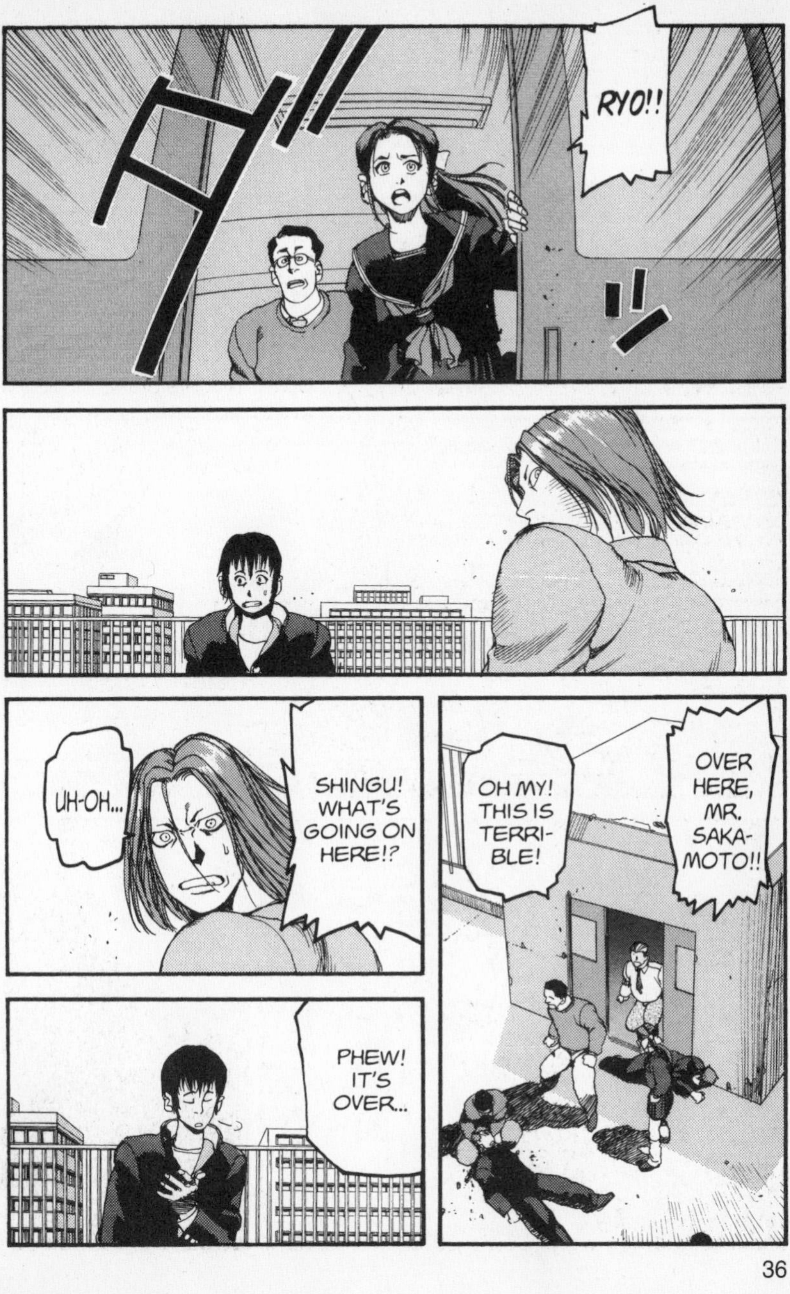
RYO!!
OVER HERE, MR. SAKA-MOTO!!
OH MY! THIS IS TERRI-BLE!
SHINGU! WHAT'S GOING ON HERE!?
UH-OH...
PHEW! IT'S OVER...

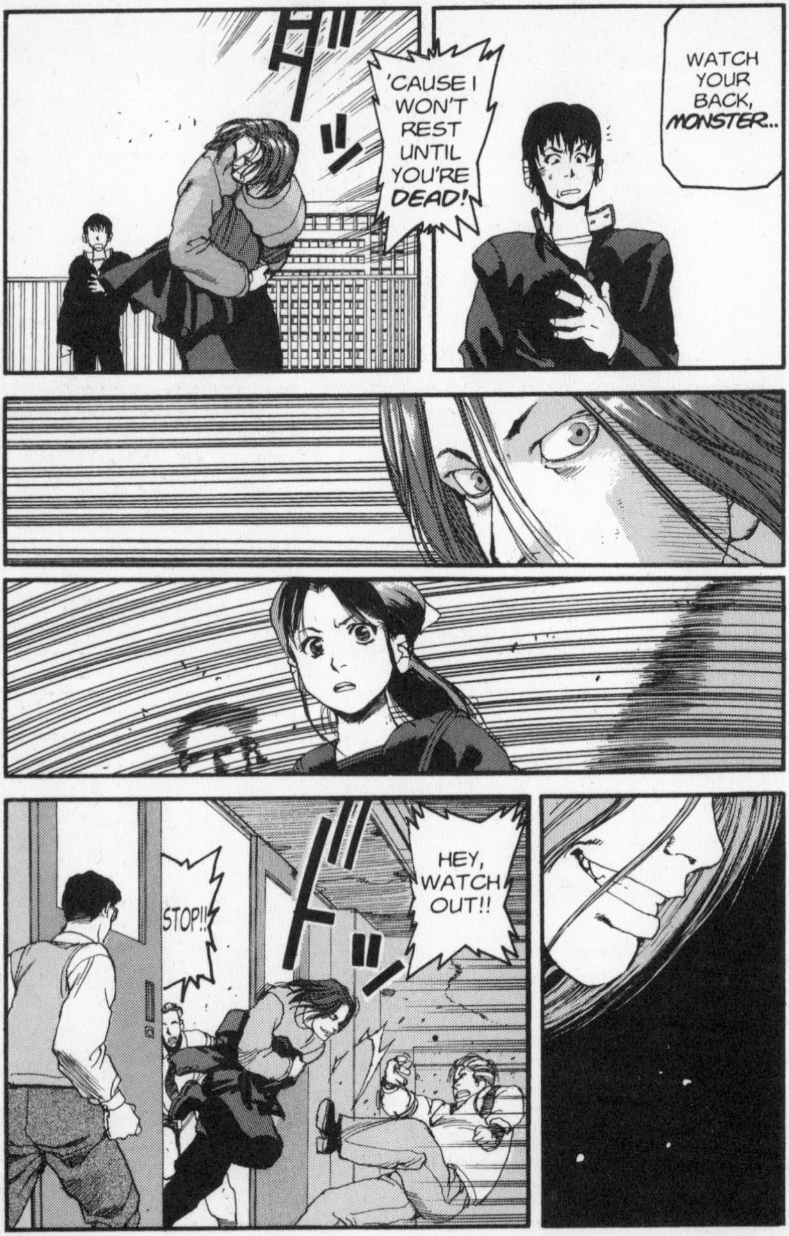
WATCH YOUR BACK, MONSTER...
ダッ
'CAUSE I WON'T REST UNTIL YOU'RE DEAD!
HEY, WATCH OUT!!
ドッ
STOP!!

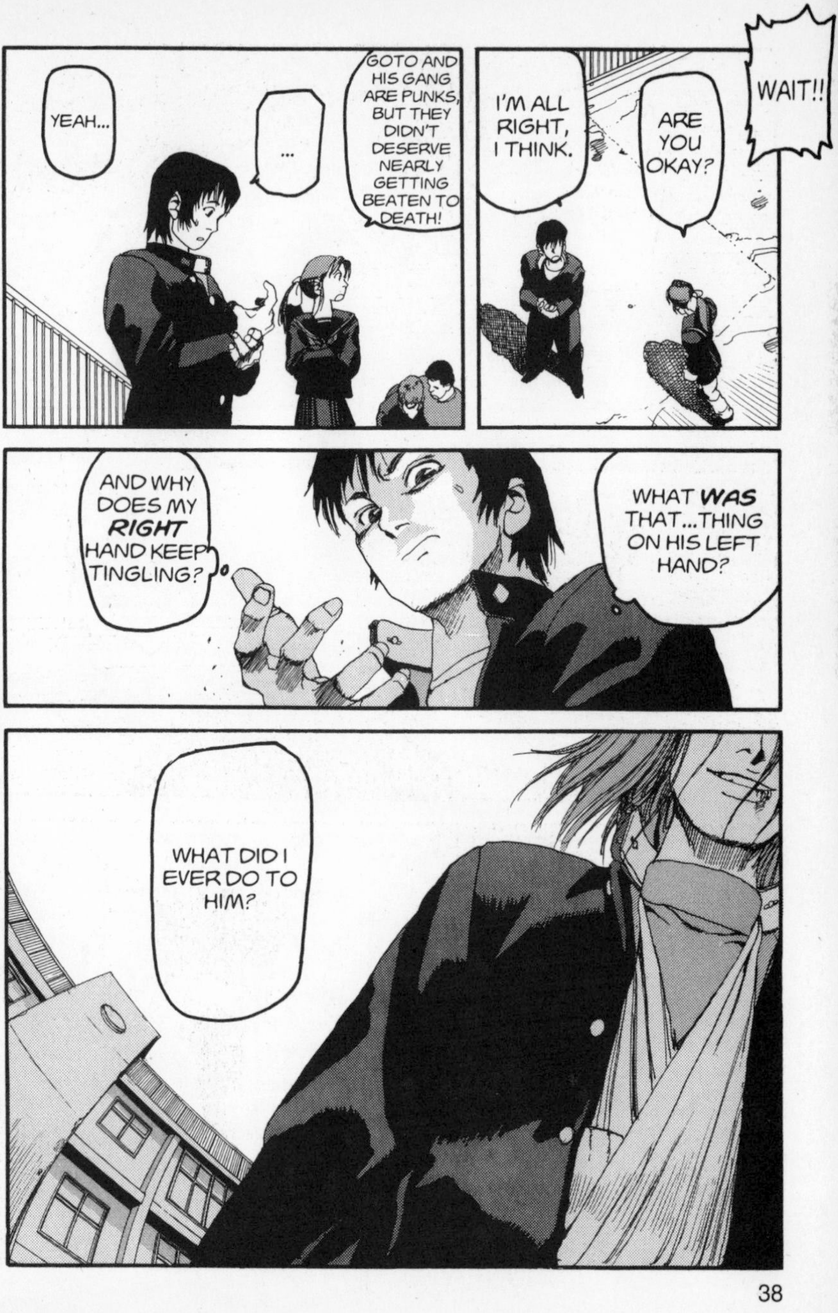
WAIT!!
ARE YOU OKAY?
I'M ALL RIGHT, I THINK.
GOTO AND HIS GANG ARE PUNKS, BUT THEY DIDN'T DESERVE NEARLY GETTING BEATEN TO DEATH!
...
YEAH...
WHAT WAS THAT...THING ON HIS LEFT HAND?
AND WHY DOES MY RIGHT HAND KEEP TINGLING?
WHAT DID I EVER DO TO HIM?

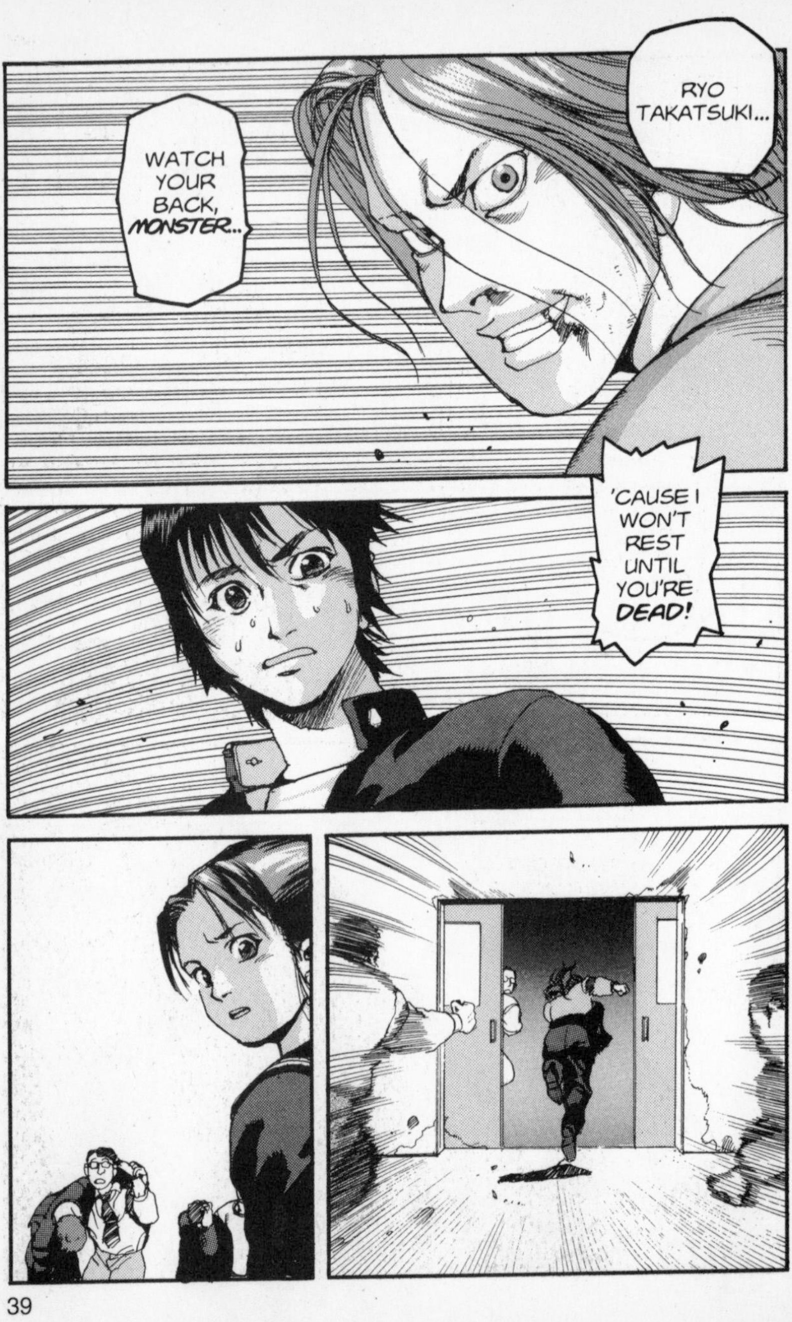
RYO TAKATSUKI...
WATCH YOUR BACK, MONSTER...
'CAUSE I WON'T REST UNTIL YOU'RE DEAD!

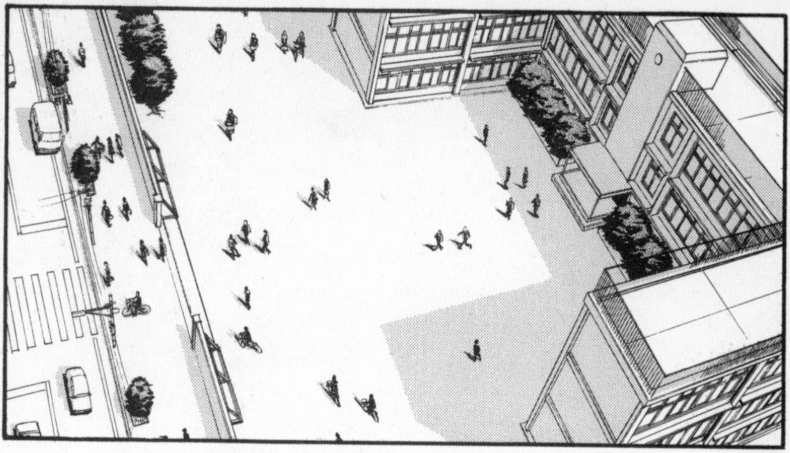

No. 2 DISAPPEARANCE

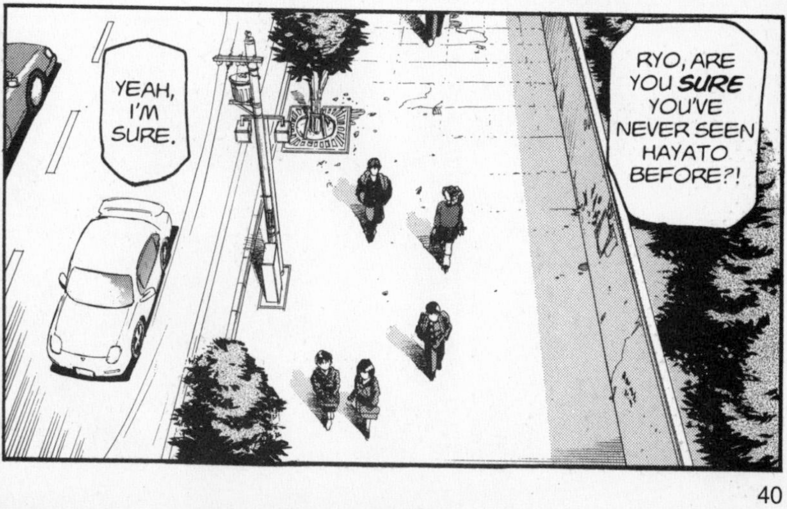
RYO, ARE YOU *SURE* YOU'VE NEVER SEEN HAYATO BEFORE?!
YEAH, I'M SURE.

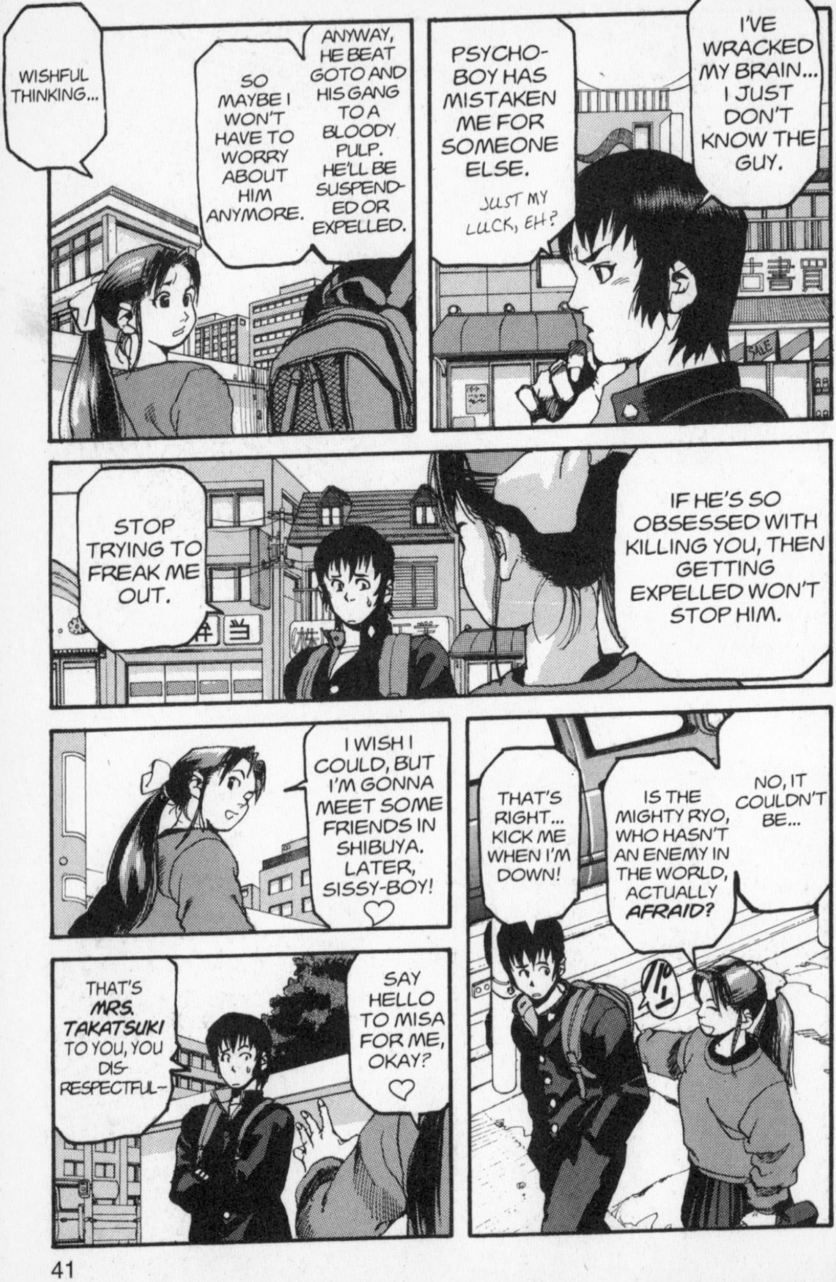
I'VE WRACKED MY BRAIN... I JUST DON'T KNOW THE GUY.
PSYCHO-BOY HAS MISTAKEN ME FOR SOMEONE ELSE.
JUST MY LUCK, EH?
ANYWAY, HE BEAT GOTO AND HIS GANG TO A BLOODY PULP. HE'LL BE SUSPENDED OR EXPELLED.
SO MAYBE I WON'T HAVE TO WORRY ABOUT HIM ANYMORE.
WISHFUL THINKING...
IF HE'S SO OBSESSED WITH KILLING YOU, THEN GETTING EXPELLED WON'T STOP HIM.
STOP TRYING TO FREAK ME OUT.
NO, IT COULDN'T BE...
IS THE MIGHTY RYO, WHO HASN'T AN ENEMY IN THE WORLD, ACTUALLY *AFRAID*?
THAT'S RIGHT... KICK ME WHEN I'M DOWN!
I WISH I COULD, BUT I'M GONNA MEET SOME FRIENDS IN SHIBUYA. LATER, SISSY-BOY! ♡
SAY HELLO TO MISA FOR ME, OKAY? ♡
THAT'S *MRS. TAKATSUKI* TO YOU, YOU DIS-RESPECTFUL-

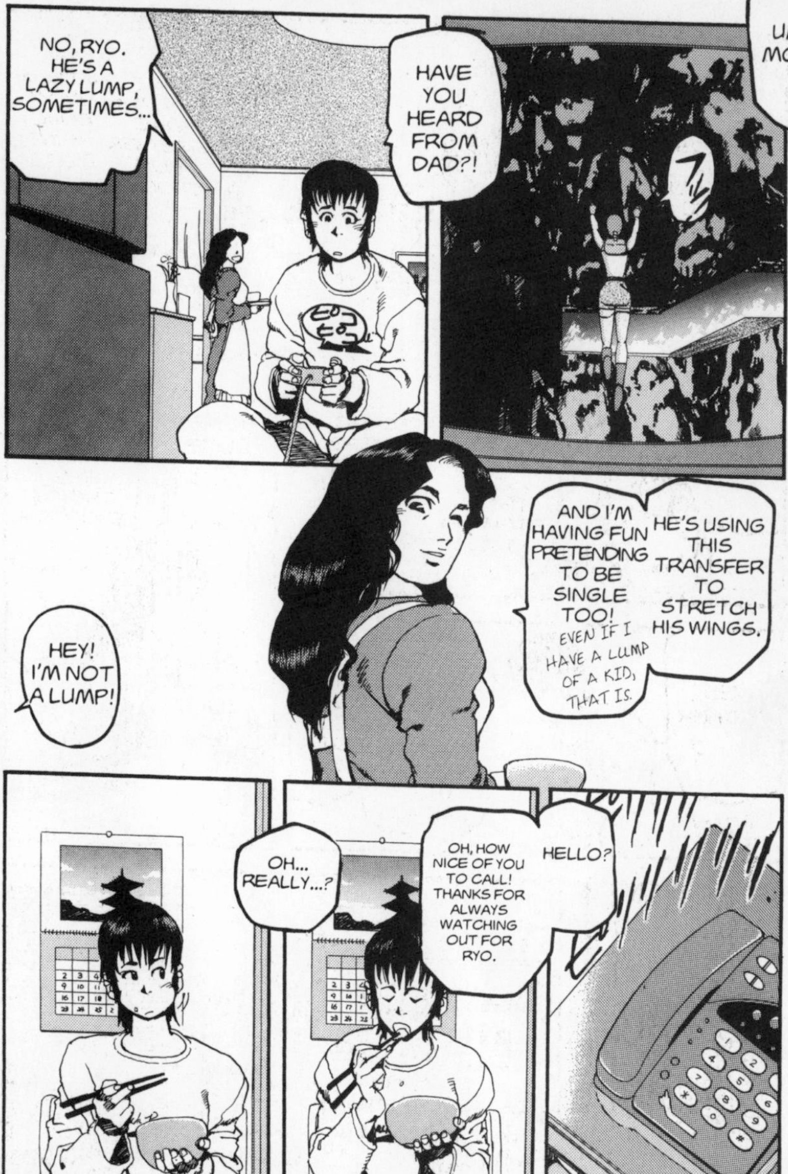
UM... MOM?
HAVE YOU HEARD FROM DAD?!
NO, RYO. HE'S A LAZY LUMP, SOMETIMES...
HE'S USING THIS TRANSFER TO STRETCH HIS WINGS.
AND I'M HAVING FUN PRETENDING TO BE SINGLE TOO! EVEN IF I HAVE A LUMP OF A KID, THAT IS.
HEY! I'M NOT A LUMP!
HELLO?
OH, HOW NICE OF YOU TO CALL! THANKS FOR ALWAYS WATCHING OUT FOR RYO.
OH... REALLY...?

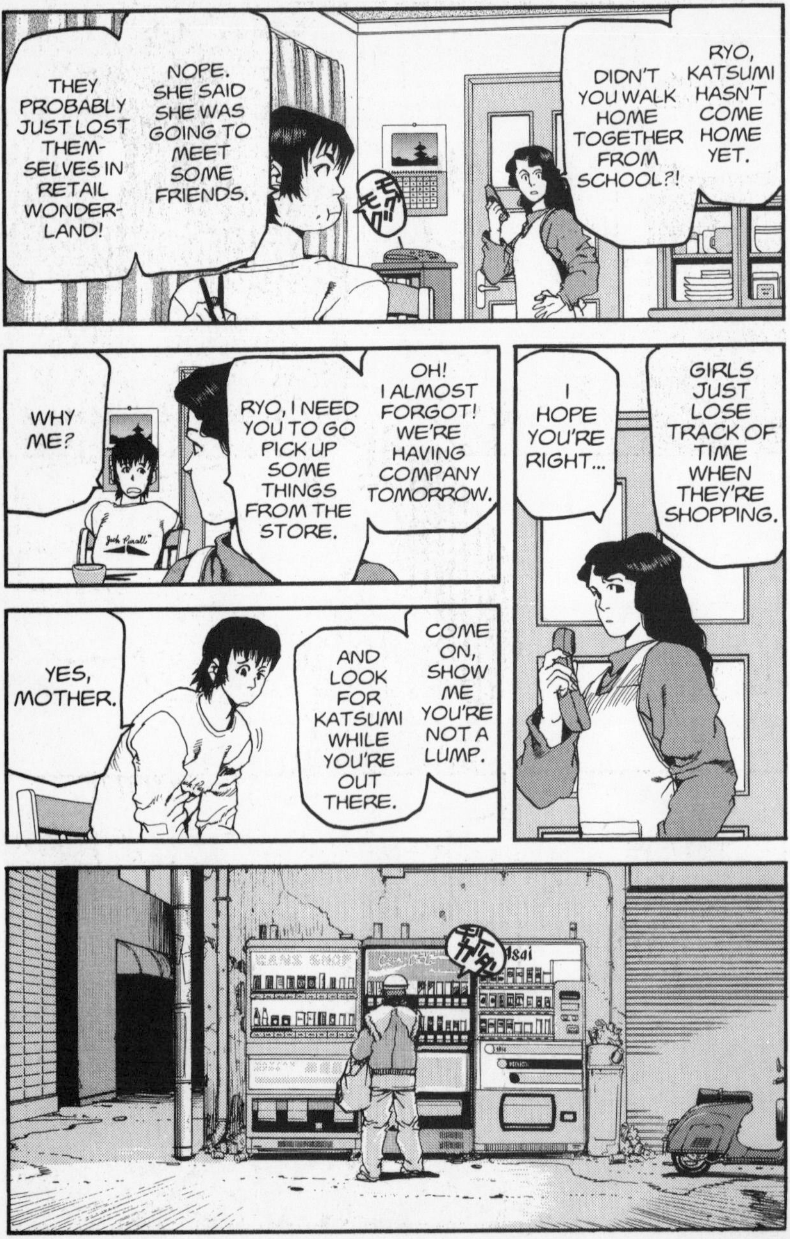
RYO, KATSUMI HASN'T COME HOME YET.
DIDN'T YOU WALK HOME TOGETHER FROM SCHOOL?!
NOPE. SHE SAID SHE WAS GOING TO MEET SOME FRIENDS.
THEY PROBABLY JUST LOST THEM-SELVES IN RETAIL WONDER-LAND!
GIRLS JUST LOSE TRACK OF TIME WHEN THEY'RE SHOPPING.
I HOPE YOU'RE RIGHT...
OH! I ALMOST FORGOT! WE'RE HAVING COMPANY TOMORROW.
RYO, I NEED YOU TO GO PICK UP SOME THINGS FROM THE STORE.
WHY ME?
COME ON, SHOW ME YOU'RE NOT A LUMP.
AND LOOK FOR KATSUMI WHILE YOU'RE OUT THERE.
YES, MOTHER.

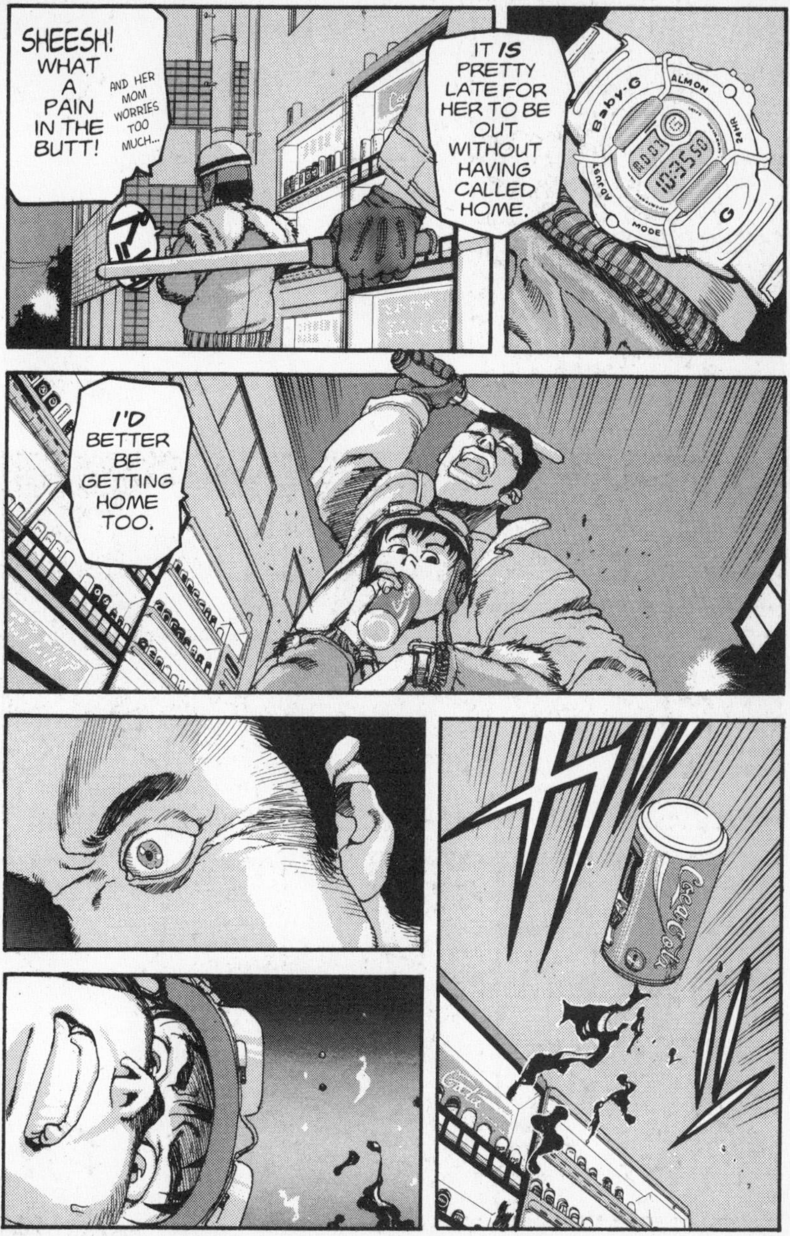
IT IS PRETTY LATE FOR HER TO BE OUT WITHOUT HAVING CALLED HOME.
SHEESH! WHAT A PAIN IN THE BUTT!
AND HER MOM WORRIES TOO MUCH...
I'D BETTER BE GETTING HOME TOO.

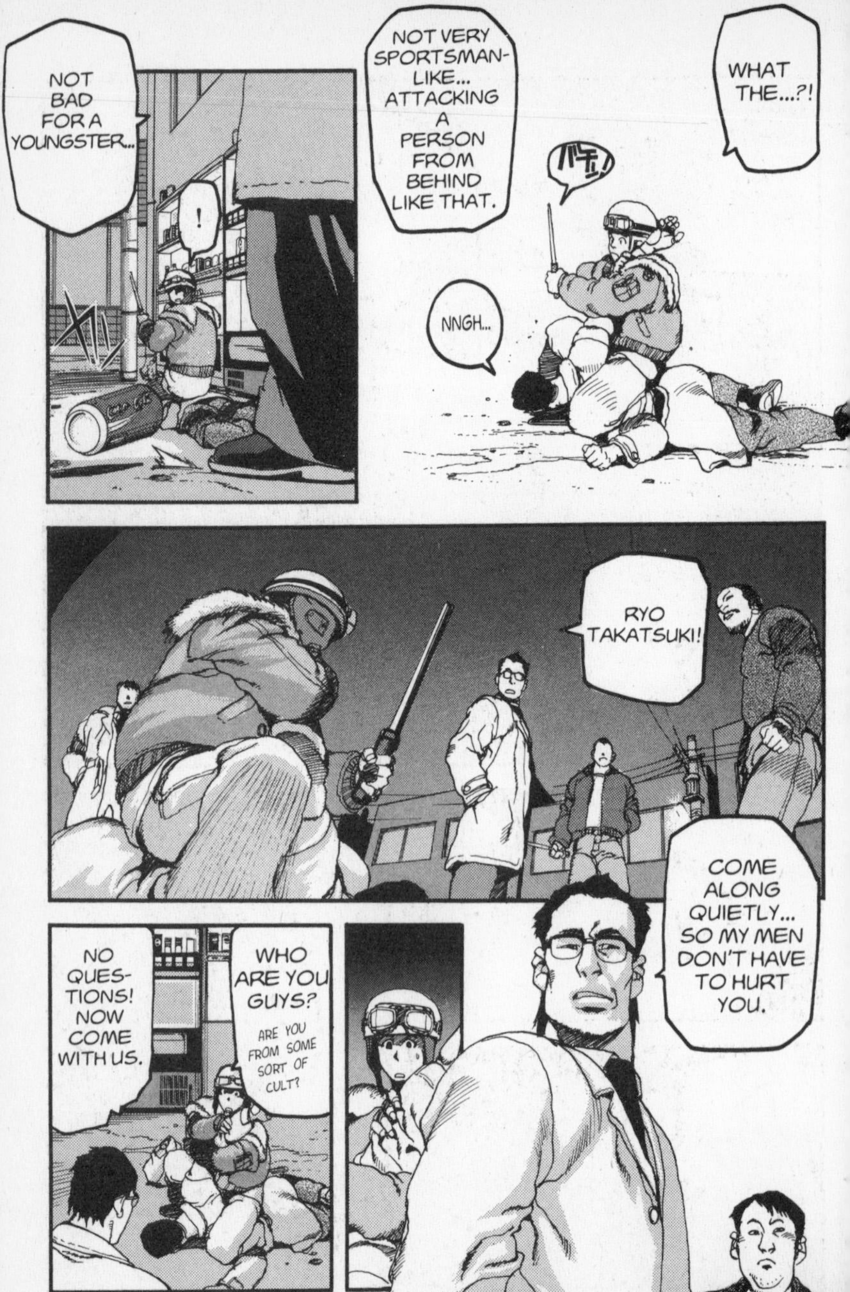
WHAT THE...?!
NOT VERY SPORTSMAN-LIKE... ATTACKING A PERSON FROM BEHIND LIKE THAT.
NNGH...
!
NOT BAD FOR A YOUNGSTER...
RYO TAKATSUKI!
COME ALONG QUIETLY... SO MY MEN DON'T HAVE TO HURT YOU.
WHO ARE YOU GUYS?
ARE YOU FROM SOME SORT OF CULT?
NO QUES-TIONS! NOW COME WITH US.

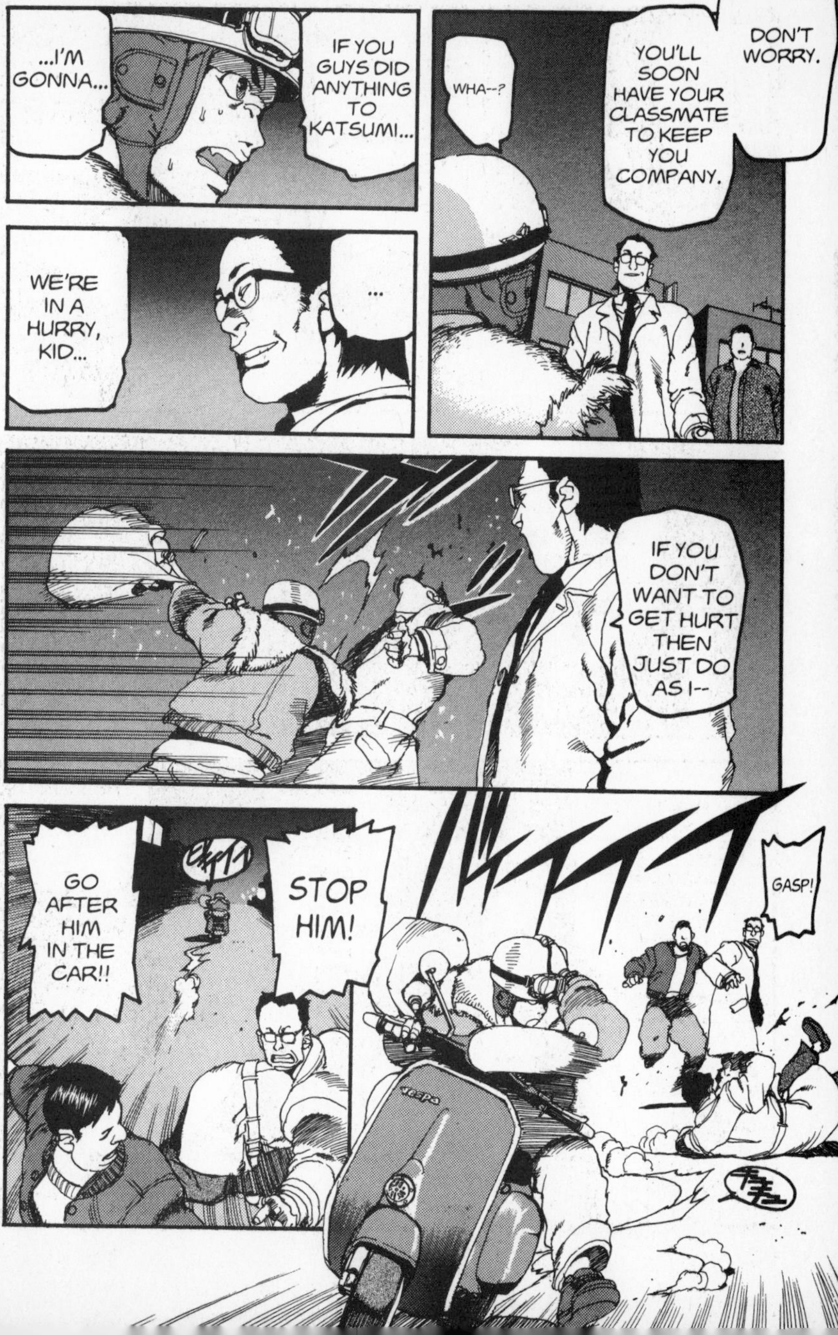
...I'M GONNA...
IF YOU GUYS DID ANYTHING TO KATSUMI...
WE'RE IN A HURRY, KID...
...
DON'T WORRY.
YOU'LL SOON HAVE YOUR CLASSMATE TO KEEP YOU COMPANY.
WHA--?
IF YOU DON'T WANT TO GET HURT THEN JUST DO AS I--
GO AFTER HIM IN THE CAR!!
STOP HIM!
GASP!

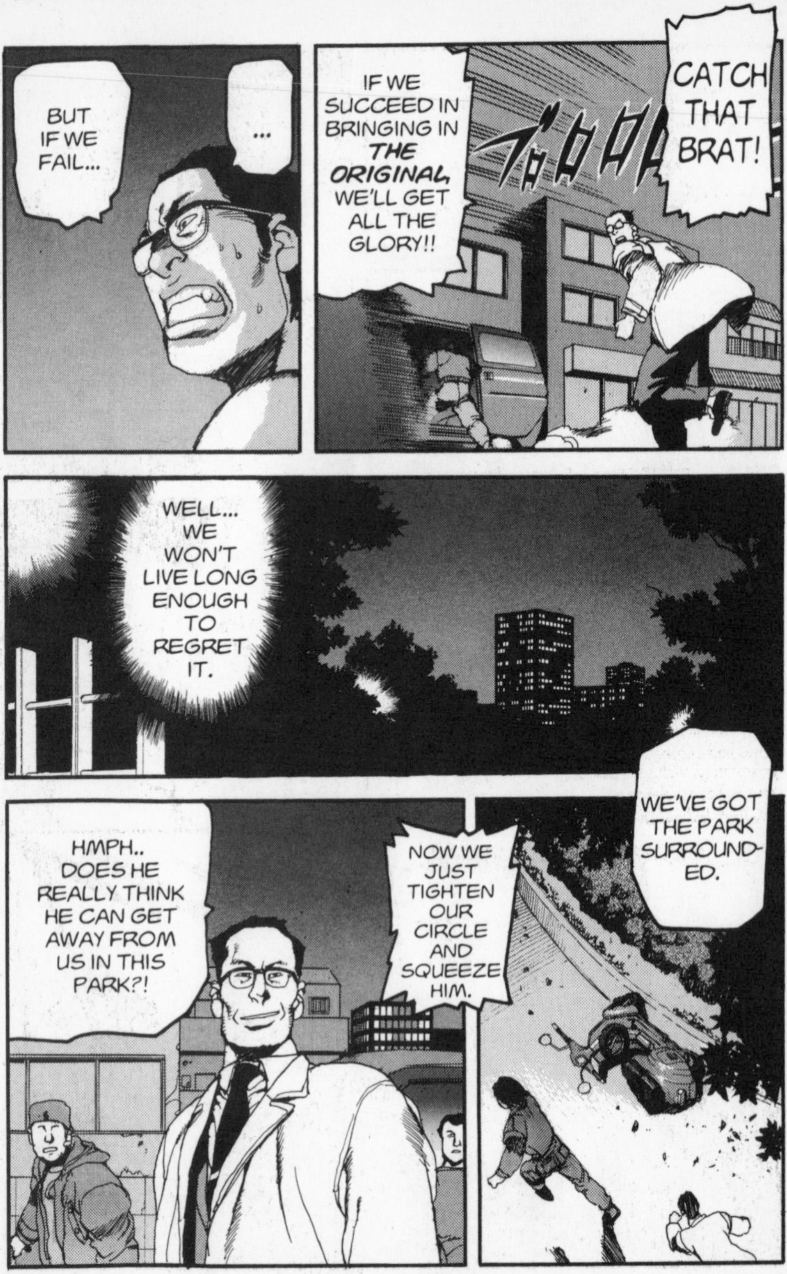
CATCH THAT BRAT!
IF WE SUCCEED IN BRINGING IN THE ORIGINAL, WE'LL GET ALL THE GLORY!!
...
BUT IF WE FAIL...
WELL... WE WON'T LIVE LONG ENOUGH TO REGRET IT.
WE'VE GOT THE PARK SURROUND-ED.
NOW WE JUST TIGHTEN OUR CIRCLE AND SQUEEZE HIM.
HMPH.. DOES HE REALLY THINK HE CAN GET AWAY FROM US IN THIS PARK?!

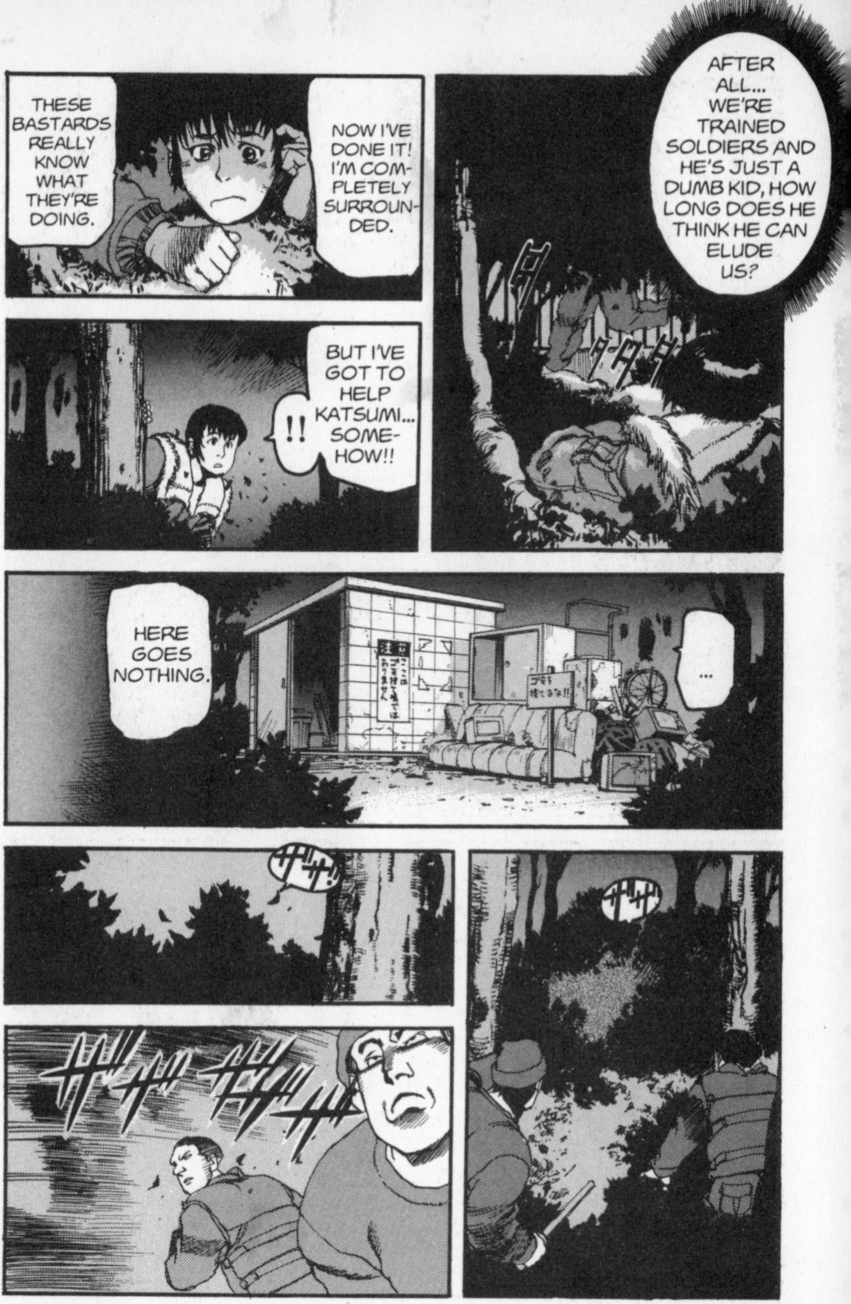
AFTER ALL... WE'RE TRAINED SOLDIERS AND HE'S JUST A DUMB KID, HOW LONG DOES HE THINK HE CAN ELUDE US?
NOW I'VE DONE IT! I'M COMPLETELY SURROUNDED.
THESE BASTARDS REALLY KNOW WHAT THEY'RE DOING.
BUT I'VE GOT TO HELP KATSUMI... SOMEHOW!!
!!
...
HERE GOES NOTHING.

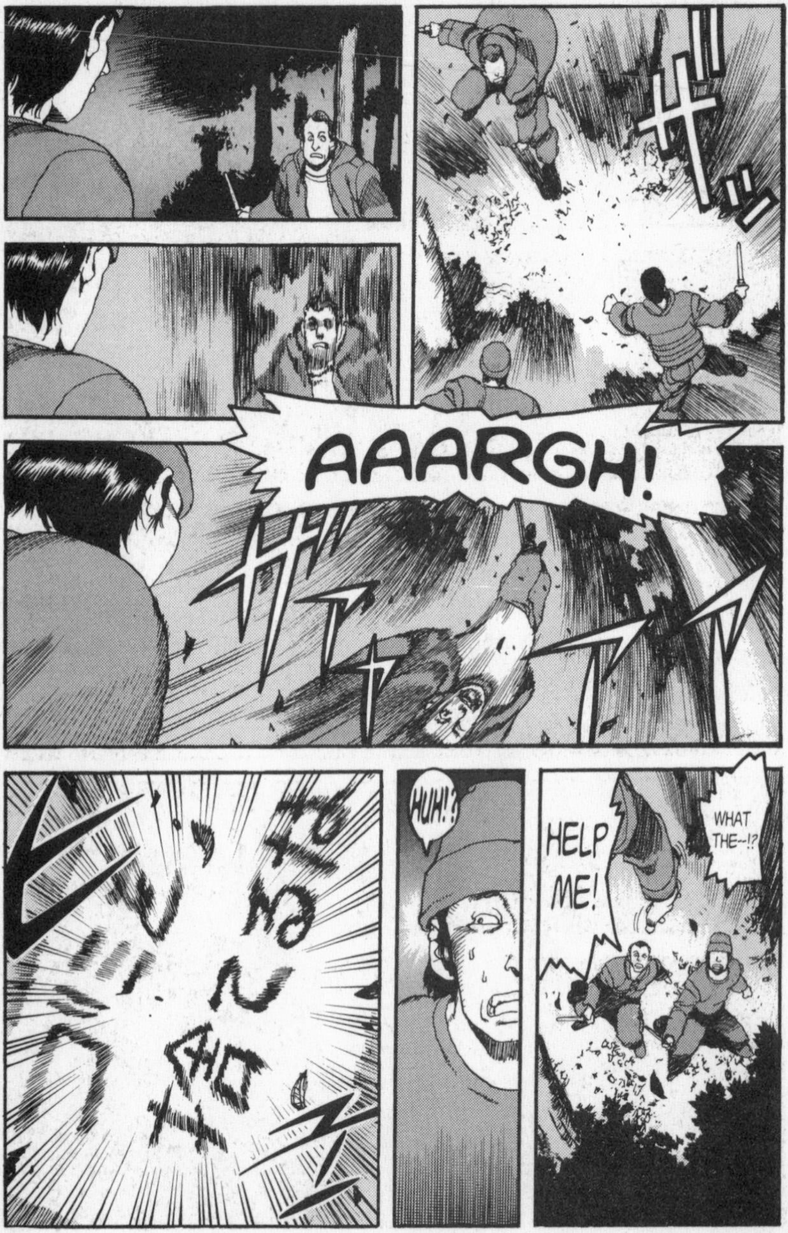
AAARGH!
WHAT THE--!?
HELP ME!
HUH!?

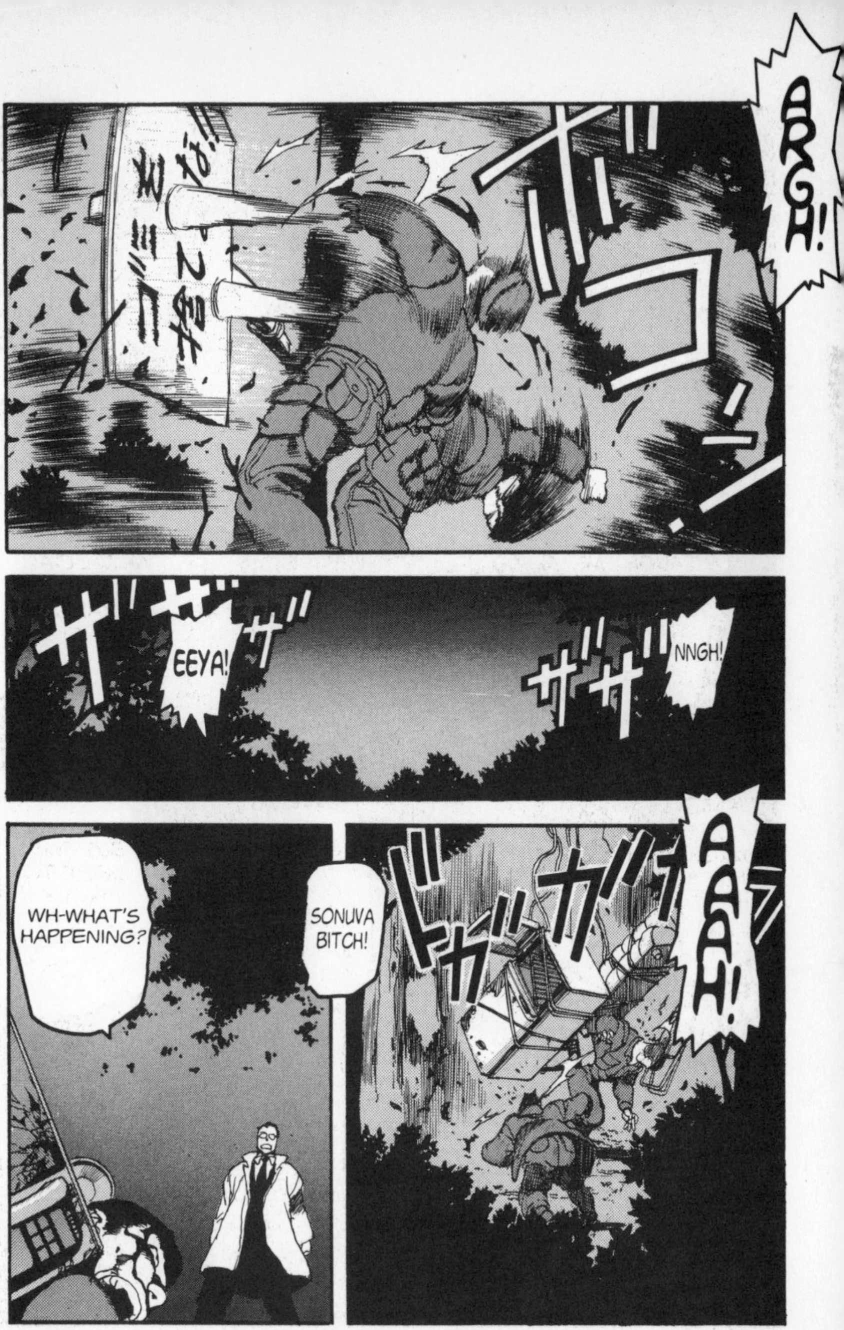
ARGH!
NNGH!
EEYA!
AAAAH!
SONUVA BITCH!
WH-WHAT'S HAPPENING?

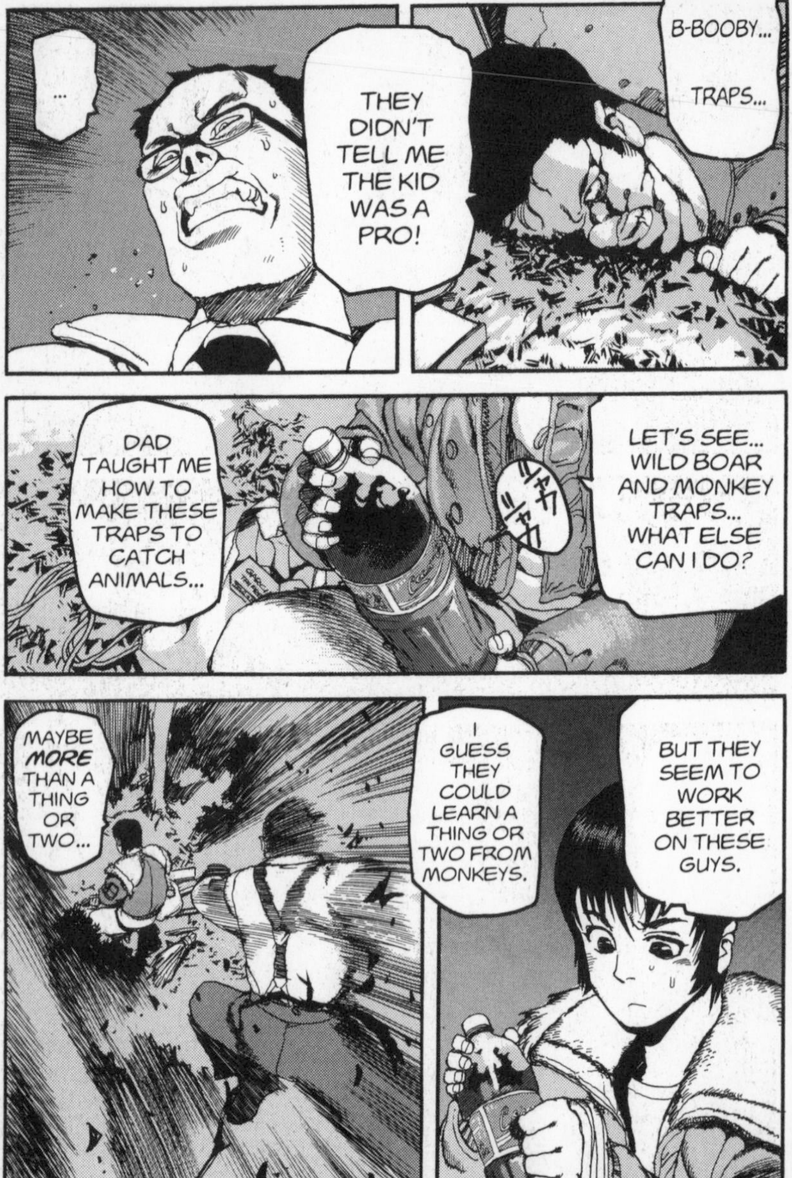
B-BOOBY... TRAPS...
THEY DIDN'T TELL ME THE KID WAS A PRO!
...
LET'S SEE... WILD BOAR AND MONKEY TRAPS... WHAT ELSE CAN I DO?
シャカシャカ
DAD TAUGHT ME HOW TO MAKE THESE TRAPS TO CATCH ANIMALS...
BUT THEY SEEM TO WORK BETTER ON THESE GUYS.
I GUESS THEY COULD LEARN A THING OR TWO FROM MONKEYS.
MAYBE **MORE** THAN A THING OR TWO...

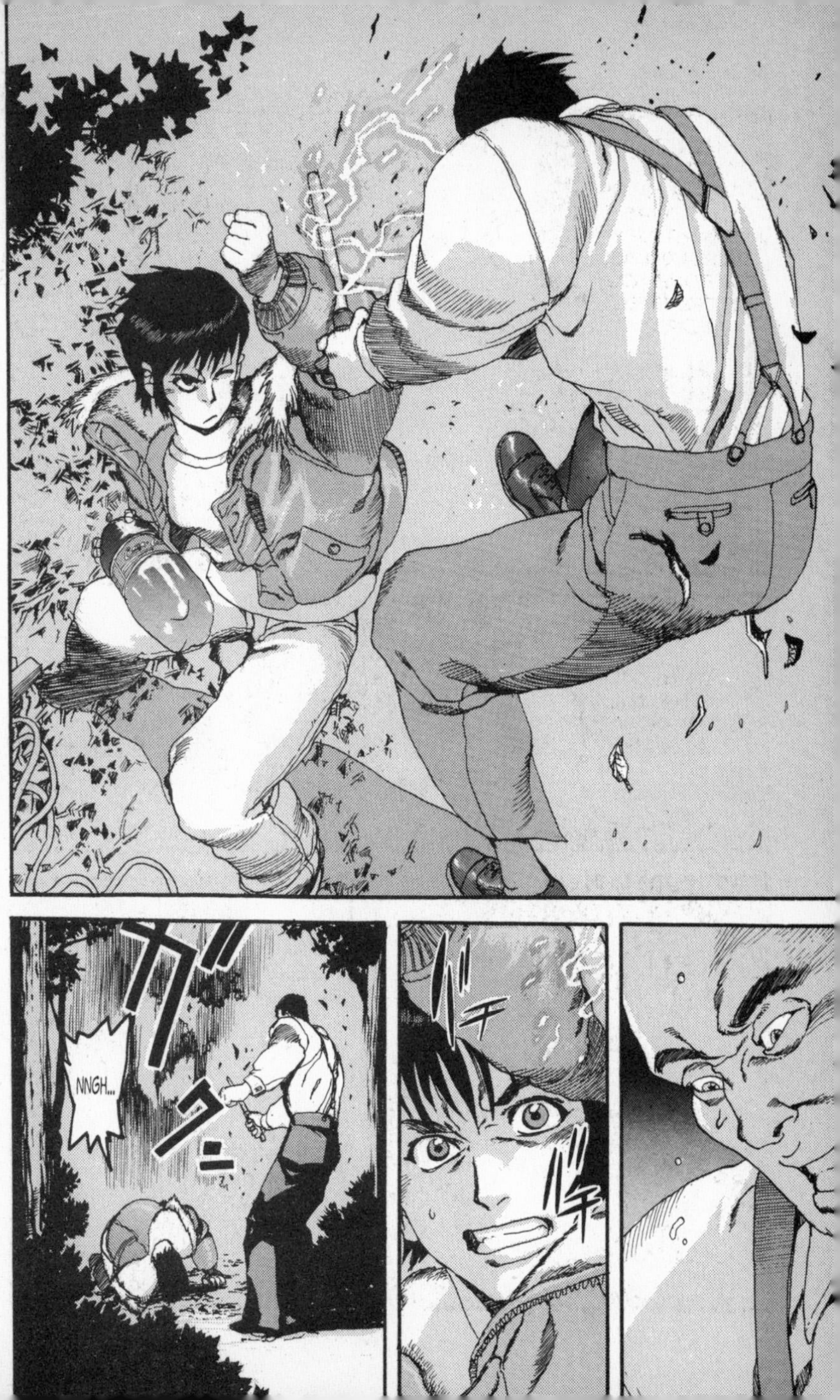
バチ
バチ
NNGH...

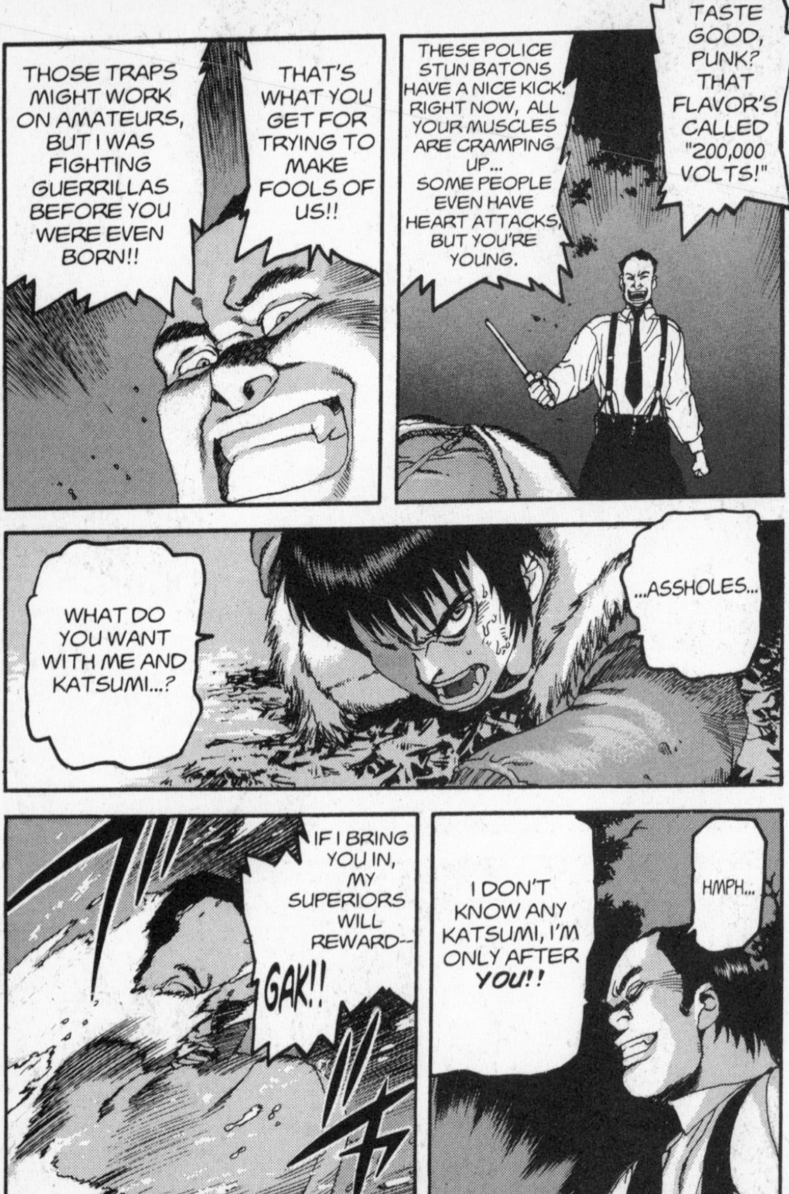
TASTE GOOD, PUNK? THAT FLAVOR'S CALLED "200,000 VOLTS!"
THESE POLICE STUN BATONS HAVE A NICE KICK! RIGHT NOW, ALL YOUR MUSCLES ARE CRAMPING UP... SOME PEOPLE EVEN HAVE HEART ATTACKS, BUT YOU'RE YOUNG.
THAT'S WHAT YOU GET FOR TRYING TO MAKE FOOLS OF US!!
THOSE TRAPS MIGHT WORK ON AMATEURS, BUT I WAS FIGHTING GUERRILLAS BEFORE YOU WERE EVEN BORN!!
...ASSHOLES...
WHAT DO YOU WANT WITH ME AND KATSUMI...?
HMPH...
I DON'T KNOW ANY KATSUMI, I'M ONLY AFTER YOU!!
IF I BRING YOU IN, MY SUPERIORS WILL REWARD--
GAK!!

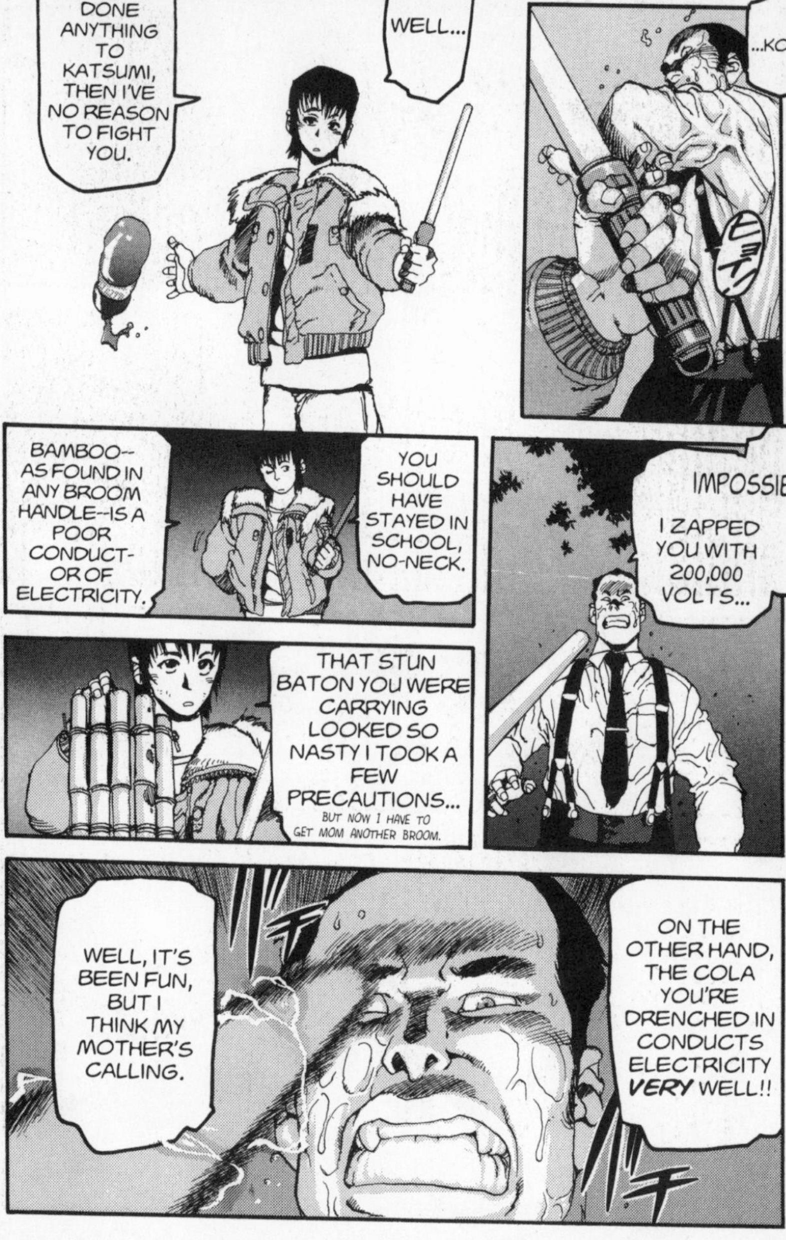
...KOF...
WELL...
IF YOU HAVEN'T DONE ANYTHING TO KATSUMI, THEN I'VE NO REASON TO FIGHT YOU.
IMPOSSIBLE!
I ZAPPED YOU WITH 200,000 VOLTS...
YOU SHOULD HAVE STAYED IN SCHOOL, NO-NECK.
BAMBOO--AS FOUND IN ANY BROOM HANDLE--IS A POOR CONDUCT-OR OF ELECTRICITY.
THAT STUN BATON YOU WERE CARRYING LOOKED SO NASTY I TOOK A FEW PRECAUTIONS...
BUT NOW I HAVE TO GET MOM ANOTHER BROOM.
ON THE OTHER HAND, THE COLA YOU'RE DRENCHED IN CONDUCTS ELECTRICITY *VERY* WELL!!
WELL, IT'S BEEN FUN, BUT I THINK MY MOTHER'S CALLING.

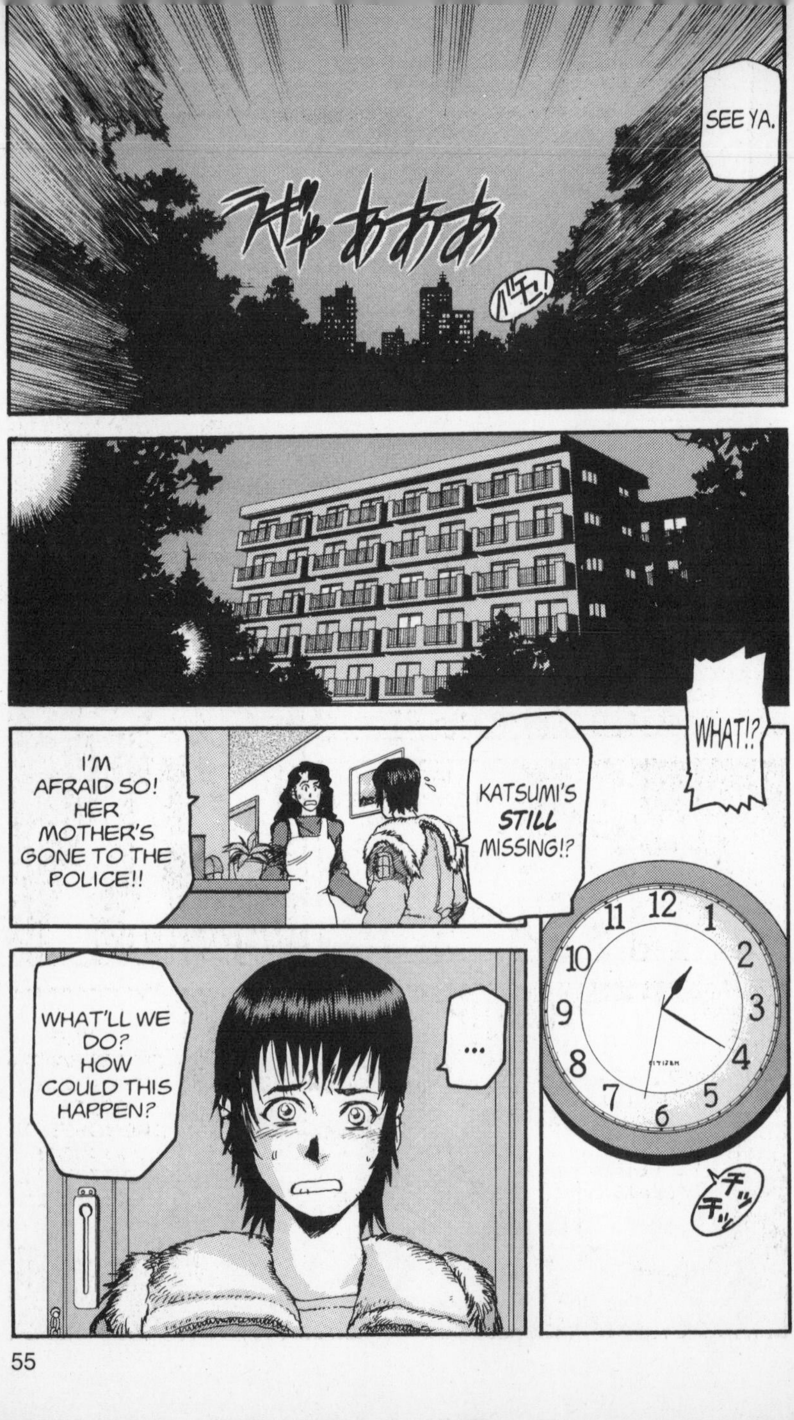
SEE YA.
WHAT!?
チッ チッ
KATSUMI'S STILL MISSING!?
I'M AFRAID SO! HER MOTHER'S GONE TO THE POLICE!!
...
WHAT'LL WE DO? HOW COULD THIS HAPPEN?

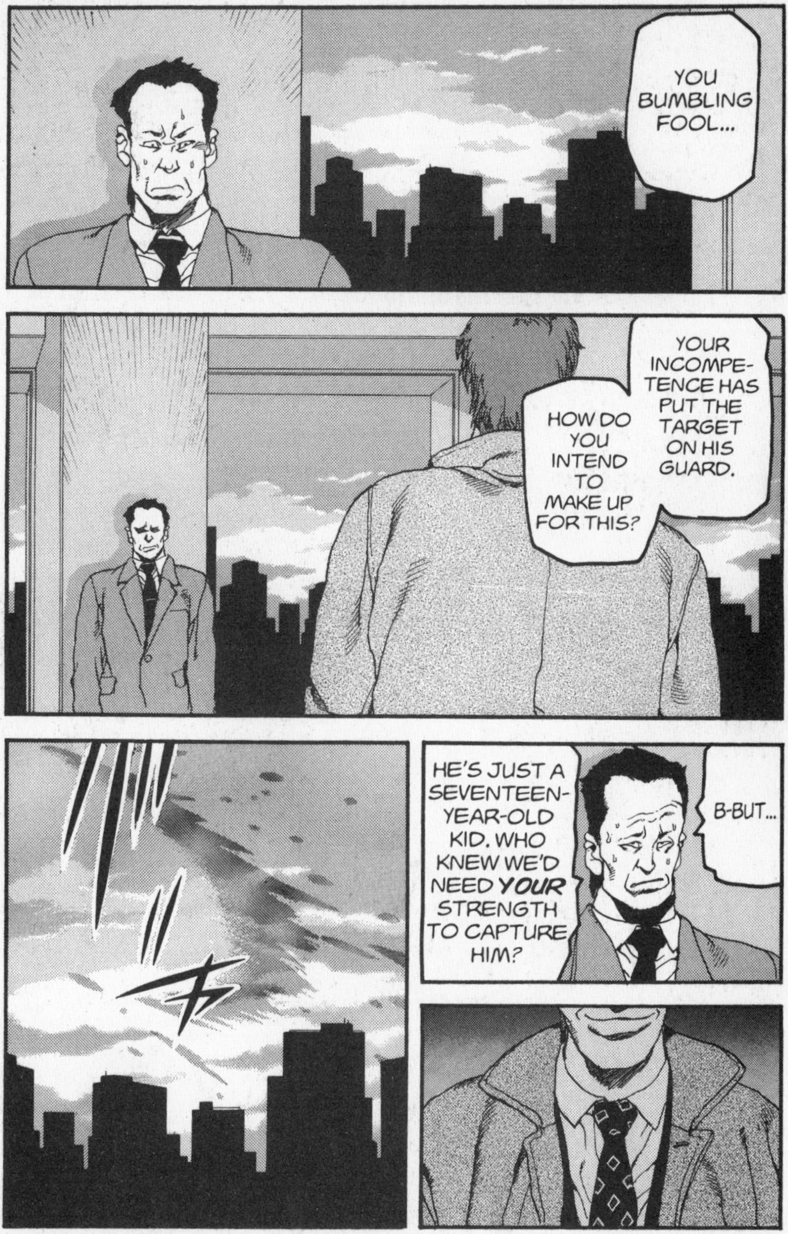
YOU BUMBLING FOOL...
YOUR INCOMPETENCE HAS PUT THE TARGET ON HIS GUARD.
HOW DO YOU INTEND TO MAKE UP FOR THIS?
B-BUT...
HE'S JUST A SEVENTEEN-YEAR-OLD KID. WHO KNEW WE'D NEED ***YOUR*** STRENGTH TO CAPTURE HIM?

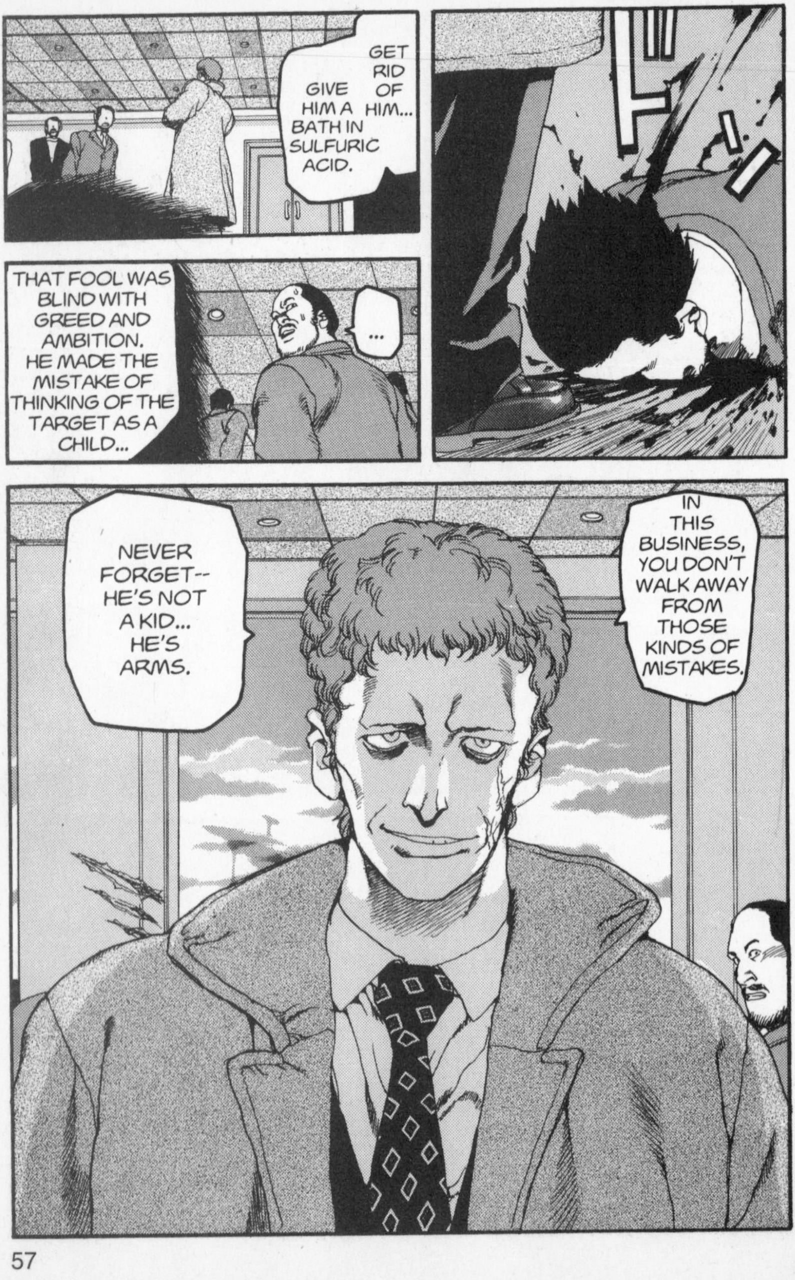
GET RID OF HIM...
GIVE HIM A BATH IN SULFURIC ACID.
...
THAT FOOL WAS BLIND WITH GREED AND AMBITION. HE MADE THE MISTAKE OF THINKING OF THE TARGET AS A CHILD...
IN THIS BUSINESS, YOU DON'T WALK AWAY FROM THOSE KINDS OF MISTAKES.
NEVER FORGET-- HE'S NOT A KID... HE'S ARMS.

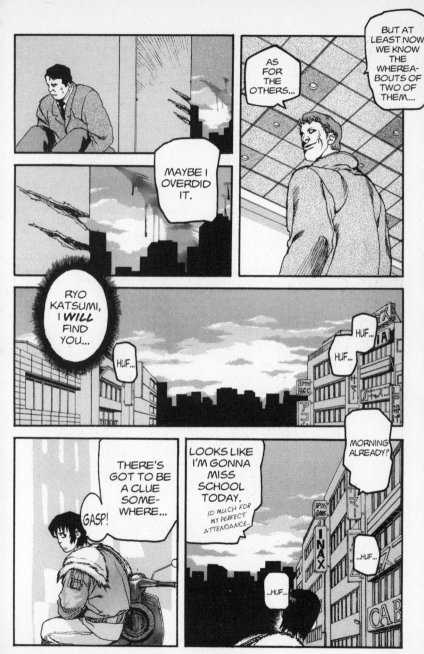

AS FOR THE OTHERS...

BUT AT LEAST NOW WE KNOW THE WHERE-ABOUTS OF TWO OF THEM....

MAYBE I OVERDID IT.

RYO KATSUMI, I *WILL* FIND YOU...

HUF...

HUF...

HUF...

MORNING ALREADY?

...HUF...

THERE'S GOT TO BE A CLUE SOME-WHERE...

GASP!

LOOKS LIKE I'M GONNA MISS SCHOOL TODAY.

SO MUCH FOR MY PERFECT ATTENDANCE...

...HUF...

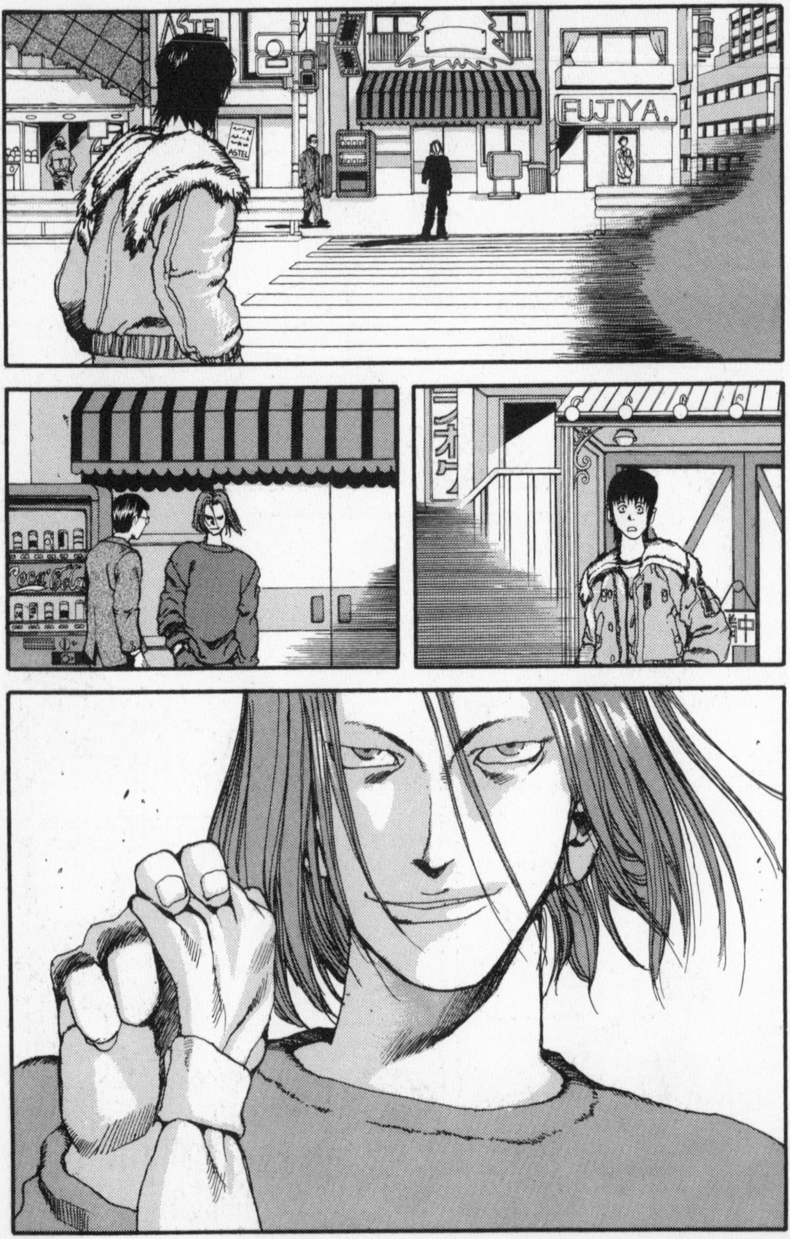
FUJIYA.
ASTEL

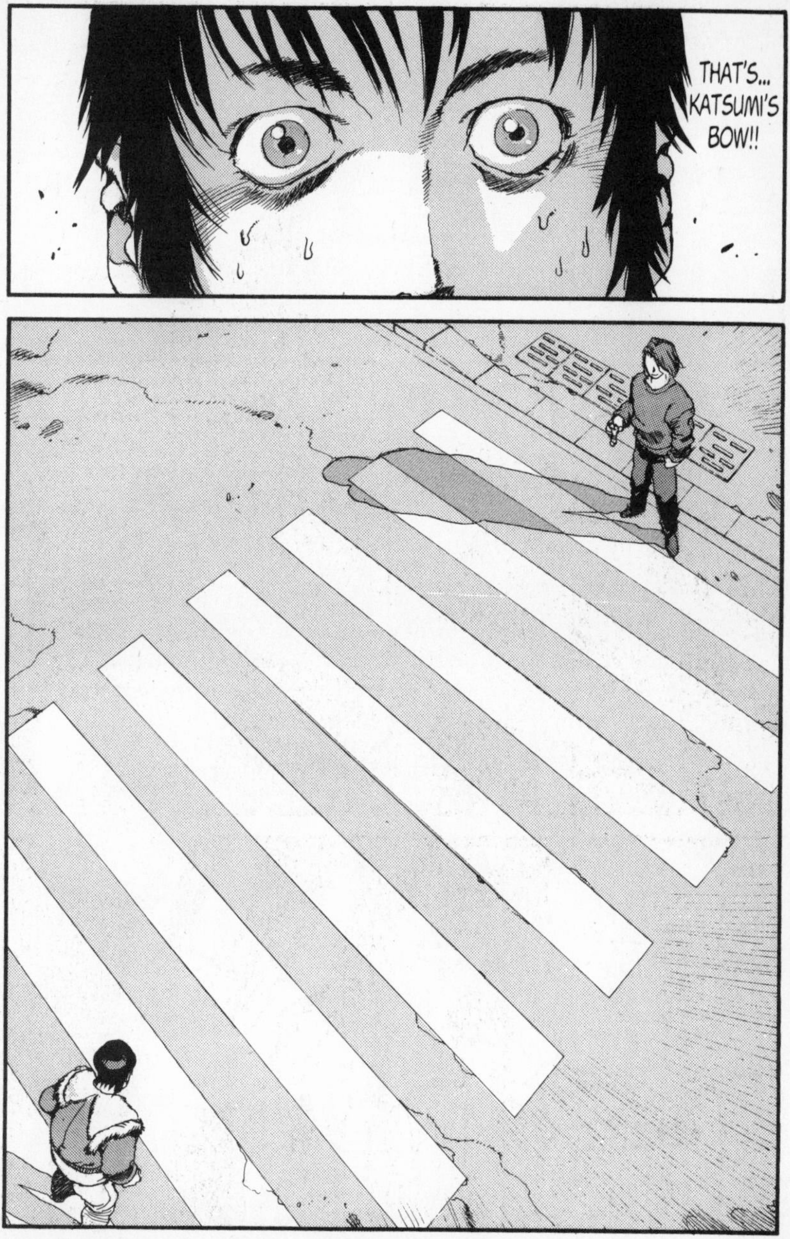
THAT'S... KATSUMI'S BOW!!

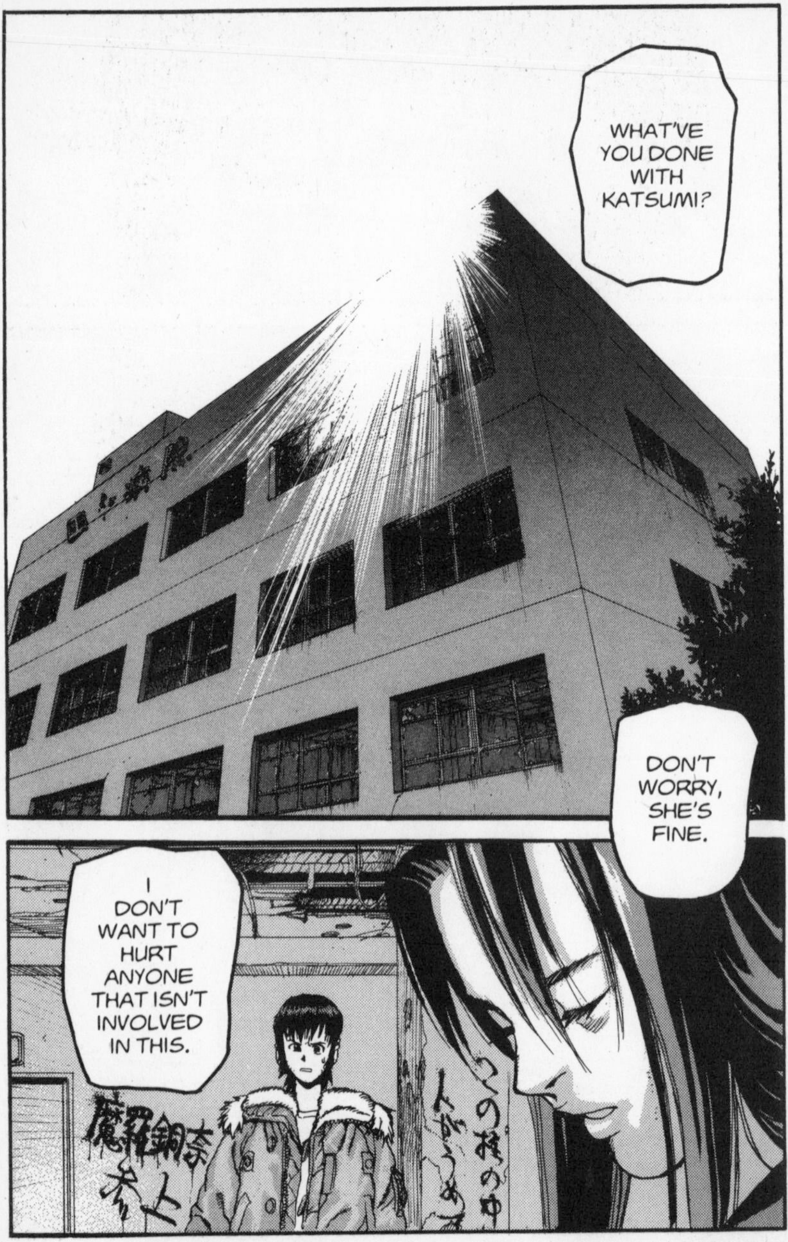
WHAT'VE YOU DONE WITH KATSUMI?
DON'T WORRY, SHE'S FINE.
I DON'T WANT TO HURT ANYONE THAT ISN'T INVOLVED IN THIS.

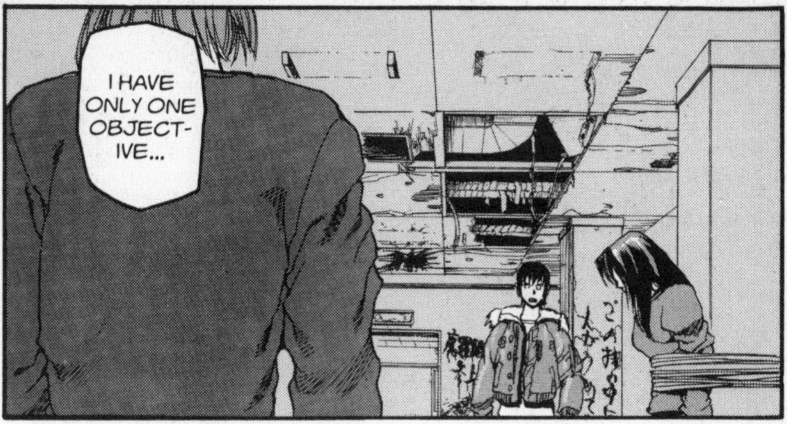
I HAVE ONLY ONE OBJECT-IVE...

No. 3 RESONANCE

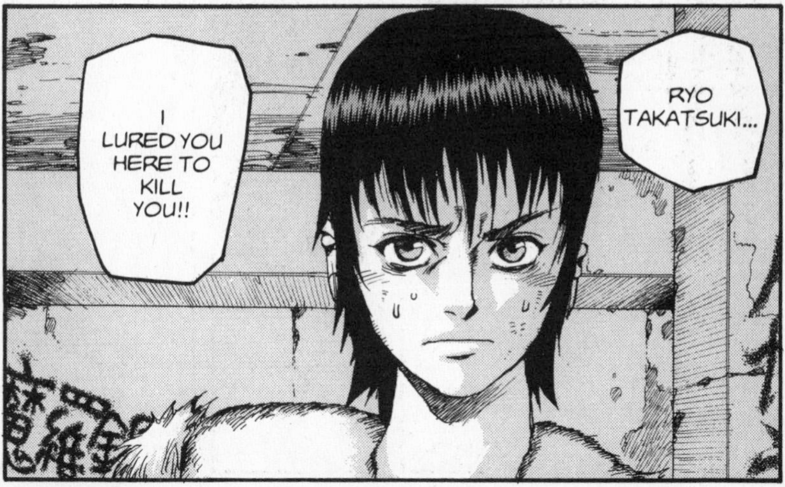
RYO TAKATSUKI...
I LURED YOU HERE TO KILL YOU!!

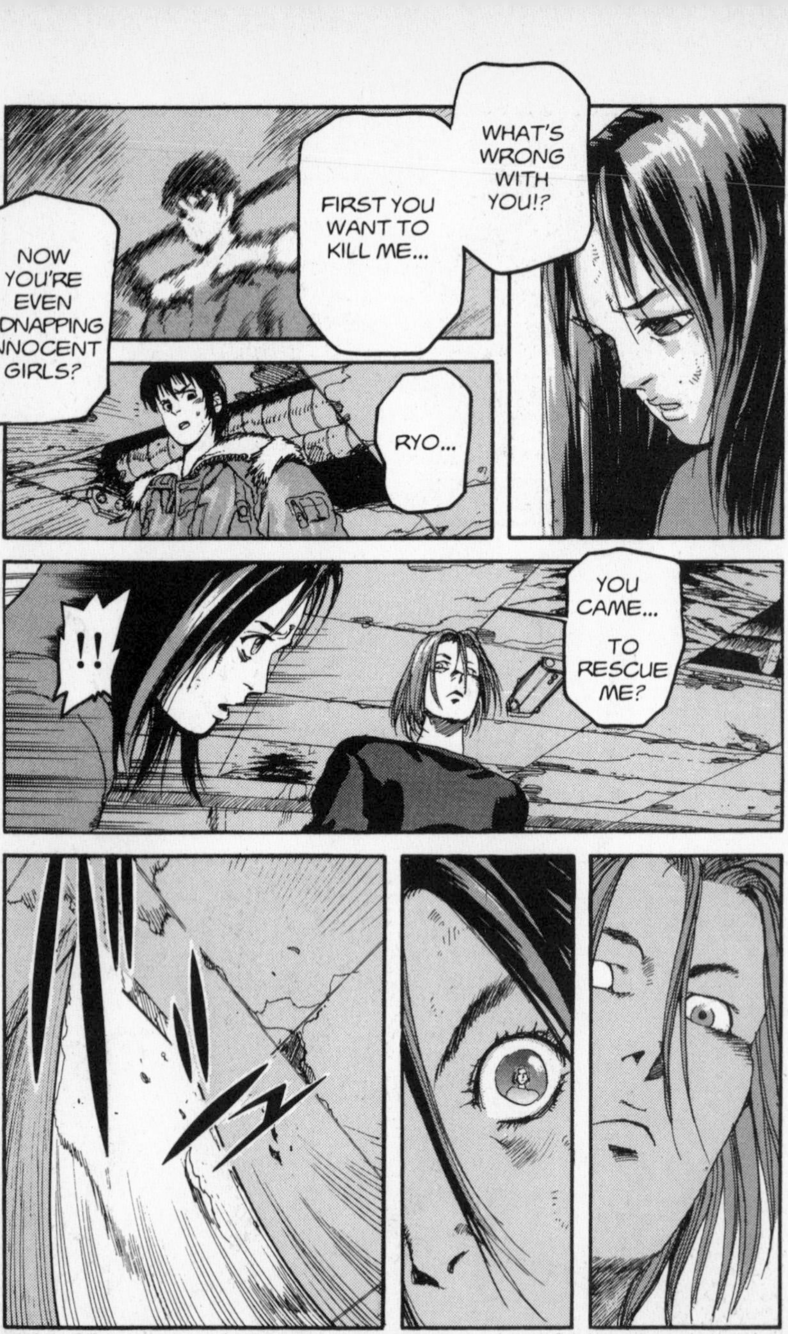
WHAT'S WRONG WITH YOU!?
FIRST YOU WANT TO KILL ME...
NOW YOU'RE EVEN KIDNAPPING INNOCENT GIRLS?
RYO...
YOU CAME... TO RESCUE ME?
!!

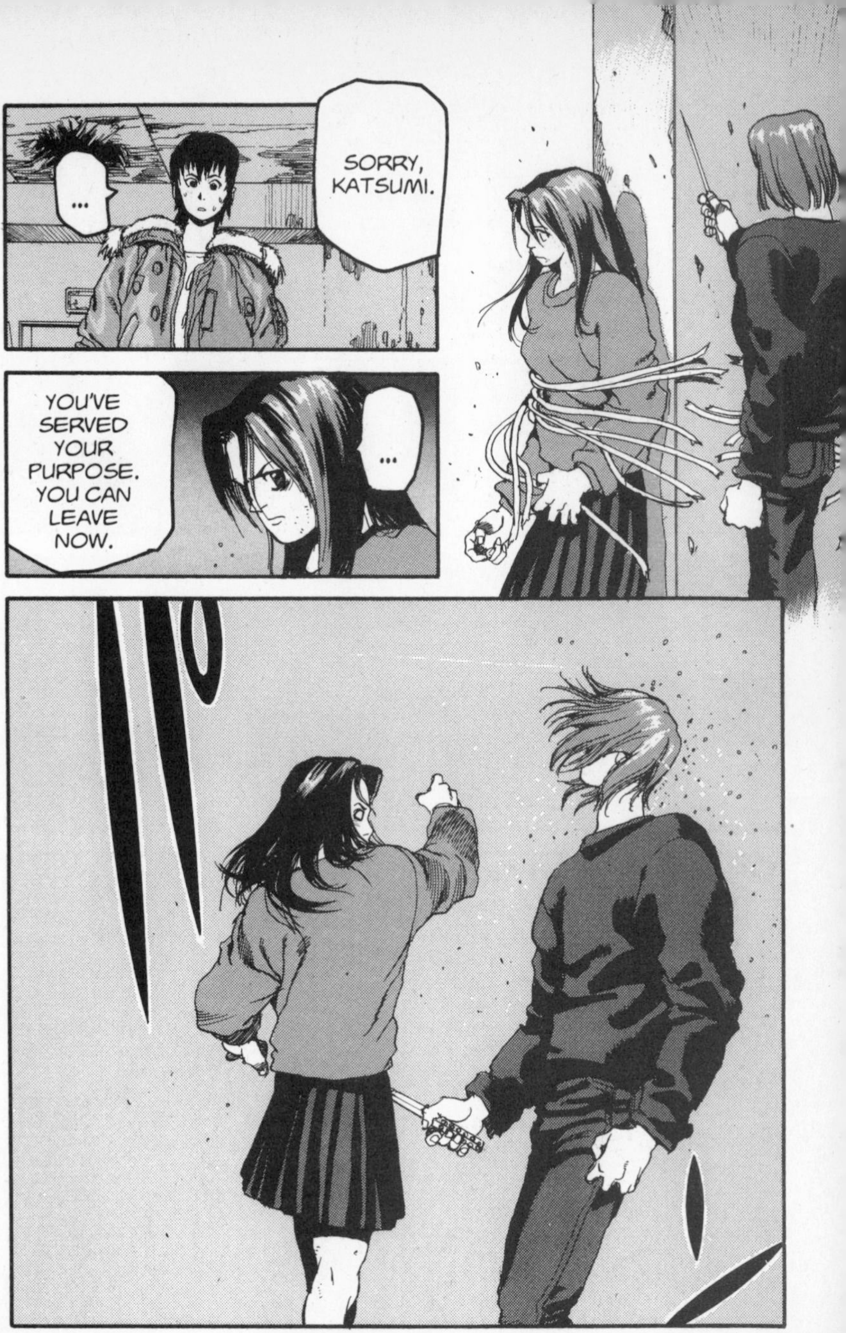
SORRY, KATSUMI.
...
...
YOU'VE SERVED YOUR PURPOSE. YOU CAN LEAVE NOW.

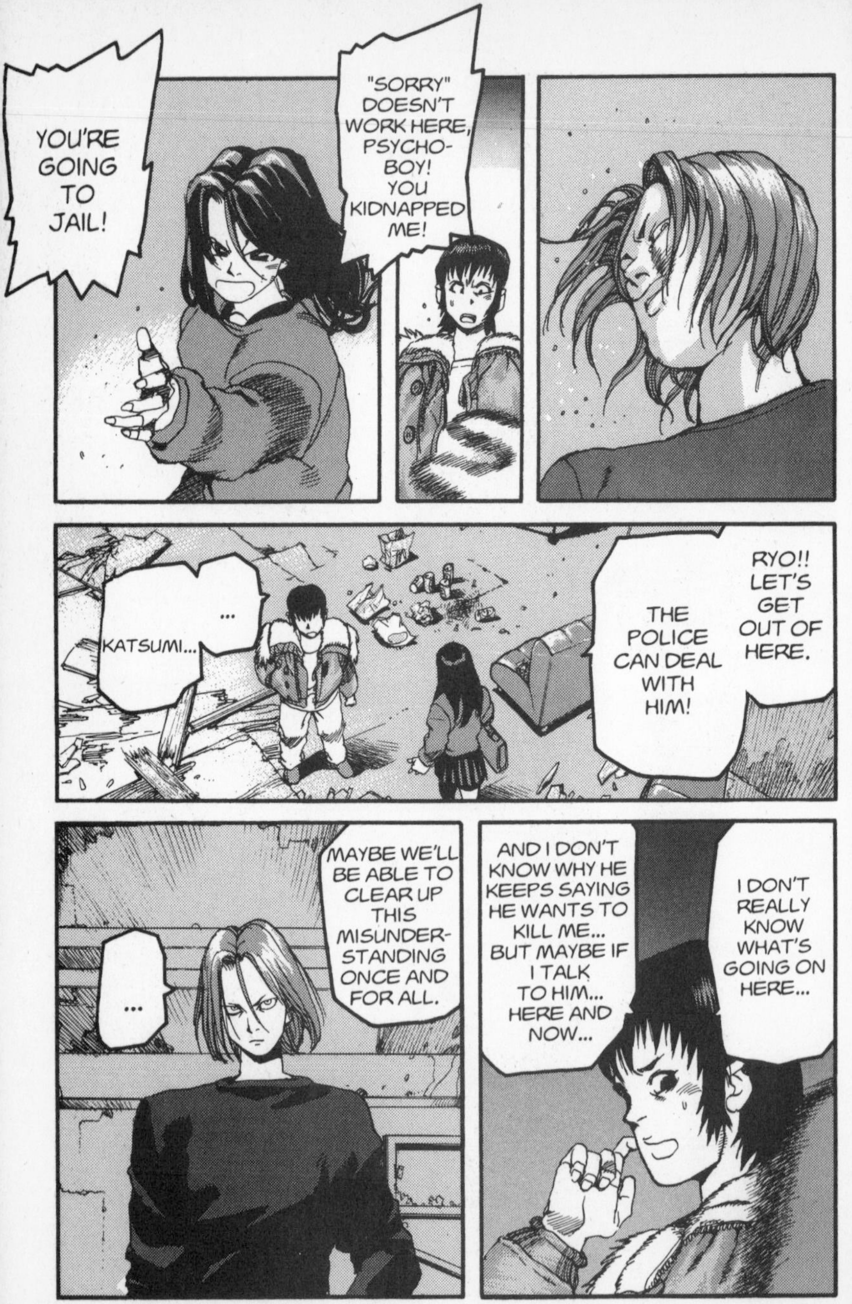
"SORRY" DOESN'T WORK HERE, PSYCHO-BOY! YOU KIDNAPPED ME!
YOU'RE GOING TO JAIL!
RYO!! LET'S GET OUT OF HERE.
THE POLICE CAN DEAL WITH HIM!
...
KATSUMI...
I DON'T REALLY KNOW WHAT'S GOING ON HERE...
AND I DON'T KNOW WHY HE KEEPS SAYING HE WANTS TO KILL ME... BUT MAYBE IF I TALK TO HIM... HERE AND NOW...
MAYBE WE'LL BE ABLE TO CLEAR UP THIS MISUNDERSTANDING ONCE AND FOR ALL.
...

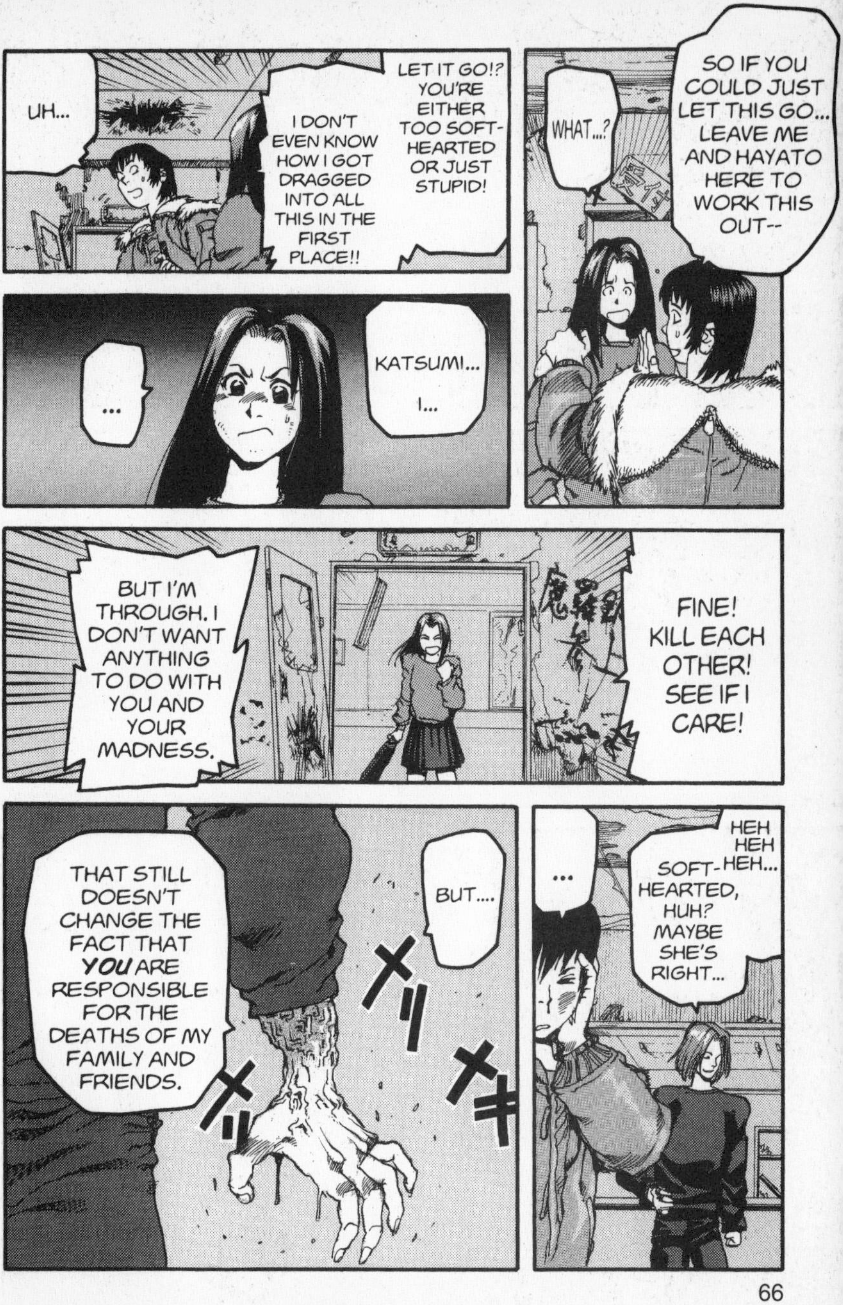
SO IF YOU COULD JUST LET THIS GO... LEAVE ME AND HAYATO HERE TO WORK THIS OUT--
WHAT...?
LET IT GO!? YOU'RE EITHER TOO SOFT-HEARTED OR JUST STUPID!
I DON'T EVEN KNOW HOW I GOT DRAGGED INTO ALL THIS IN THE FIRST PLACE!!
UH...
KATSUMI... I...
...
FINE! KILL EACH OTHER! SEE IF I CARE!
BUT I'M THROUGH. I DON'T WANT ANYTHING TO DO WITH YOU AND YOUR MADNESS.
HEH HEH HEH...
SOFT-HEARTED, HUH? MAYBE SHE'S RIGHT...
...
BUT....
THAT STILL DOESN'T CHANGE THE FACT THAT ***YOU*** ARE RESPONSIBLE FOR THE DEATHS OF MY FAMILY AND FRIENDS.

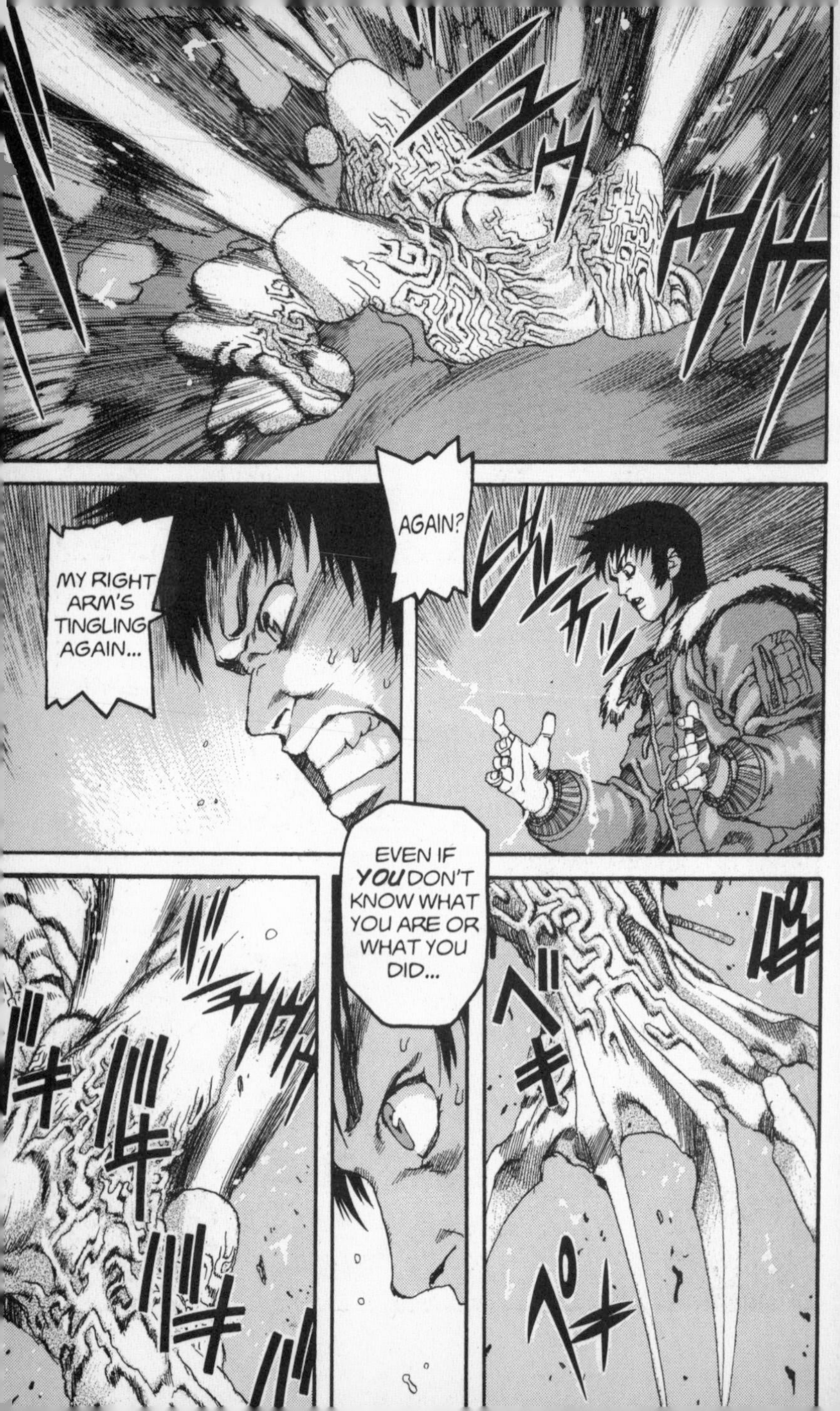
AGAIN?
MY RIGHT ARM'S TINGLING AGAIN...
EVEN IF *YOU* DON'T KNOW WHAT YOU ARE OR WHAT YOU DID...

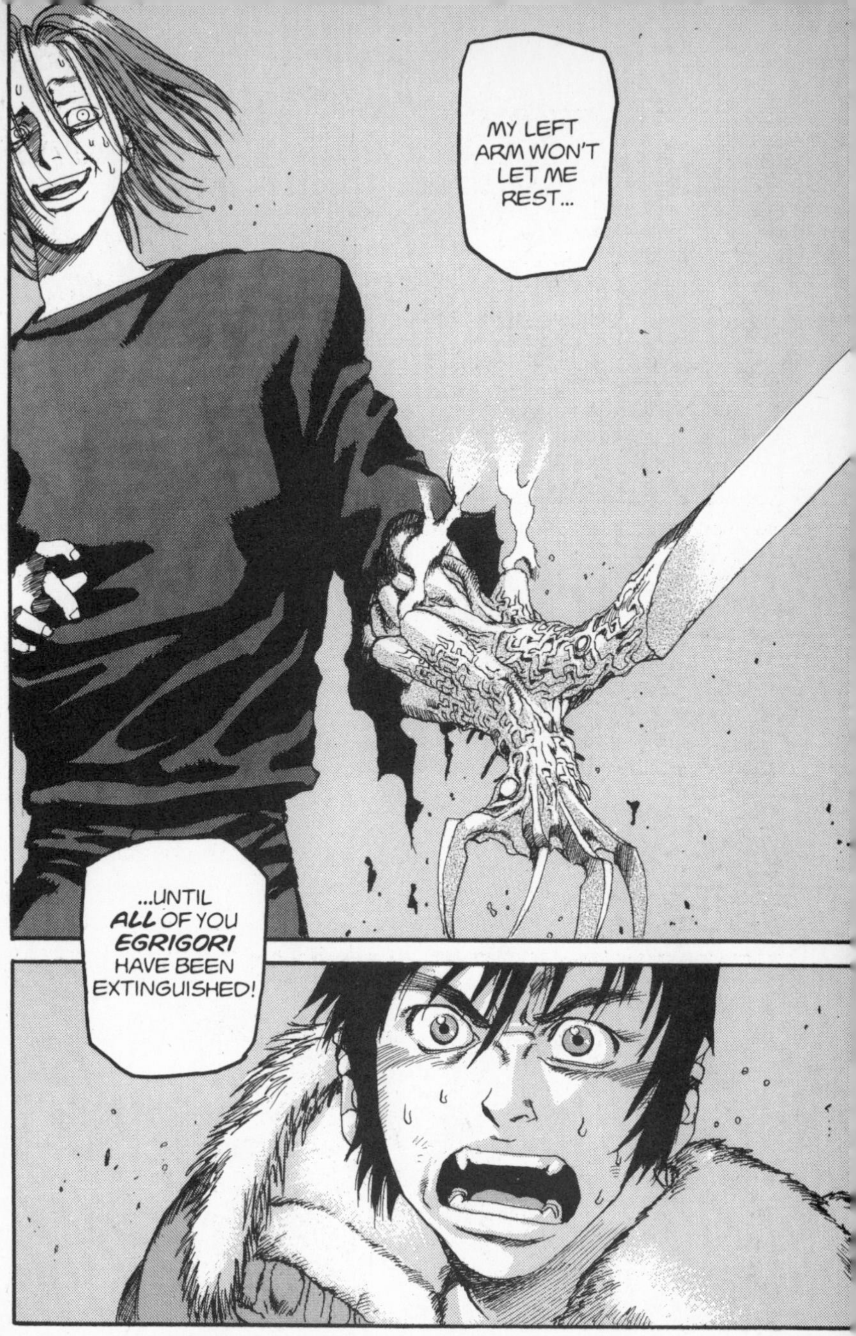
MY LEFT ARM WON'T LET ME REST...
...UNTIL **ALL** OF YOU ***EGRIGORI*** HAVE BEEN EXTINGUISHED!

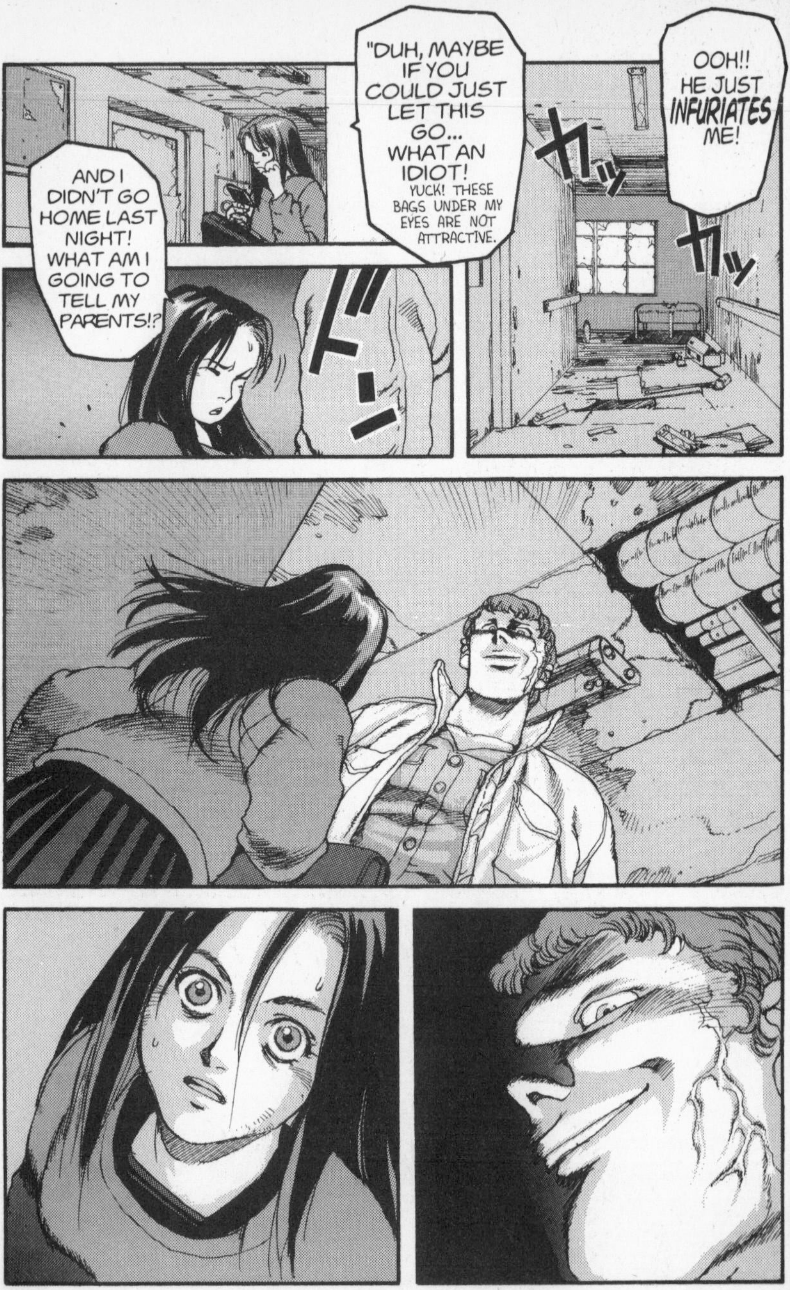

OOH!! HE JUST INFURIATES ME!
カッ
カッ
"DUH, MAYBE IF YOU COULD JUST LET THIS GO... WHAT AN IDIOT!
YUCK! THESE BAGS UNDER MY EYES ARE NOT ATTRACTIVE.
AND I DIDN'T GO HOME LAST NIGHT! WHAT AM I GOING TO TELL MY PARENTS!?
ドーン

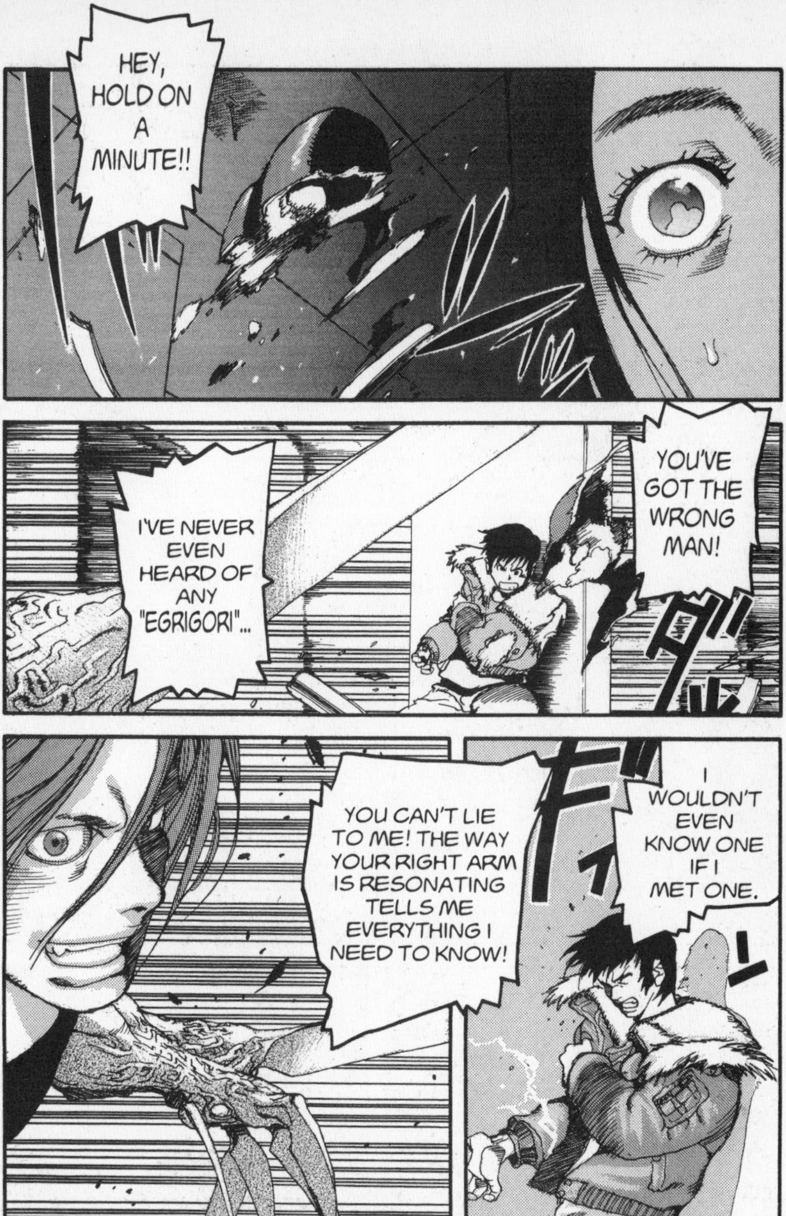
HEY, HOLD ON A MINUTE!!
YOU'VE GOT THE WRONG MAN!
I'VE NEVER EVEN HEARD OF ANY "EGRIGORI"...
I WOULDN'T EVEN KNOW ONE IF I MET ONE.
YOU CAN'T LIE TO ME! THE WAY YOUR RIGHT ARM IS RESONATING TELLS ME EVERYTHING I NEED TO KNOW!

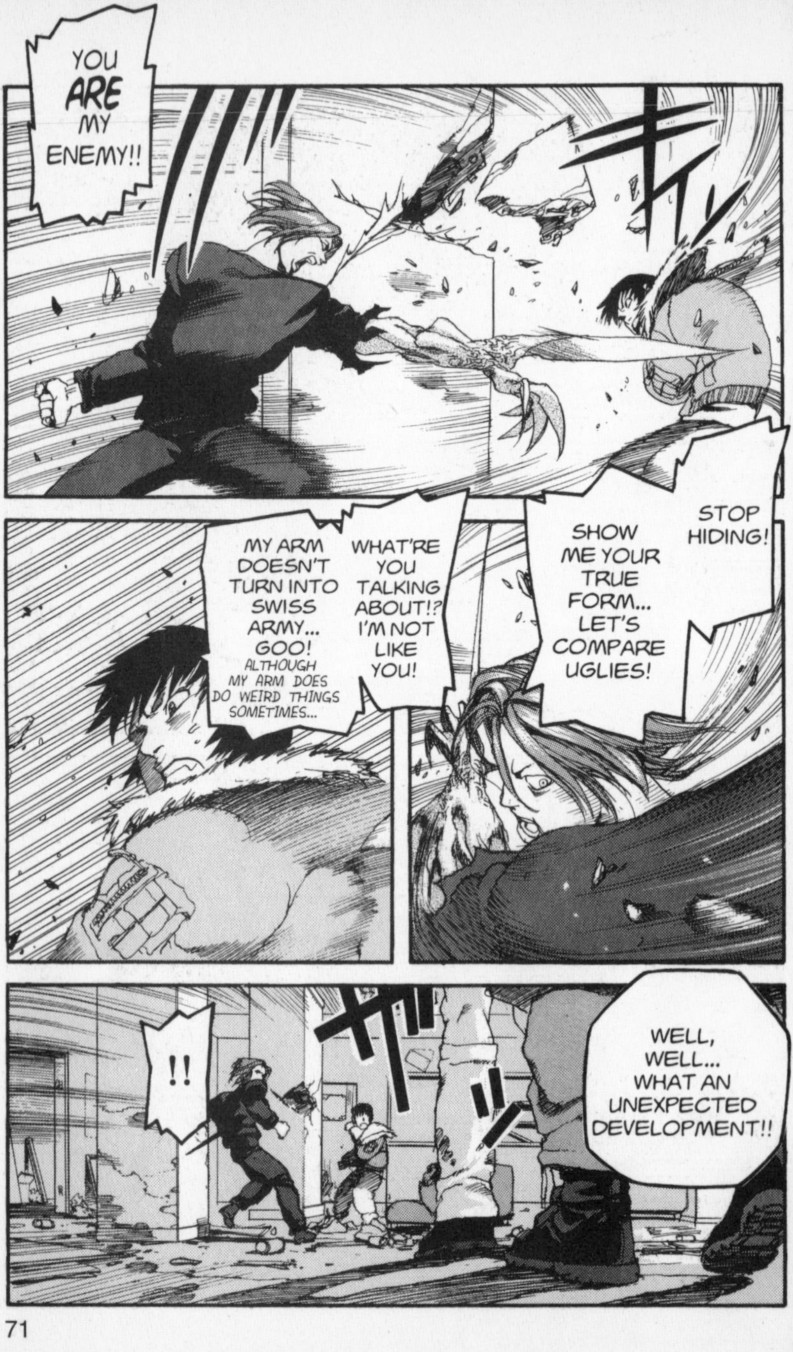
YOU ARE MY ENEMY!!
STOP HIDING!
SHOW ME YOUR TRUE FORM... LET'S COMPARE UGLIES!
WHAT'RE YOU TALKING ABOUT!? I'M NOT LIKE YOU!
MY ARM DOESN'T TURN INTO SWISS ARMY... GOO!
ALTHOUGH MY ARM DOES DO WEIRD THINGS SOMETIMES...
WELL, WELL... WHAT AN UNEXPECTED DEVELOPMENT!!
!!

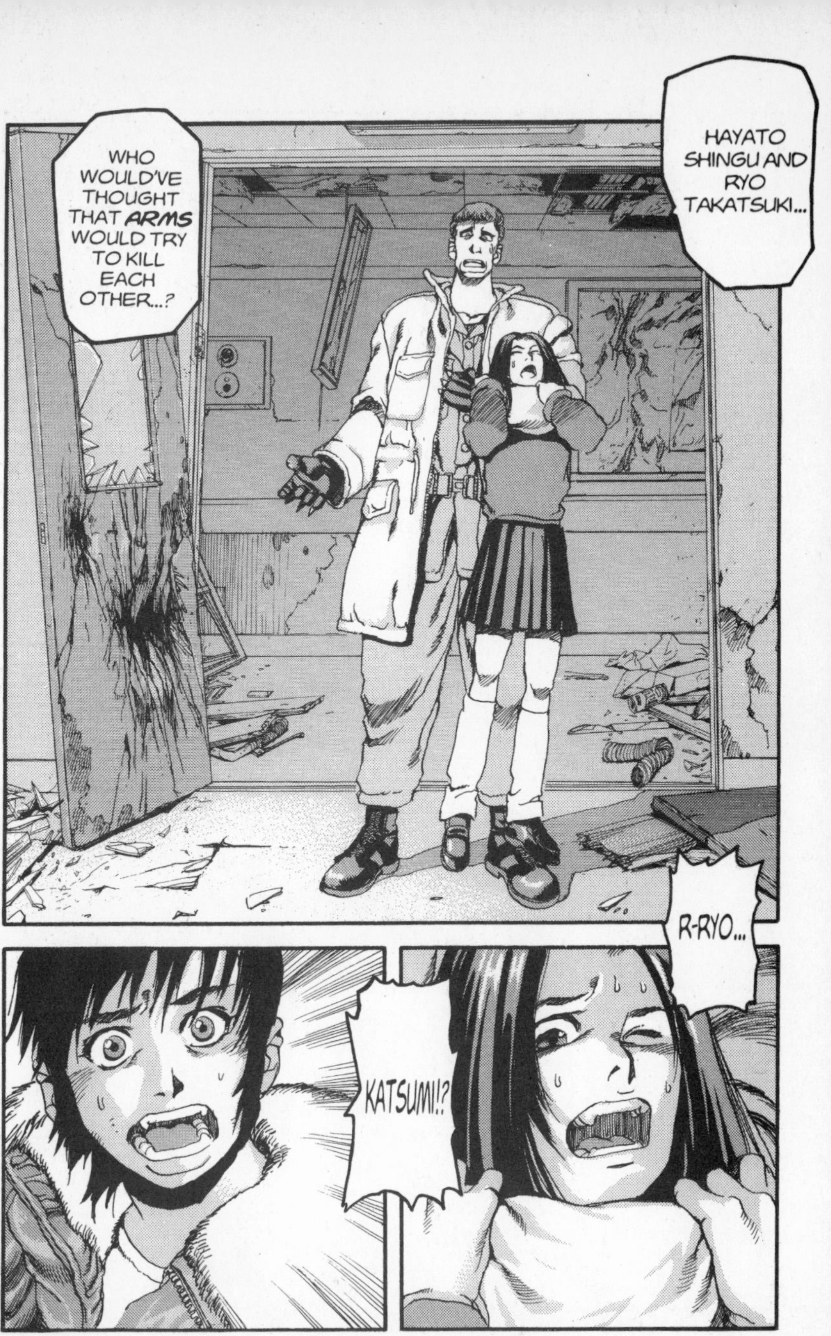

HAYATO SHINGU AND RYO TAKATSUKI...
WHO WOULD'VE THOUGHT THAT ARMS WOULD TRY TO KILL EACH OTHER...?
R-RYO...
KATSUMI!?

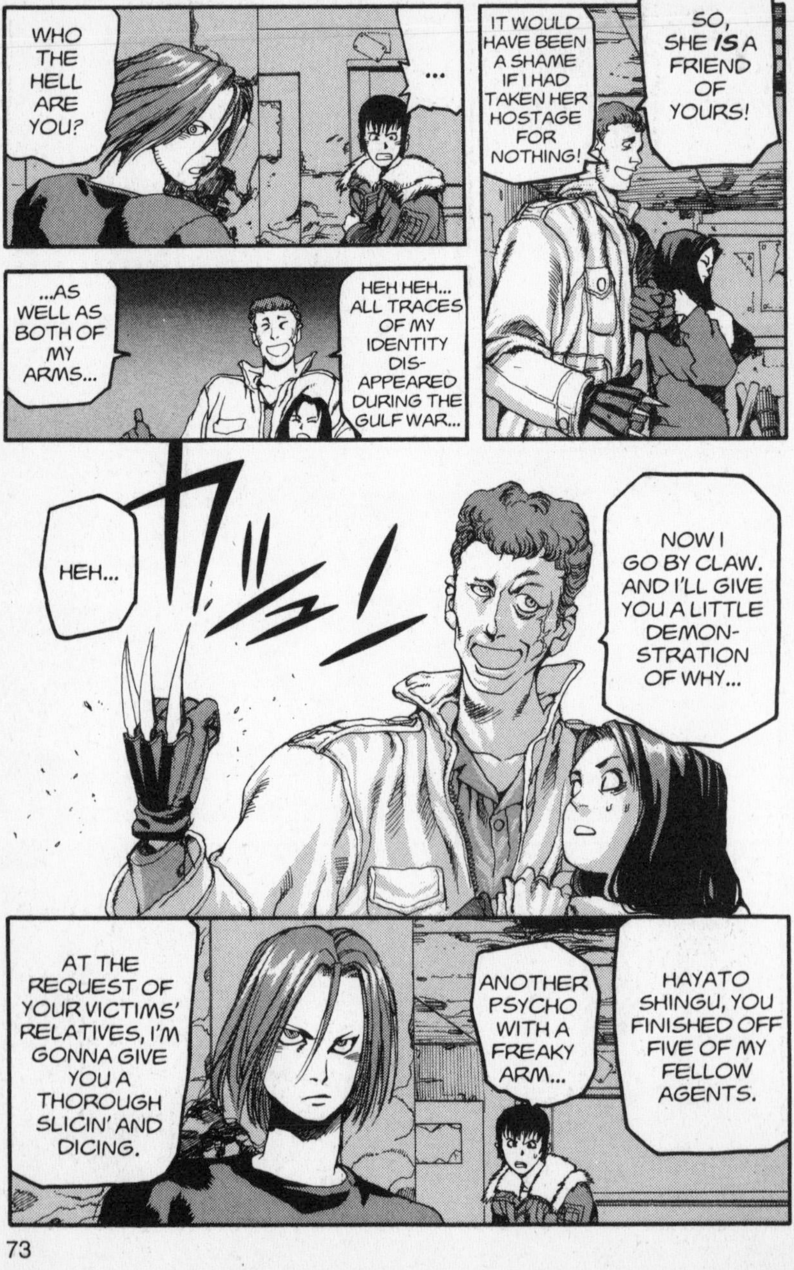
SO, SHE *IS* A FRIEND OF YOURS!
IT WOULD HAVE BEEN A SHAME IF I HAD TAKEN HER HOSTAGE FOR NOTHING!
...
WHO THE HELL ARE YOU?
HEH HEH... ALL TRACES OF MY IDENTITY DIS-APPEARED DURING THE GULF WAR...
...AS WELL AS BOTH OF MY ARMS...
NOW I GO BY CLAW. AND I'LL GIVE YOU A LITTLE DEMON-STRATION OF WHY...
HEH...
HAYATO SHINGU, YOU FINISHED OFF FIVE OF MY FELLOW AGENTS.
ANOTHER PSYCHO WITH A FREAKY ARM...
AT THE REQUEST OF YOUR VICTIMS' RELATIVES, I'M GONNA GIVE YOU A THOROUGH SLICIN' AND DICING.

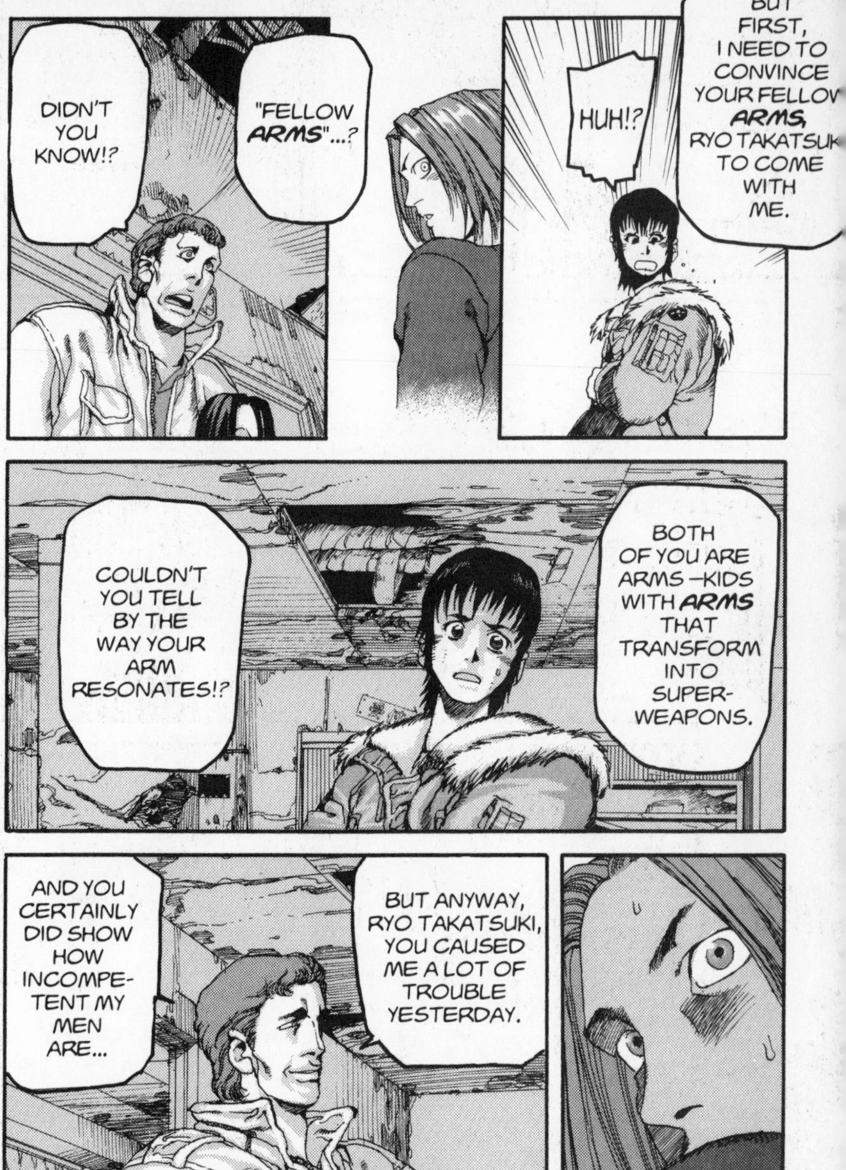
BUT FIRST, I NEED TO CONVINCE YOUR FELLOW ARMS, RYO TAKATSUK TO COME WITH ME.
HUH!?
"FELLOW ARMS"...?
DIDN'T YOU KNOW!?
BOTH OF YOU ARE ARMS—KIDS WITH ARMS THAT TRANSFORM INTO SUPER-WEAPONS.
COULDN'T YOU TELL BY THE WAY YOUR ARM RESONATES!?
BUT ANYWAY, RYO TAKATSUKI, YOU CAUSED ME A LOT OF TROUBLE YESTERDAY.
AND YOU CERTAINLY DID SHOW HOW INCOMPE-TENT MY MEN ARE...

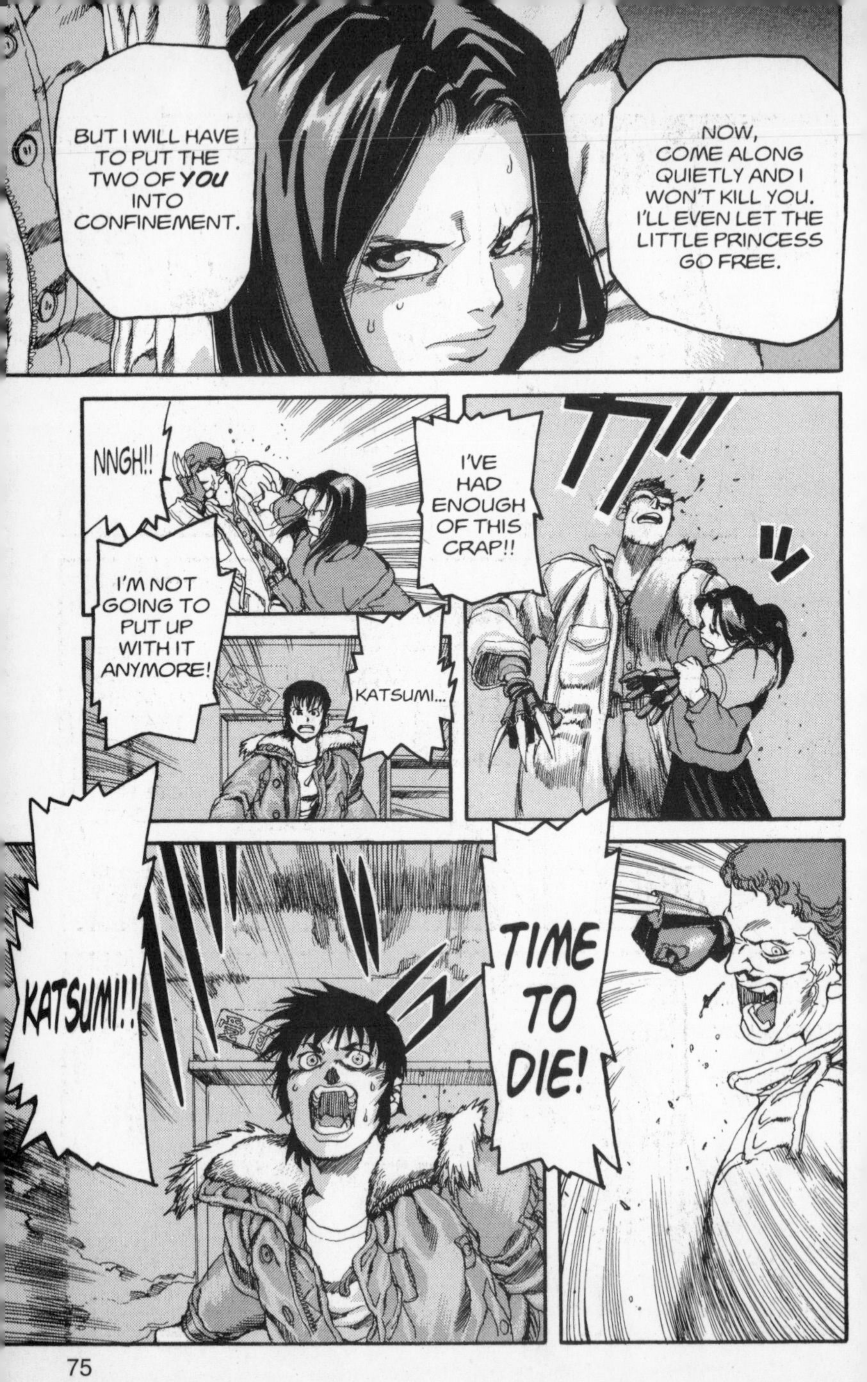
NOW, COME ALONG QUIETLY AND I WON'T KILL YOU. I'LL EVEN LET THE LITTLE PRINCESS GO FREE.
BUT I WILL HAVE TO PUT THE TWO OF *YOU* INTO CONFINEMENT.
I'VE HAD ENOUGH OF THIS CRAP!!
NNGH!!
I'M NOT GOING TO PUT UP WITH IT ANYMORE!
KATSUMI...
TIME TO DIE!
KATSUMI!!

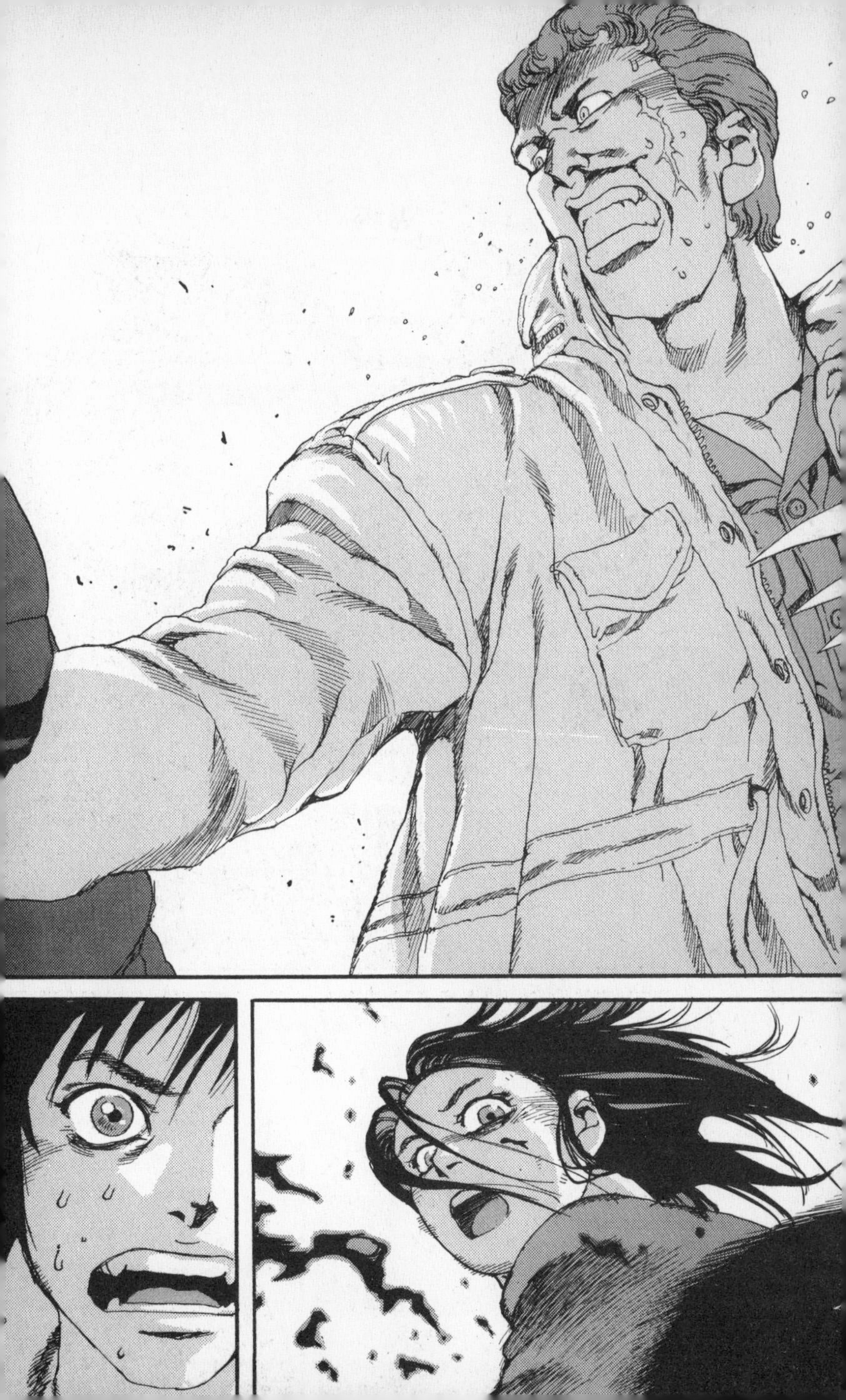

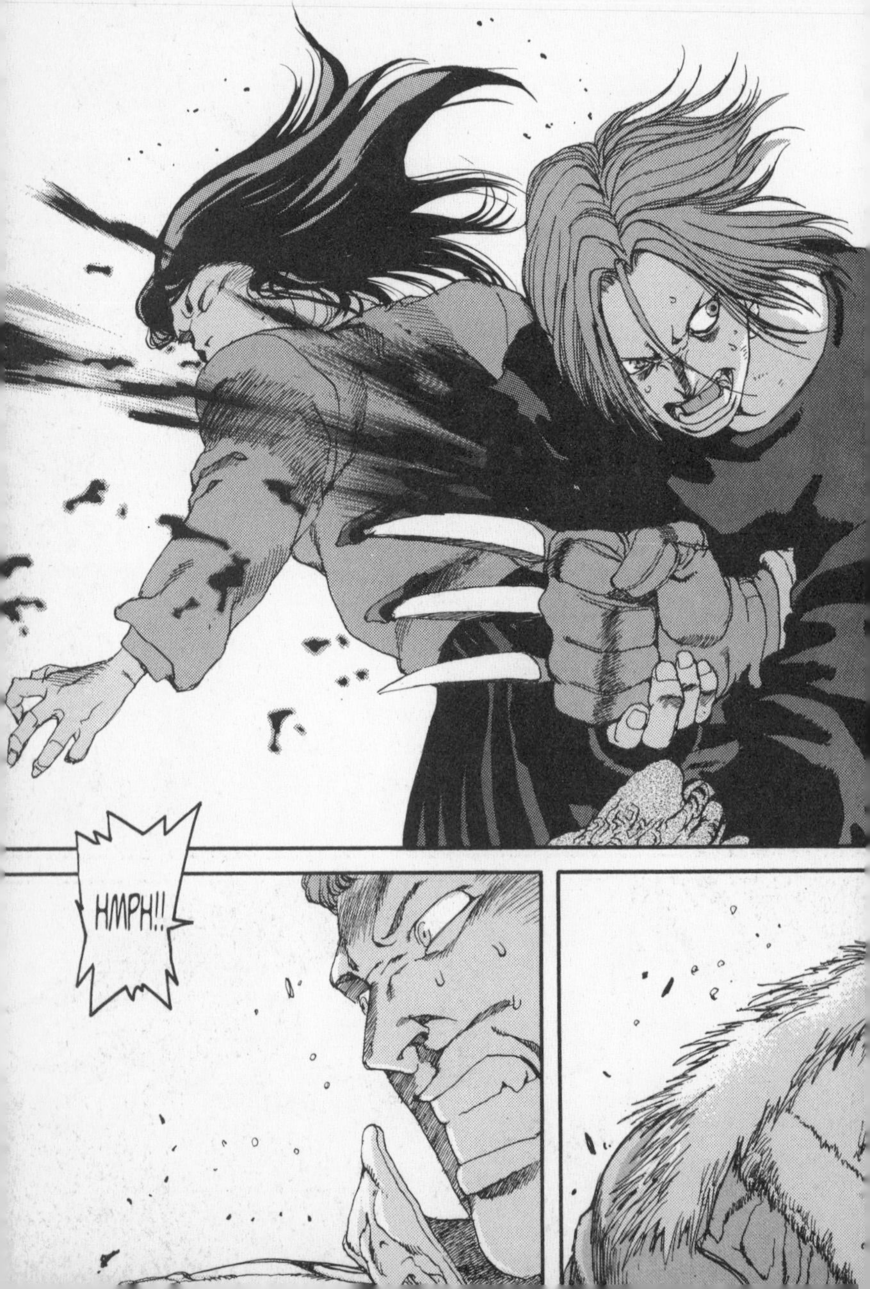
HMPH!!

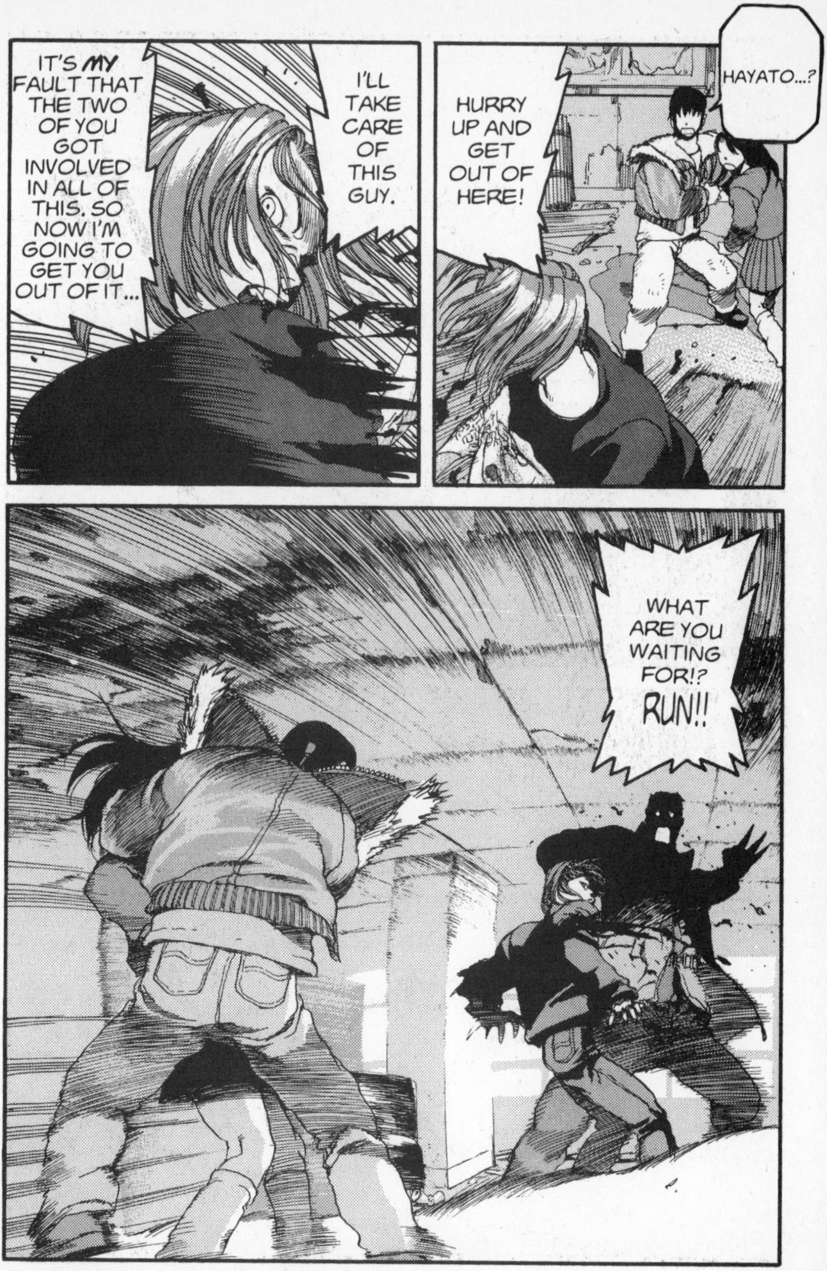
HAYATO...?
HURRY UP AND GET OUT OF HERE!
I'LL TAKE CARE OF THIS GUY.
IT'S MY FAULT THAT THE TWO OF YOU GOT INVOLVED IN ALL OF THIS. SO NOW I'M GOING TO GET YOU OUT OF IT...
WHAT ARE YOU WAITING FOR!? RUN!!

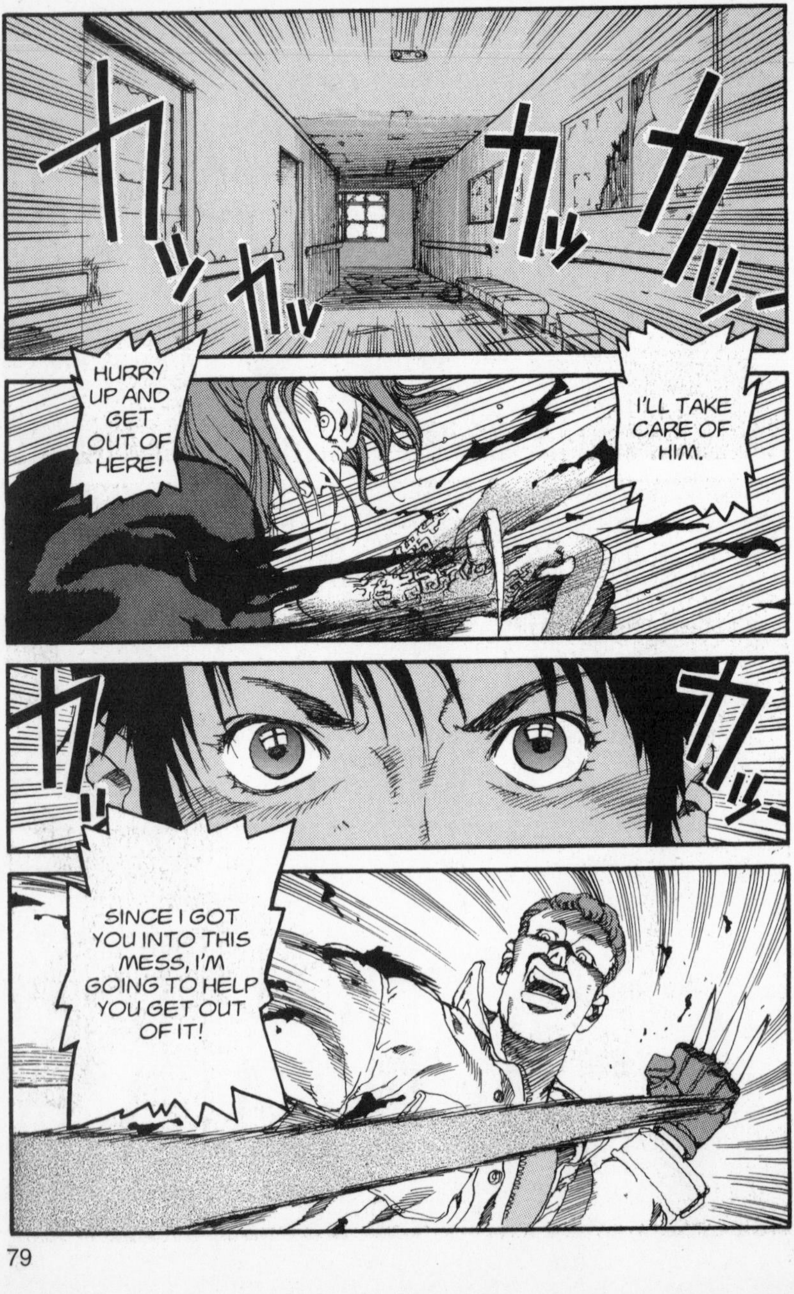
I'LL TAKE CARE OF HIM.
HURRY UP AND GET OUT OF HERE!
SINCE I GOT YOU INTO THIS MESS, I'M GOING TO HELP YOU GET OUT OF IT!

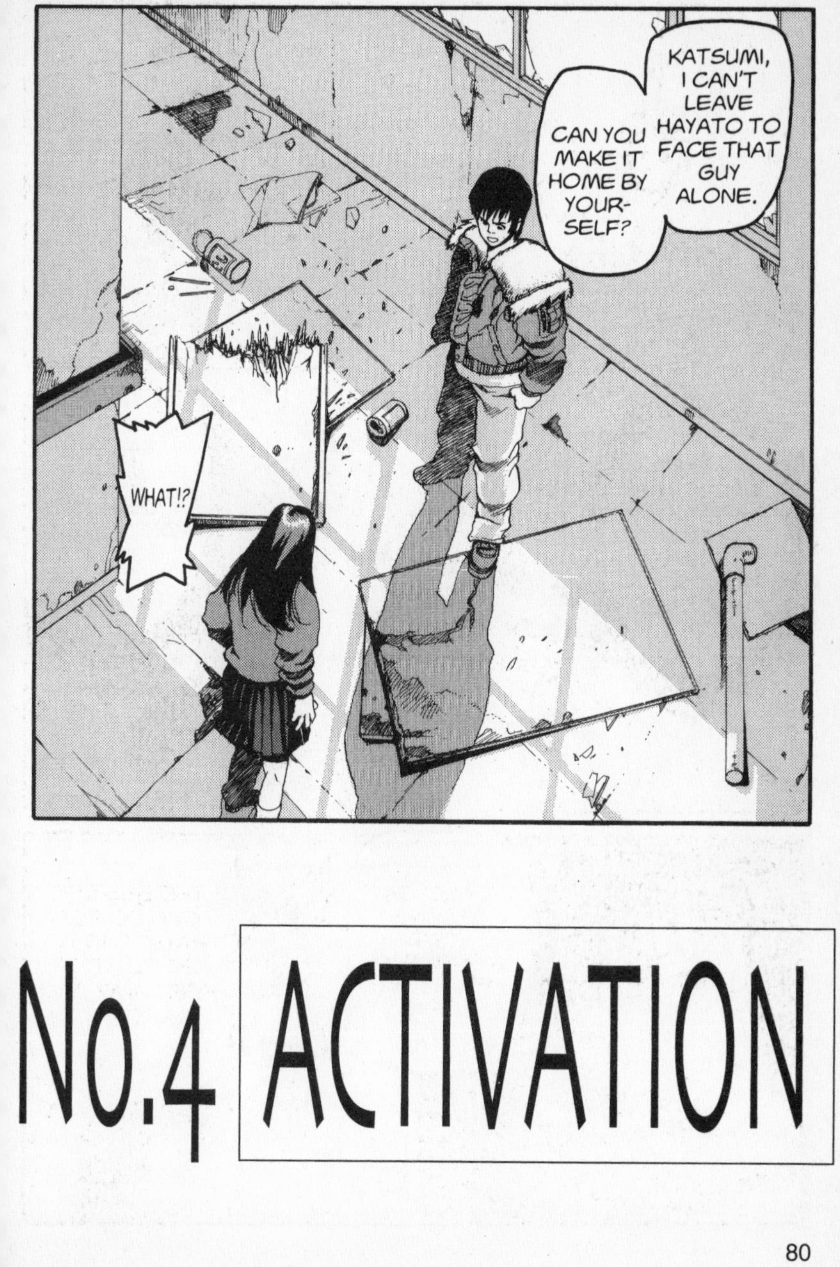
KATSUMI, I CAN'T LEAVE HAYATO TO FACE THAT GUY ALONE.
CAN YOU MAKE IT HOME BY YOUR-SELF?
WHAT!?

No.4 ACTIVATION

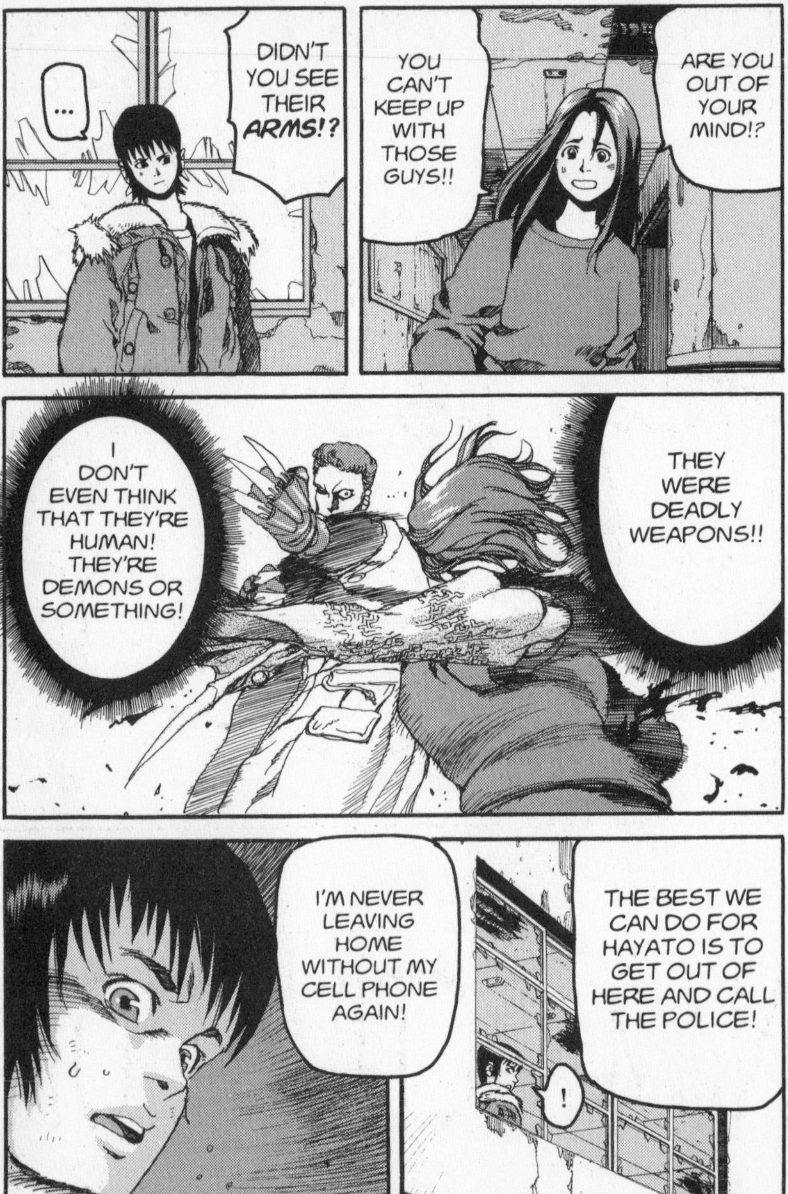
ARE YOU OUT OF YOUR MIND!?
YOU CAN'T KEEP UP WITH THOSE GUYS!!
DIDN'T YOU SEE THEIR *ARMS!?*
...
THEY WERE DEADLY WEAPONS!!
...
I DON'T EVEN THINK THAT THEY'RE HUMAN! THEY'RE DEMONS OR SOMETHING!
THE BEST WE CAN DO FOR HAYATO IS TO GET OUT OF HERE AND CALL THE POLICE!
!
I'M NEVER LEAVING HOME WITHOUT MY CELL PHONE AGAIN!

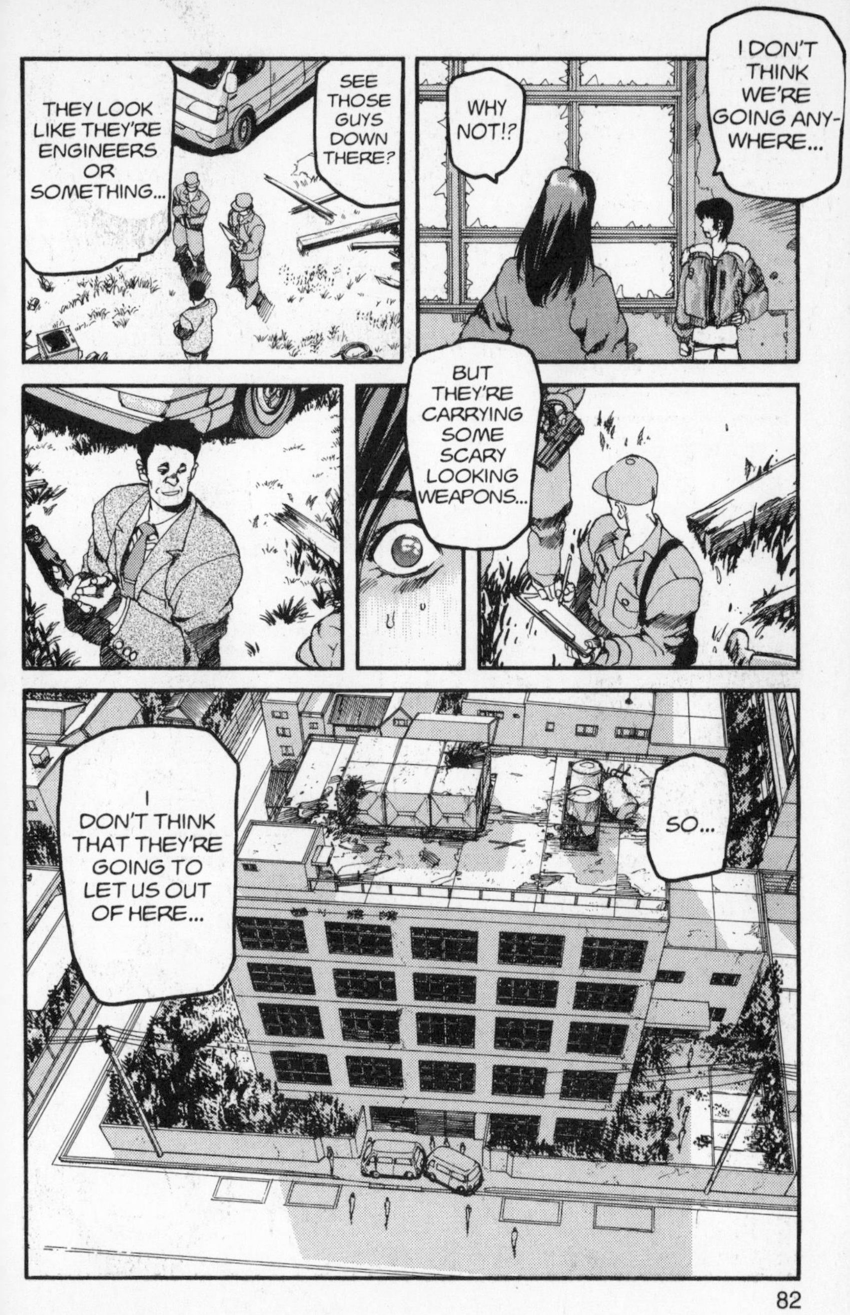
I DON'T THINK WE'RE GOING ANY-WHERE...
WHY NOT!?
SEE THOSE GUYS DOWN THERE?
THEY LOOK LIKE THEY'RE ENGINEERS OR SOMETHING...
BUT THEY'RE CARRYING SOME SCARY LOOKING WEAPONS...
SO...
I DON'T THINK THAT THEY'RE GOING TO LET US OUT OF HERE...

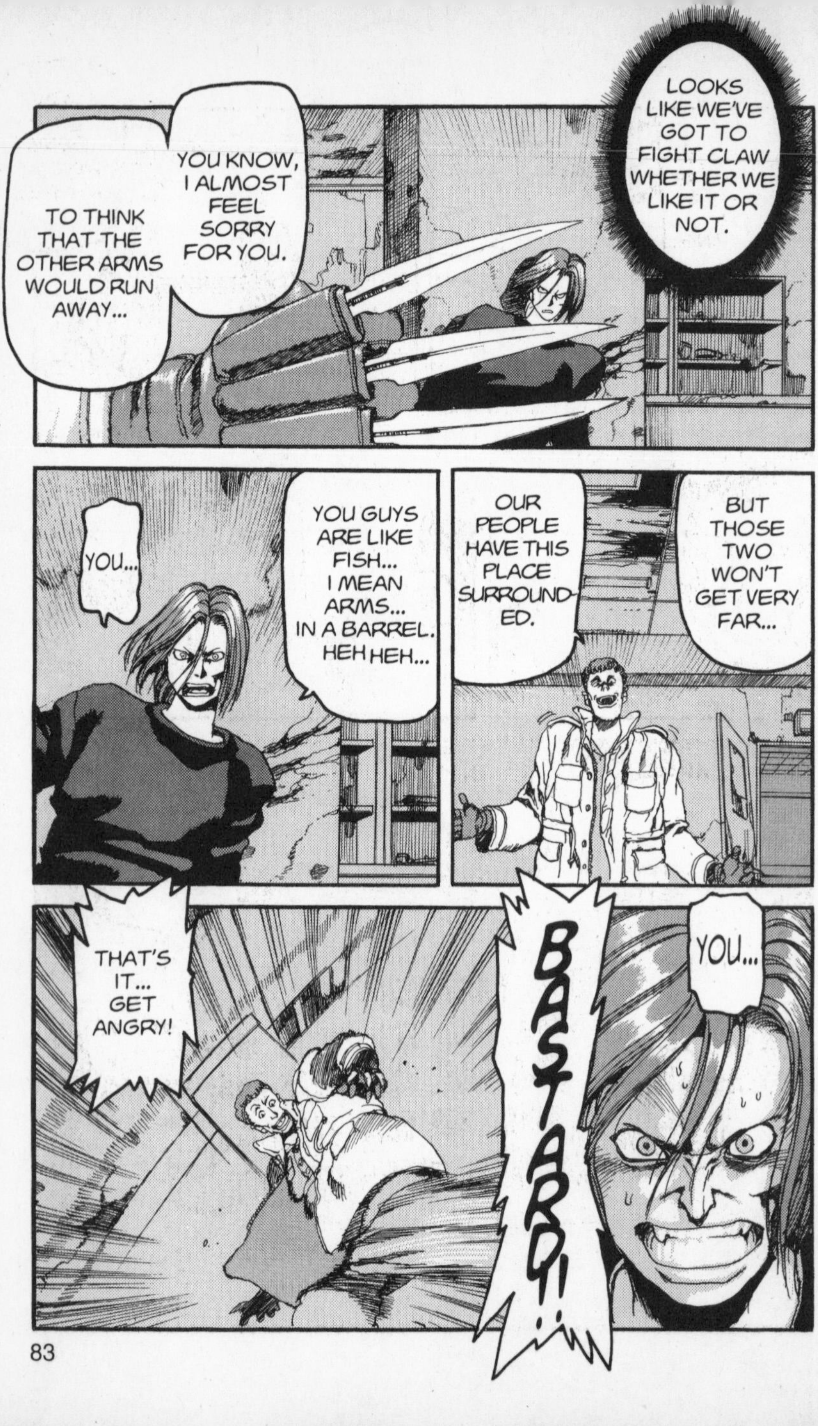
LOOKS LIKE WE'VE GOT TO FIGHT CLAW WHETHER WE LIKE IT OR NOT.
YOU KNOW, I ALMOST FEEL SORRY FOR YOU.
TO THINK THAT THE OTHER ARMS WOULD RUN AWAY...
BUT THOSE TWO WON'T GET VERY FAR...
OUR PEOPLE HAVE THIS PLACE SURROUND-ED.
YOU GUYS ARE LIKE FISH... I MEAN ARMS... IN A BARREL. HEH HEH...
YOU...
YOU...
BASTARD!!
THAT'S IT... GET ANGRY!

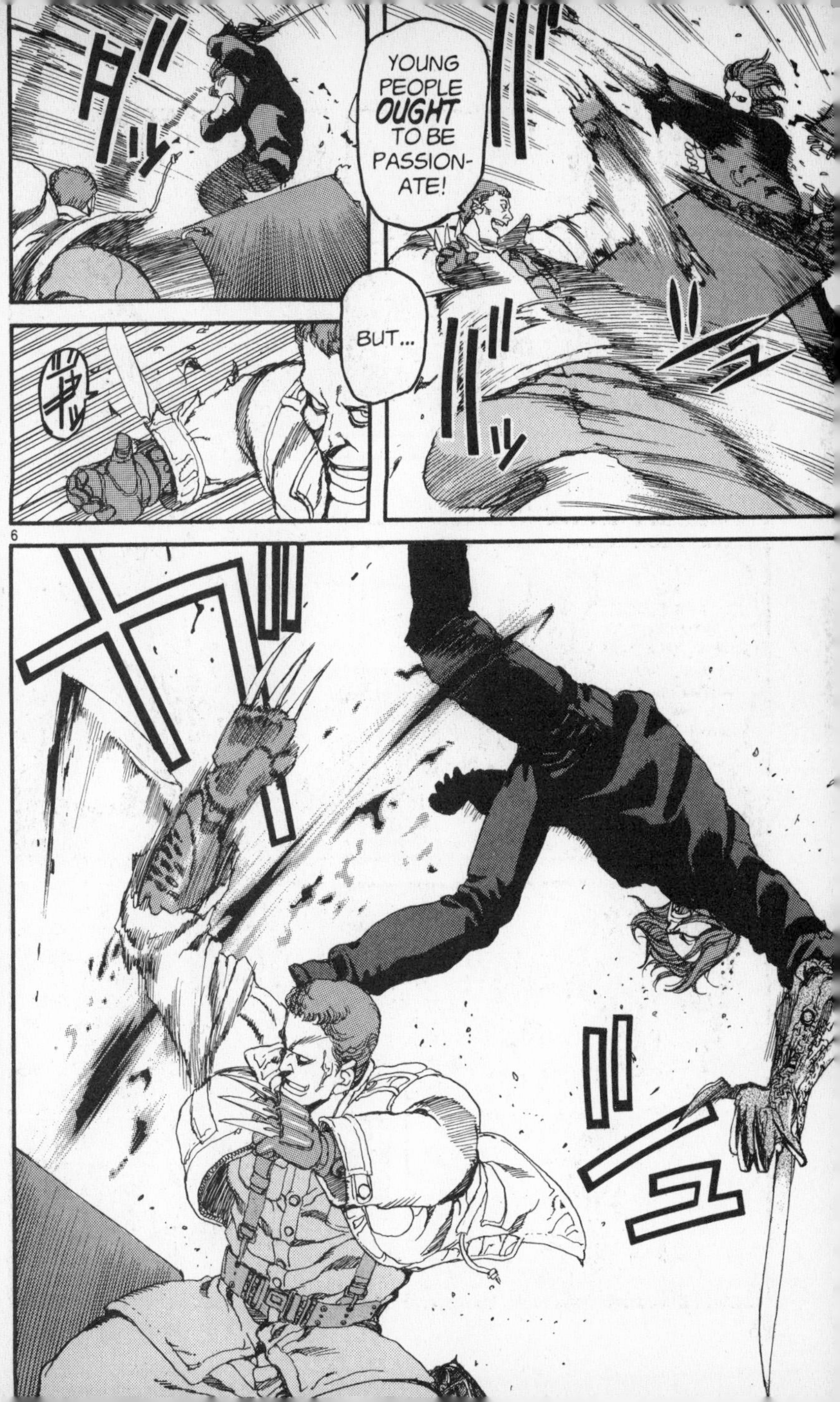
YOUNG PEOPLE OUGHT TO BE PASSION-ATE!
BUT...

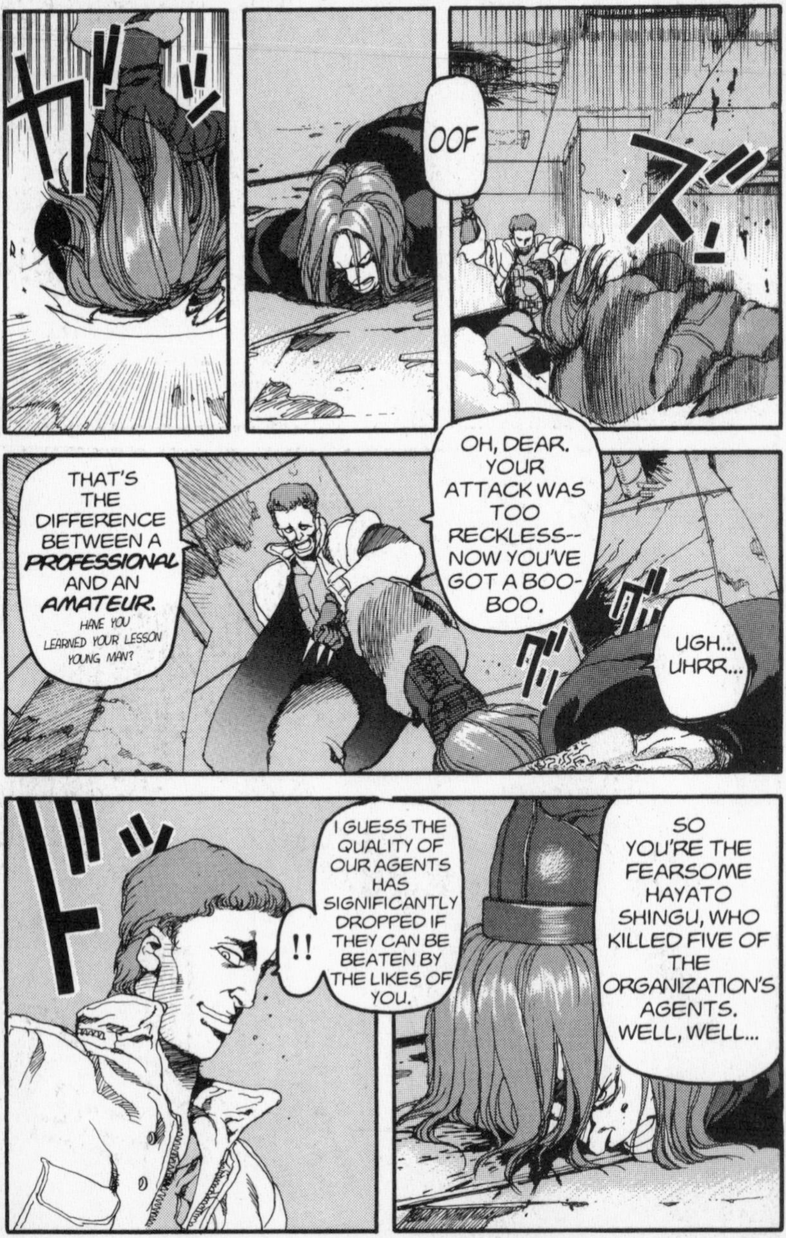
OOF
OH, DEAR. YOUR ATTACK WAS TOO RECKLESS-- NOW YOU'VE GOT A BOO-BOO.
UGH... UHRR...
THAT'S THE DIFFERENCE BETWEEN A PROFESSIONAL AND AN AMATEUR. HAVE YOU LEARNED YOUR LESSON YOUNG MAN?
SO YOU'RE THE FEARSOME HAYATO SHINGU, WHO KILLED FIVE OF THE ORGANIZATION'S AGENTS. WELL, WELL...
I GUESS THE QUALITY OF OUR AGENTS HAS SIGNIFICANTLY DROPPED IF THEY CAN BE BEATEN BY THE LIKES OF YOU.
!!

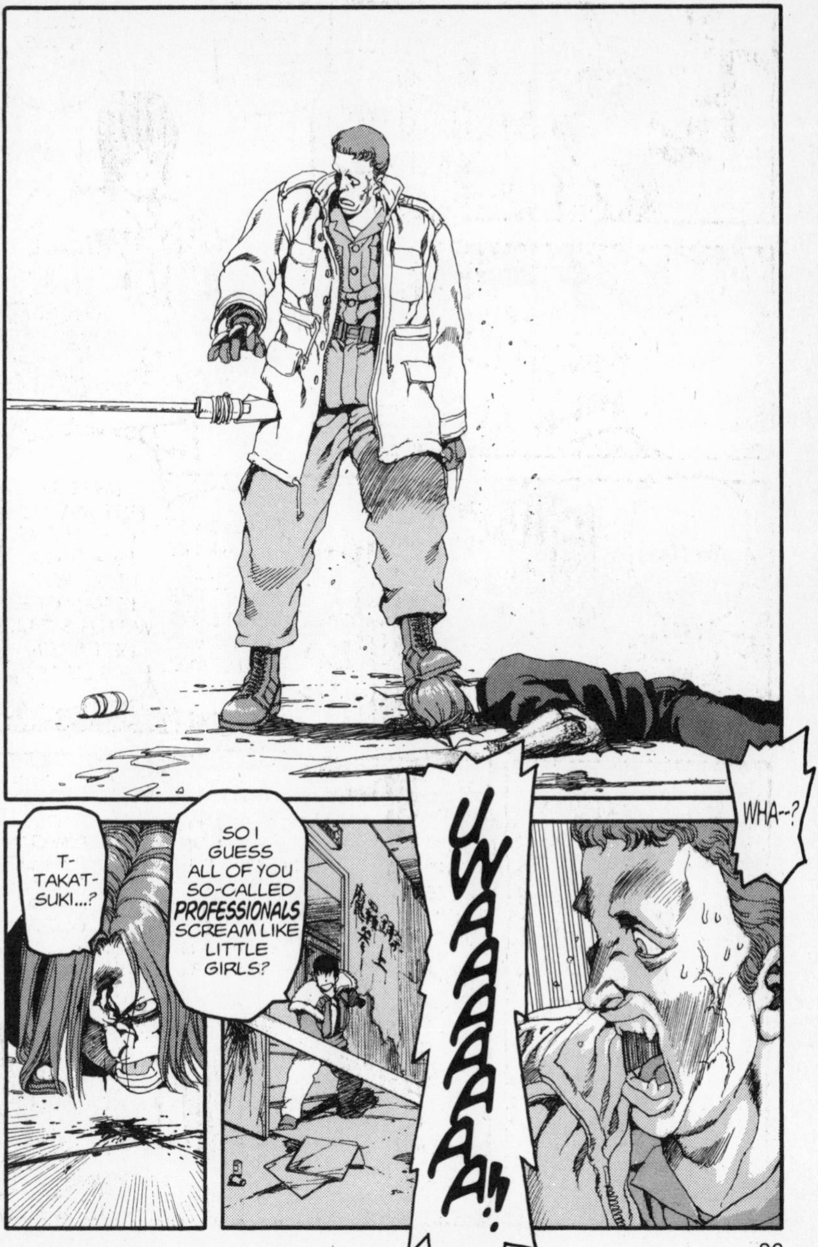
WHA--?
UWAAAAAAA!!
SO I GUESS ALL OF YOU SO-CALLED PROFESSIONALS SCREAM LIKE LITTLE GIRLS?
T-TAKATSUKI...?

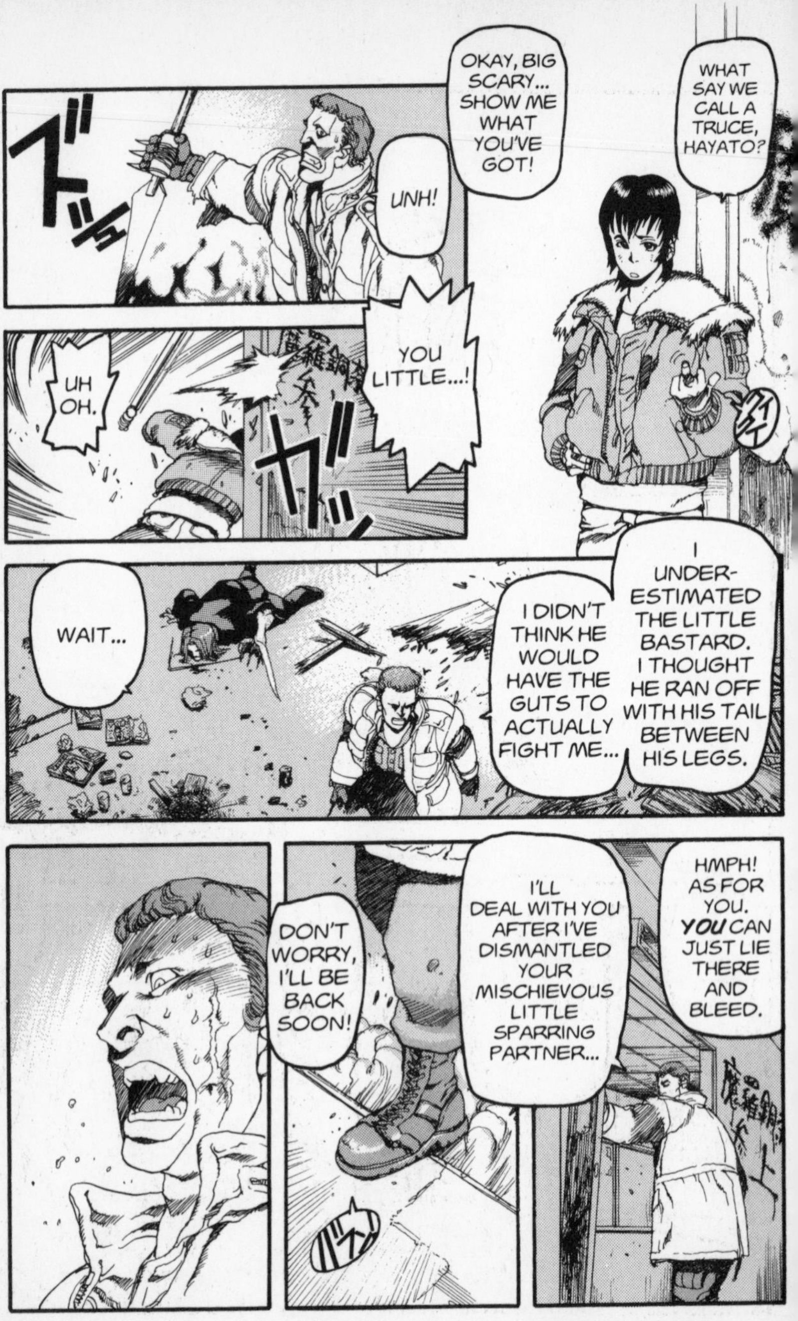
WHAT SAY WE CALL A TRUCE, HAYATO?
OKAY, BIG SCARY... SHOW ME WHAT YOU'VE GOT!
UNH!
YOU LITTLE...!
UH OH.
I UNDER-ESTIMATED THE LITTLE BASTARD. I THOUGHT HE RAN OFF WITH HIS TAIL BETWEEN HIS LEGS.
I DIDN'T THINK HE WOULD HAVE THE GUTS TO ACTUALLY FIGHT ME...
WAIT...
HMPH! AS FOR YOU. *YOU* CAN JUST LIE THERE AND BLEED.
I'LL DEAL WITH YOU AFTER I'VE DISMANTLED YOUR MISCHIEVOUS LITTLE SPARRING PARTNER...
DON'T WORRY, I'LL BE BACK SOON!

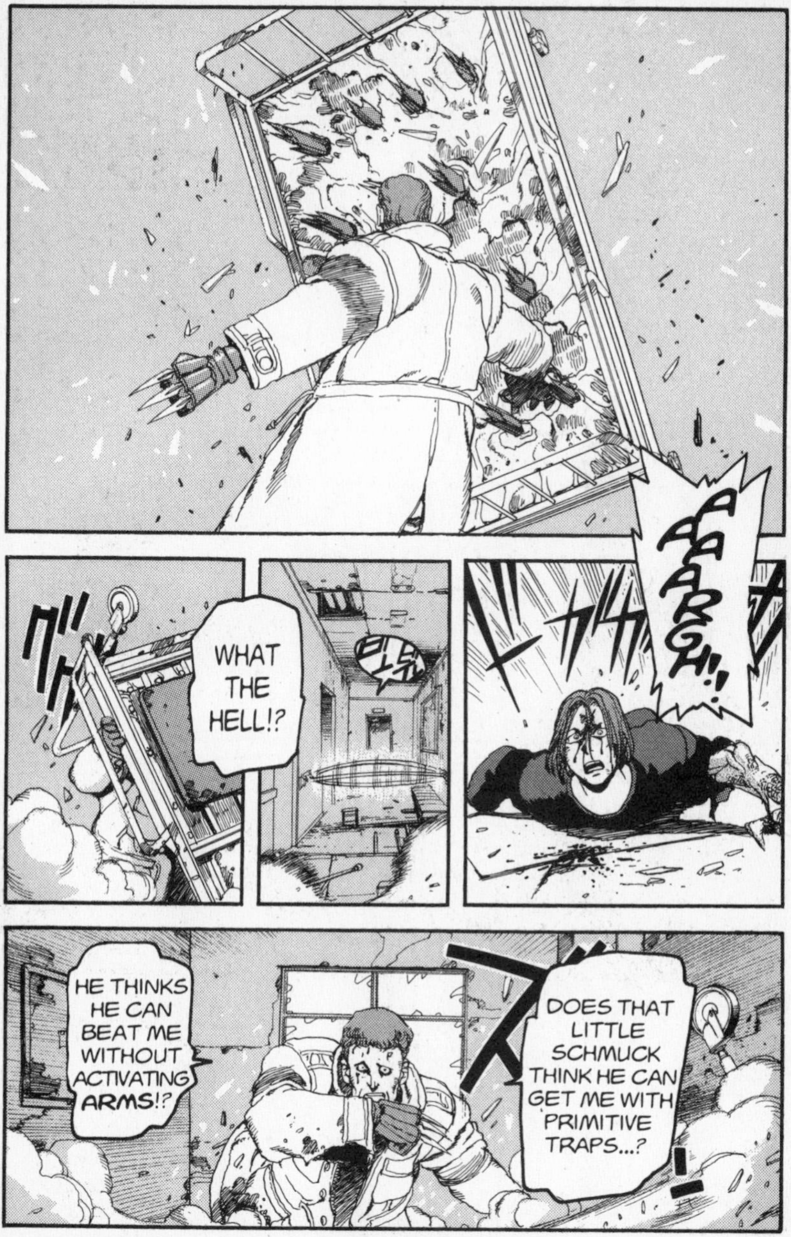
AAAARGH!!
WHAT THE HELL!?
DOES THAT LITTLE SCHMUCK THINK HE CAN GET ME WITH PRIMITIVE TRAPS...?
HE THINKS HE CAN BEAT ME WITHOUT ACTIVATING ARMS!?

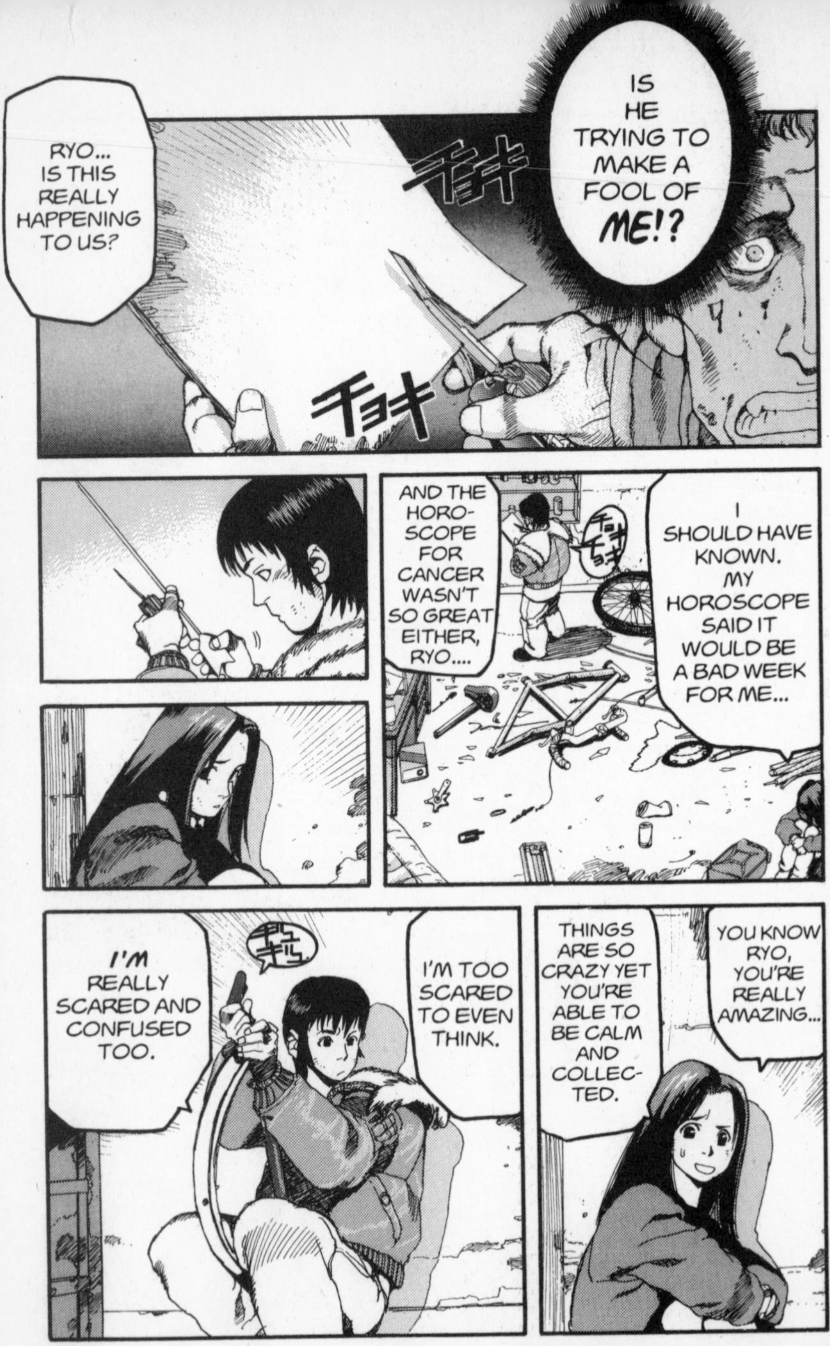
IS HE TRYING TO MAKE A FOOL OF ME!?
チョキ
RYO... IS THIS REALLY HAPPENING TO US?
チョキ
I SHOULD HAVE KNOWN. MY HOROSCOPE SAID IT WOULD BE A BAD WEEK FOR ME...
AND THE HORO-SCOPE FOR CANCER WASN'T SO GREAT EITHER, RYO....
YOU KNOW RYO, YOU'RE REALLY AMAZING...
THINGS ARE SO CRAZY YET YOU'RE ABLE TO BE CALM AND COLLECTED.
I'M TOO SCARED TO EVEN THINK.
I'M REALLY SCARED AND CONFUSED TOO.

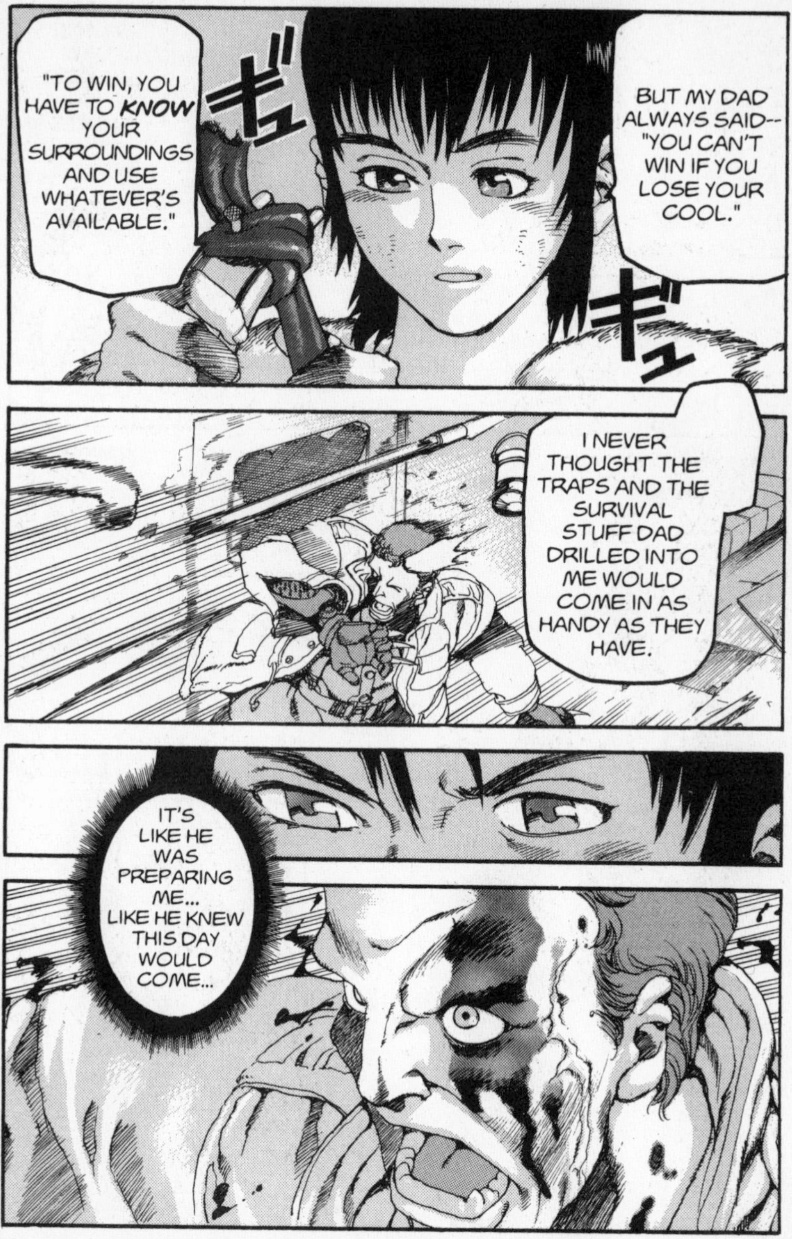
BUT MY DAD ALWAYS SAID-- "YOU CAN'T WIN IF YOU LOSE YOUR COOL."
ギュ
"TO WIN, YOU HAVE TO *KNOW* YOUR SURROUNDINGS AND USE WHATEVER'S AVAILABLE."
ギュ
I NEVER THOUGHT THE TRAPS AND THE SURVIVAL STUFF DAD DRILLED INTO ME WOULD COME IN AS HANDY AS THEY HAVE.
IT'S LIKE HE WAS PREPARING ME... LIKE HE KNEW THIS DAY WOULD COME...

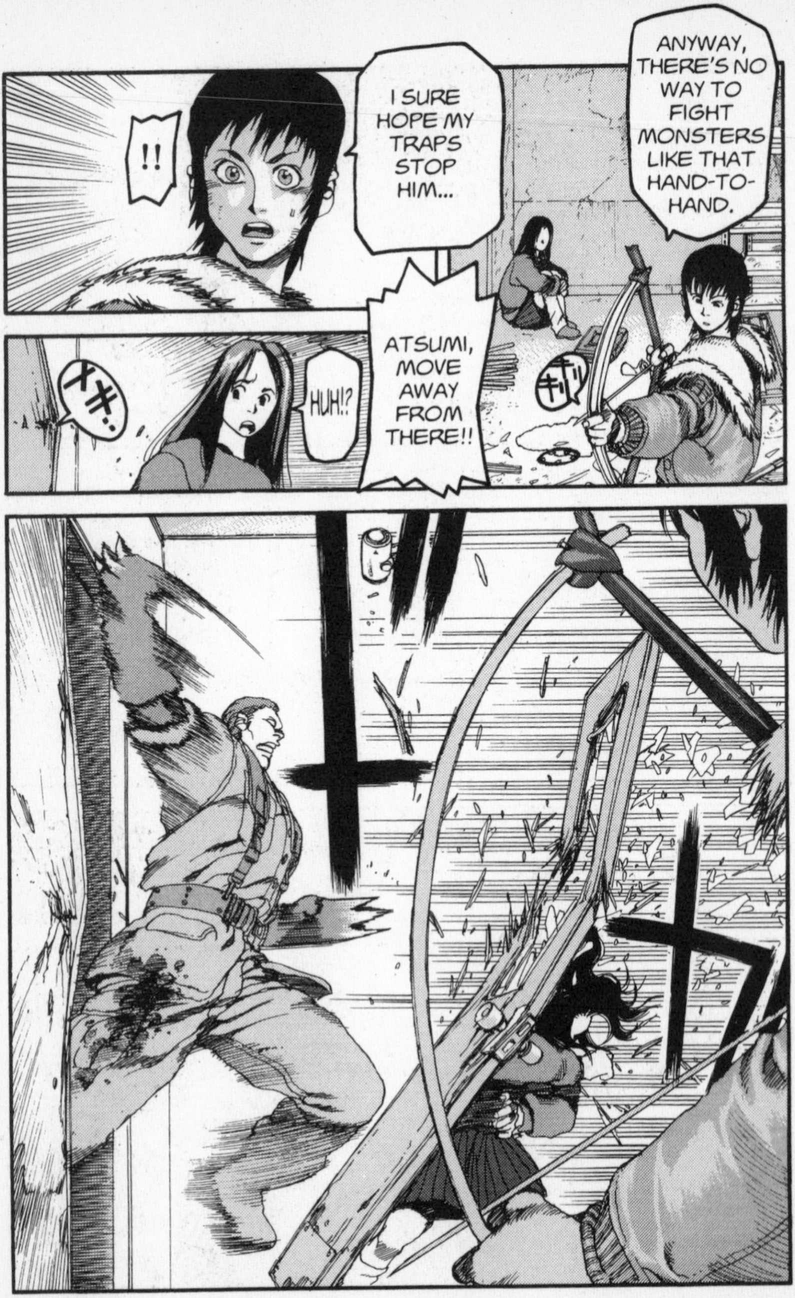
ANYWAY, THERE'S NO WAY TO FIGHT MONSTERS LIKE THAT HAND-TO-HAND.
I SURE HOPE MY TRAPS STOP HIM...
!!
ATSUMI, MOVE AWAY FROM THERE!!
キリ
HUH!?
メキ..

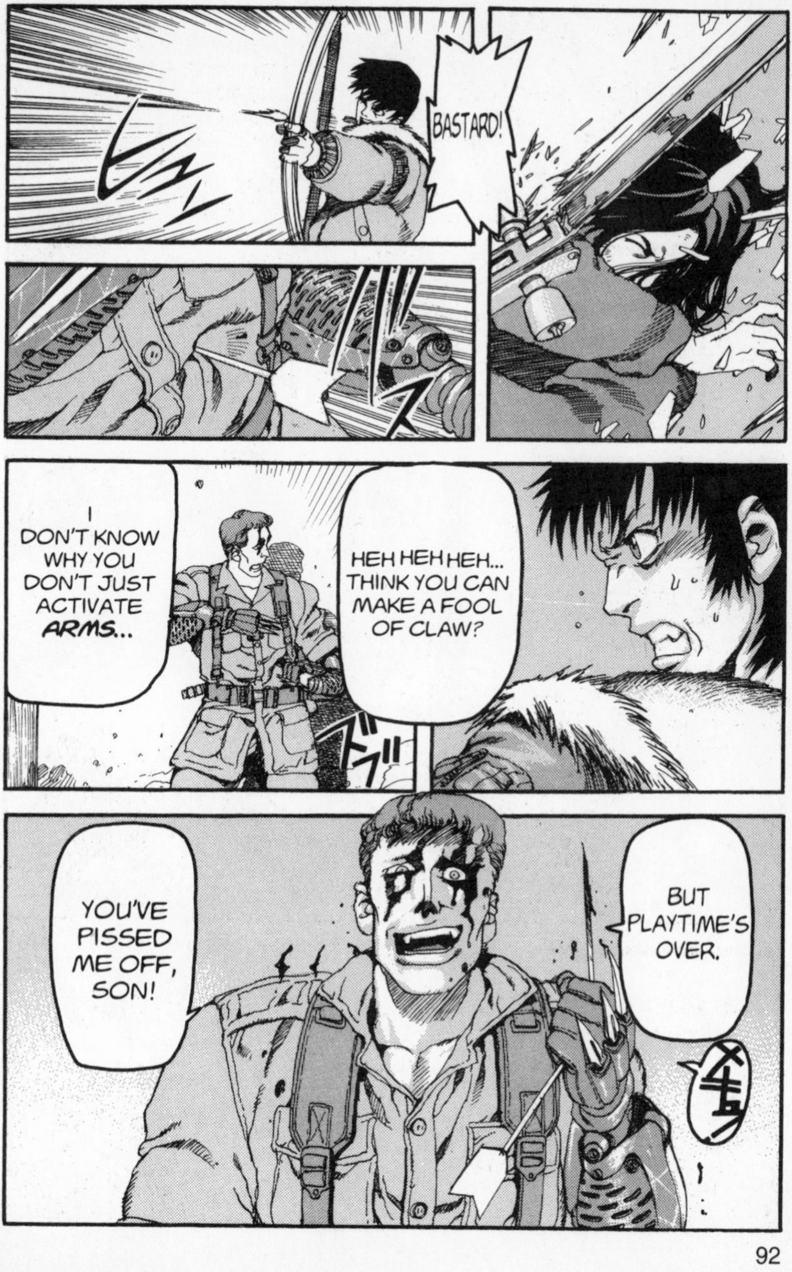
BASTARD!
HEH HEH HEH... THINK YOU CAN MAKE A FOOL OF CLAW?
I DON'T KNOW WHY YOU DON'T JUST ACTIVATE ***ARMS***...
BUT PLAYTIME'S OVER.
YOU'VE PISSED ME OFF, SON!

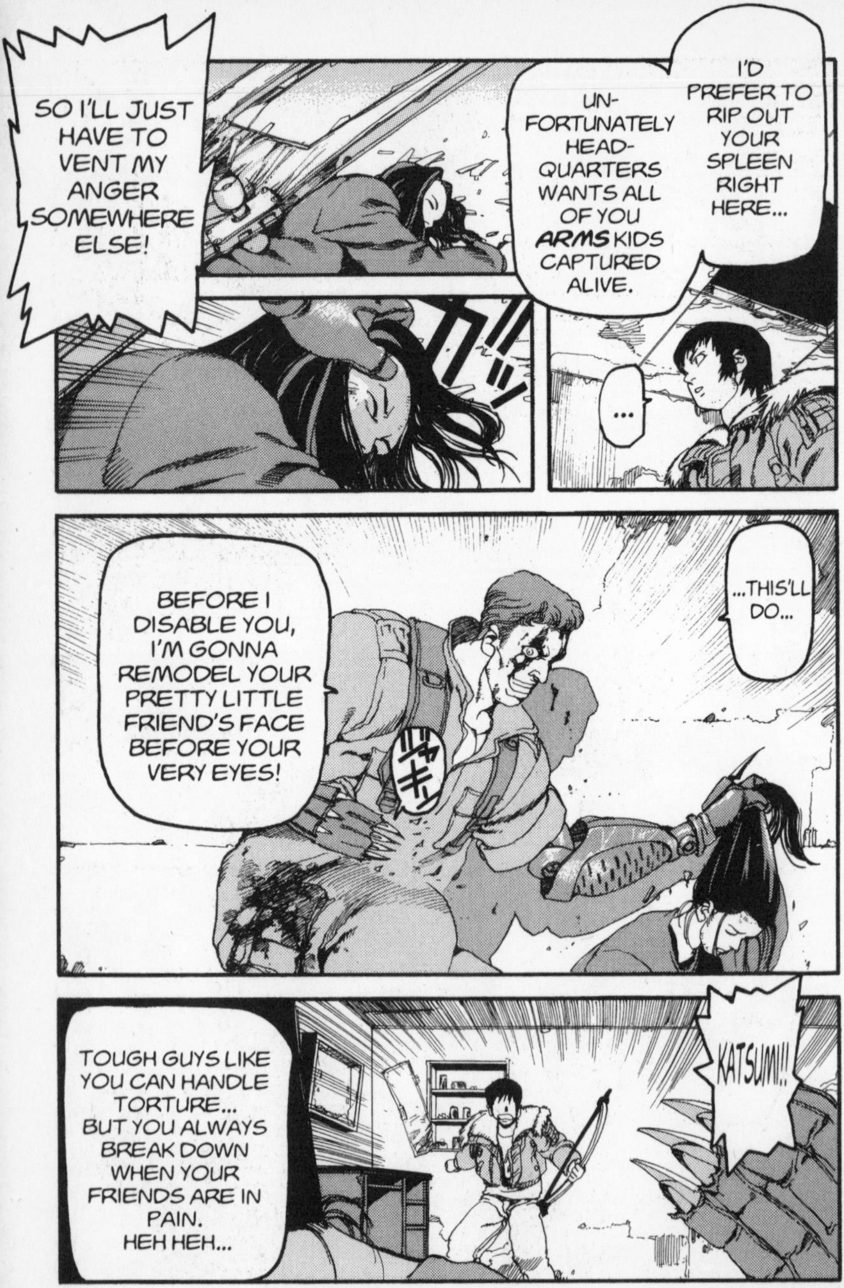
I'D PREFER TO RIP OUT YOUR SPLEEN RIGHT HERE...
UN-FORTUNATELY HEAD-QUARTERS WANTS ALL OF YOU ARMS KIDS CAPTURED ALIVE.
...
SO I'LL JUST HAVE TO VENT MY ANGER SOMEWHERE ELSE!
...THIS'LL DO...
BEFORE I DISABLE YOU, I'M GONNA REMODEL YOUR PRETTY LITTLE FRIEND'S FACE BEFORE YOUR VERY EYES!
KATSUMI!!
TOUGH GUYS LIKE YOU CAN HANDLE TORTURE... BUT YOU ALWAYS BREAK DOWN WHEN YOUR FRIENDS ARE IN PAIN. HEH HEH...

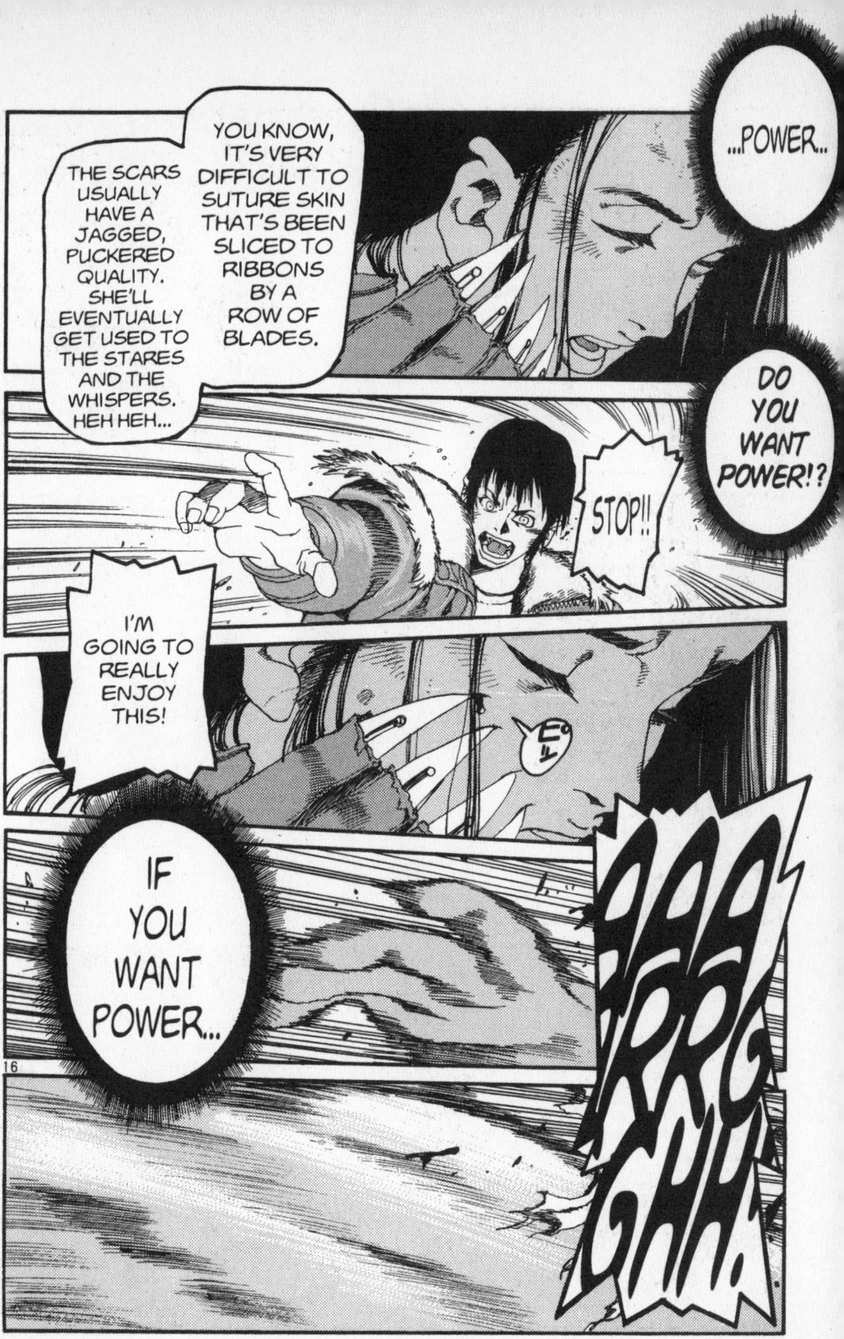
...POWER...
YOU KNOW, IT'S VERY DIFFICULT TO SUTURE SKIN THAT'S BEEN SLICED TO RIBBONS BY A ROW OF BLADES.
THE SCARS USUALLY HAVE A JAGGED, PUCKERED QUALITY. SHE'LL EVENTUALLY GET USED TO THE STARES AND THE WHISPERS. HEH HEH...
DO YOU WANT POWER!?
STOP!!
I'M GOING TO REALLY ENJOY THIS!
IF YOU WANT POWER...

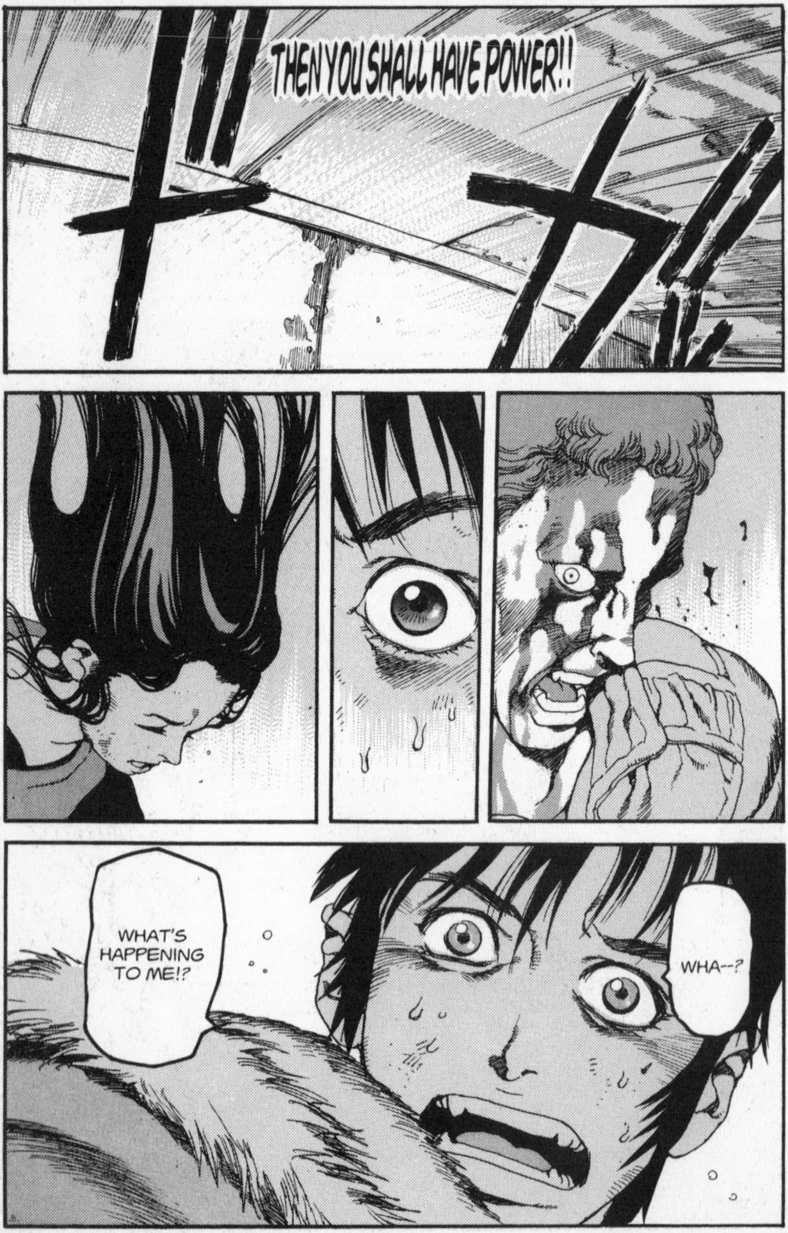
THEN YOU SHALL HAVE POWER!!
WHA--?
WHAT'S HAPPENING TO ME!?

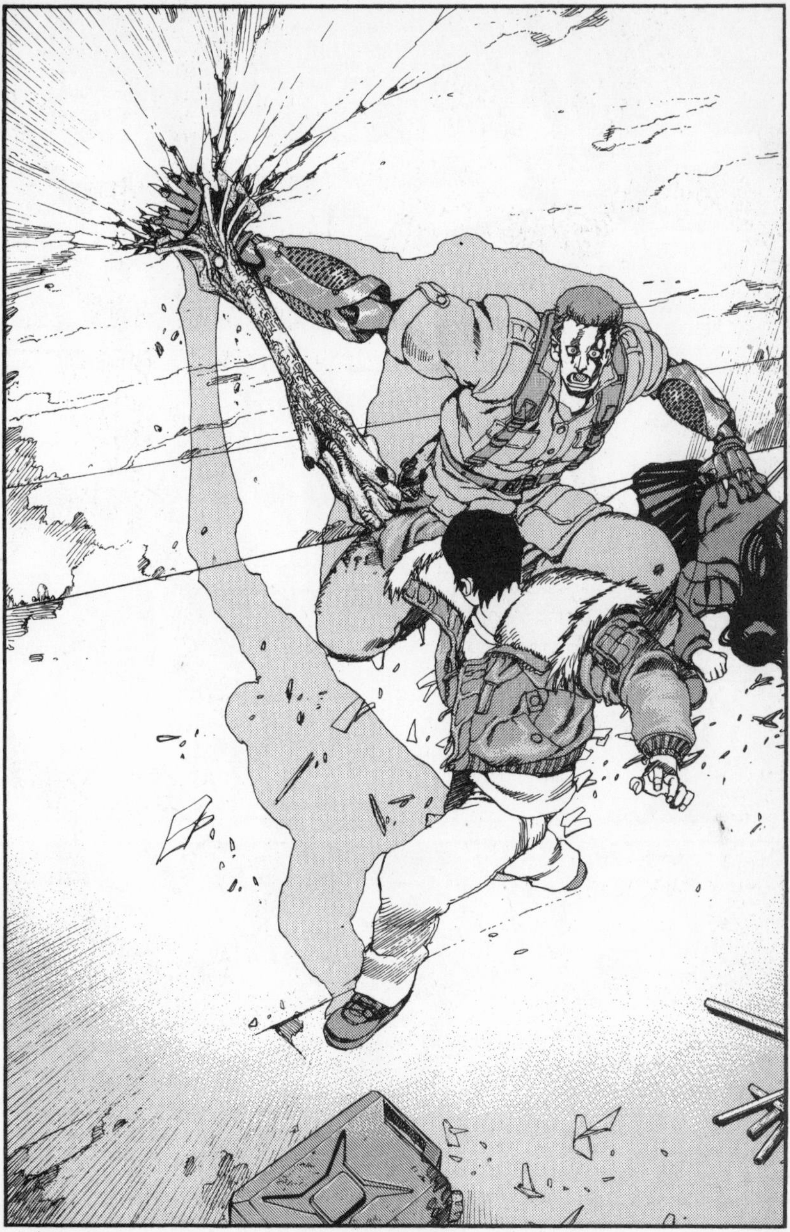

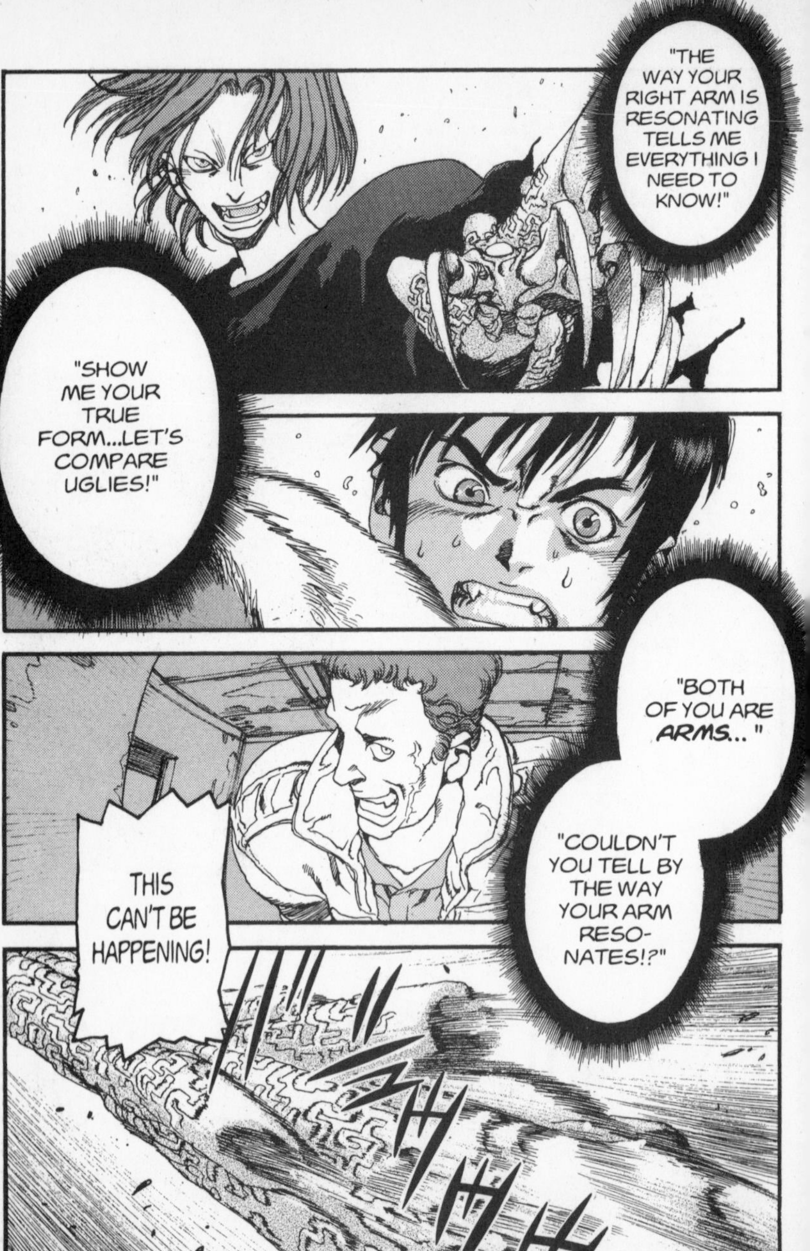
"THE WAY YOUR RIGHT ARM IS RESONATING TELLS ME EVERYTHING I NEED TO KNOW!"
"SHOW ME YOUR TRUE FORM...LET'S COMPARE UGLIES!"
"BOTH OF YOU ARE ***ARMS...*** "
"COULDN'T YOU TELL BY THE WAY YOUR ARM RESO-NATES!?"
THIS CAN'T BE HAPPENING!

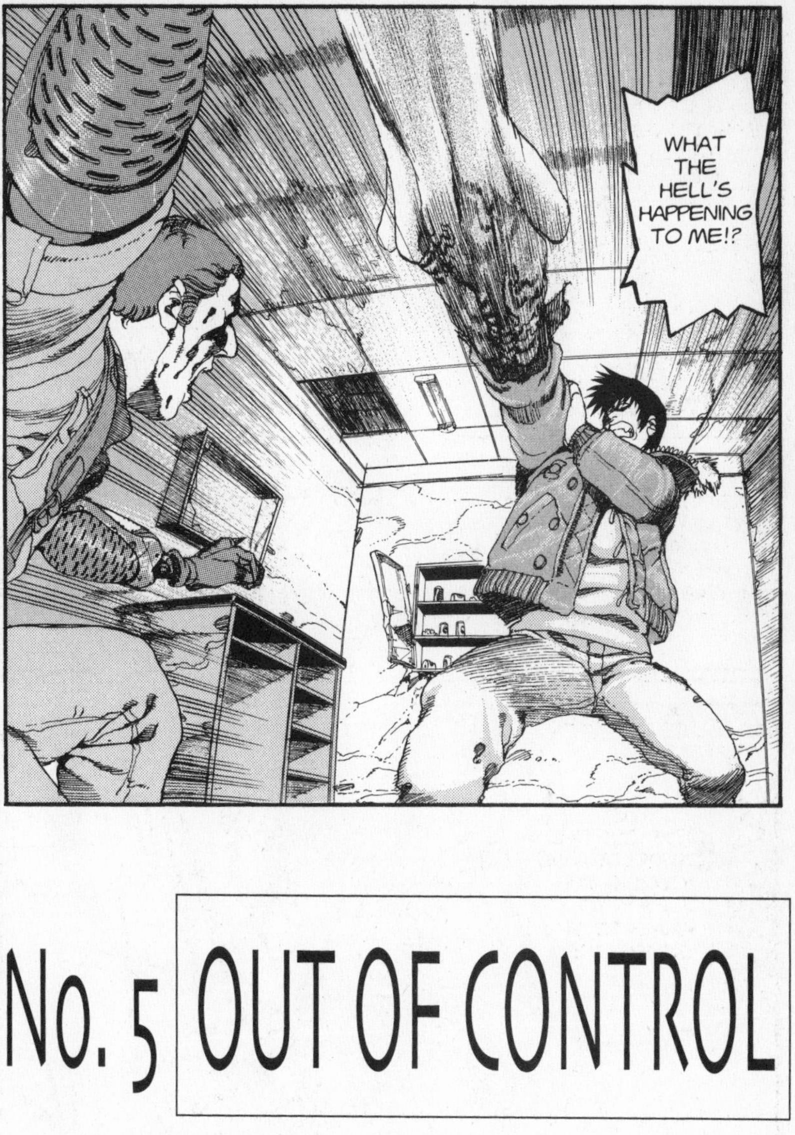
WHAT THE HELL'S HAPPENING TO ME!?

No. 5 OUT OF CONTROL

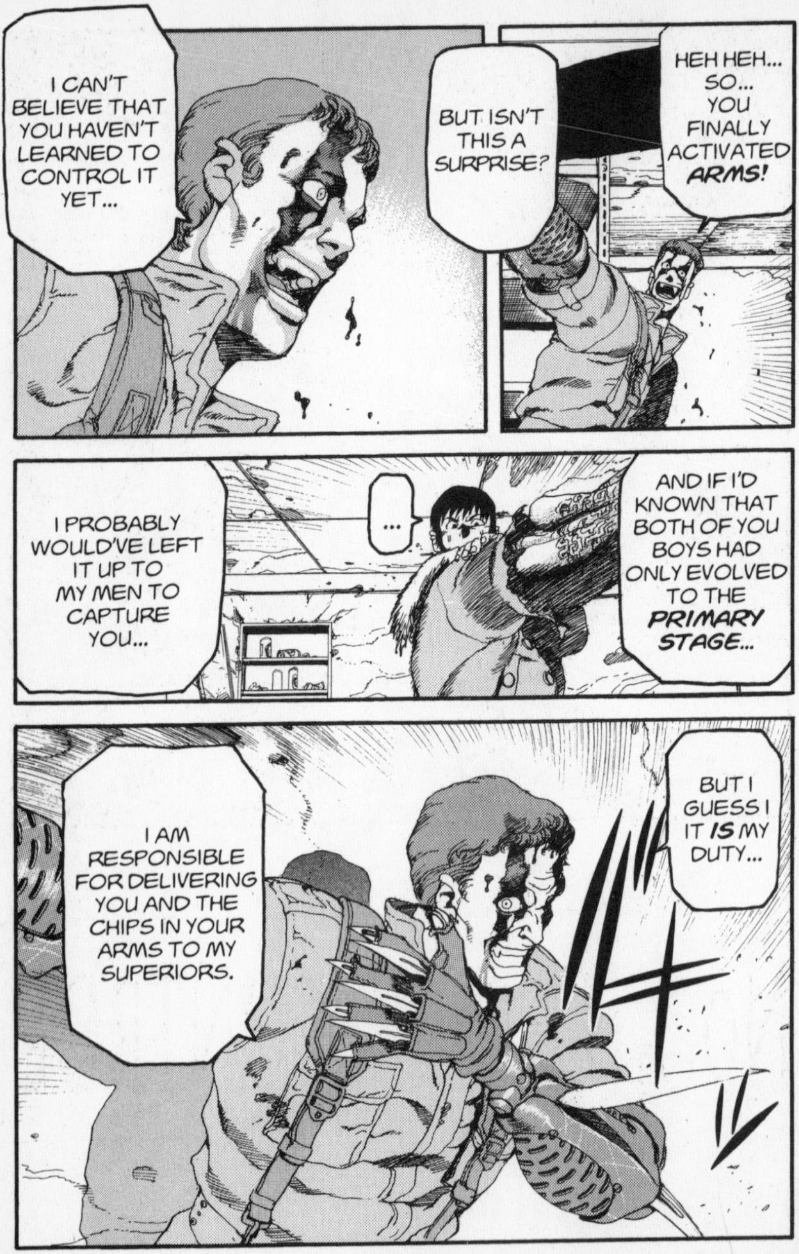
HEH HEH... SO... YOU FINALLY ACTIVATED ***ARMS!***
BUT ISN'T THIS A SURPRISE?
I CAN'T BELIEVE THAT YOU HAVEN'T LEARNED TO CONTROL IT YET...
AND IF I'D KNOWN THAT BOTH OF YOU BOYS HAD ONLY EVOLVED TO THE ***PRIMARY STAGE...***
...
I PROBABLY WOULD'VE LEFT IT UP TO MY MEN TO CAPTURE YOU...
BUT I GUESS IT ***IS*** MY DUTY...
I AM RESPONSIBLE FOR DELIVERING YOU AND THE CHIPS IN YOUR ARMS TO MY SUPERIORS.

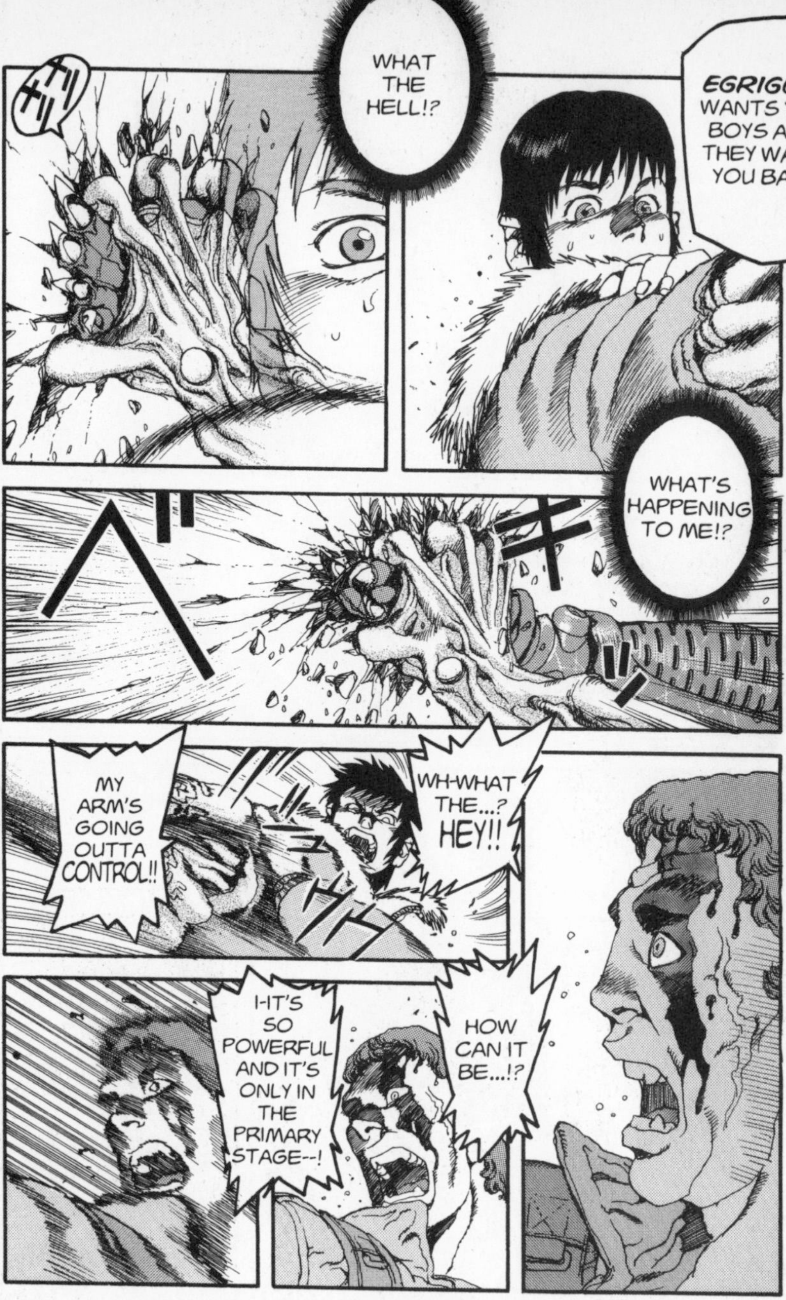
EGRIGORI WANTS YOU BOYS AND THEY WANT YOU BAD!
WHAT THE HELL!?
WHAT'S HAPPENING TO ME!?
WH-WHAT THE...? HEY!!
MY ARM'S GOING OUTTA CONTROL!!
HOW CAN IT BE...!?
I-IT'S SO POWERFUL AND IT'S ONLY IN THE PRIMARY STAGE--!

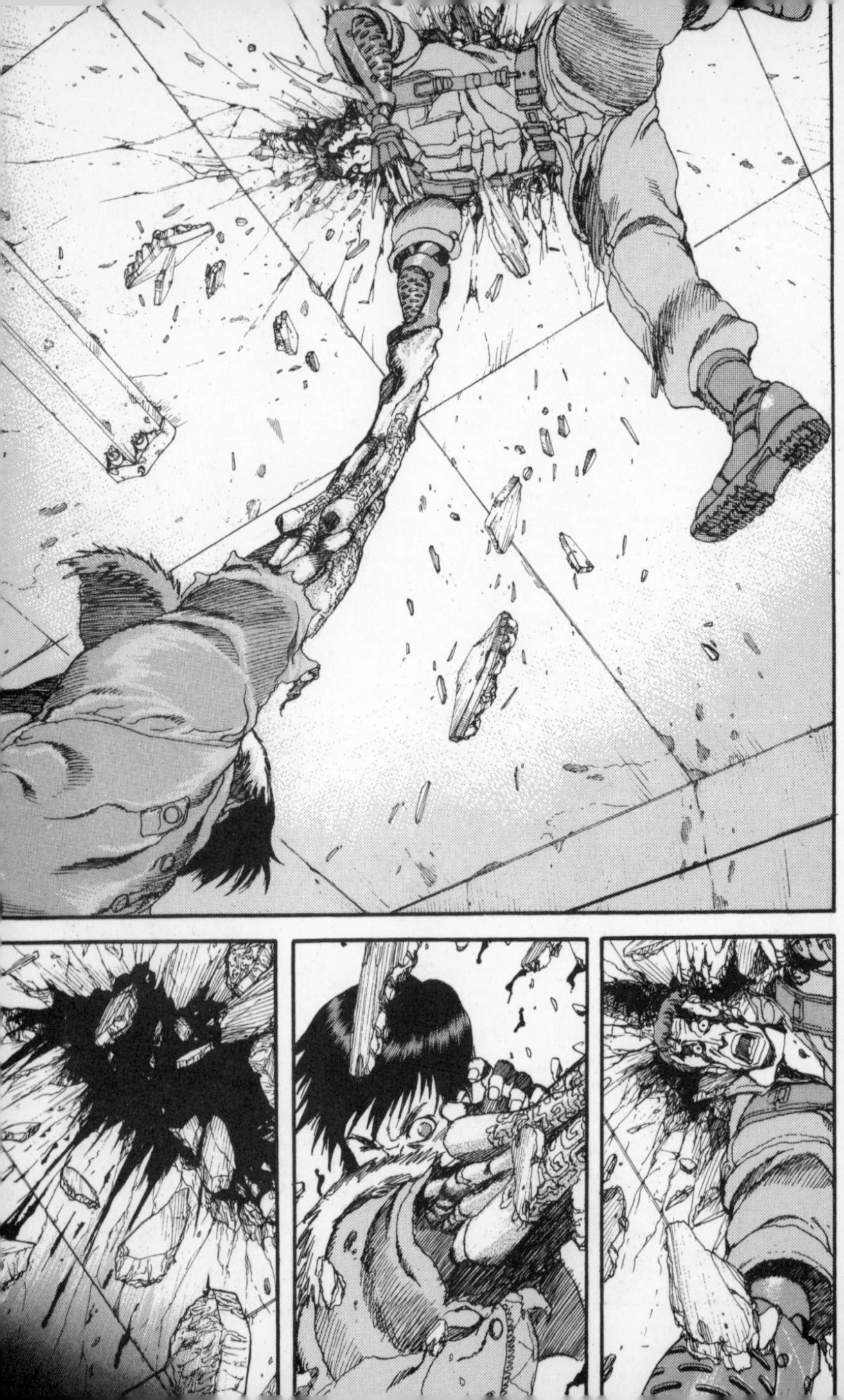

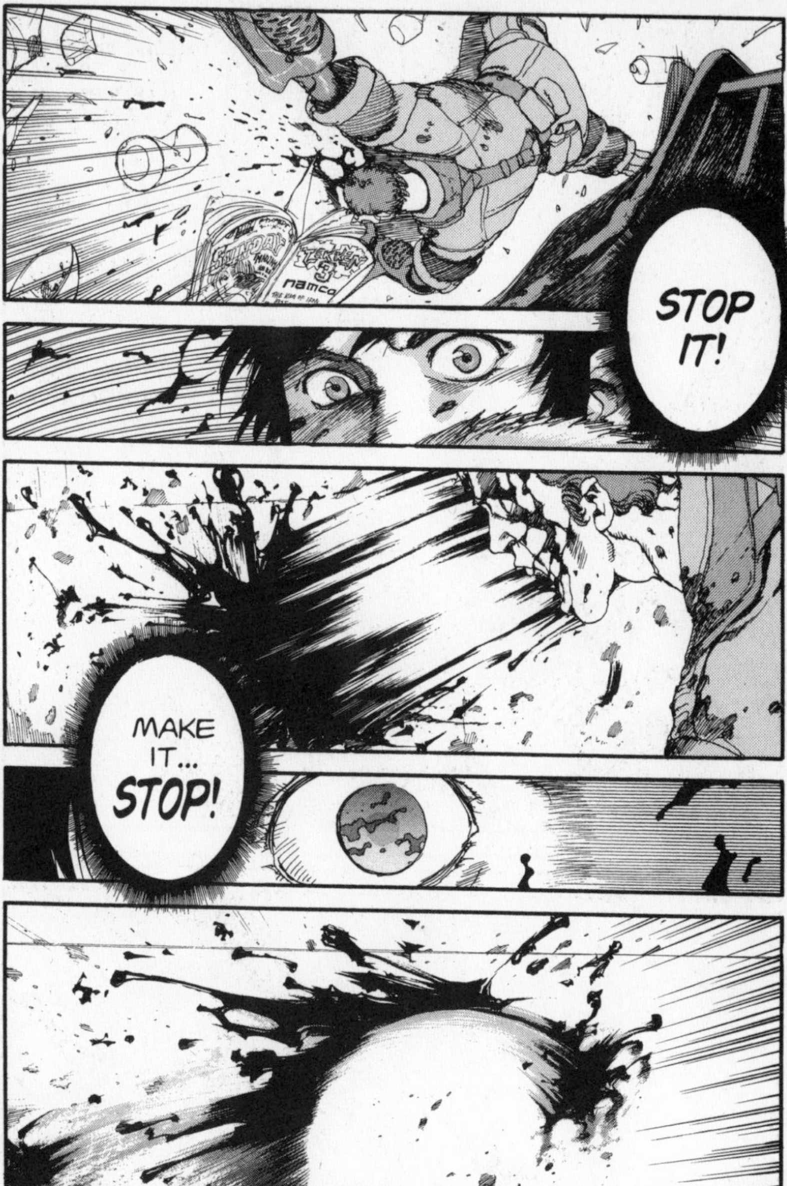
TEKKEN 3
namco
SUNDAY
STOP IT!
MAKE IT... STOP!

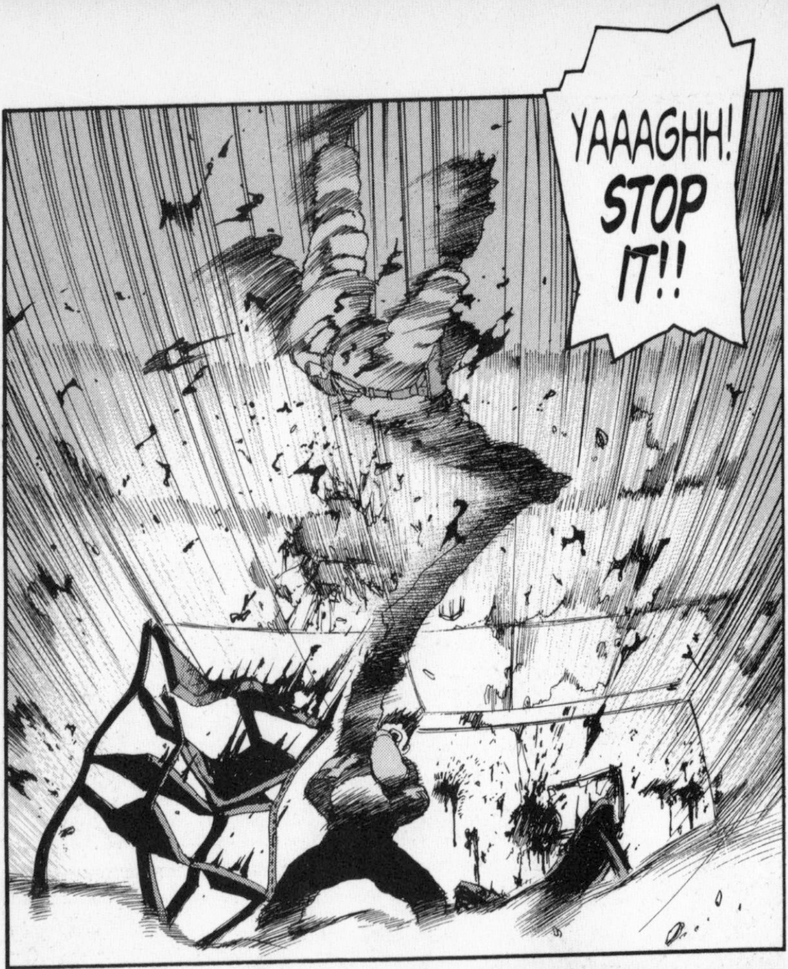
YAAAGHH! STOP IT!!

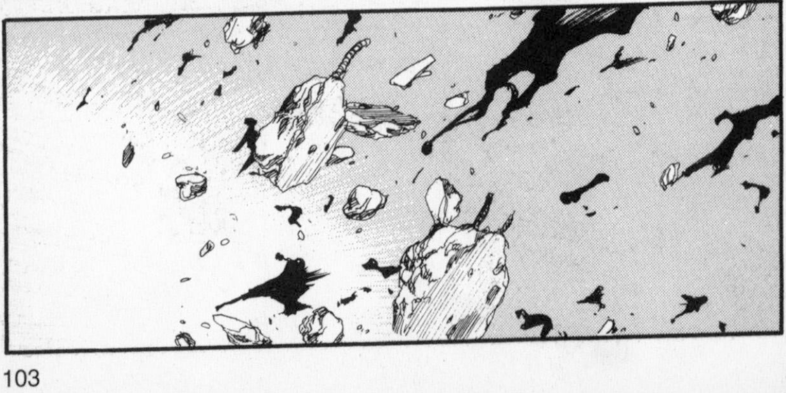

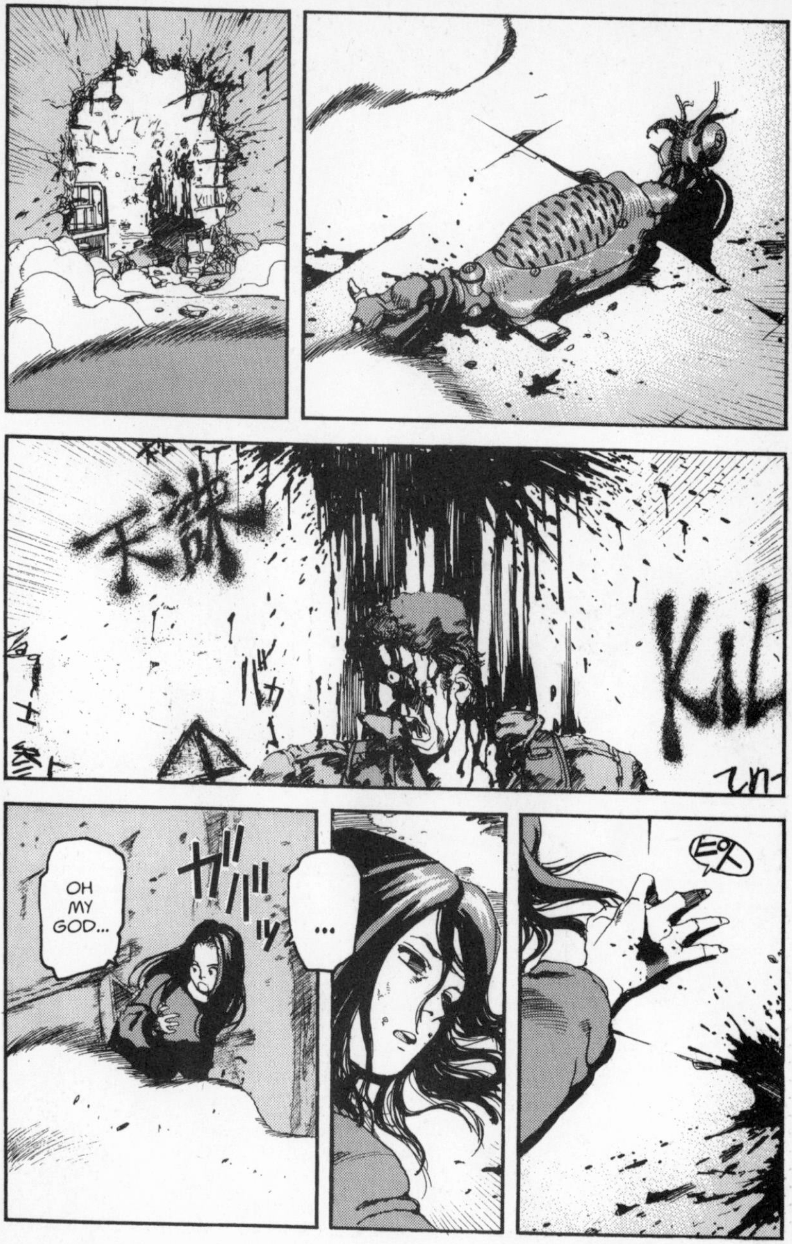
...
OH MY GOD...

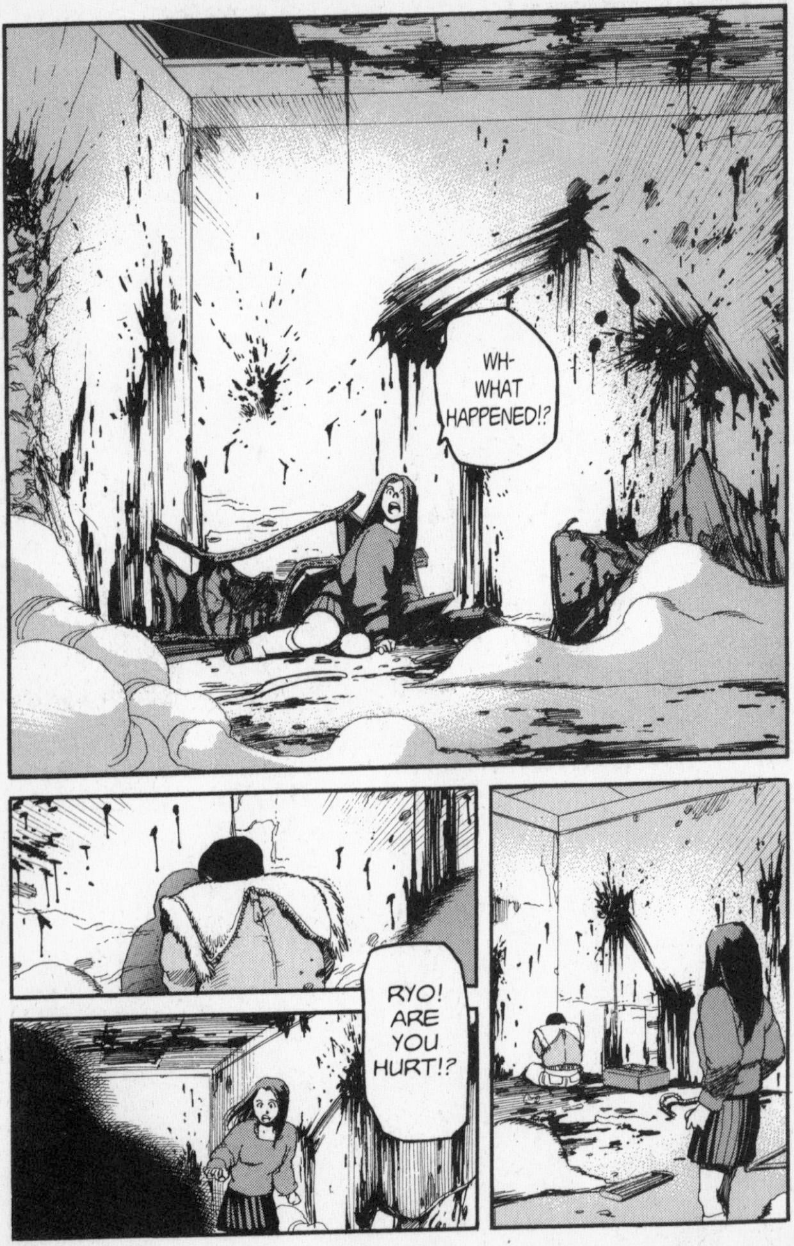
WH- WHAT HAPPENED!?
RYO! ARE YOU HURT!?

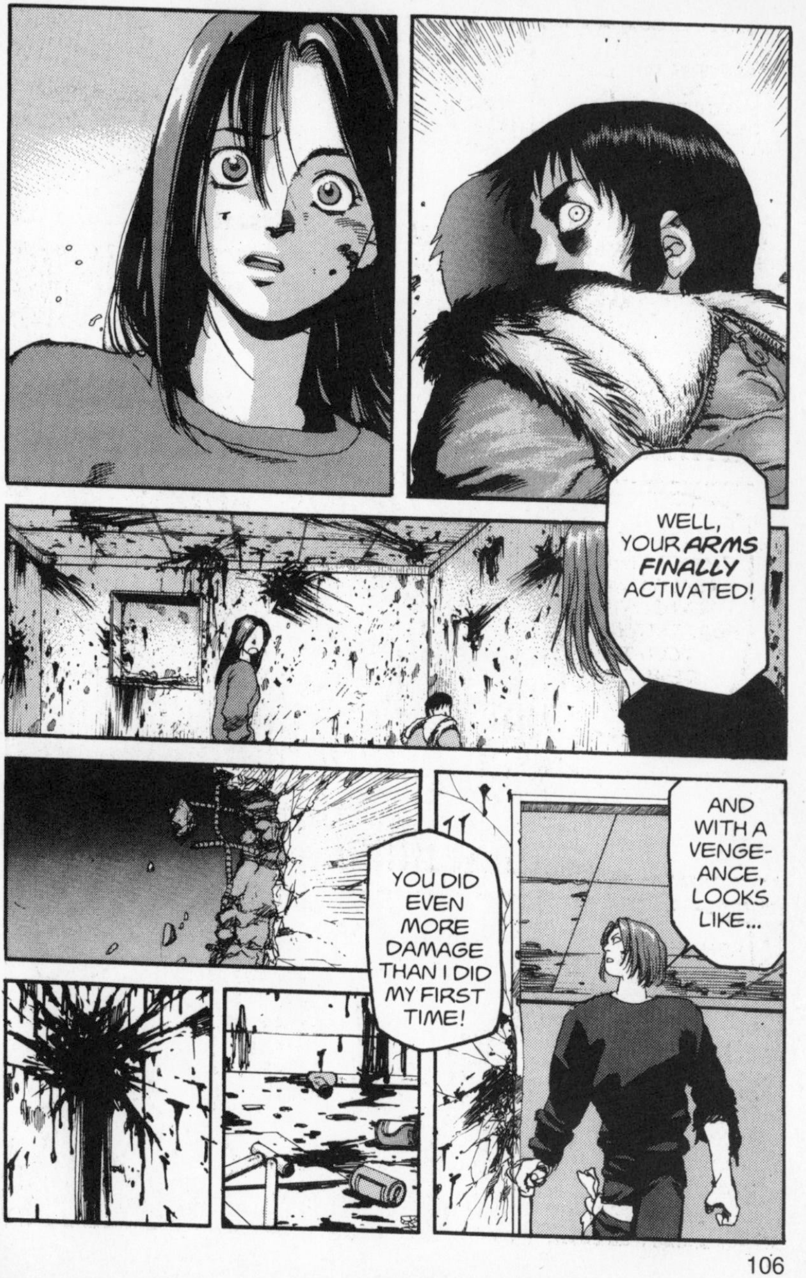
WELL, YOUR ARMS FINALLY ACTIVATED!
AND WITH A VENGE-ANCE, LOOKS LIKE...
YOU DID EVEN MORE DAMAGE THAN I DID MY FIRST TIME!

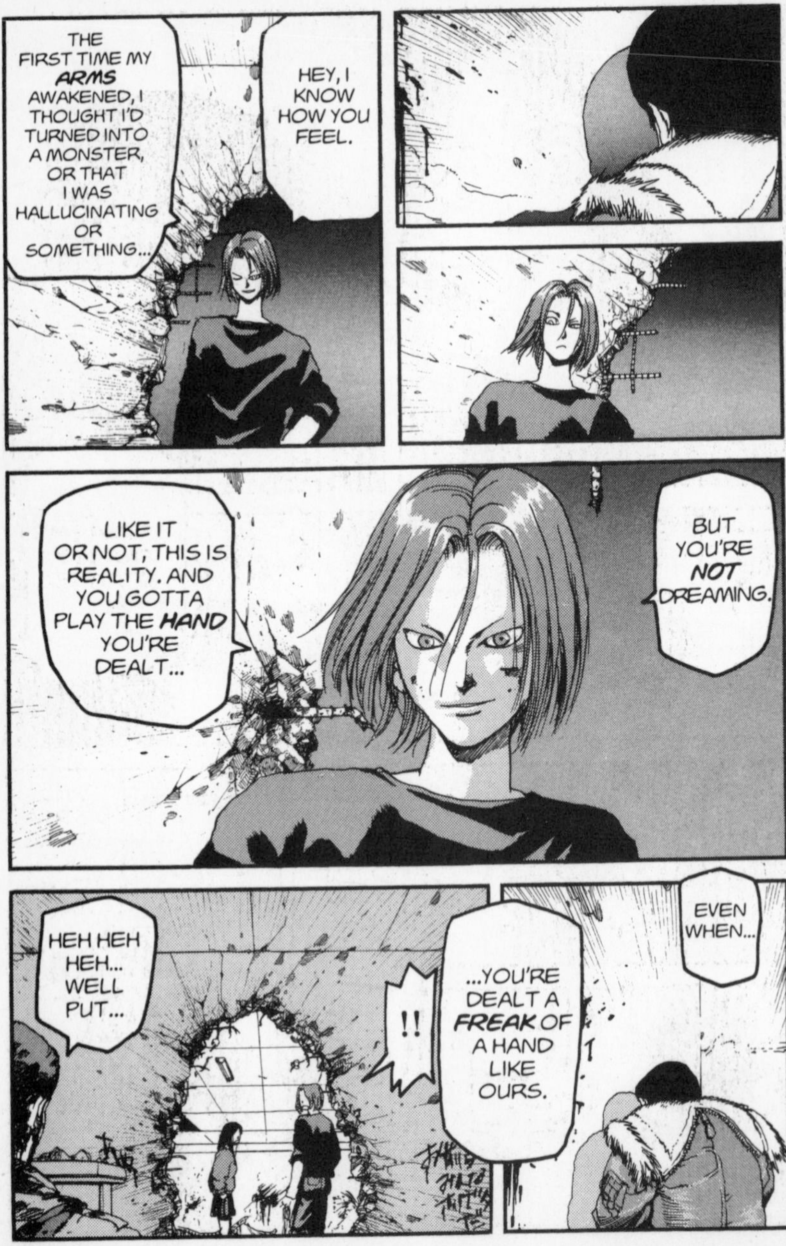
HEY, I KNOW HOW YOU FEEL.
THE FIRST TIME MY ARMS AWAKENED, I THOUGHT I'D TURNED INTO A MONSTER, OR THAT I WAS HALLUCINATING OR SOMETHING...
BUT YOU'RE NOT DREAMING.
LIKE IT OR NOT, THIS IS REALITY. AND YOU GOTTA PLAY THE HAND YOU'RE DEALT...
EVEN WHEN...
...YOU'RE DEALT A FREAK OF A HAND LIKE OURS.
!!
HEH HEH HEH... WELL PUT...

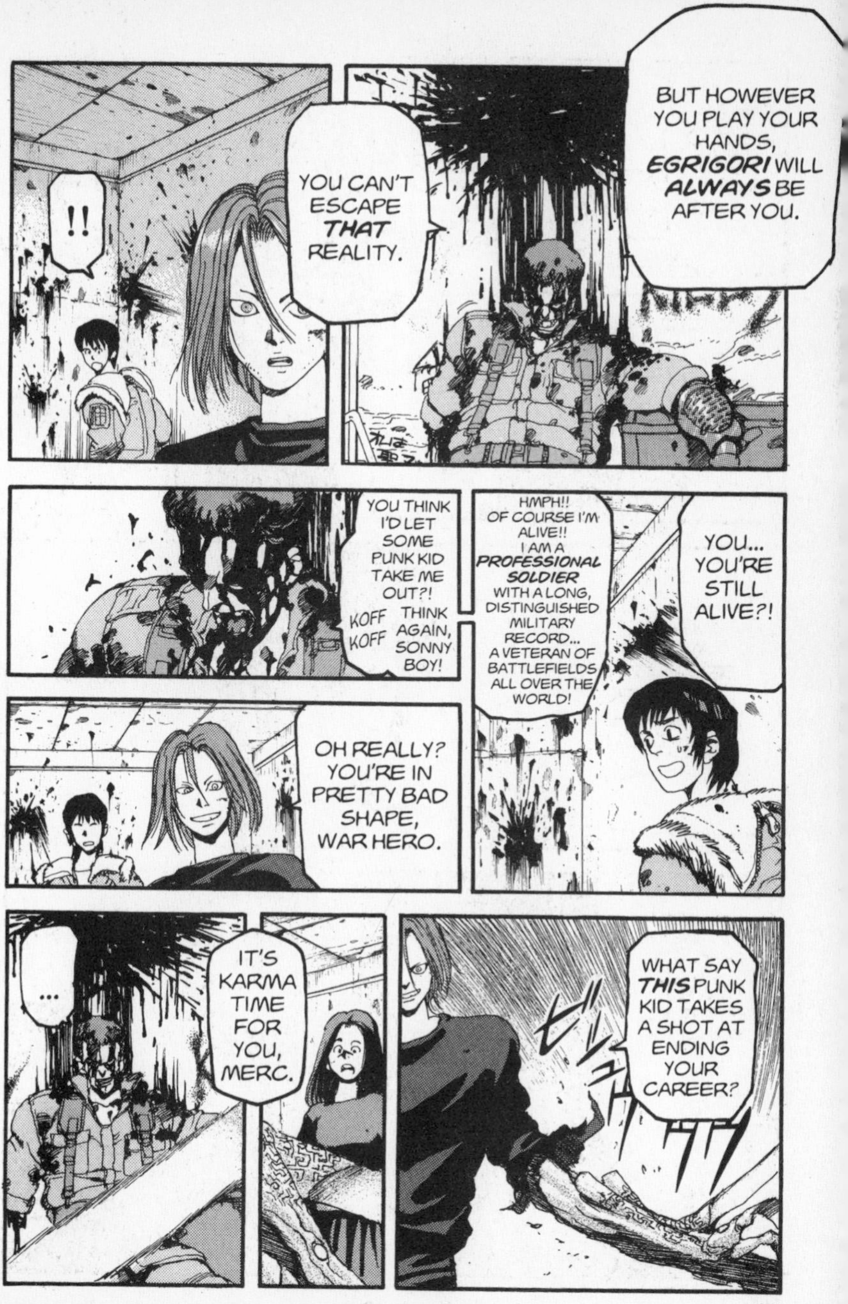
BUT HOWEVER YOU PLAY YOUR HANDS, EGRIGORI WILL ALWAYS BE AFTER YOU.
YOU CAN'T ESCAPE THAT REALITY.
!!
YOU... YOU'RE STILL ALIVE?!
HMPH!! OF COURSE I'M ALIVE!! I AM A PROFESSIONAL SOLDIER WITH A LONG, DISTINGUISHED MILITARY RECORD... A VETERAN OF BATTLEFIELDS ALL OVER THE WORLD!
YOU THINK I'D LET SOME PUNK KID TAKE ME OUT?!
KOFF KOFF
THINK AGAIN, SONNY BOY!
OH REALLY? YOU'RE IN PRETTY BAD SHAPE, WAR HERO.
WHAT SAY THIS PUNK KID TAKES A SHOT AT ENDING YOUR CAREER?
IT'S KARMA TIME FOR YOU, MERC.
...

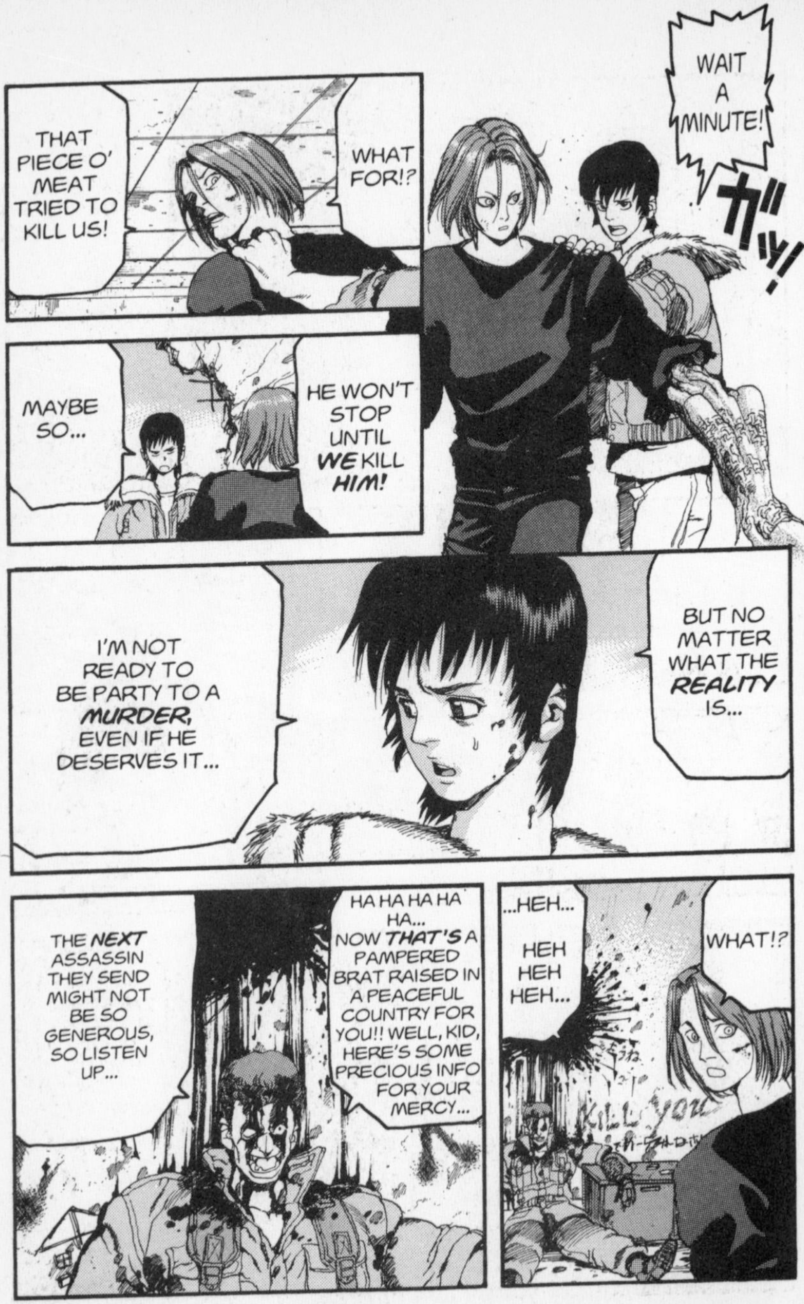
WAIT A MINUTE!
ガッ!
WHAT FOR!?
THAT PIECE O' MEAT TRIED TO KILL US!
HE WON'T STOP UNTIL WE KILL HIM!
MAYBE SO...
BUT NO MATTER WHAT THE REALITY IS...
I'M NOT READY TO BE PARTY TO A MURDER, EVEN IF HE DESERVES IT...
WHAT!?
...HEH...
HEH HEH HEH...
HA HA HA HA HA... NOW THAT'S A PAMPERED BRAT RAISED IN A PEACEFUL COUNTRY FOR YOU!! WELL, KID, HERE'S SOME PRECIOUS INFO FOR YOUR MERCY...
THE NEXT ASSASSIN THEY SEND MIGHT NOT BE SO GENEROUS, SO LISTEN UP...

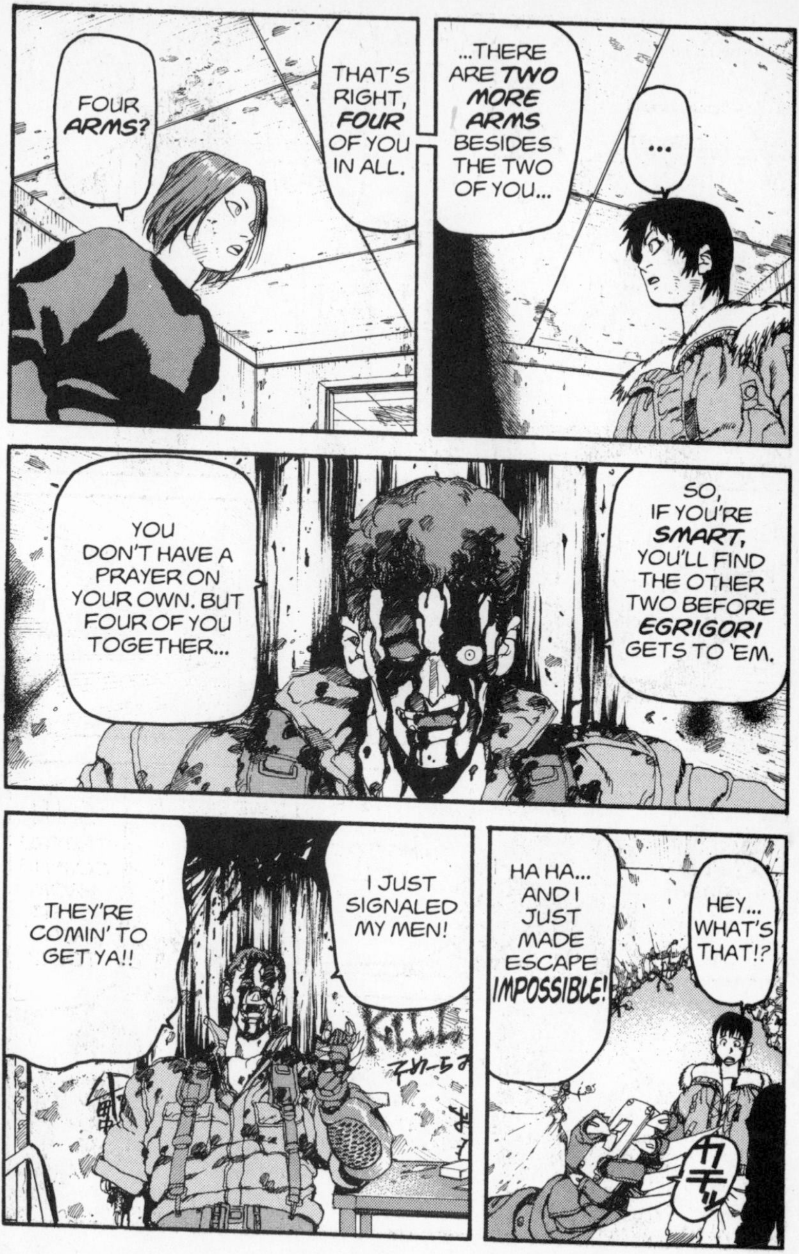
...THERE ARE TWO MORE ARMS BESIDES THE TWO OF YOU...
...
THAT'S RIGHT, FOUR OF YOU IN ALL.
FOUR ARMS?
SO, IF YOU'RE SMART, YOU'LL FIND THE OTHER TWO BEFORE EGRIGORI GETS TO 'EM.
YOU DON'T HAVE A PRAYER ON YOUR OWN. BUT FOUR OF YOU TOGETHER...
HEY... WHAT'S THAT!?
HA HA... AND I JUST MADE ESCAPE IMPOSSIBLE!
I JUST SIGNALED MY MEN!
THEY'RE COMIN' TO GET YA!!
KILL

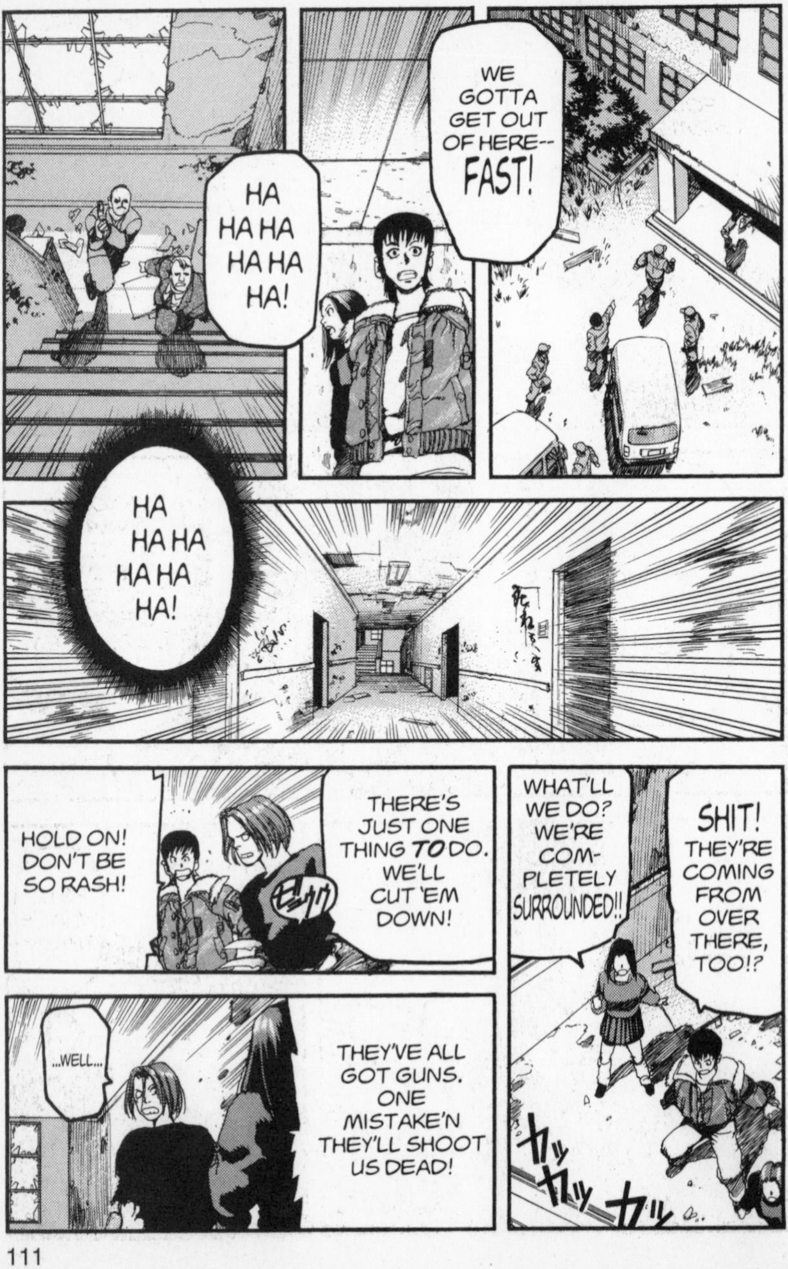
WE GOTTA GET OUT OF HERE-- FAST!
HA HA HA HA HA HA!
HA HA HA HA HA HA!
SHIT! THEY'RE COMING FROM OVER THERE, TOO!?
WHAT'LL WE DO? WE'RE COM- PLETELY SURROUNDED!!
THERE'S JUST ONE THING *TO* DO. WE'LL CUT 'EM DOWN!
HOLD ON! DON'T BE SO RASH!
THEY'VE ALL GOT GUNS. ONE MISTAKE'N THEY'LL SHOOT US DEAD!
...WELL...

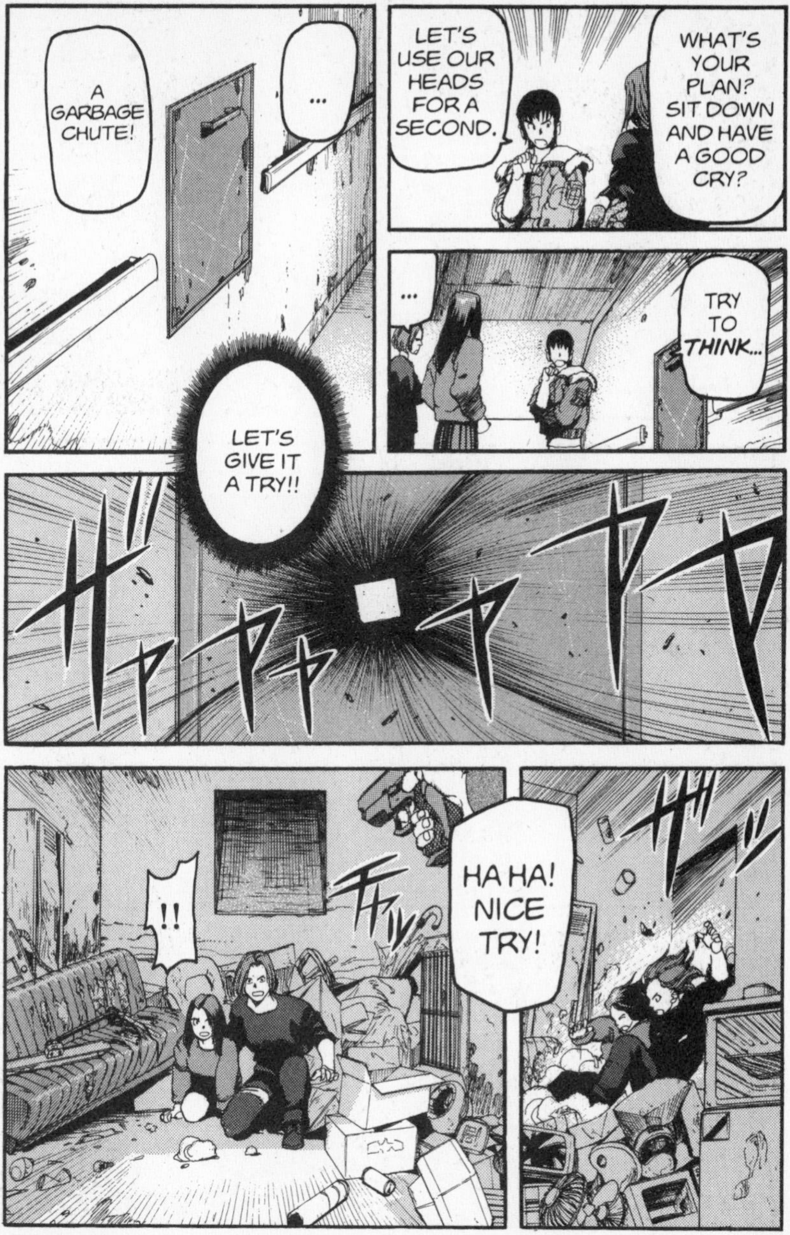
WHAT'S YOUR PLAN? SIT DOWN AND HAVE A GOOD CRY?
LET'S USE OUR HEADS FOR A SECOND.
TRY TO THINK...
...
...
A GARBAGE CHUTE!
LET'S GIVE IT A TRY!!
HA HA! NICE TRY!
!!

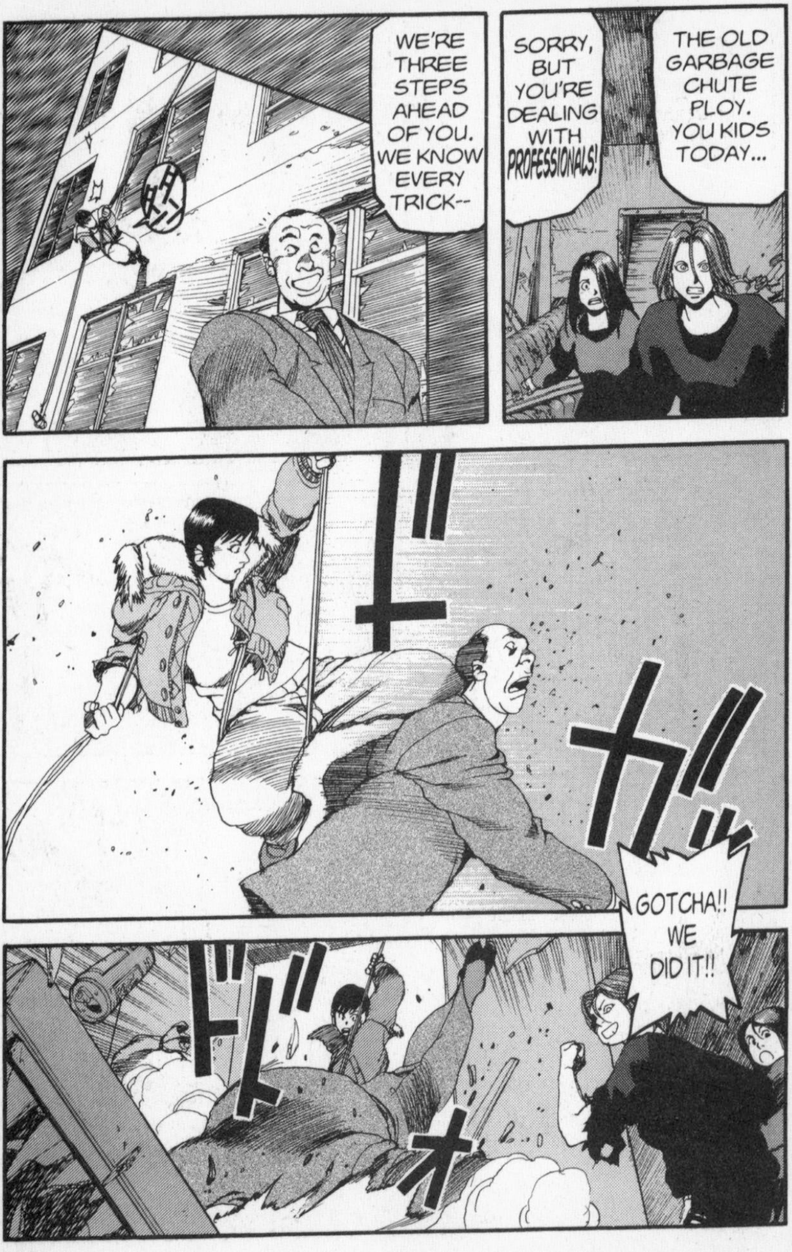
THE OLD GARBAGE CHUTE PLOY. YOU KIDS TODAY...
SORRY, BUT YOU'RE DEALING WITH PROFESSIONALS!
WE'RE THREE STEPS AHEAD OF YOU. WE KNOW EVERY TRICK--
GOTCHA!! WE DID IT!!

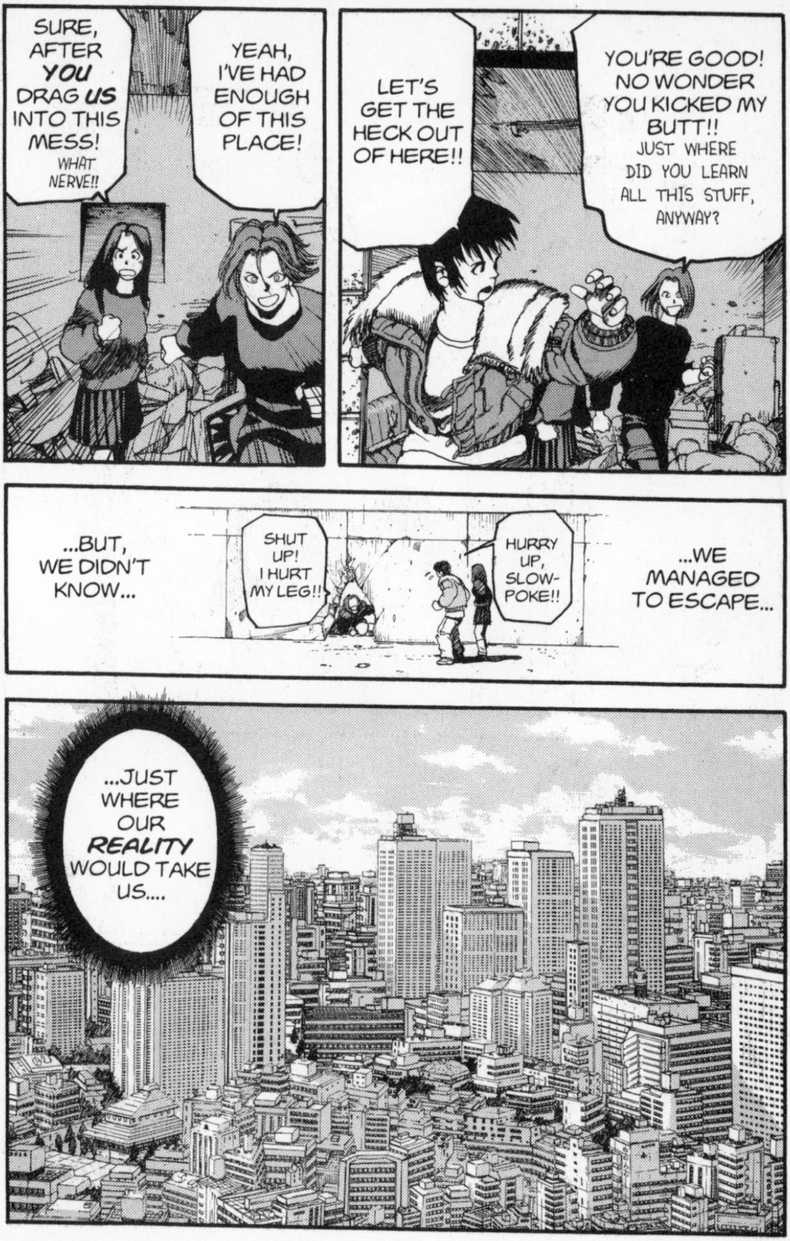
YOU'RE GOOD! NO WONDER YOU KICKED MY BUTT!!
JUST WHERE DID YOU LEARN ALL THIS STUFF, ANYWAY?
LET'S GET THE HECK OUT OF HERE!!
YEAH, I'VE HAD ENOUGH OF THIS PLACE!
SURE, AFTER YOU DRAG US INTO THIS MESS!
WHAT NERVE!!
...WE MANAGED TO ESCAPE...
HURRY UP, SLOW-POKE!!
SHUT UP! I HURT MY LEG!!
...BUT, WE DIDN'T KNOW...
...JUST WHERE OUR REALITY WOULD TAKE US....

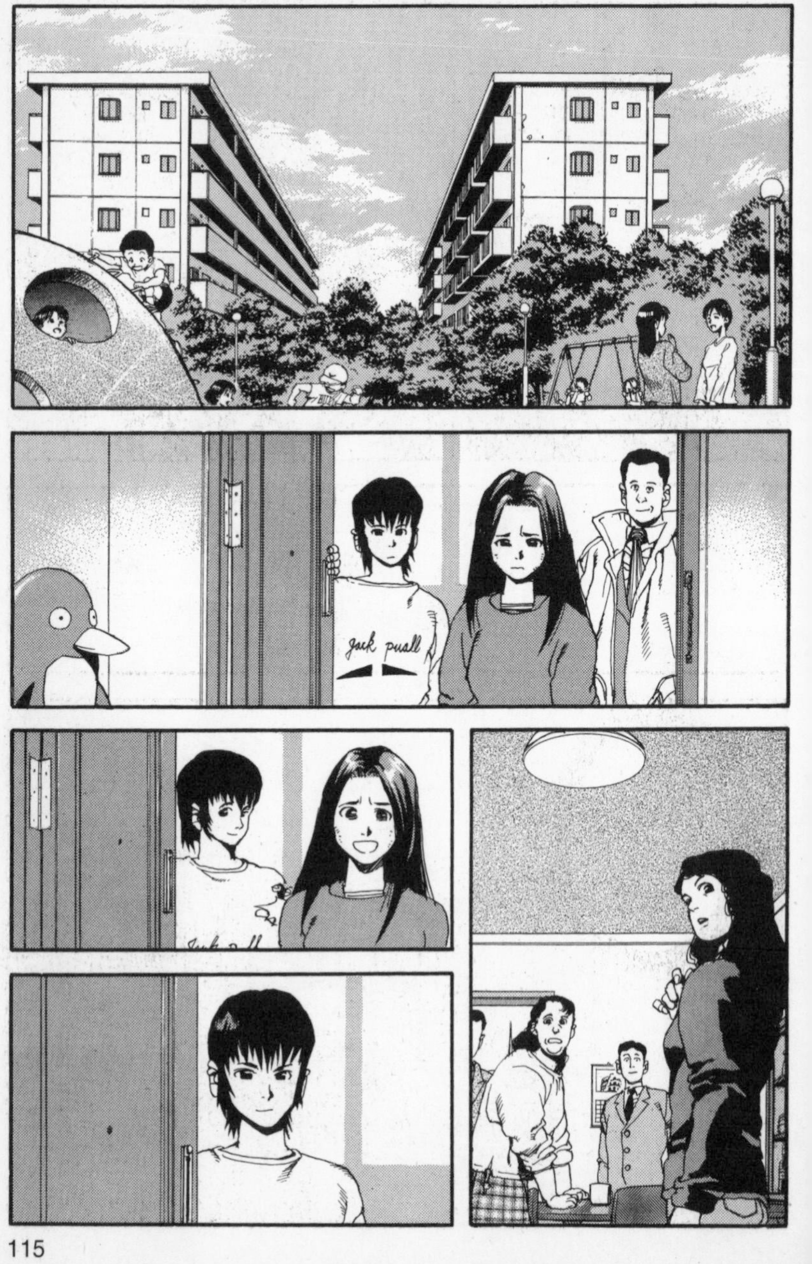
Jack puall

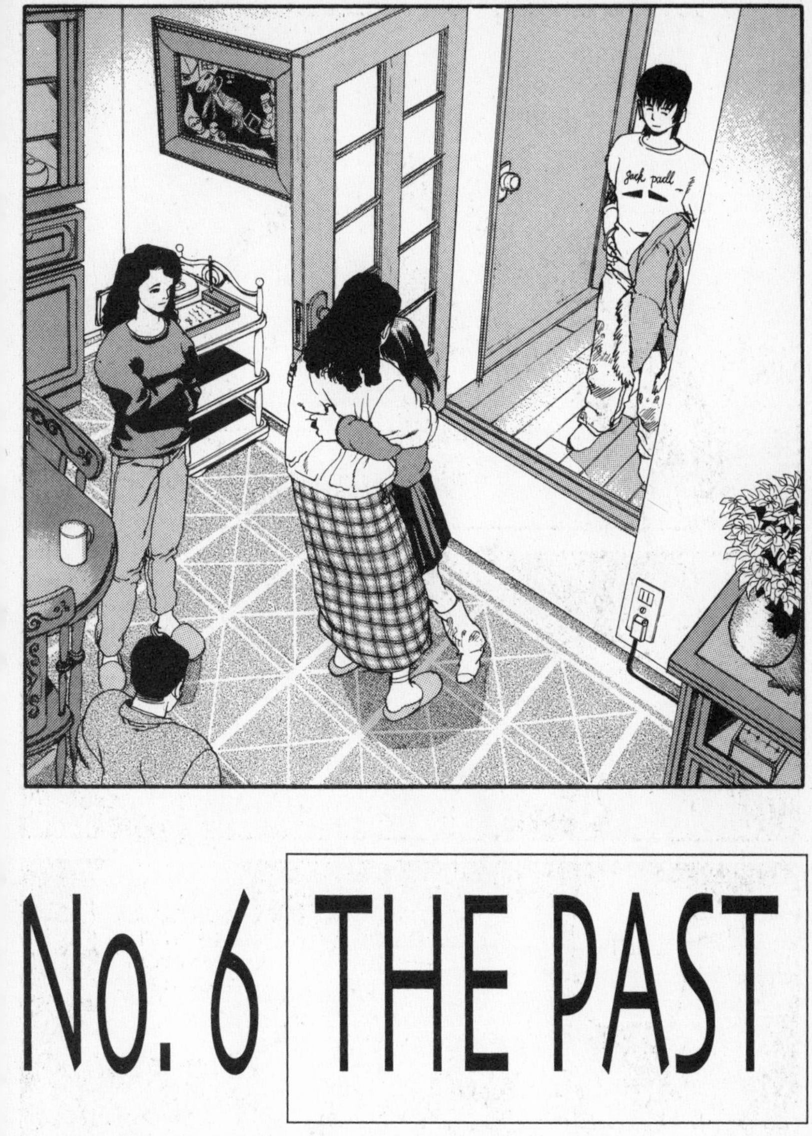

No. 6 THE PAST

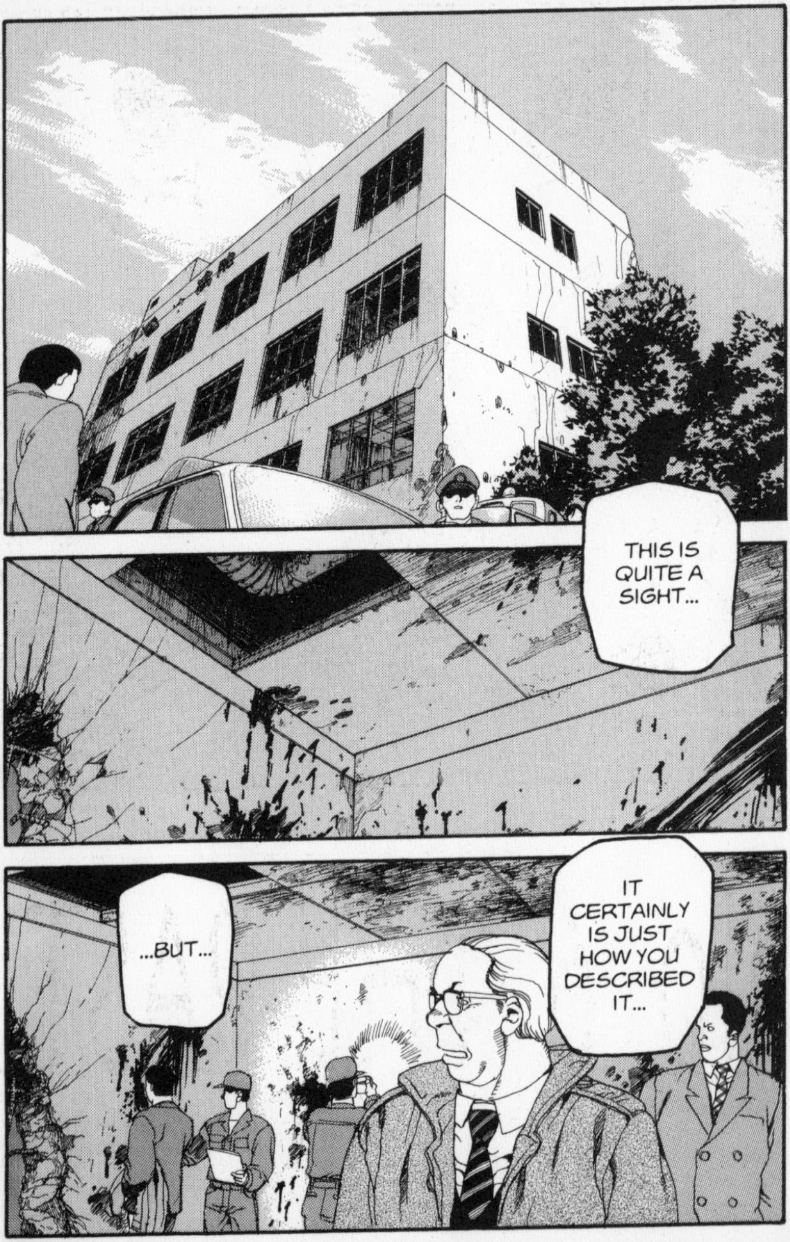
THIS IS QUITE A SIGHT...
IT CERTAINLY IS JUST HOW YOU DESCRIBED IT...
...BUT...

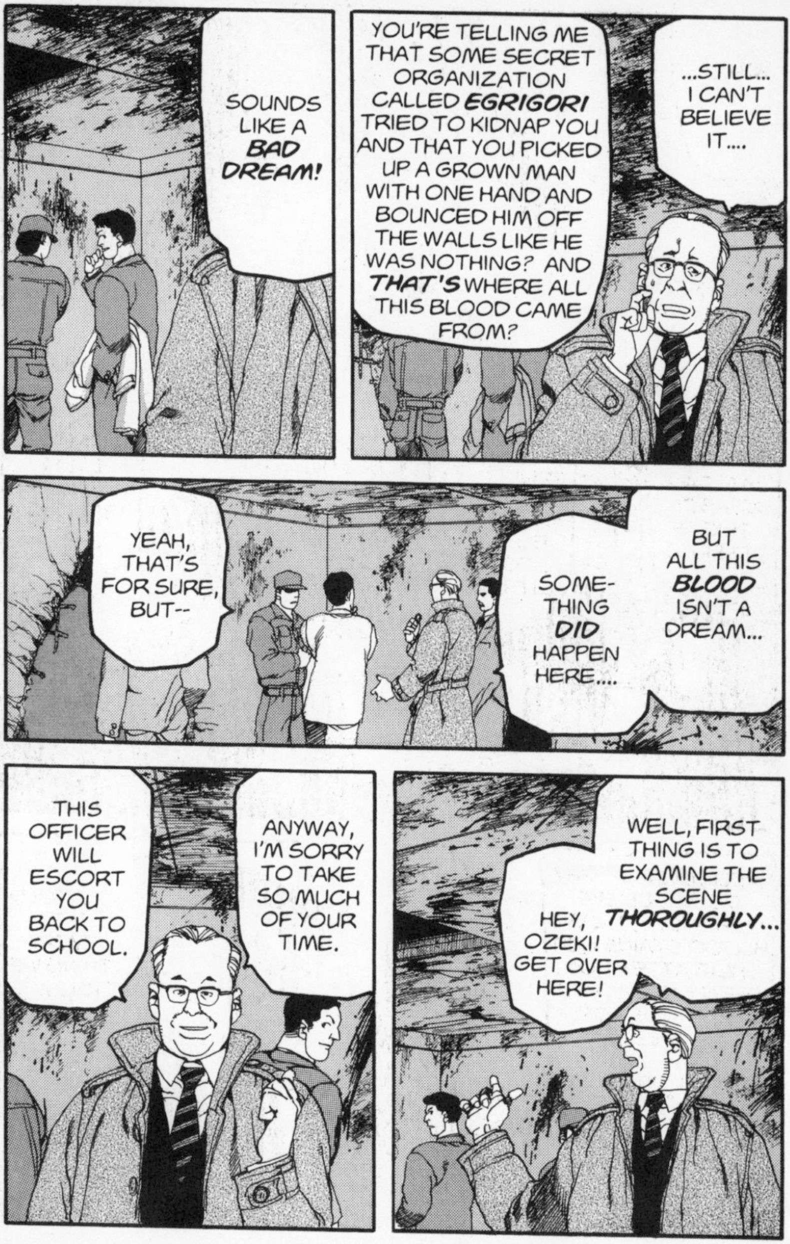
YOU'RE TELLING ME THAT SOME SECRET ORGANIZATION CALLED EGRIGORI TRIED TO KIDNAP YOU AND THAT YOU PICKED UP A GROWN MAN WITH ONE HAND AND BOUNCED HIM OFF THE WALLS LIKE HE WAS NOTHING? AND THAT'S WHERE ALL THIS BLOOD CAME FROM?
...STILL... I CAN'T BELIEVE IT....
SOUNDS LIKE A BAD DREAM!
BUT ALL THIS BLOOD ISN'T A DREAM...
SOME-THING DID HAPPEN HERE....
YEAH, THAT'S FOR SURE, BUT--
WELL, FIRST THING IS TO EXAMINE THE SCENE THOROUGHLY...
HEY, OZEKI! GET OVER HERE!
ANYWAY, I'M SORRY TO TAKE SO MUCH OF YOUR TIME.
THIS OFFICER WILL ESCORT YOU BACK TO SCHOOL.

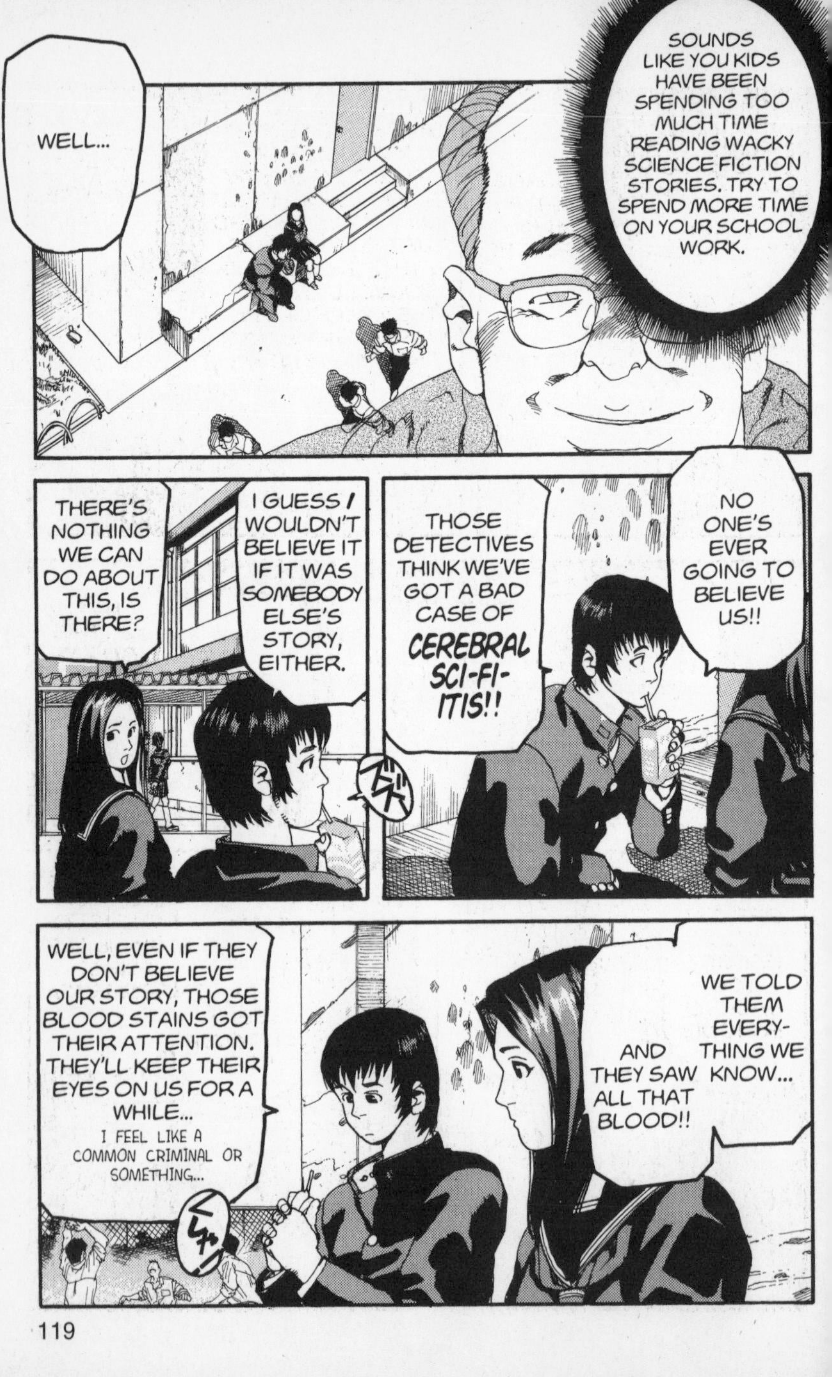
SOUNDS LIKE YOU KIDS HAVE BEEN SPENDING TOO MUCH TIME READING WACKY SCIENCE FICTION STORIES. TRY TO SPEND MORE TIME ON YOUR SCHOOL WORK.
WELL...
NO ONE'S EVER GOING TO BELIEVE US!!
THOSE DETECTIVES THINK WE'VE GOT A BAD CASE OF CEREBRAL SCI-FI-ITIS!!
I GUESS I WOULDN'T BELIEVE IT IF IT WAS SOMEBODY ELSE'S STORY, EITHER.
THERE'S NOTHING WE CAN DO ABOUT THIS, IS THERE?
WE TOLD THEM EVERYTHING WE KNOW...
AND THEY SAW ALL THAT BLOOD!!
WELL, EVEN IF THEY DON'T BELIEVE OUR STORY, THOSE BLOOD STAINS GOT THEIR ATTENTION. THEY'LL KEEP THEIR EYES ON US FOR A WHILE...
I FEEL LIKE A COMMON CRIMINAL OR SOMETHING...

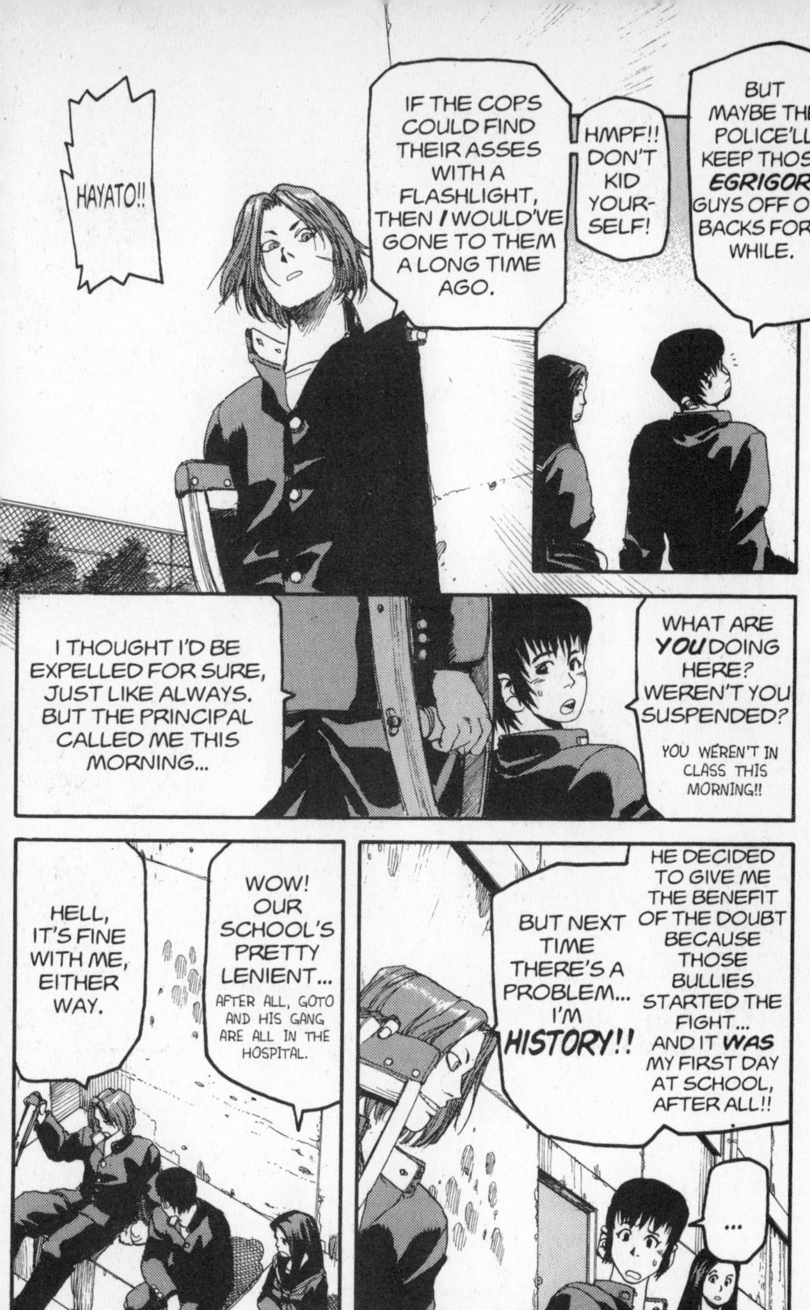
BUT MAYBE THE POLICE'LL KEEP THOSE ***EGRIGORI*** GUYS OFF OUR BACKS FOR A WHILE.
HMPF!! DON'T KID YOUR-SELF!
IF THE COPS COULD FIND THEIR ASSES WITH A FLASHLIGHT, THEN ***I*** WOULD'VE GONE TO THEM A LONG TIME AGO.
HAYATO!!
WHAT ARE ***YOU*** DOING HERE? WEREN'T YOU SUSPENDED?
YOU WEREN'T IN CLASS THIS MORNING!!
I THOUGHT I'D BE EXPELLED FOR SURE, JUST LIKE ALWAYS. BUT THE PRINCIPAL CALLED ME THIS MORNING...
HE DECIDED TO GIVE ME THE BENEFIT OF THE DOUBT BECAUSE THOSE BULLIES STARTED THE FIGHT... AND IT ***WAS*** MY FIRST DAY AT SCHOOL, AFTER ALL!!
BUT NEXT TIME THERE'S A PROBLEM... I'M ***HISTORY!!***
...
WOW! OUR SCHOOL'S PRETTY LENIENT...
AFTER ALL, GOTO AND HIS GANG ARE ALL IN THE HOSPITAL.
HELL, IT'S FINE WITH ME, EITHER WAY.

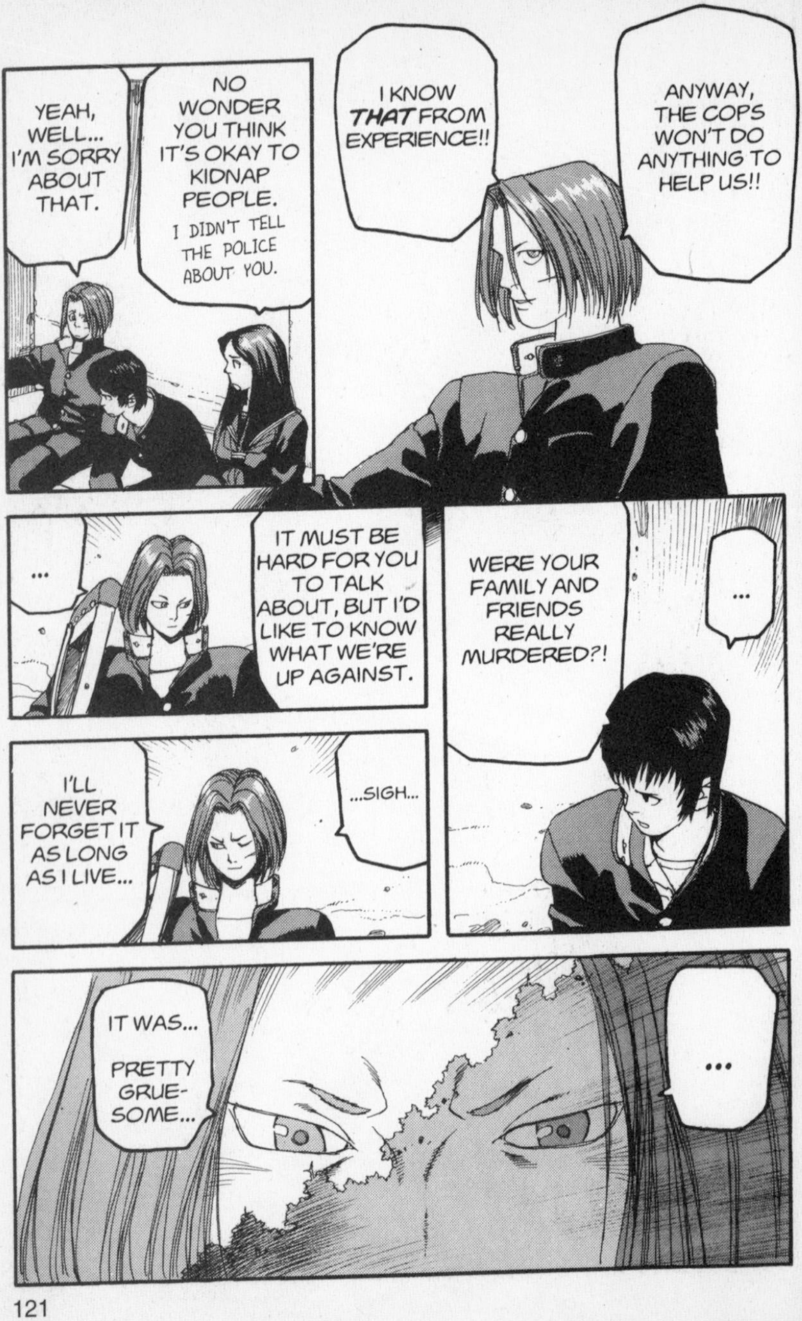
ANYWAY, THE COPS WON'T DO ANYTHING TO HELP US!!
I KNOW *THAT* FROM EXPERIENCE!!
NO WONDER YOU THINK IT'S OKAY TO KIDNAP PEOPLE.
I DIDN'T TELL THE POLICE ABOUT YOU.
YEAH, WELL... I'M SORRY ABOUT THAT.
...
WERE YOUR FAMILY AND FRIENDS REALLY MURDERED?!
IT MUST BE HARD FOR YOU TO TALK ABOUT, BUT I'D LIKE TO KNOW WHAT WE'RE UP AGAINST.
...
...SIGH...
I'LL NEVER FORGET IT AS LONG AS I LIVE...
...
IT WAS...
PRETTY GRUESOME...

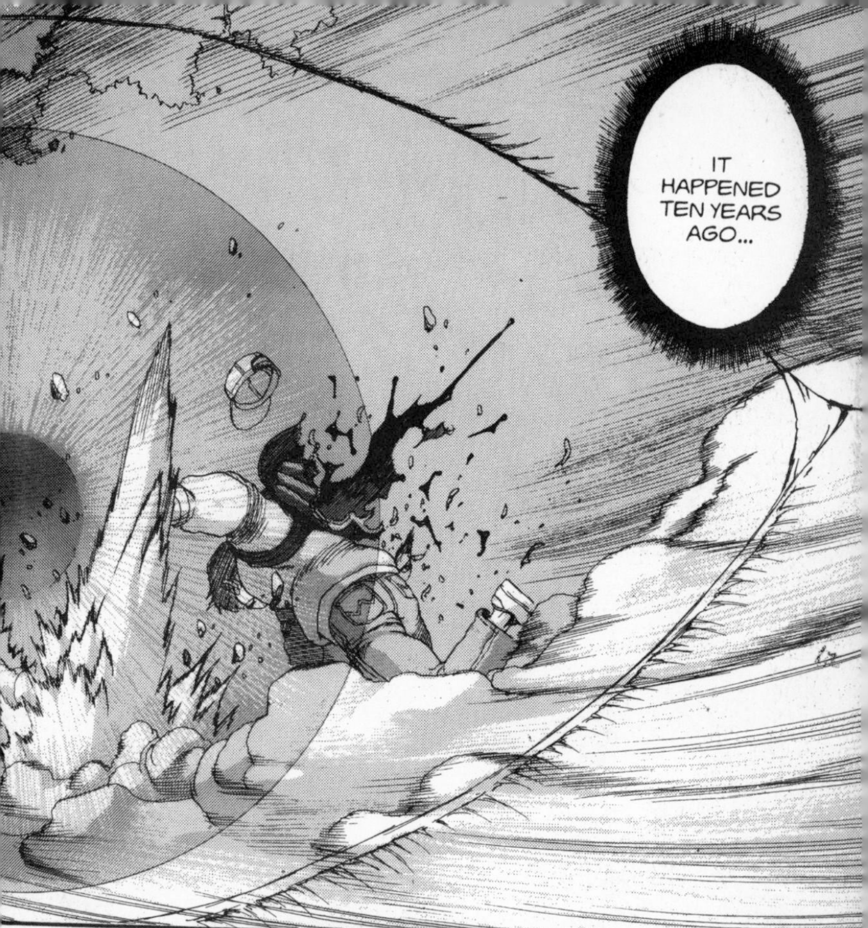
IT HAPPENED TEN YEARS AGO...
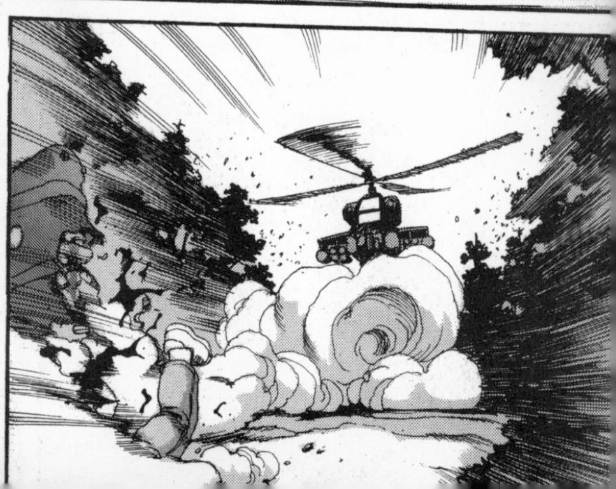
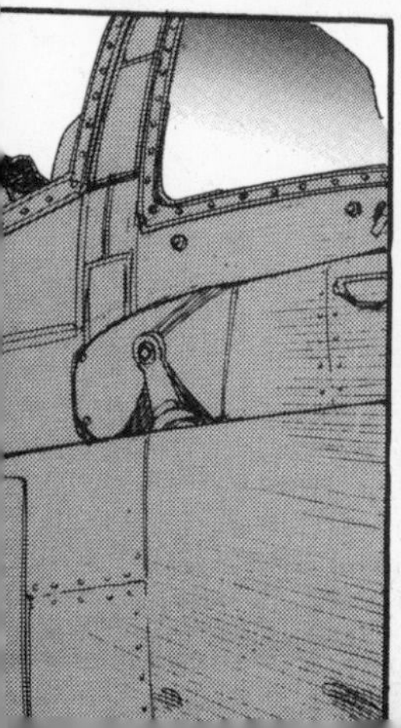

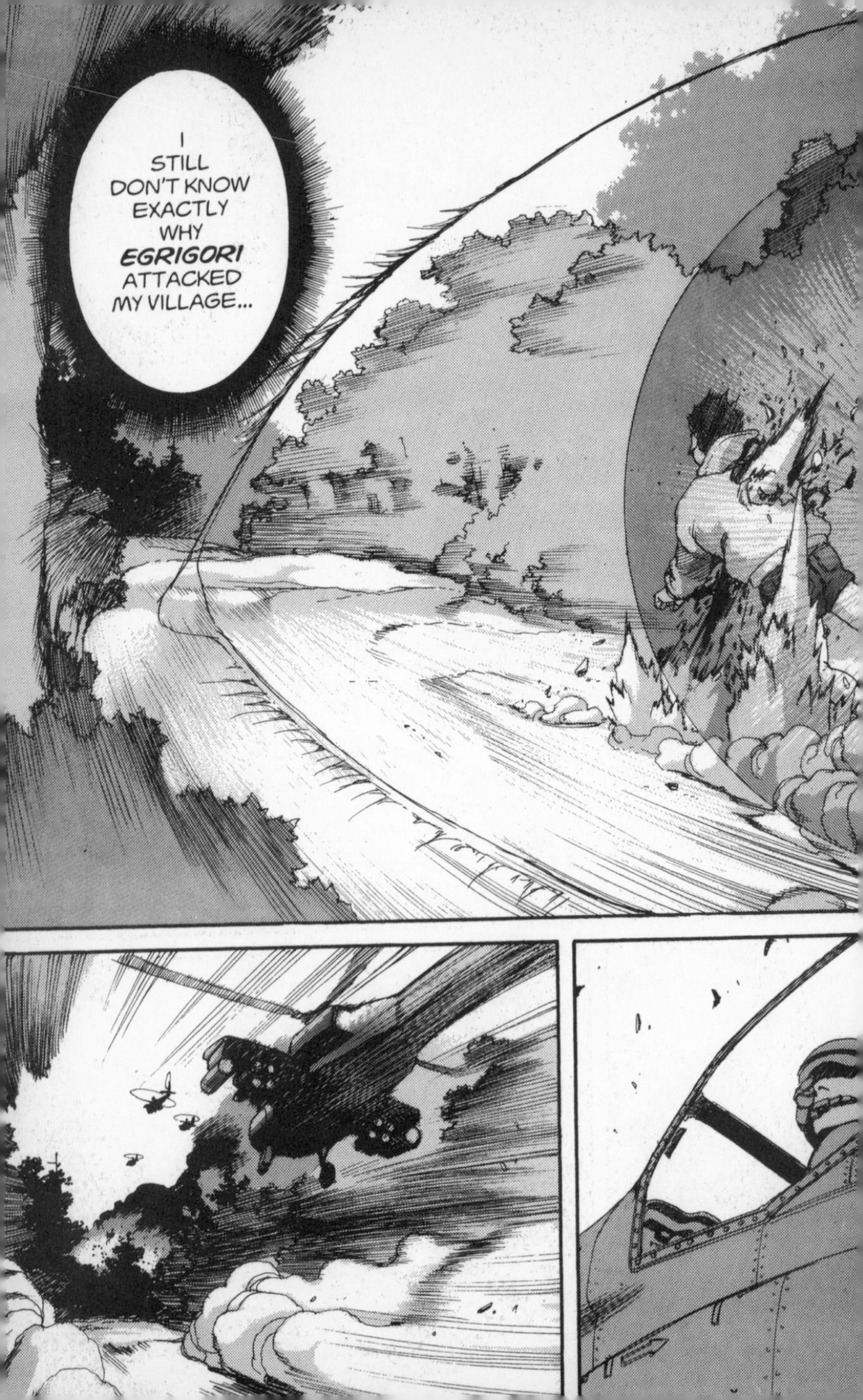
I STILL DON'T KNOW EXACTLY WHY *EGRIGORI* ATTACKED MY VILLAGE...

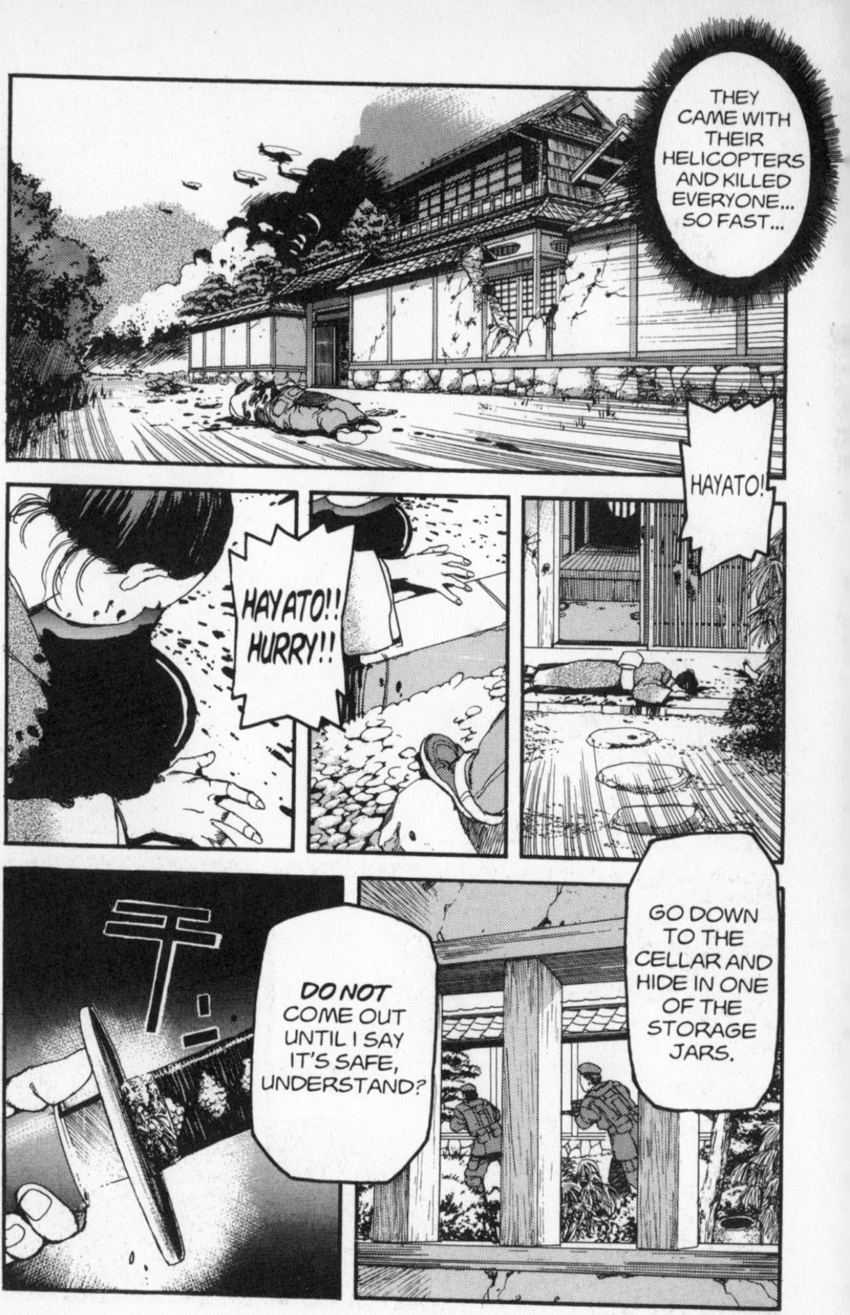
THEY CAME WITH THEIR HELICOPTERS AND KILLED EVERYONE... SO FAST...
HAYATO!
HAYATO!! HURRY!!
GO DOWN TO THE CELLAR AND HIDE IN ONE OF THE STORAGE JARS.
DO NOT COME OUT UNTIL I SAY IT'S SAFE, UNDERSTAND?

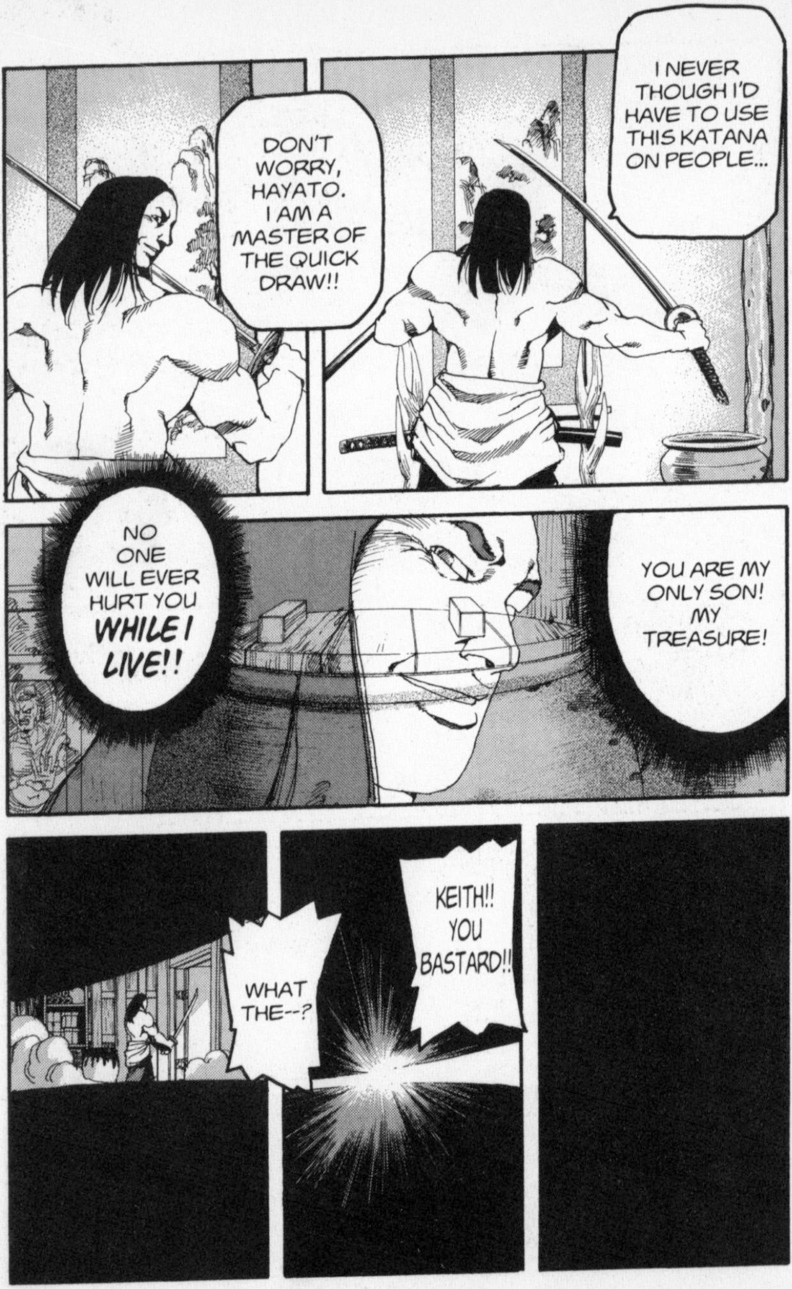
I NEVER THOUGH I'D HAVE TO USE THIS KATANA ON PEOPLE...
DON'T WORRY, HAYATO. I AM A MASTER OF THE QUICK DRAW!!
YOU ARE MY ONLY SON! MY TREASURE!
NO ONE WILL EVER HURT YOU WHILE I LIVE!!
KEITH!! YOU BASTARD!!
WHAT THE--?

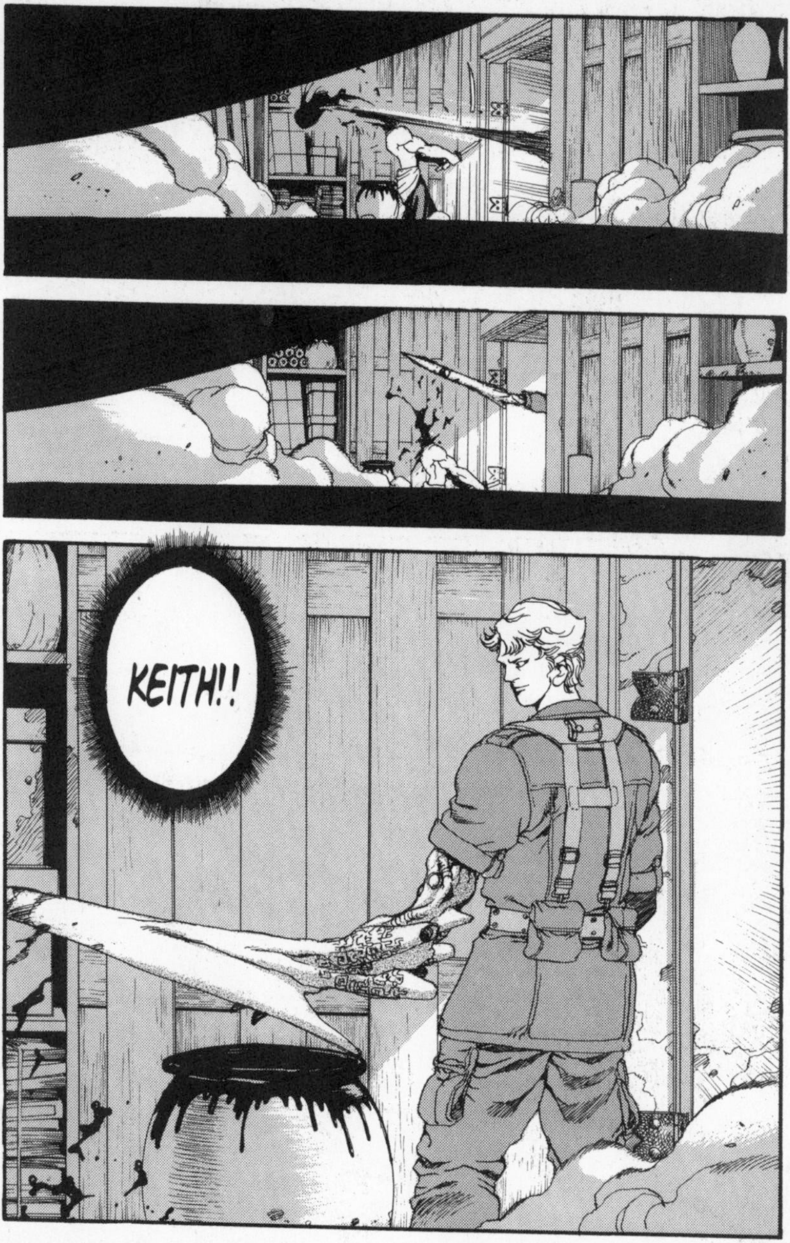
KEITH!!

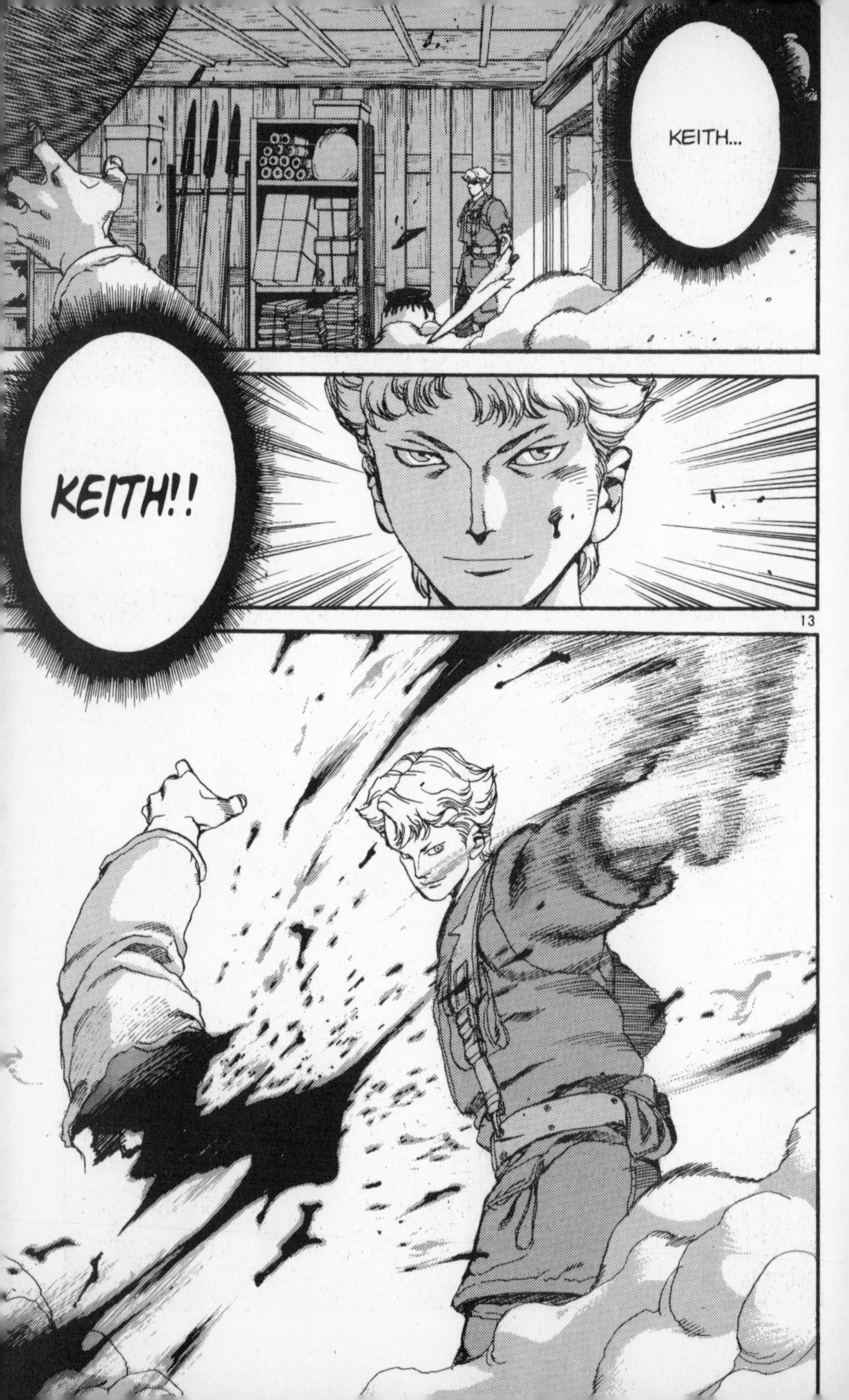
KEITH...
KEITH!!

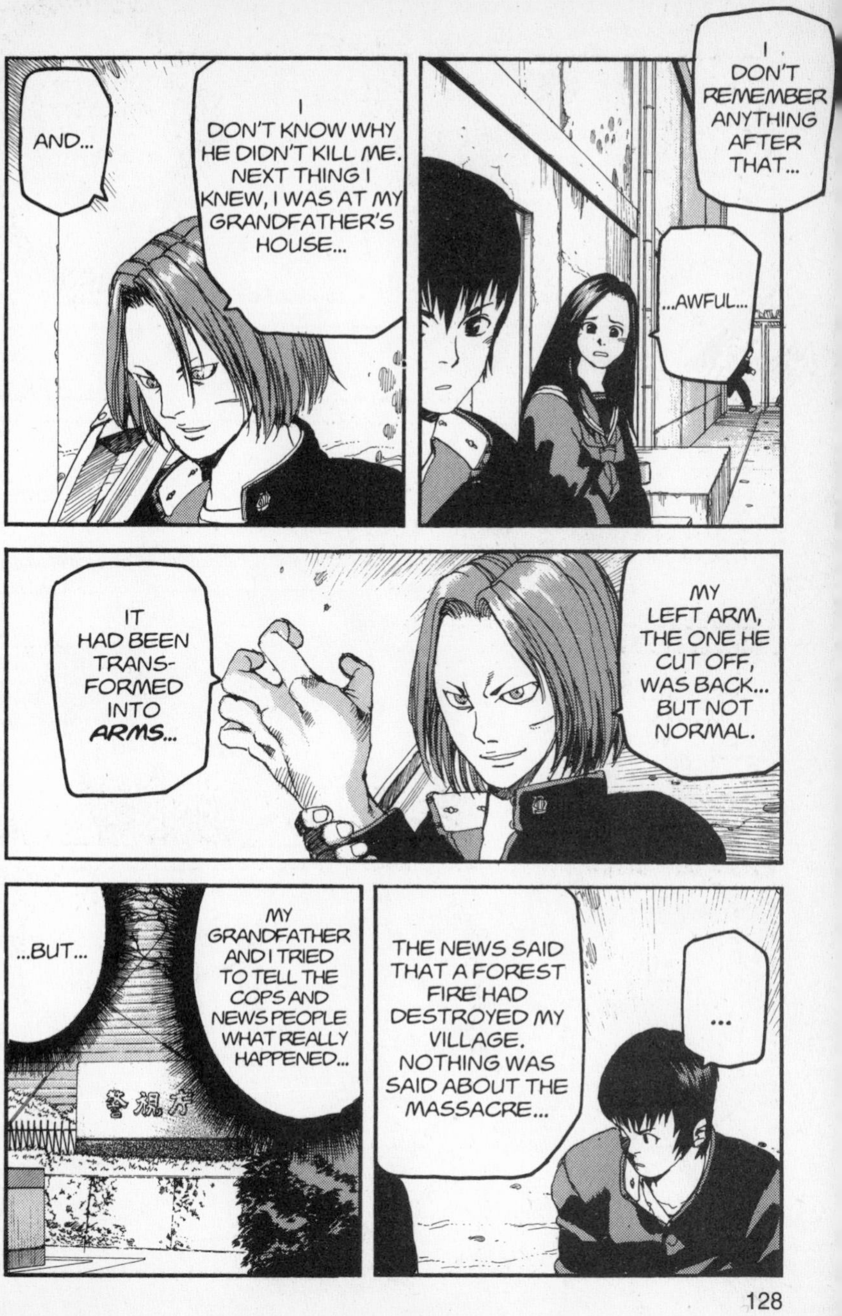
I DON'T REMEMBER ANYTHING AFTER THAT...
...AWFUL...
I DON'T KNOW WHY HE DIDN'T KILL ME. NEXT THING I KNEW, I WAS AT MY GRANDFATHER'S HOUSE...
AND...
MY LEFT ARM, THE ONE HE CUT OFF, WAS BACK... BUT NOT NORMAL.
IT HAD BEEN TRANS-FORMED INTO ARMS...
...
THE NEWS SAID THAT A FOREST FIRE HAD DESTROYED MY VILLAGE. NOTHING WAS SAID ABOUT THE MASSACRE...
MY GRANDFATHER AND I TRIED TO TELL THE COPS AND NEWS PEOPLE WHAT REALLY HAPPENED...
...BUT...
警視庁

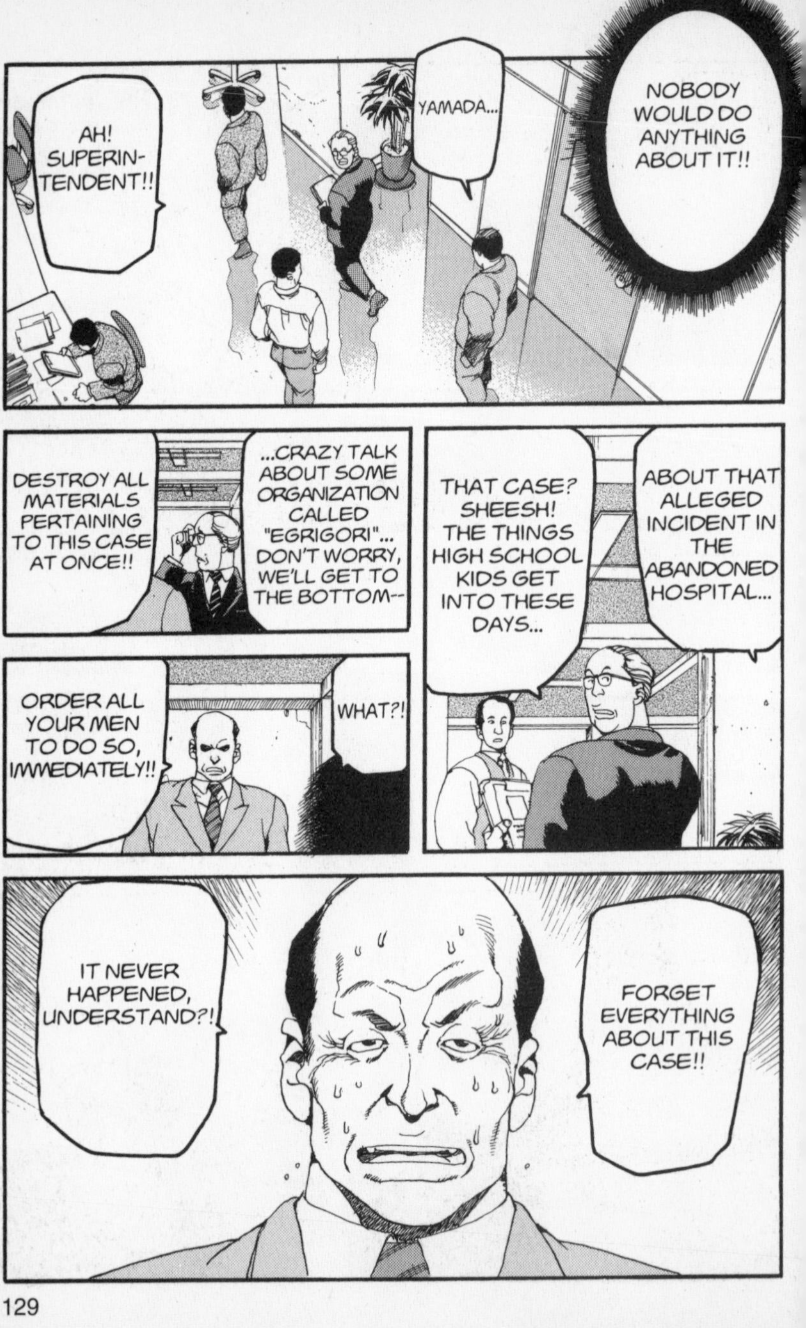
NOBODY WOULD DO ANYTHING ABOUT IT!!
YAMADA...
AH! SUPERIN-TENDENT!!
ABOUT THAT ALLEGED INCIDENT IN THE ABANDONED HOSPITAL...
THAT CASE? SHEESH! THE THINGS HIGH SCHOOL KIDS GET INTO THESE DAYS...
...CRAZY TALK ABOUT SOME ORGANIZATION CALLED "EGRIGORI"... DON'T WORRY, WE'LL GET TO THE BOTTOM--
DESTROY ALL MATERIALS PERTAINING TO THIS CASE AT ONCE!!
WHAT?!
ORDER ALL YOUR MEN TO DO SO, IMMEDIATELY!!
FORGET EVERYTHING ABOUT THIS CASE!!
IT NEVER HAPPENED, UNDERSTAND?!

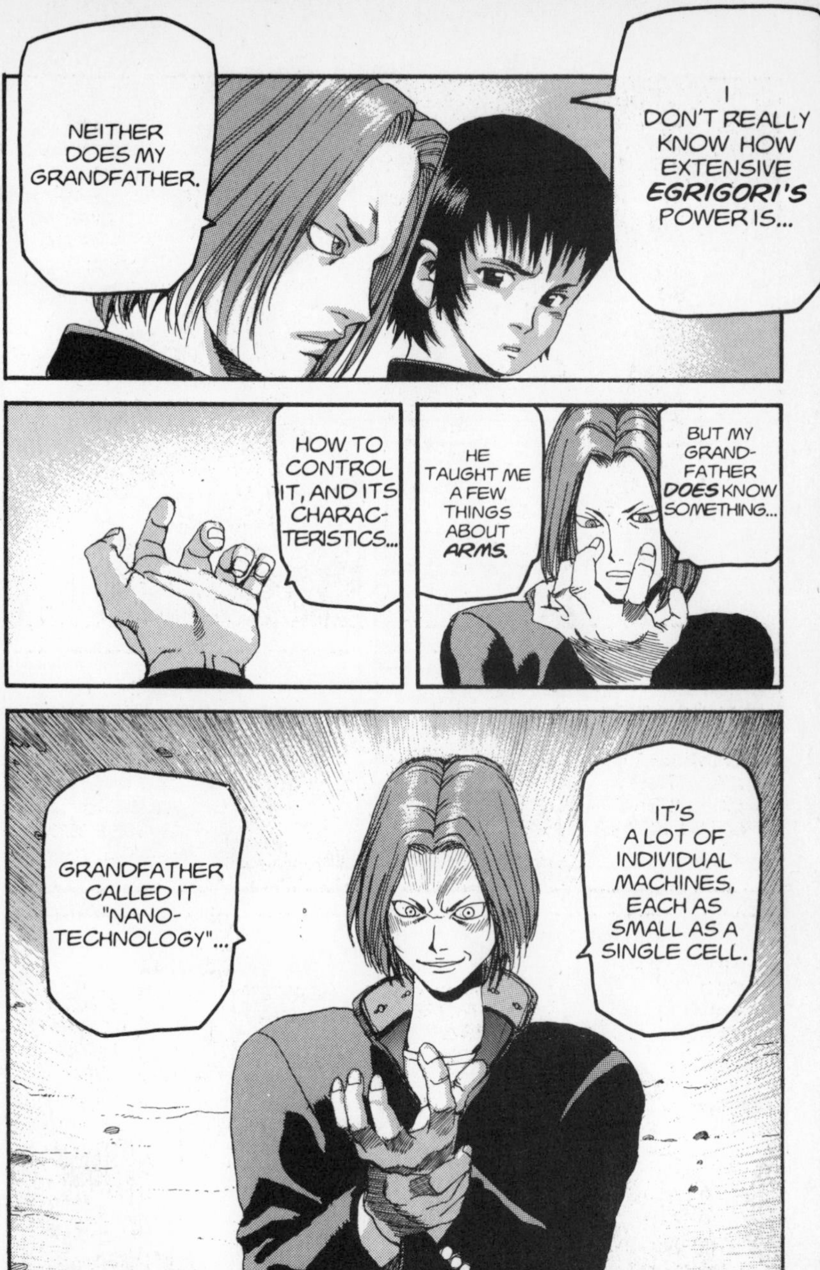
I DON'T REALLY KNOW HOW EXTENSIVE EGRIGORI'S POWER IS...
NEITHER DOES MY GRANDFATHER.
BUT MY GRAND-FATHER DOES KNOW SOMETHING...
HE TAUGHT ME A FEW THINGS ABOUT ARMS.
HOW TO CONTROL IT, AND ITS CHARAC-TERISTICS...
IT'S A LOT OF INDIVIDUAL MACHINES, EACH AS SMALL AS A SINGLE CELL.
GRANDFATHER CALLED IT "NANO-TECHNOLOGY"...

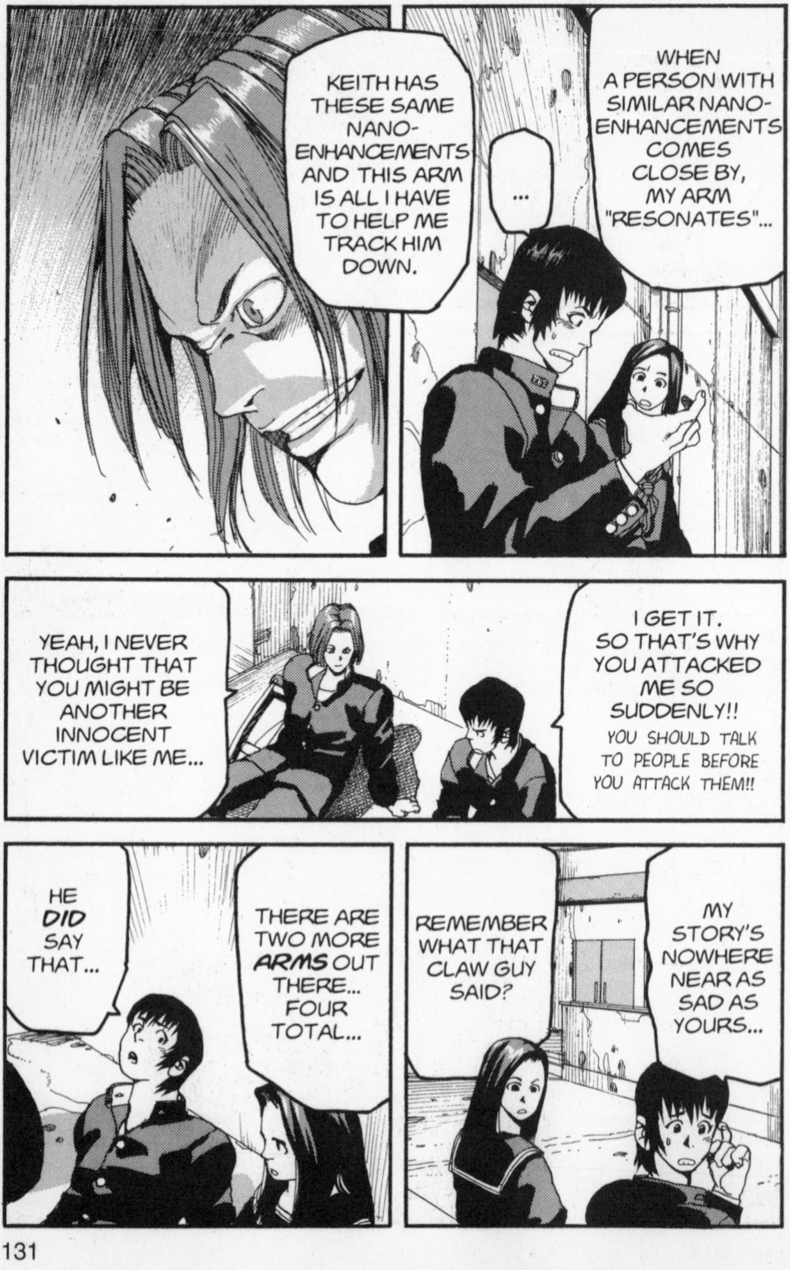
WHEN A PERSON WITH SIMILAR NANO-ENHANCEMENTS COMES CLOSE BY, MY ARM "RESONATES"...
...
KEITH HAS THESE SAME NANO-ENHANCEMENTS AND THIS ARM IS ALL I HAVE TO HELP ME TRACK HIM DOWN.
I GET IT. SO THAT'S WHY YOU ATTACKED ME SO SUDDENLY!! YOU SHOULD TALK TO PEOPLE BEFORE YOU ATTACK THEM!!
YEAH, I NEVER THOUGHT THAT YOU MIGHT BE ANOTHER INNOCENT VICTIM LIKE ME...
MY STORY'S NOWHERE NEAR AS SAD AS YOURS...
REMEMBER WHAT THAT CLAW GUY SAID?
THERE ARE TWO MORE ***ARMS*** OUT THERE... FOUR TOTAL...
HE ***DID*** SAY THAT...

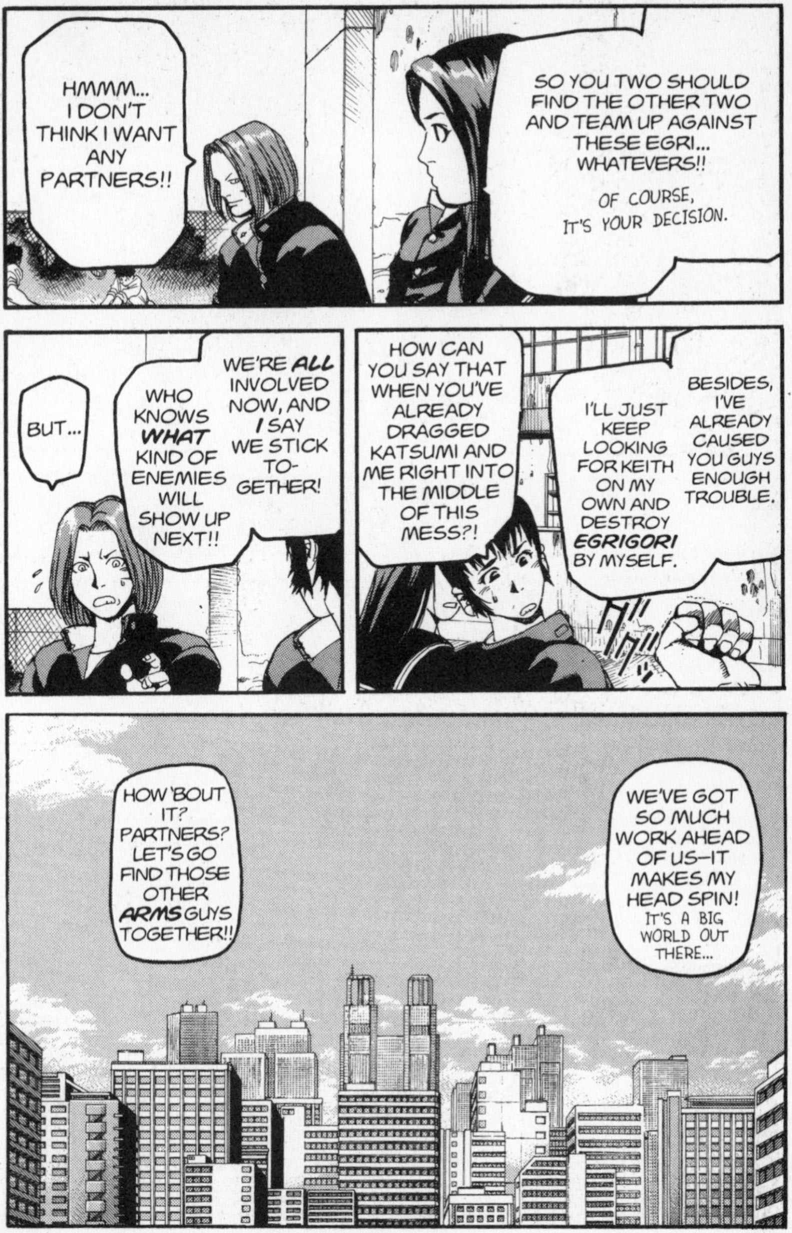
SO YOU TWO SHOULD FIND THE OTHER TWO AND TEAM UP AGAINST THESE EGRI... WHATEVERS!!
OF COURSE, IT'S YOUR DECISION.
HMMM... I DON'T THINK I WANT ANY PARTNERS!!
BESIDES, I'VE ALREADY CAUSED YOU GUYS ENOUGH TROUBLE.
I'LL JUST KEEP LOOKING FOR KEITH ON MY OWN AND DESTROY EGRIGORI BY MYSELF.
HOW CAN YOU SAY THAT WHEN YOU'VE ALREADY DRAGGED KATSUMI AND ME RIGHT INTO THE MIDDLE OF THIS MESS?!
WE'RE ALL INVOLVED NOW, AND I SAY WE STICK TO-GETHER!
WHO KNOWS WHAT KIND OF ENEMIES WILL SHOW UP NEXT!!
BUT...
WE'VE GOT SO MUCH WORK AHEAD OF US—IT MAKES MY HEAD SPIN!
IT'S A BIG WORLD OUT THERE...
HOW 'BOUT IT? PARTNERS? LET'S GO FIND THOSE OTHER ARMS GUYS TOGETHER!!

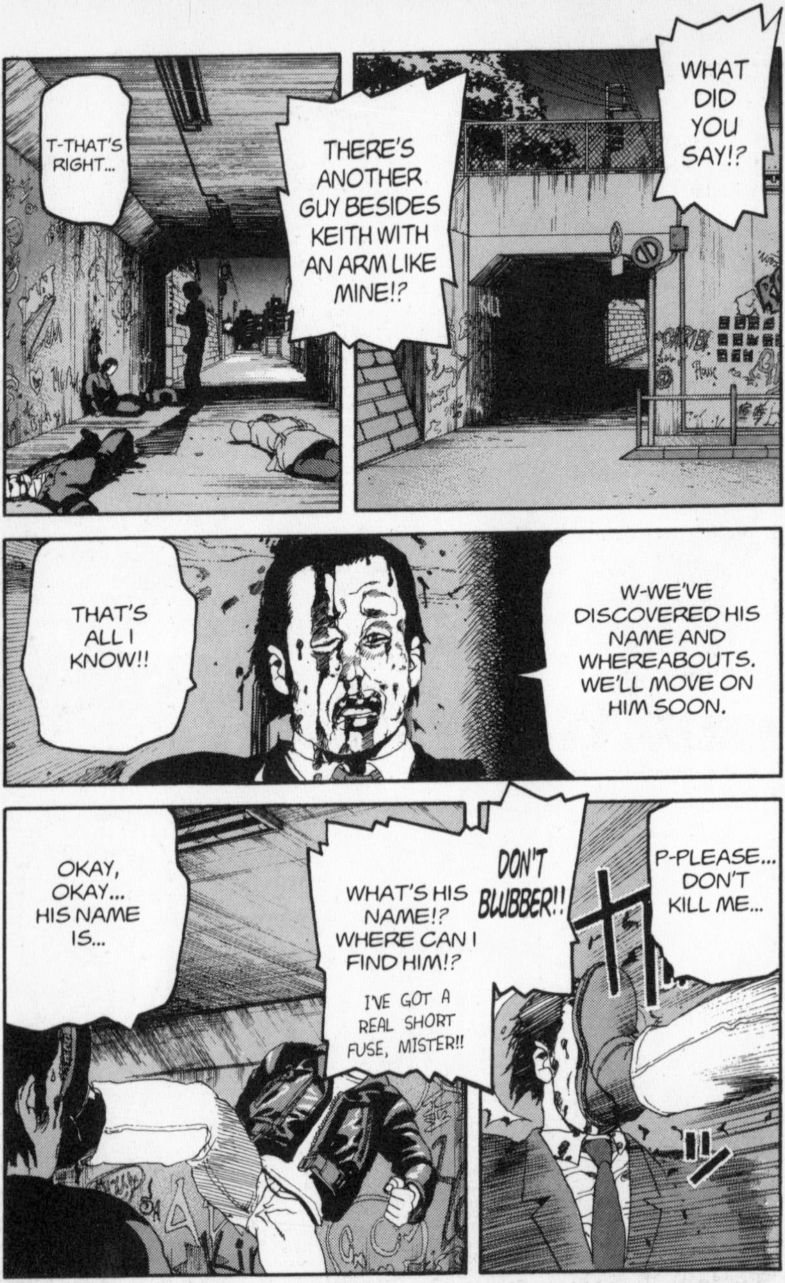
WHAT DID YOU SAY!?
THERE'S ANOTHER GUY BESIDES KEITH WITH AN ARM LIKE MINE!?
T-THAT'S RIGHT...
W-WE'VE DISCOVERED HIS NAME AND WHEREABOUTS. WE'LL MOVE ON HIM SOON.
THAT'S ALL I KNOW!!
P-PLEASE... DON'T KILL ME...
DON'T BLUBBER!!
WHAT'S HIS NAME!? WHERE CAN I FIND HIM!?
I'VE GOT A REAL SHORT FUSE, MISTER!!
OKAY, OKAY... HIS NAME IS...

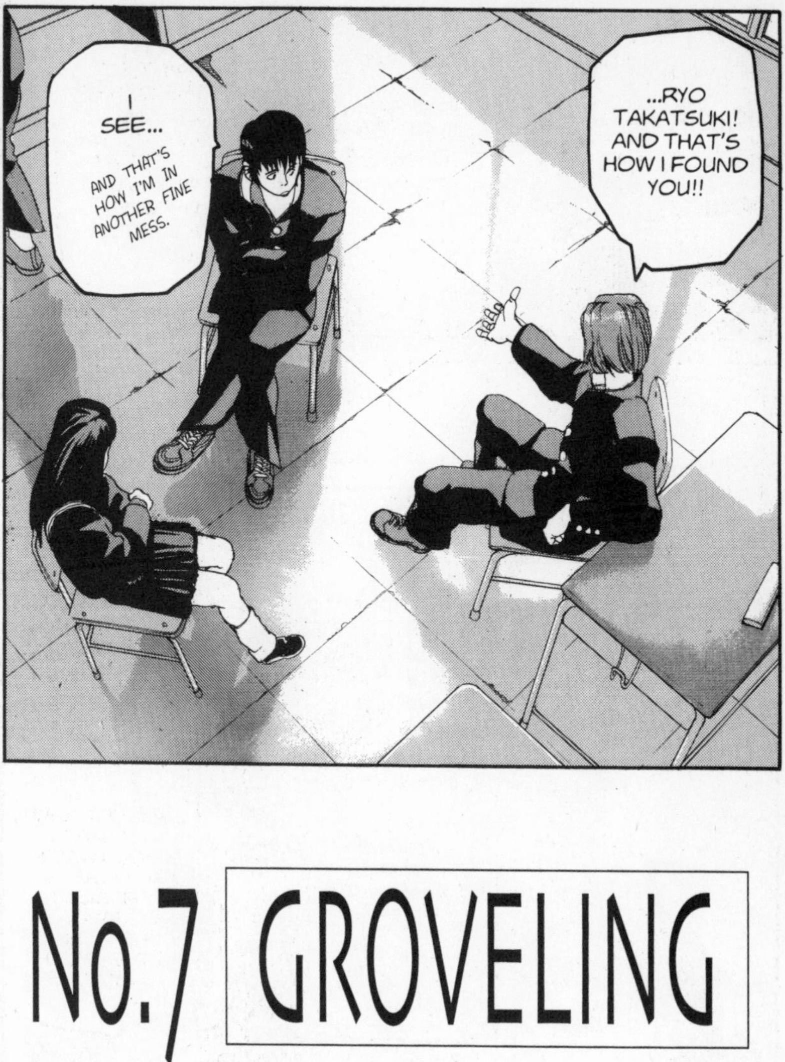
...RYO TAKATSUKI! AND THAT'S HOW I FOUND YOU!!
I SEE...
AND THAT'S HOW I'M IN ANOTHER FINE MESS.

No.7 GROVELING

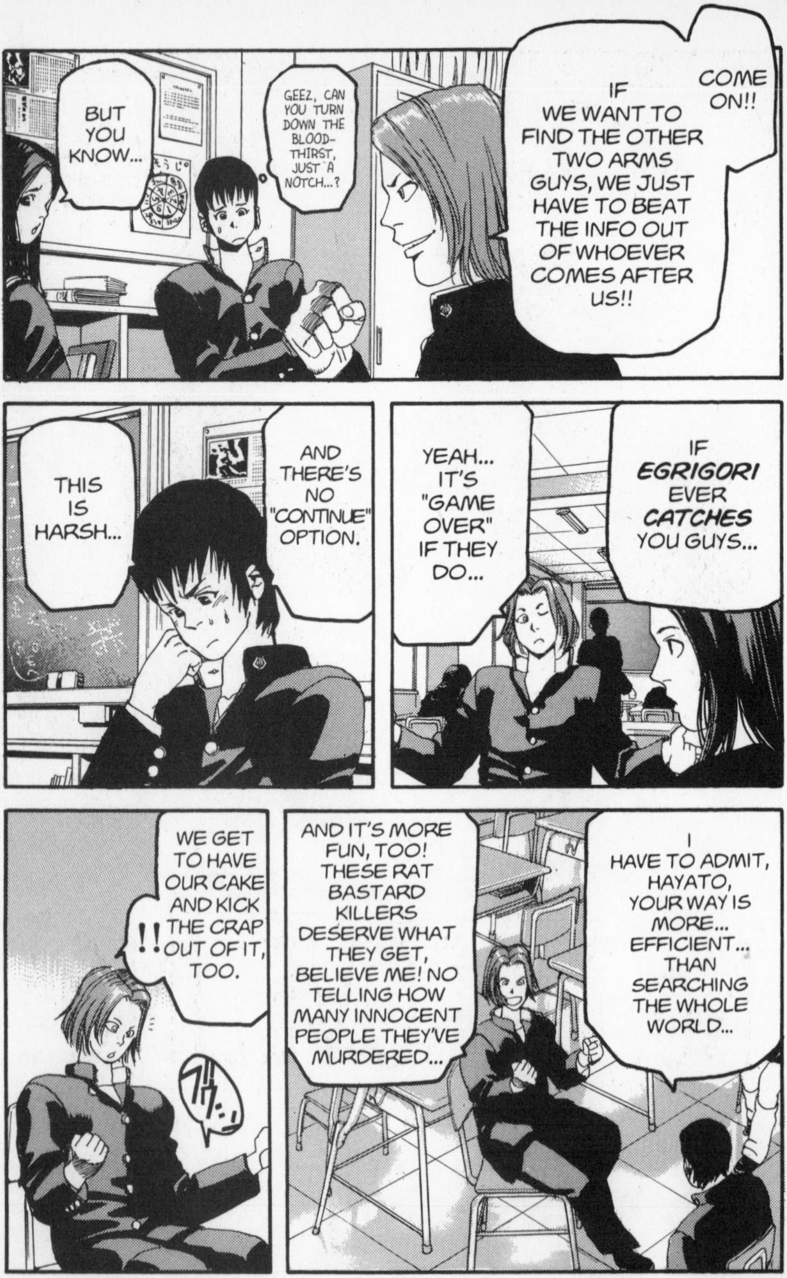

COME ON!!
IF WE WANT TO FIND THE OTHER TWO ARMS GUYS, WE JUST HAVE TO BEAT THE INFO OUT OF WHOEVER COMES AFTER US!!
GEEZ, CAN YOU TURN DOWN THE BLOOD-THIRST, JUST A NOTCH...?
BUT YOU KNOW...
IF EGRIGORI EVER CATCHES YOU GUYS...
YEAH... IT'S "GAME OVER" IF THEY DO...
AND THERE'S NO "CONTINUE" OPTION.
THIS IS HARSH...
I HAVE TO ADMIT, HAYATO, YOUR WAY IS MORE... EFFICIENT... THAN SEARCHING THE WHOLE WORLD...
AND IT'S MORE FUN, TOO! THESE RAT BASTARD KILLERS DESERVE WHAT THEY GET, BELIEVE ME! NO TELLING HOW MANY INNOCENT PEOPLE THEY'VE MURDERED...
WE GET TO HAVE OUR CAKE AND KICK THE CRAP OUT OF IT, TOO.
!!

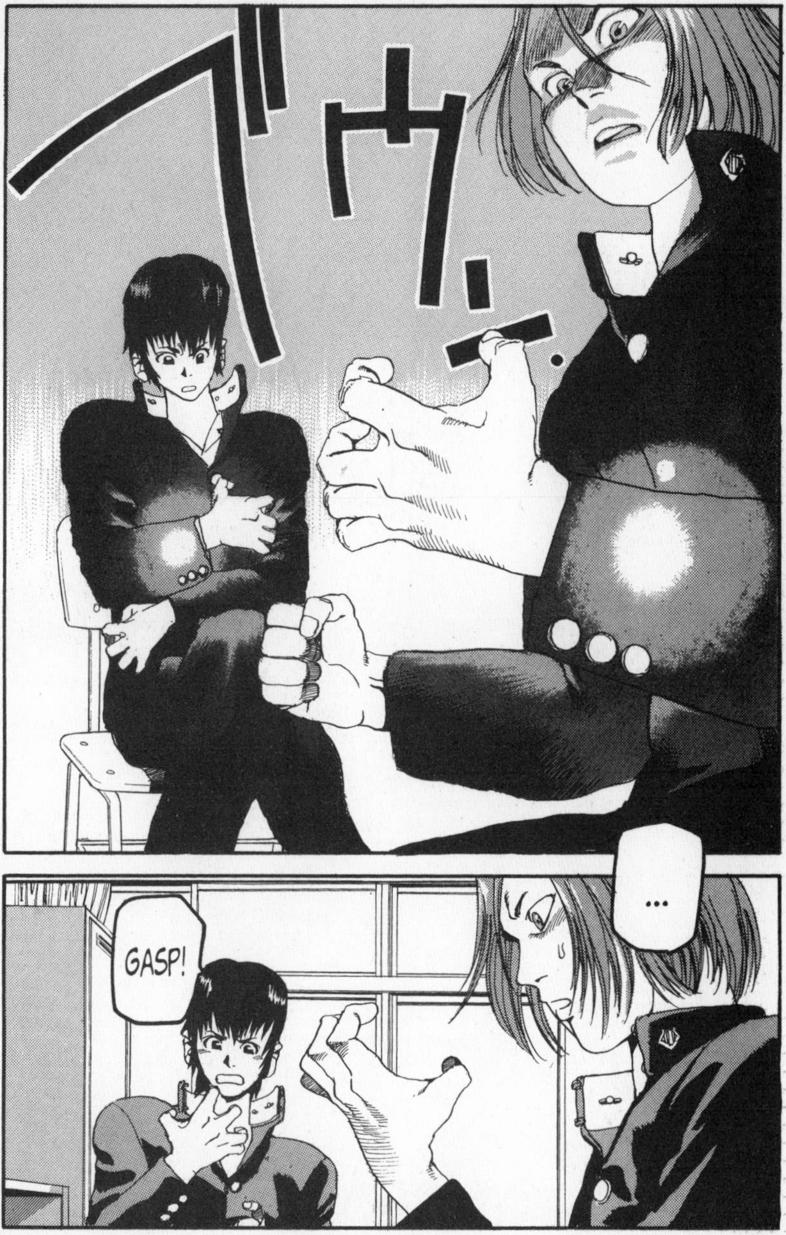
ブウ
...
GASP!

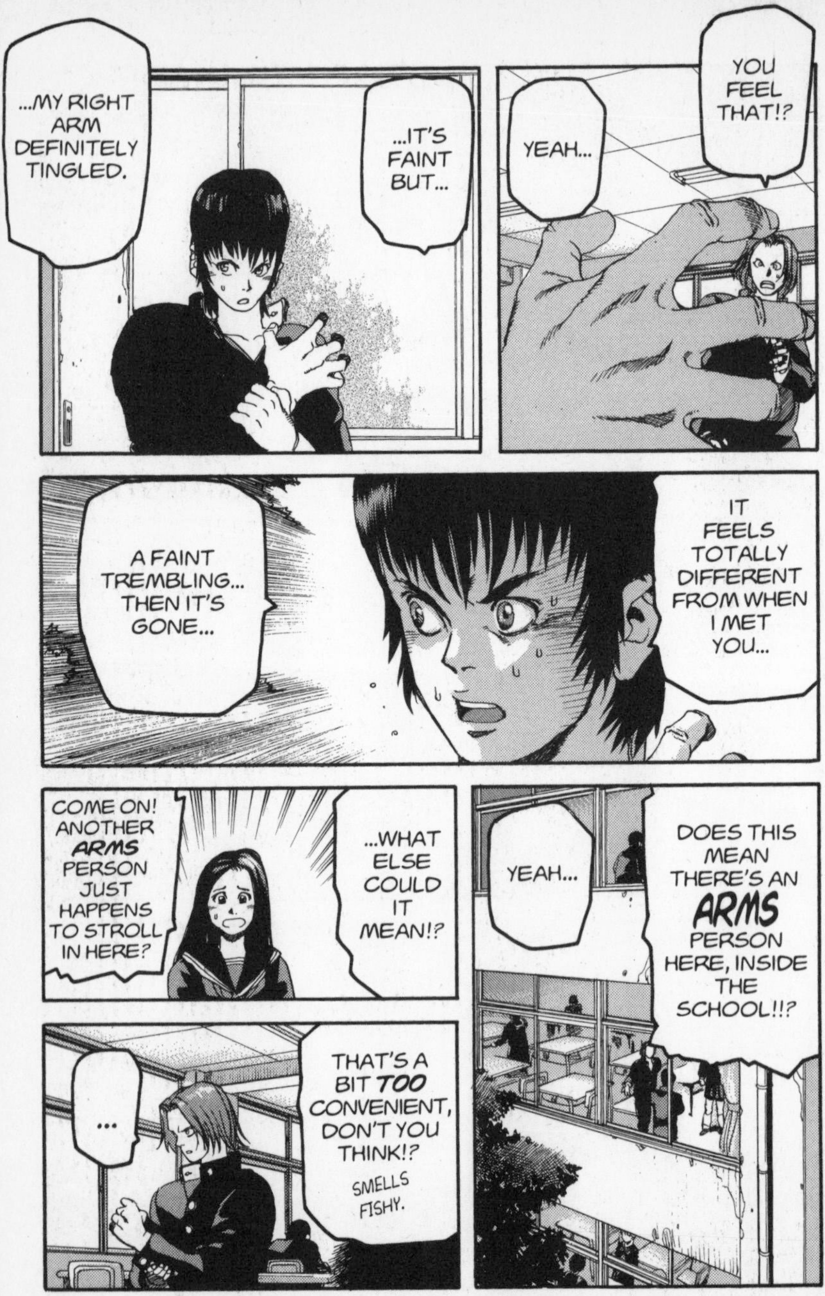
YOU FEEL THAT!?
YEAH...
...IT'S FAINT BUT...
...MY RIGHT ARM DEFINITELY TINGLED.
IT FEELS TOTALLY DIFFERENT FROM WHEN I MET YOU...
A FAINT TREMBLING... THEN IT'S GONE...
DOES THIS MEAN THERE'S AN ARMS PERSON HERE, INSIDE THE SCHOOL!!?
YEAH...
...WHAT ELSE COULD IT MEAN!?
COME ON! ANOTHER ARMS PERSON JUST HAPPENS TO STROLL IN HERE?
THAT'S A BIT TOO CONVENIENT, DON'T YOU THINK!?
SMELLS FISHY.
...

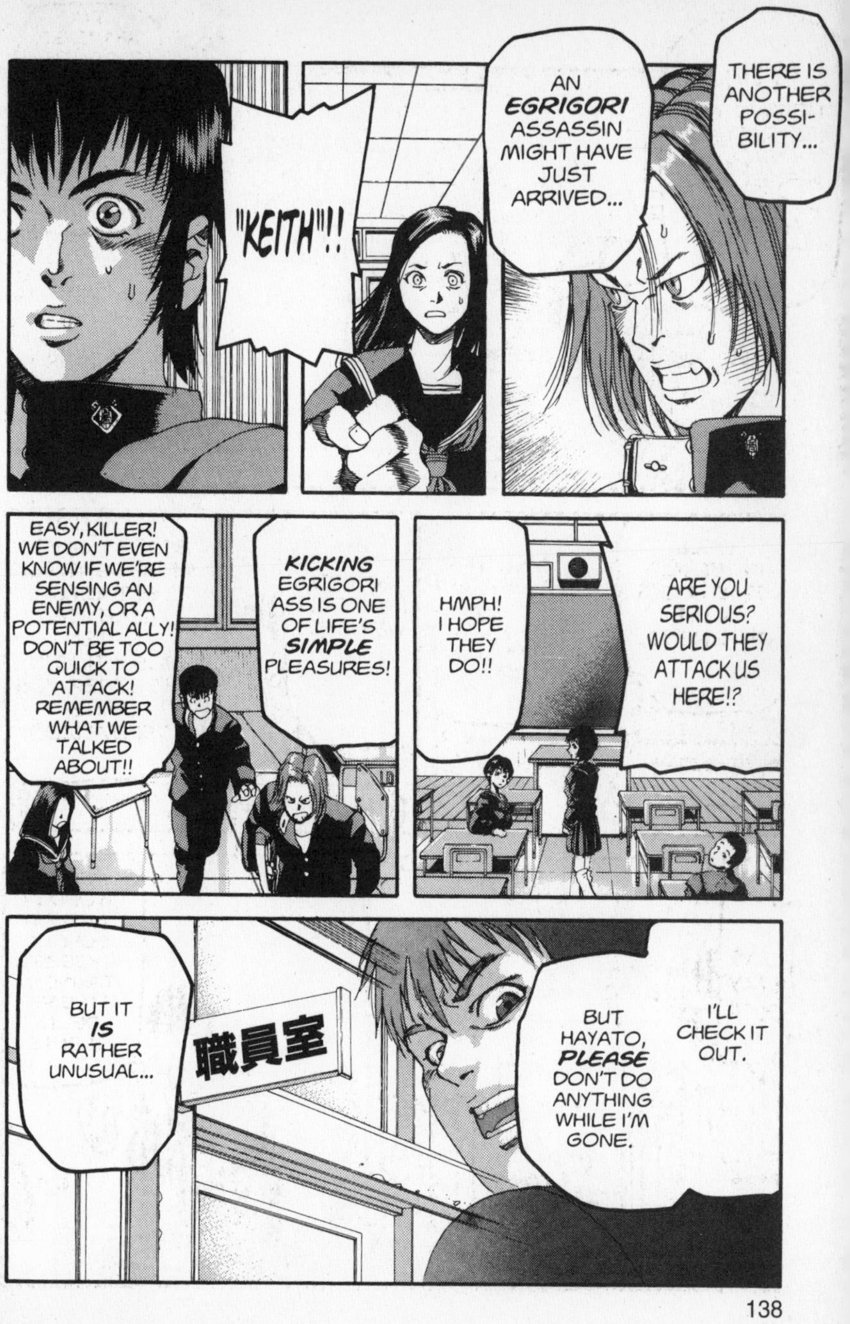
THERE IS ANOTHER POSSI-BILITY...
AN EGRIGORI ASSASSIN MIGHT HAVE JUST ARRIVED...
"KEITH"!!
ARE YOU SERIOUS? WOULD THEY ATTACK US HERE!?
HMPH! I HOPE THEY DO!!
KICKING EGRIGORI ASS IS ONE OF LIFE'S SIMPLE PLEASURES!
EASY, KILLER! WE DON'T EVEN KNOW IF WE'RE SENSING AN ENEMY, OR A POTENTIAL ALLY! DON'T BE TOO QUICK TO ATTACK! REMEMBER WHAT WE TALKED ABOUT!!
I'LL CHECK IT OUT.
BUT HAYATO, PLEASE DON'T DO ANYTHING WHILE I'M GONE.
職員室
BUT IT IS RATHER UNUSUAL...

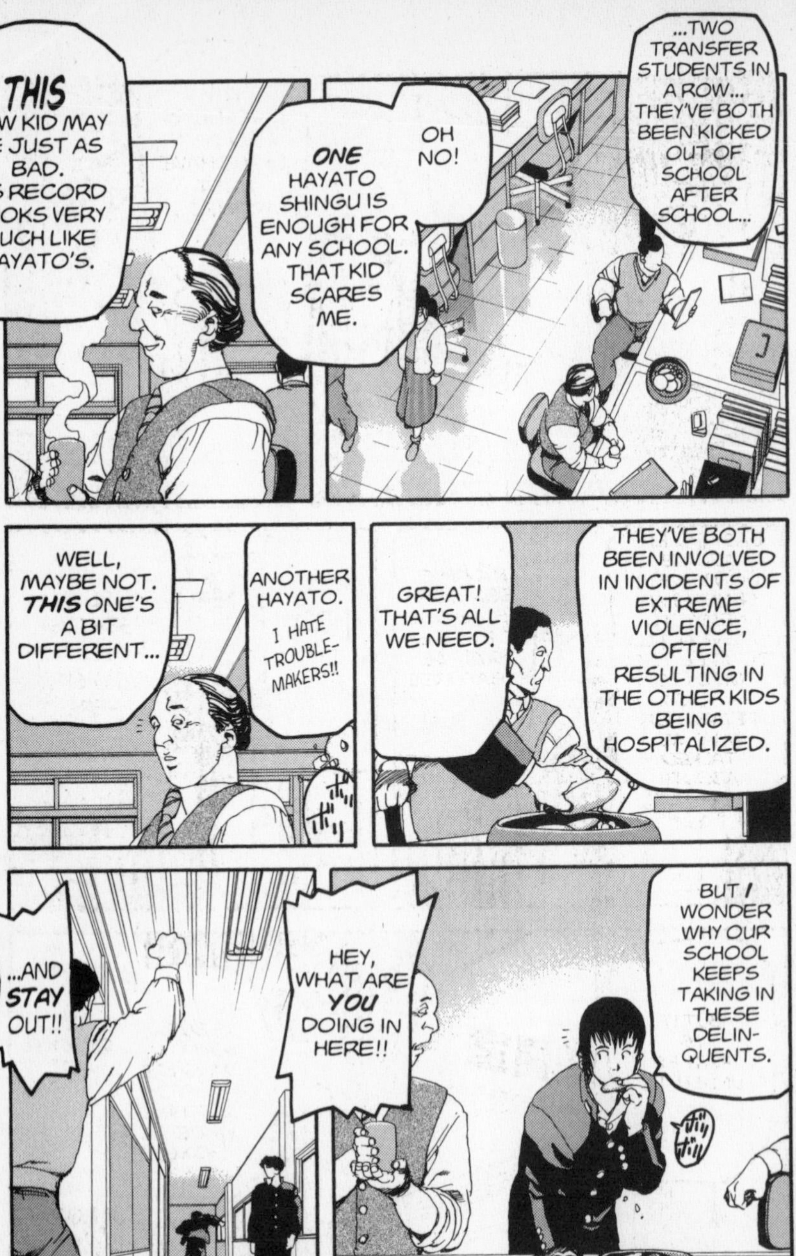
...TWO TRANSFER STUDENTS IN A ROW... THEY'VE BOTH BEEN KICKED OUT OF SCHOOL AFTER SCHOOL...
OH NO!
ONE HAYATO SHINGU IS ENOUGH FOR ANY SCHOOL. THAT KID SCARES ME.
THIS NEW KID MAY BE JUST AS BAD. HIS RECORD LOOKS VERY MUCH LIKE HAYATO'S.
THEY'VE BOTH BEEN INVOLVED IN INCIDENTS OF EXTREME VIOLENCE, OFTEN RESULTING IN THE OTHER KIDS BEING HOSPITALIZED.
GREAT! THAT'S ALL WE NEED.
ANOTHER HAYATO.
I HATE TROUBLE-MAKERS!!
WELL, MAYBE NOT. THIS ONE'S A BIT DIFFERENT...
BUT I WONDER WHY OUR SCHOOL KEEPS TAKING IN THESE DELIN-QUENTS.
HEY, WHAT ARE YOU DOING IN HERE!!
...AND STAY OUT!!

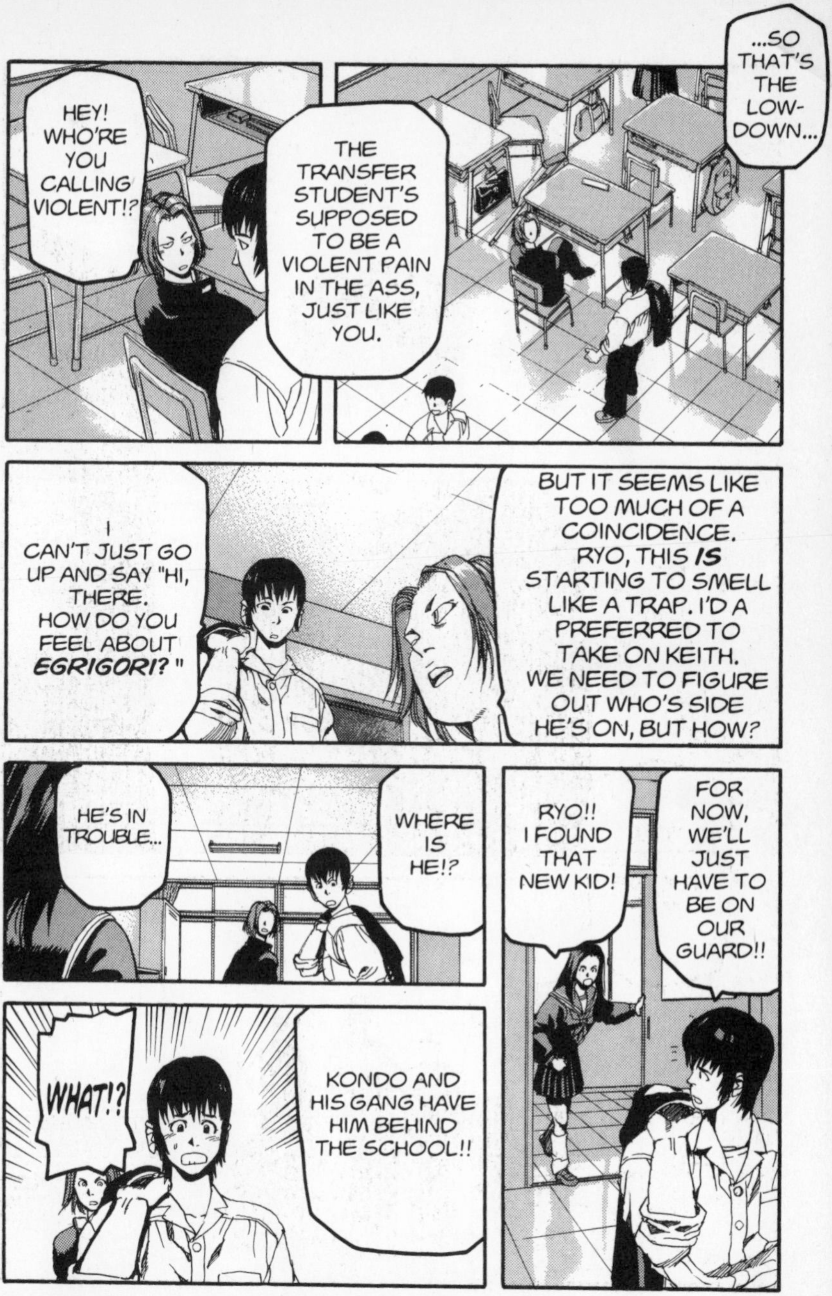
...SO THAT'S THE LOW-DOWN...
THE TRANSFER STUDENT'S SUPPOSED TO BE A VIOLENT PAIN IN THE ASS, JUST LIKE YOU.
HEY! WHO'RE YOU CALLING VIOLENT!?
BUT IT SEEMS LIKE TOO MUCH OF A COINCIDENCE. RYO, THIS ***IS*** STARTING TO SMELL LIKE A TRAP. I'D A PREFERRED TO TAKE ON KEITH. WE NEED TO FIGURE OUT WHO'S SIDE HE'S ON, BUT HOW?
I CAN'T JUST GO UP AND SAY "HI, THERE. HOW DO YOU FEEL ABOUT ***EGRIGORI?***"
FOR NOW, WE'LL JUST HAVE TO BE ON OUR GUARD!!
RYO!! I FOUND THAT NEW KID!
WHERE IS HE!?
HE'S IN TROUBLE...
KONDO AND HIS GANG HAVE HIM BEHIND THE SCHOOL!!
WHAT!?

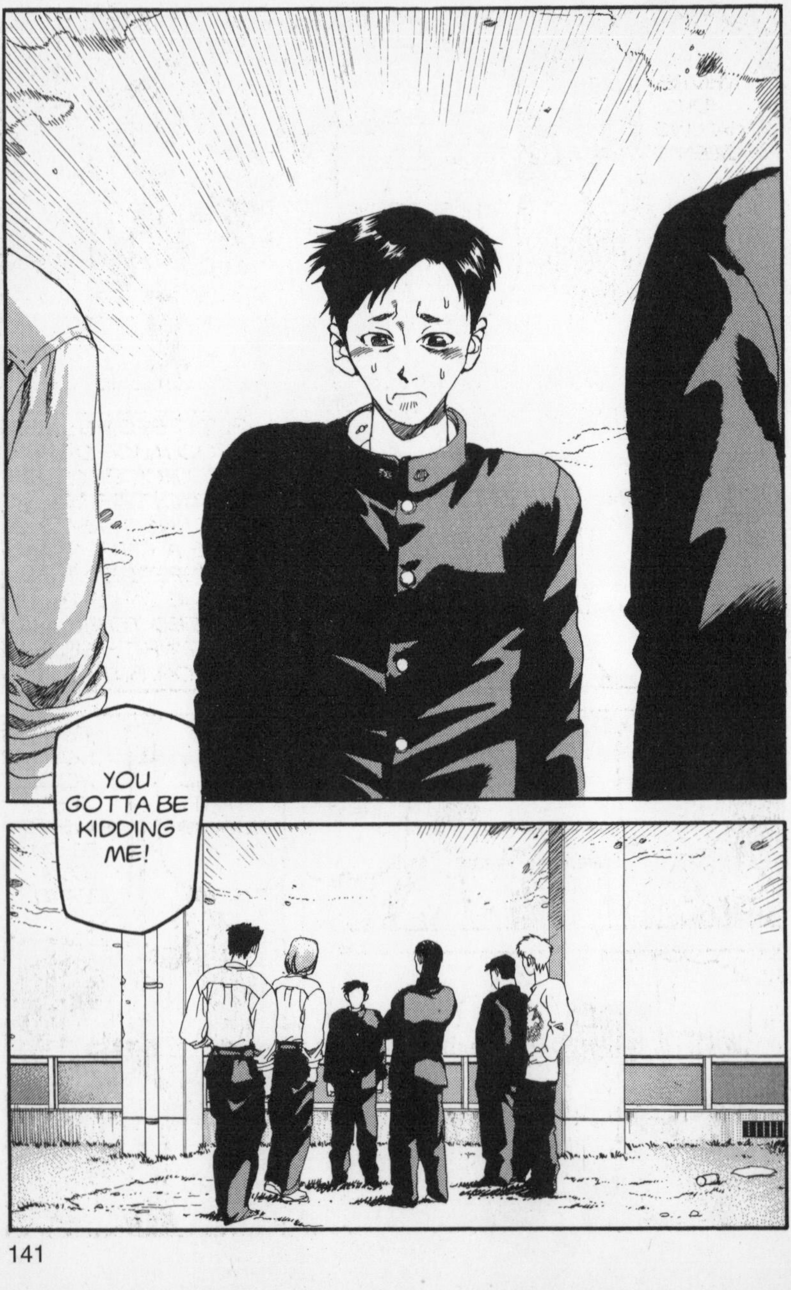
YOU GOTTA BE KIDDING ME!

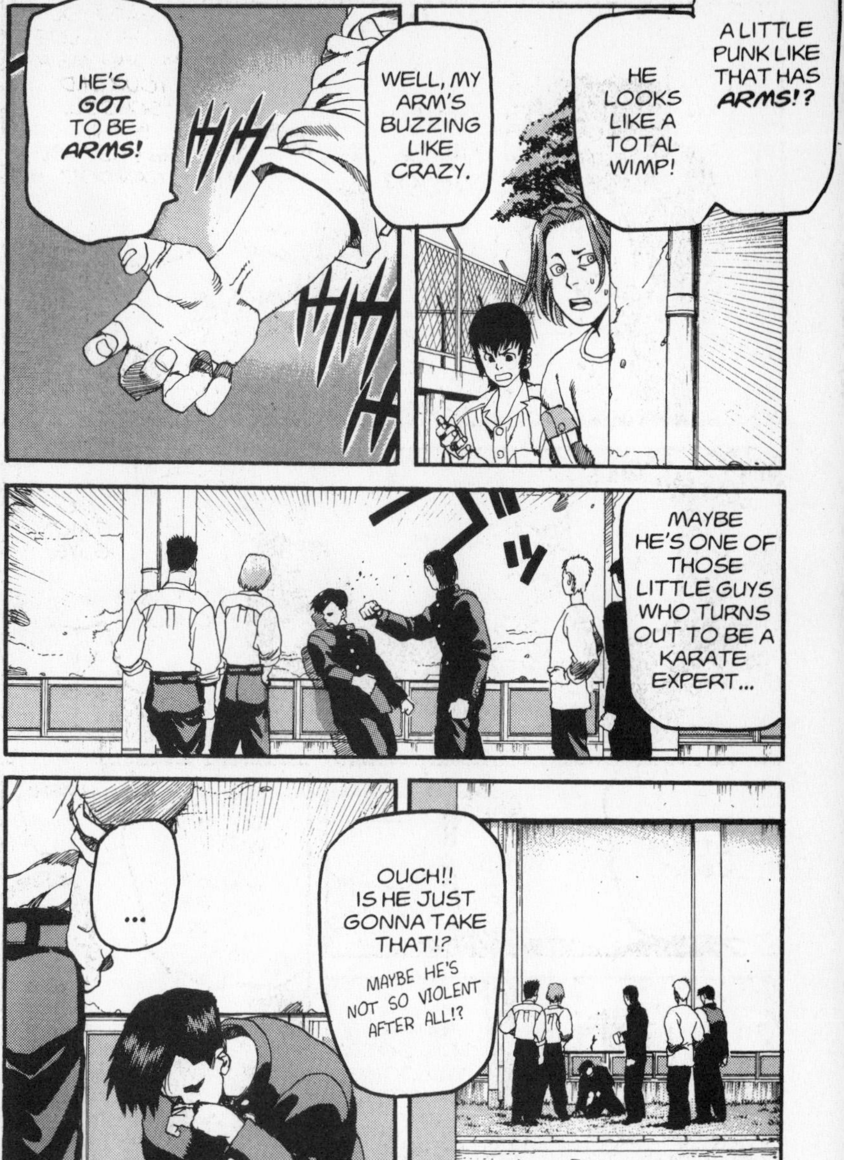
A LITTLE PUNK LIKE THAT HAS ARMS!?
HE LOOKS LIKE A TOTAL WIMP!
WELL, MY ARM'S BUZZING LIKE CRAZY.
HE'S GOT TO BE ARMS!
MAYBE HE'S ONE OF THOSE LITTLE GUYS WHO TURNS OUT TO BE A KARATE EXPERT...
OUCH!! IS HE JUST GONNA TAKE THAT!?
MAYBE HE'S NOT SO VIOLENT AFTER ALL!?
...

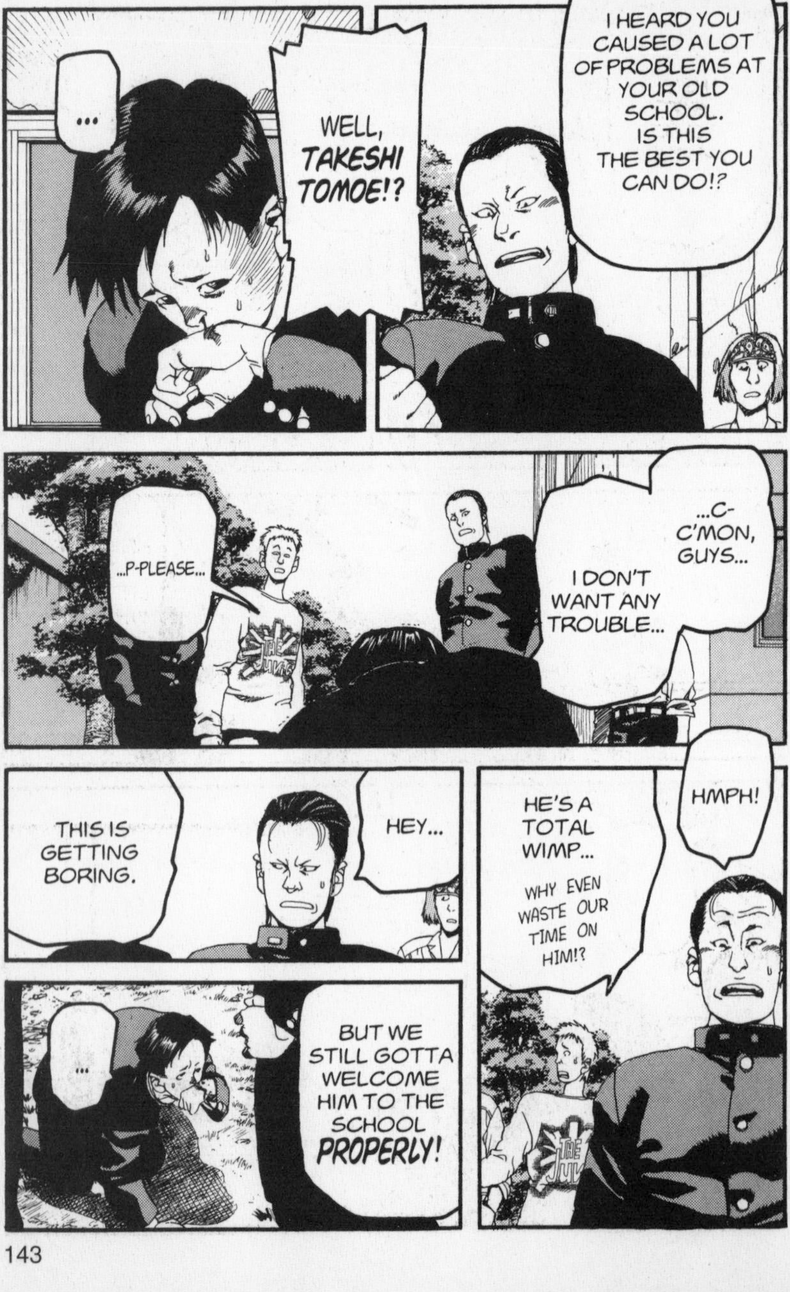

I HEARD YOU CAUSED A LOT OF PROBLEMS AT YOUR OLD SCHOOL. IS THIS THE BEST YOU CAN DO!?
WELL, TAKESHI TOMOE!?
...
...C- C'MON, GUYS...
I DON'T WANT ANY TROUBLE...
...P-PLEASE...
HMPH!
HE'S A TOTAL WIMP...
WHY EVEN WASTE OUR TIME ON HIM!?
HEY...
THIS IS GETTING BORING.
BUT WE STILL GOTTA WELCOME HIM TO THE SCHOOL PROPERLY!
...

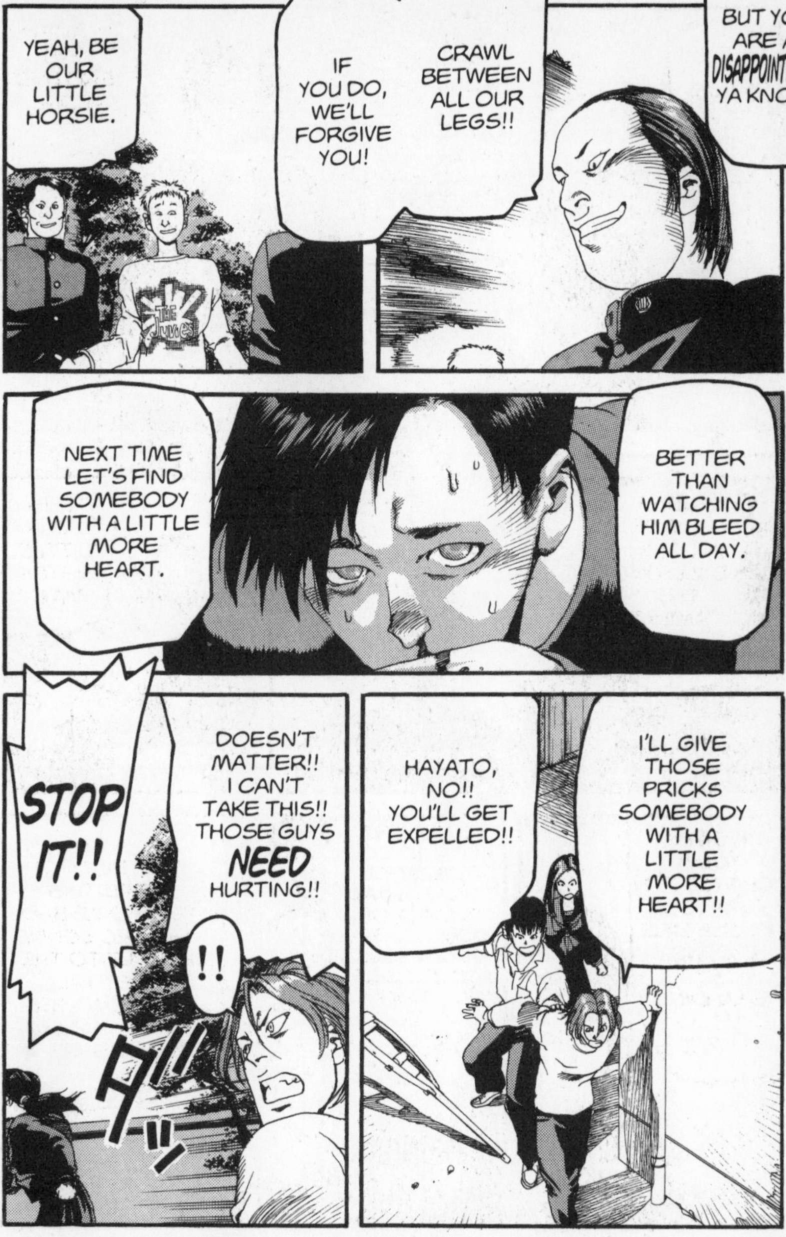
BUT YOU ARE A DISAPPOINTMENT, YA KNOW?
CRAWL BETWEEN ALL OUR LEGS!!
IF YOU DO, WE'LL FORGIVE YOU!
YEAH, BE OUR LITTLE HORSIE.
THE JUVIES
BETTER THAN WATCHING HIM BLEED ALL DAY.
NEXT TIME LET'S FIND SOMEBODY WITH A LITTLE MORE HEART.
I'LL GIVE THOSE PRICKS SOMEBODY WITH A LITTLE MORE HEART!!
HAYATO, NO!! YOU'LL GET EXPELLED!!
DOESN'T MATTER!! I CAN'T TAKE THIS!! THOSE GUYS NEED HURTING!!
STOP IT!!
!!

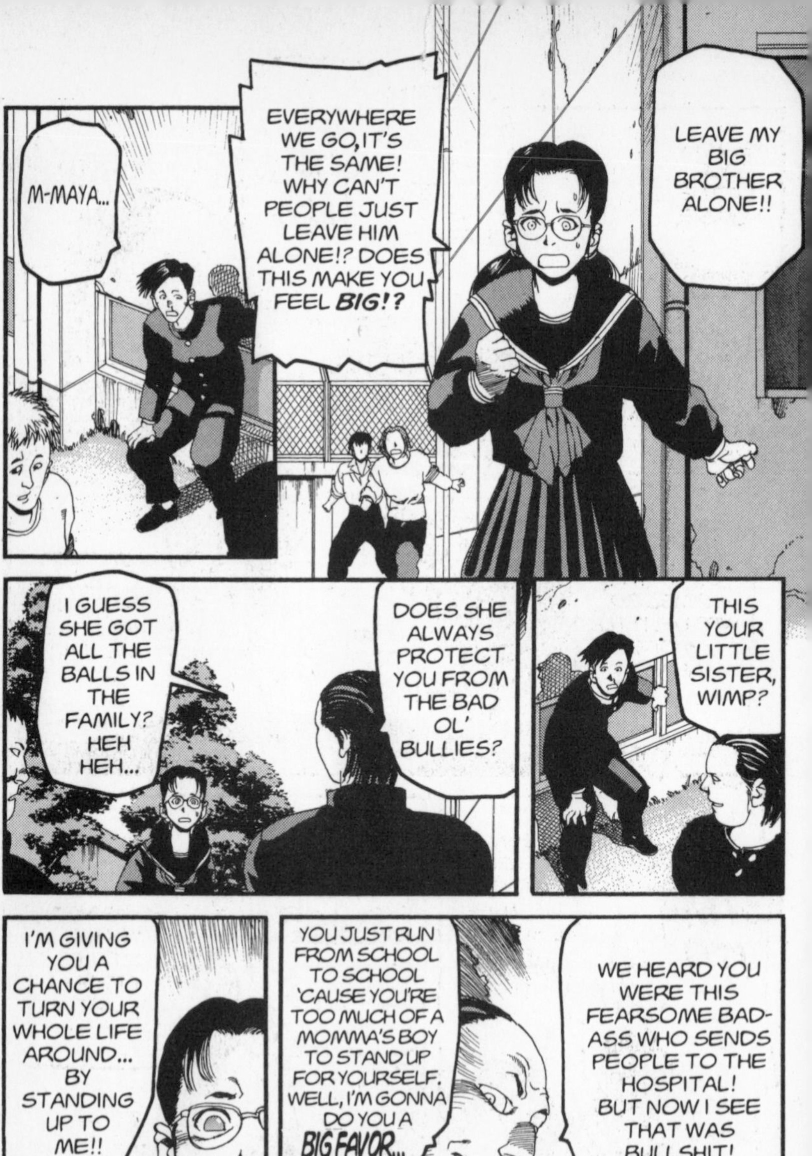
LEAVE MY BIG BROTHER ALONE!!
EVERYWHERE WE GO, IT'S THE SAME! WHY CAN'T PEOPLE JUST LEAVE HIM ALONE!? DOES THIS MAKE YOU FEEL BIG!?
M-MAYA...
THIS YOUR LITTLE SISTER, WIMP?
DOES SHE ALWAYS PROTECT YOU FROM THE BAD OL' BULLIES?
I GUESS SHE GOT ALL THE BALLS IN THE FAMILY? HEH HEH...
WE HEARD YOU WERE THIS FEARSOME BAD-ASS WHO SENDS PEOPLE TO THE HOSPITAL! BUT NOW I SEE THAT WAS BULLSHIT!
YOU JUST RUN FROM SCHOOL TO SCHOOL 'CAUSE YOU'RE TOO MUCH OF A MOMMA'S BOY TO STAND UP FOR YOURSELF. WELL, I'M GONNA DO YOU A BIG FAVOR...
I'M GIVING YOU A CHANCE TO TURN YOUR WHOLE LIFE AROUND... BY STANDING UP TO ME!!

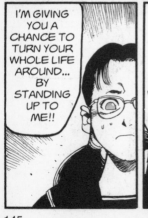

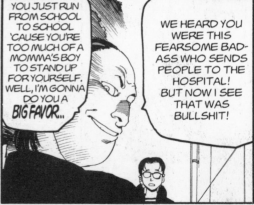

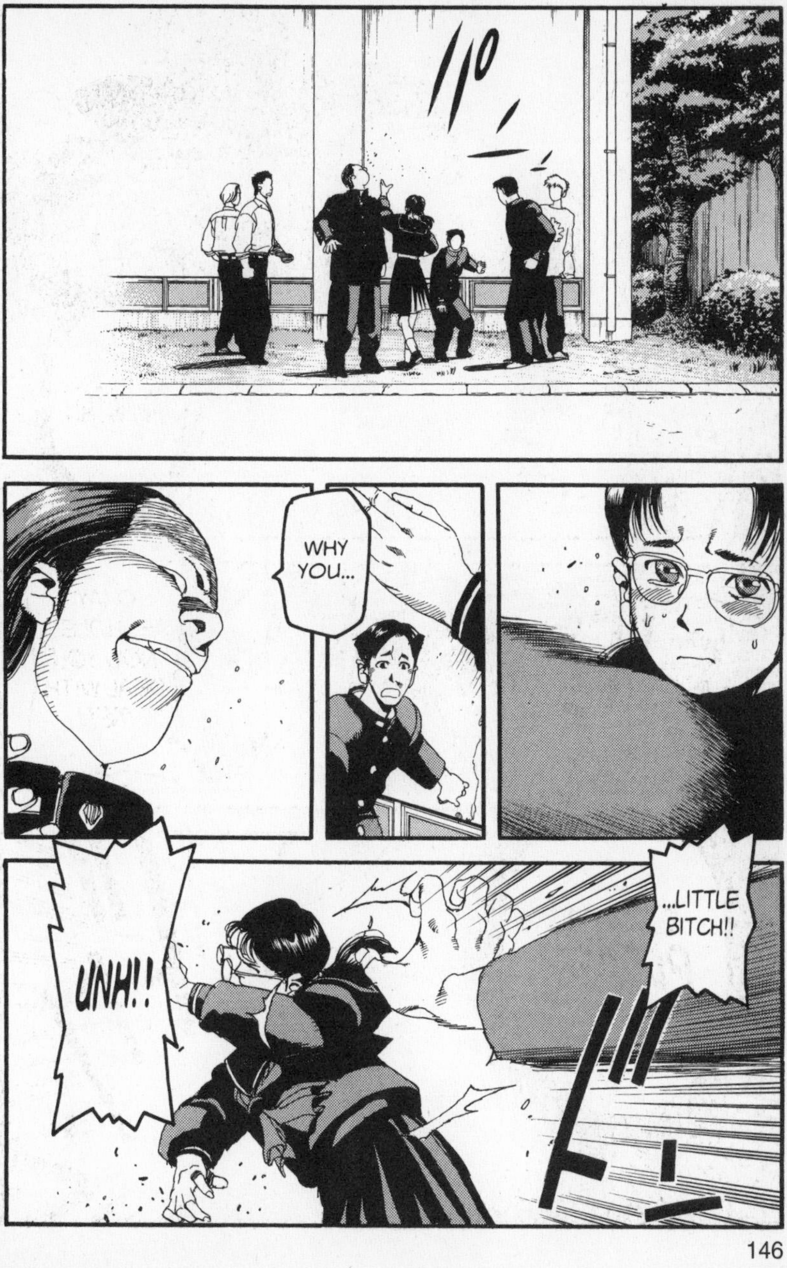
WHY YOU...
...LITTLE BITCH!!
UNH!!

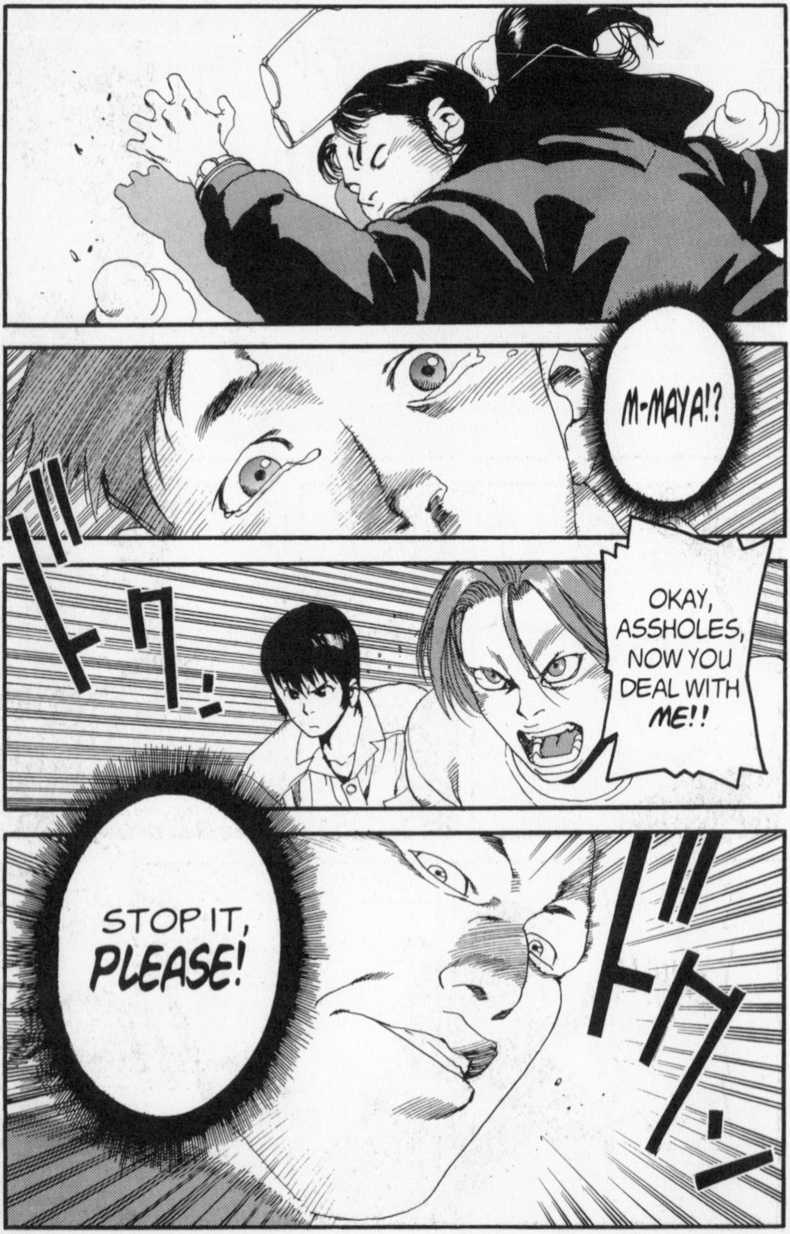
M-MAYA!?
OKAY, ASSHOLES, NOW YOU DEAL WITH ME!!
STOP IT, PLEASE!

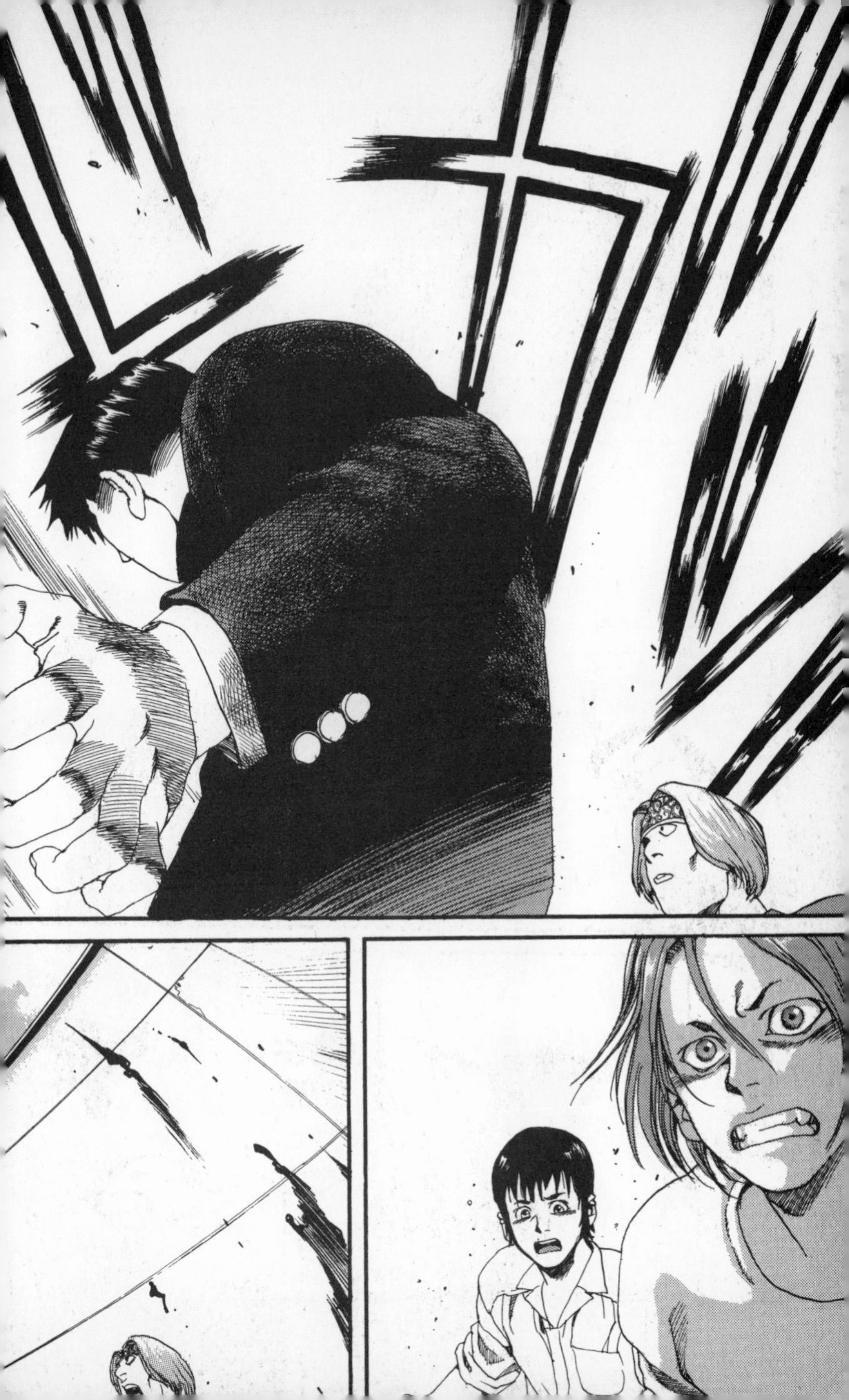

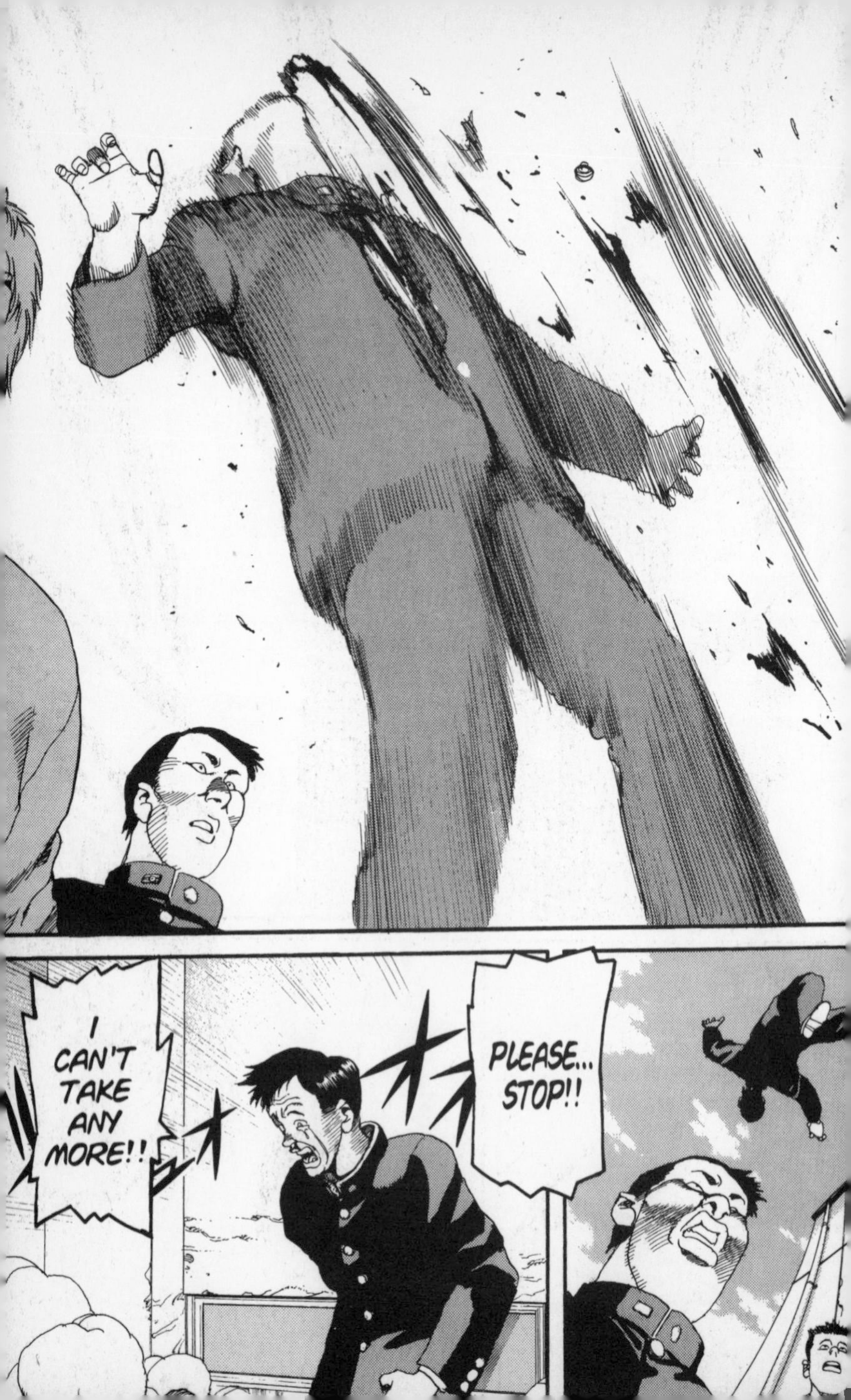
PLEASE... STOP!!
I CAN'T TAKE ANY MORE!!

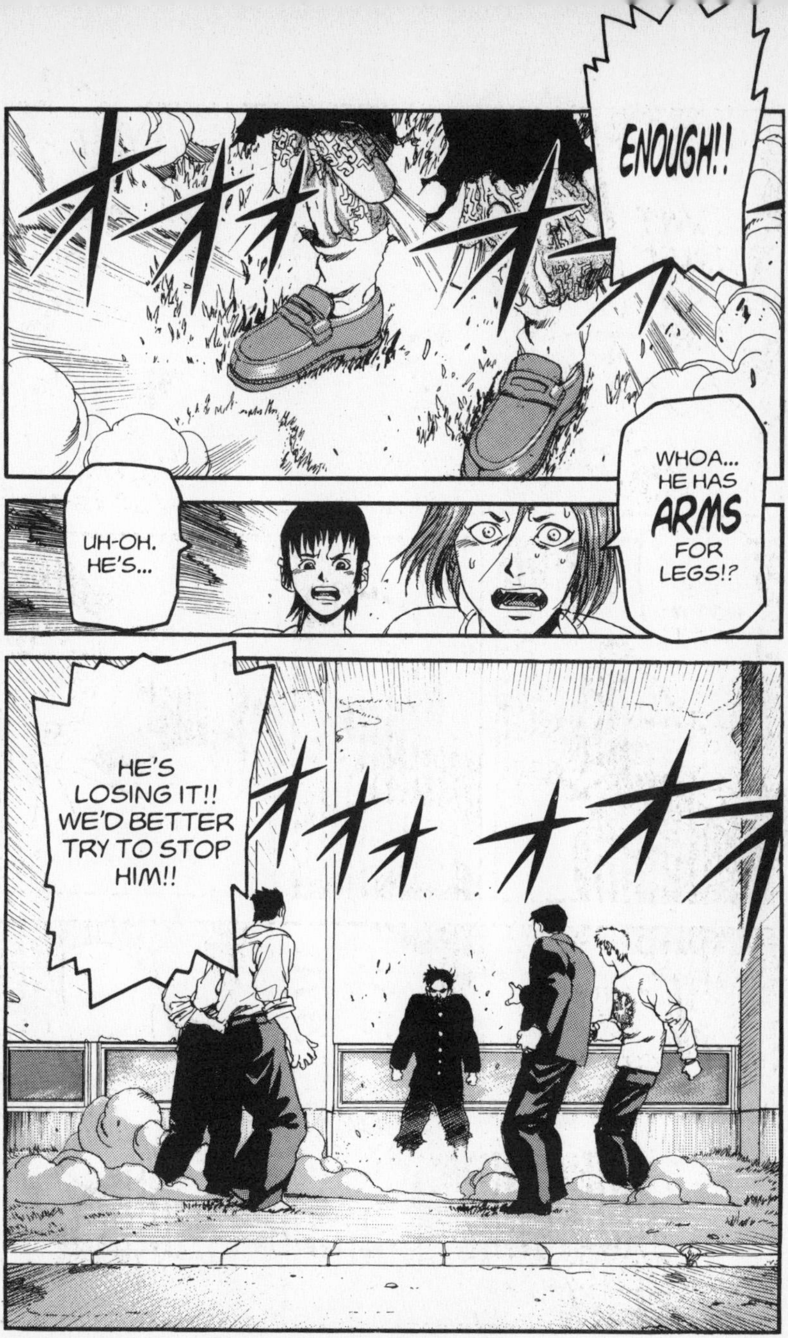
ENOUGH!!
WHOA... HE HAS ARMS FOR LEGS!?
UH-OH. HE'S...
HE'S LOSING IT!! WE'D BETTER TRY TO STOP HIM!!

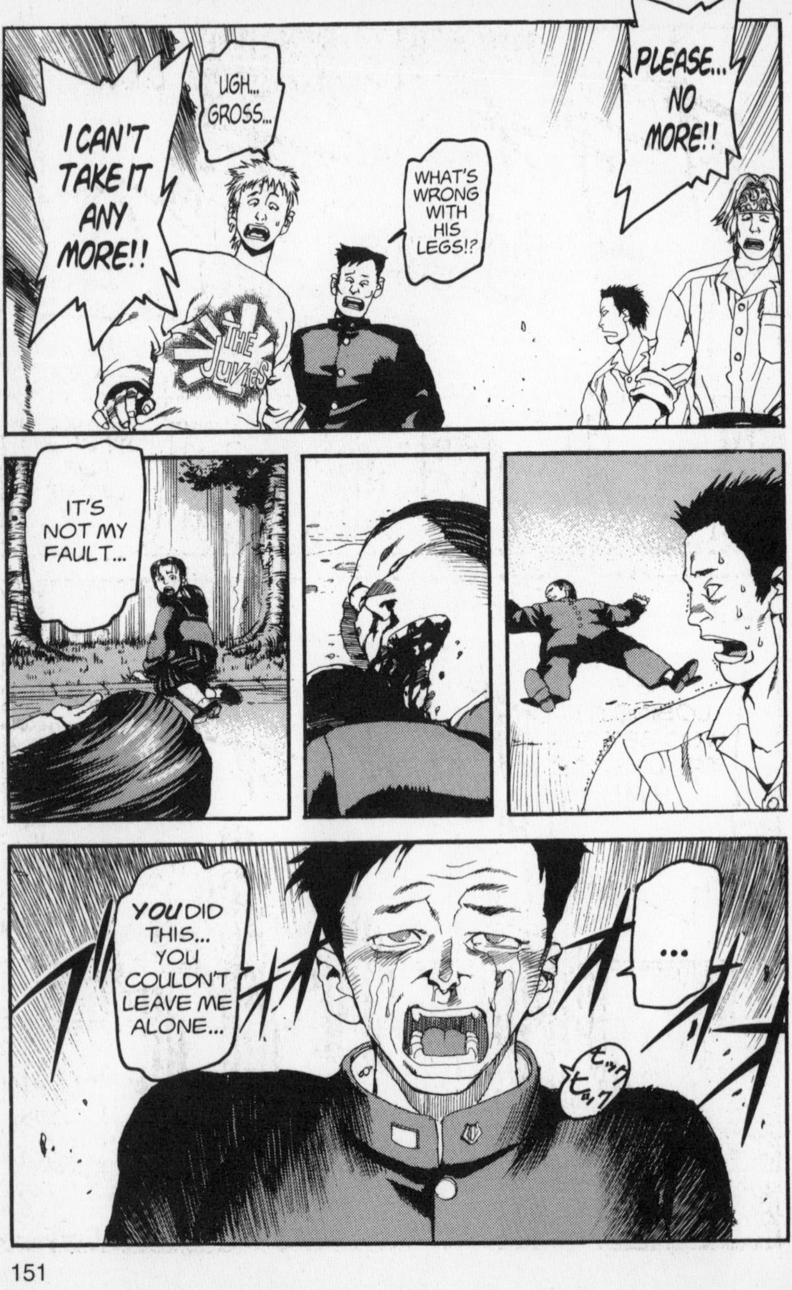
PLEASE... NO MORE!!
WHAT'S WRONG WITH HIS LEGS!?
UGH... GROSS...
I CAN'T TAKE IT ANY MORE!!
IT'S NOT MY FAULT...
...
YOU DID THIS... YOU COULDN'T LEAVE ME ALONE...

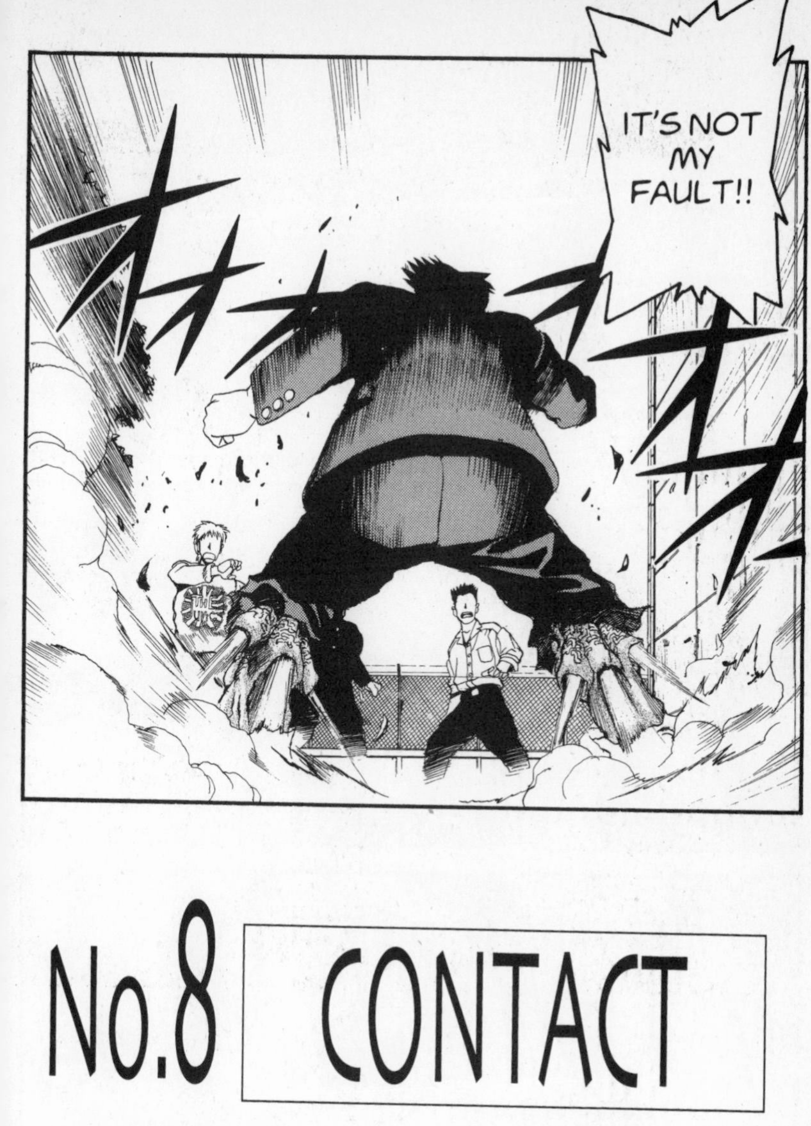
IT'S NOT MY FAULT!!

No.8 CONTACT

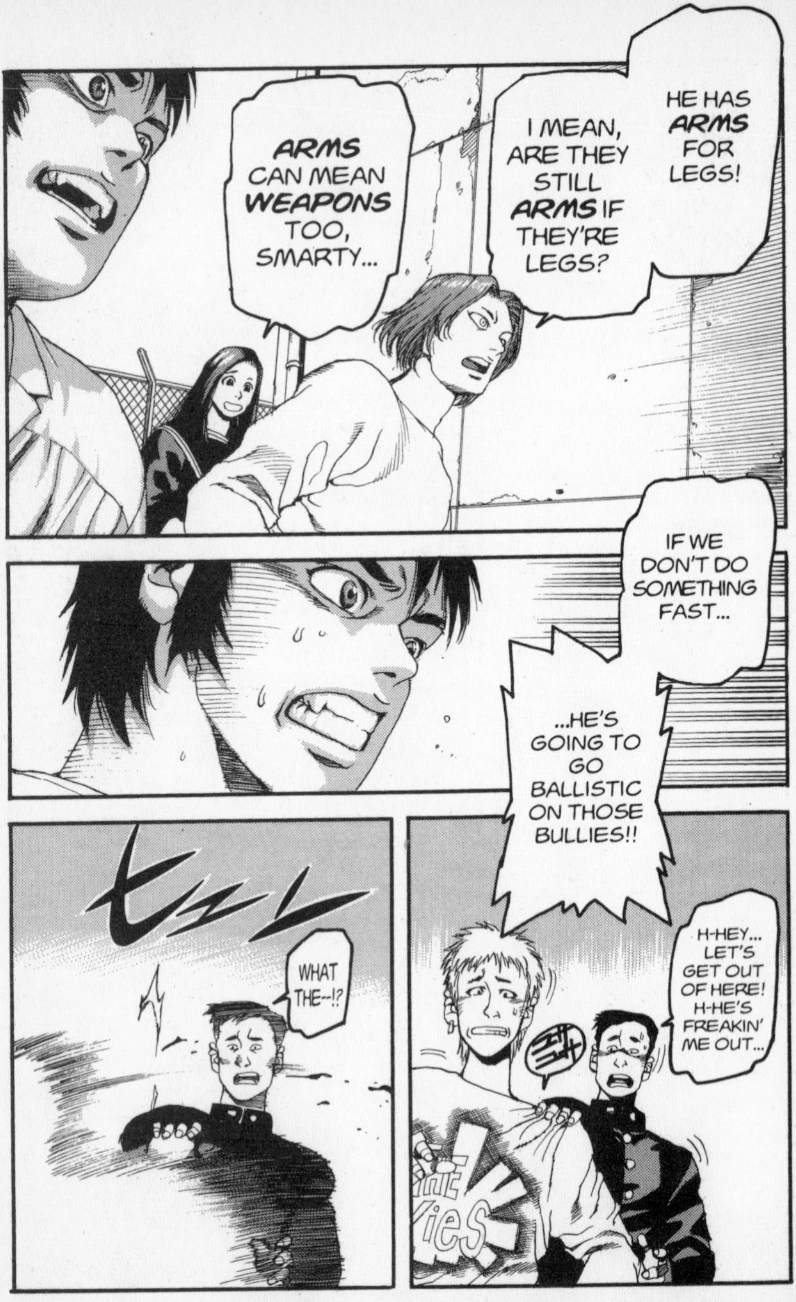
HE HAS ARMS FOR LEGS!
I MEAN, ARE THEY STILL ARMS IF THEY'RE LEGS?
ARMS CAN MEAN WEAPONS TOO, SMARTY...
IF WE DON'T DO SOMETHING FAST...
...HE'S GOING TO GO BALLISTIC ON THOSE BULLIES!!
H-HEY... LET'S GET OUT OF HERE! H-HE'S FREAKIN' ME OUT...
WHAT THE--!?

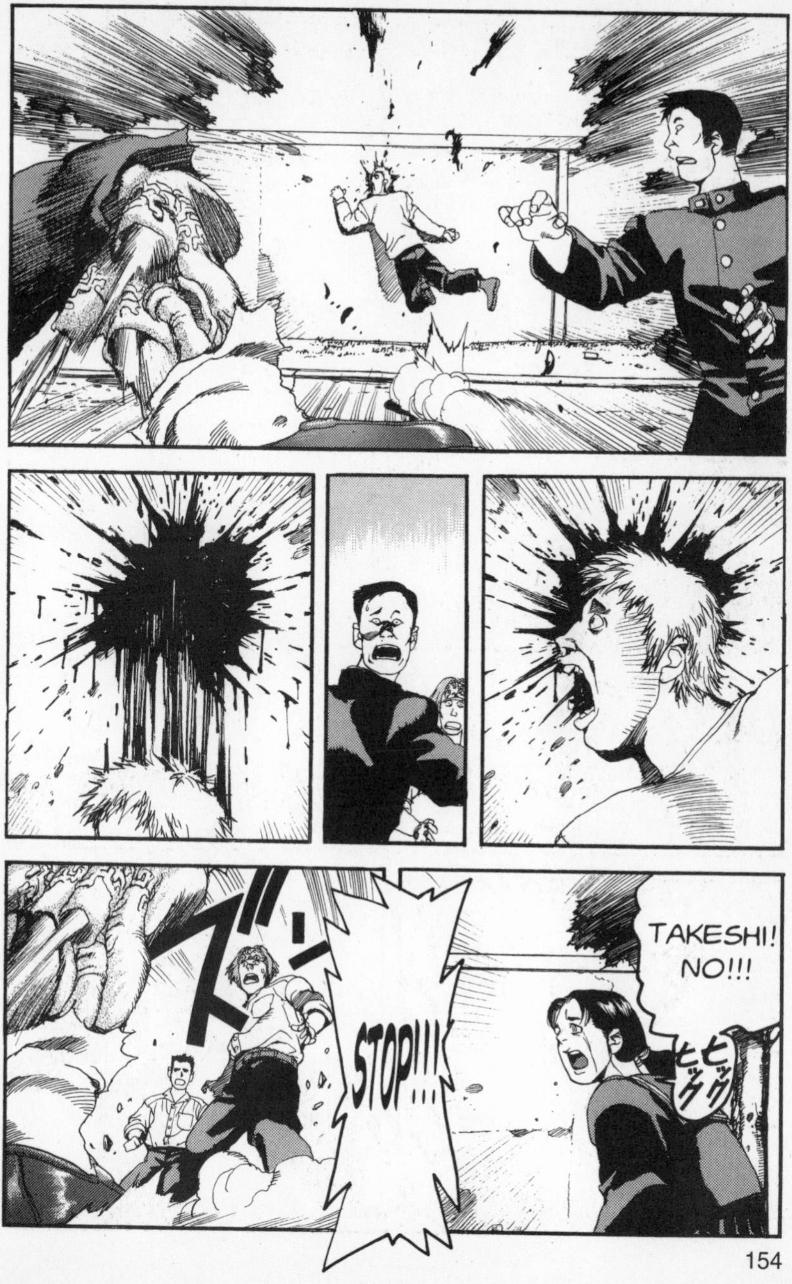
TAKESHI! NO!!!
ヒック ヒック
STOP!!!!

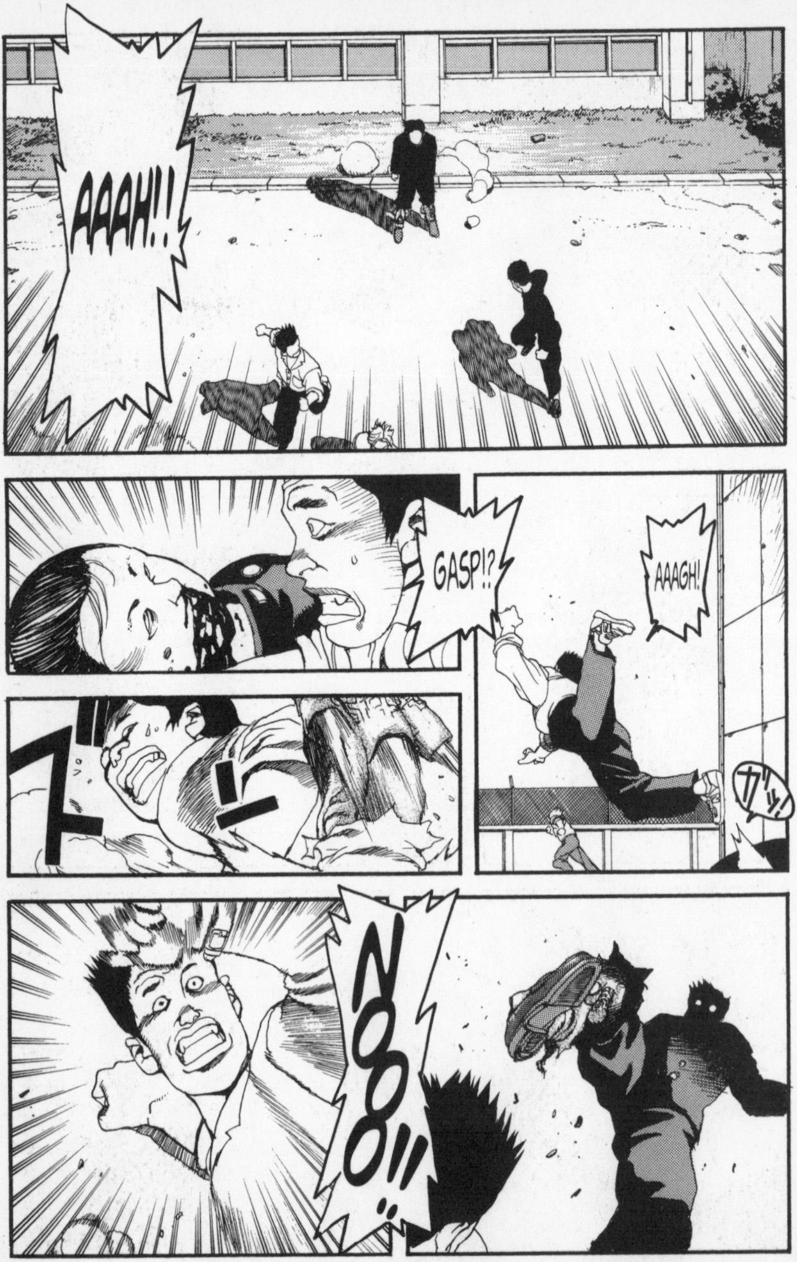
AAAH!!
AAAGH!
ガッ!
GASP!?
NOOO!!

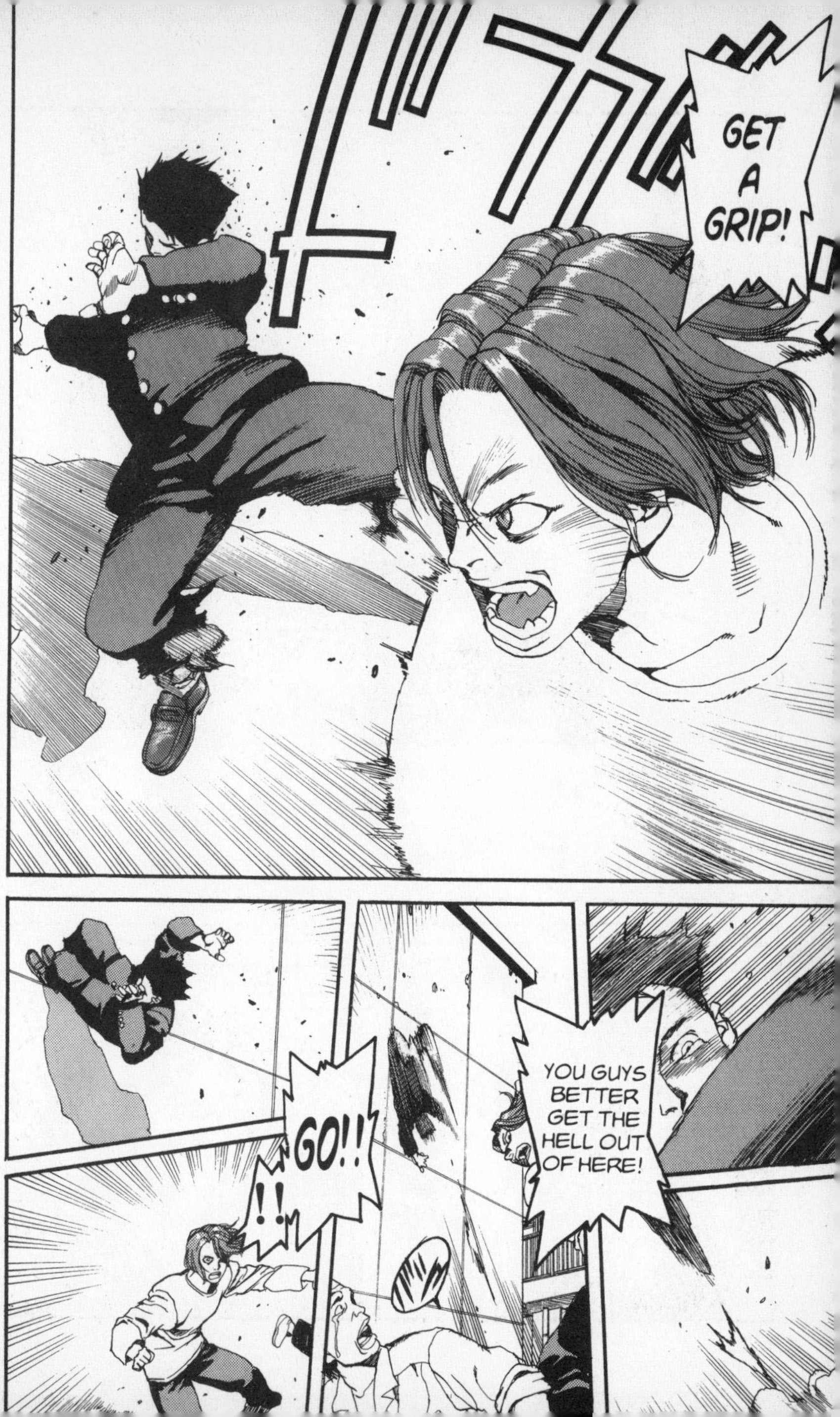
GET A GRIP!
YOU GUYS BETTER GET THE HELL OUT OF HERE!
GO!!
!!

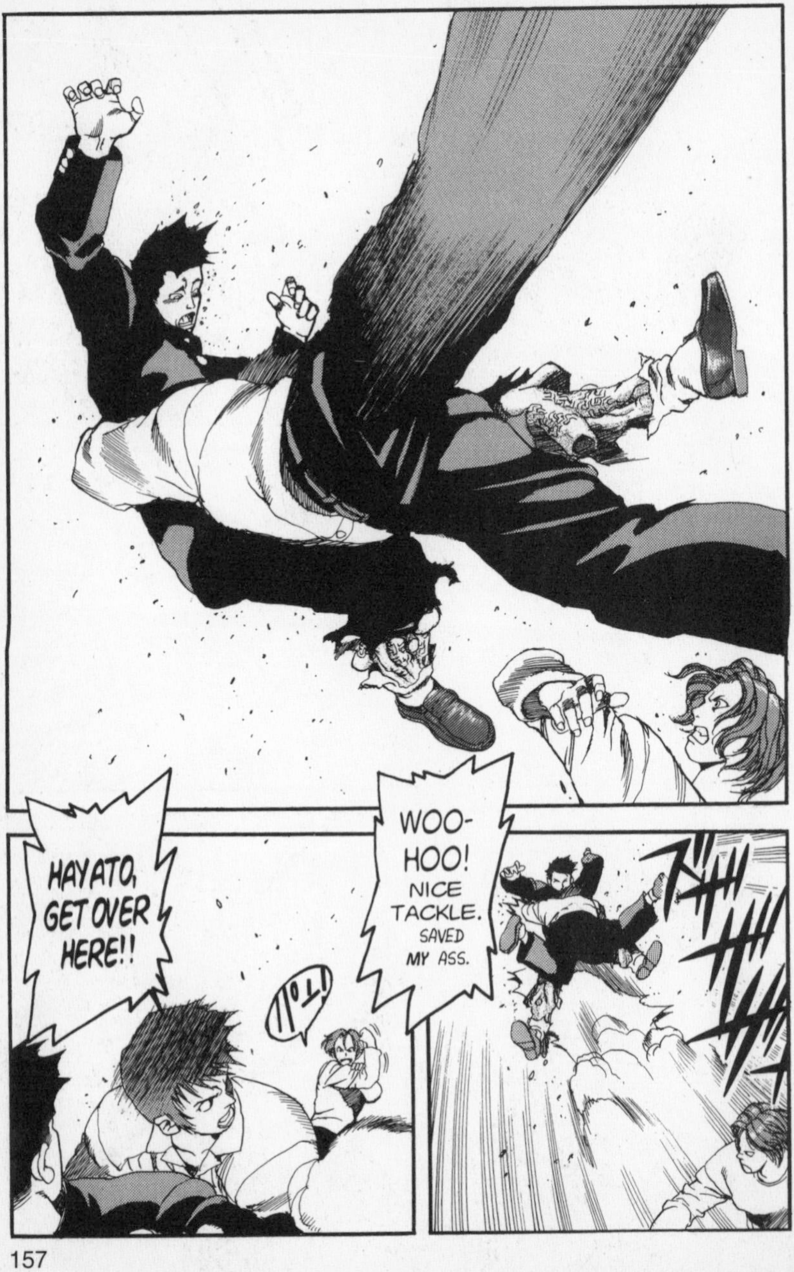
WOO-HOO! NICE TACKLE. SAVED MY ASS.
HAYATO, GET OVER HERE!!

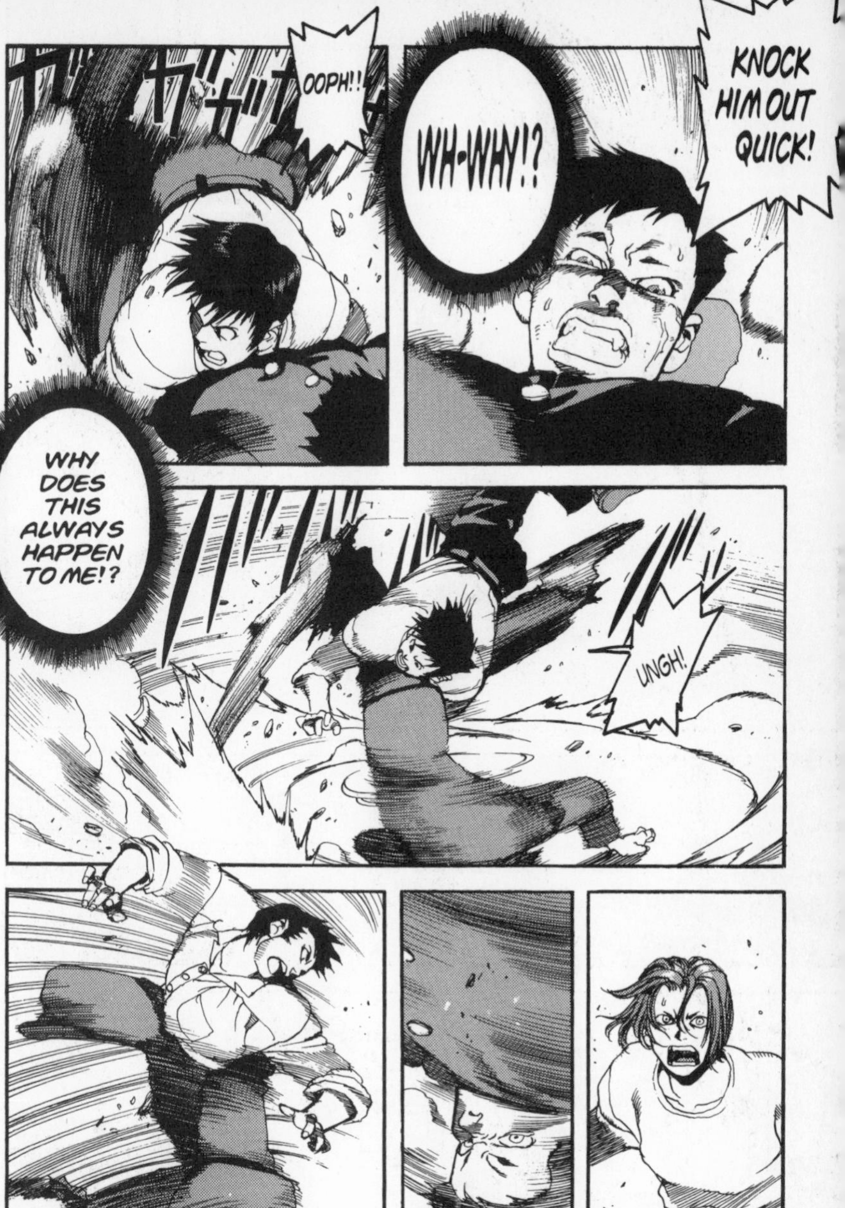
KNOCK HIM OUT QUICK!
WH-WHY!?
OOPH!!
WHY DOES THIS ALWAYS HAPPEN TO ME!?
UNGH!

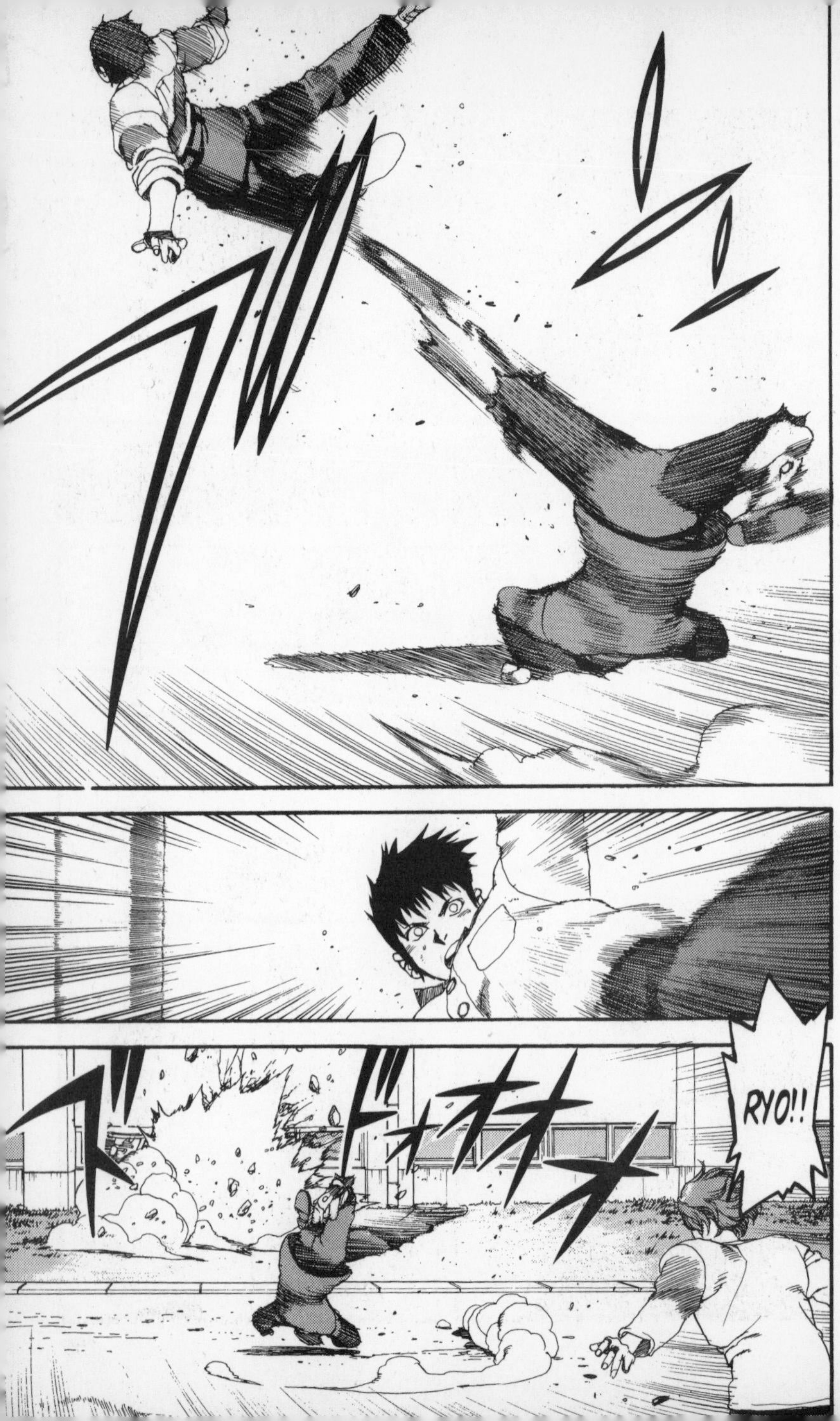
RYO!!

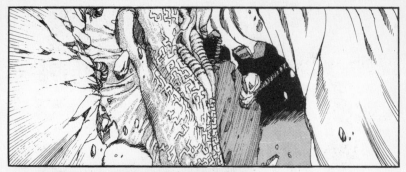

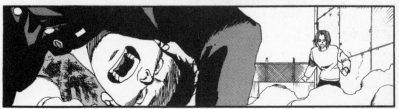

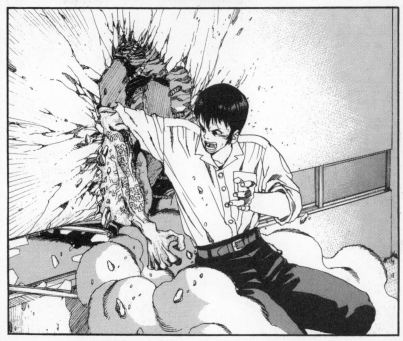

160

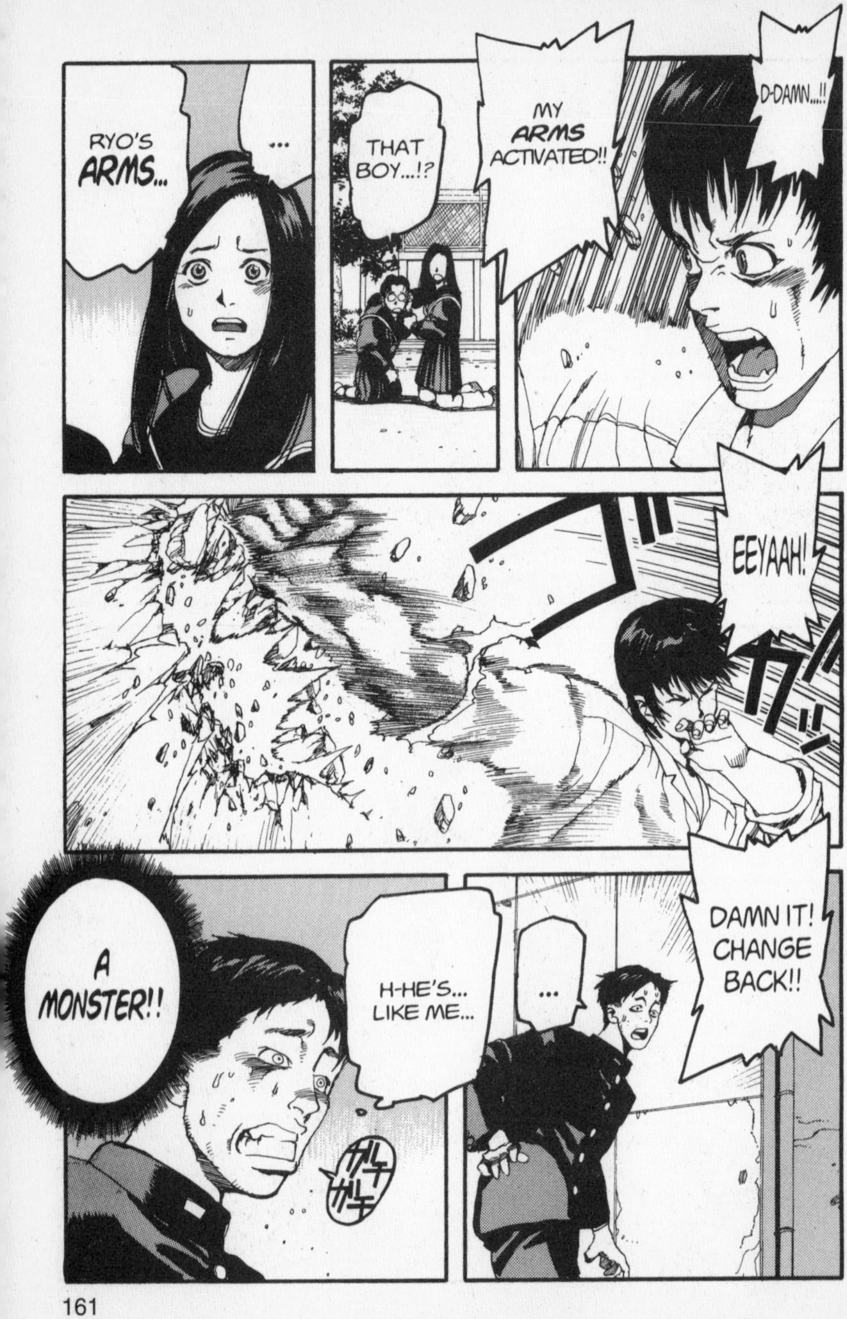
D-DAMN...!!
MY ARMS ACTIVATED!!
THAT BOY...!?
...
RYO'S ARMS...
EEYAAH!
DAMN IT! CHANGE BACK!!
...
H-HE'S... LIKE ME...
A MONSTER!!

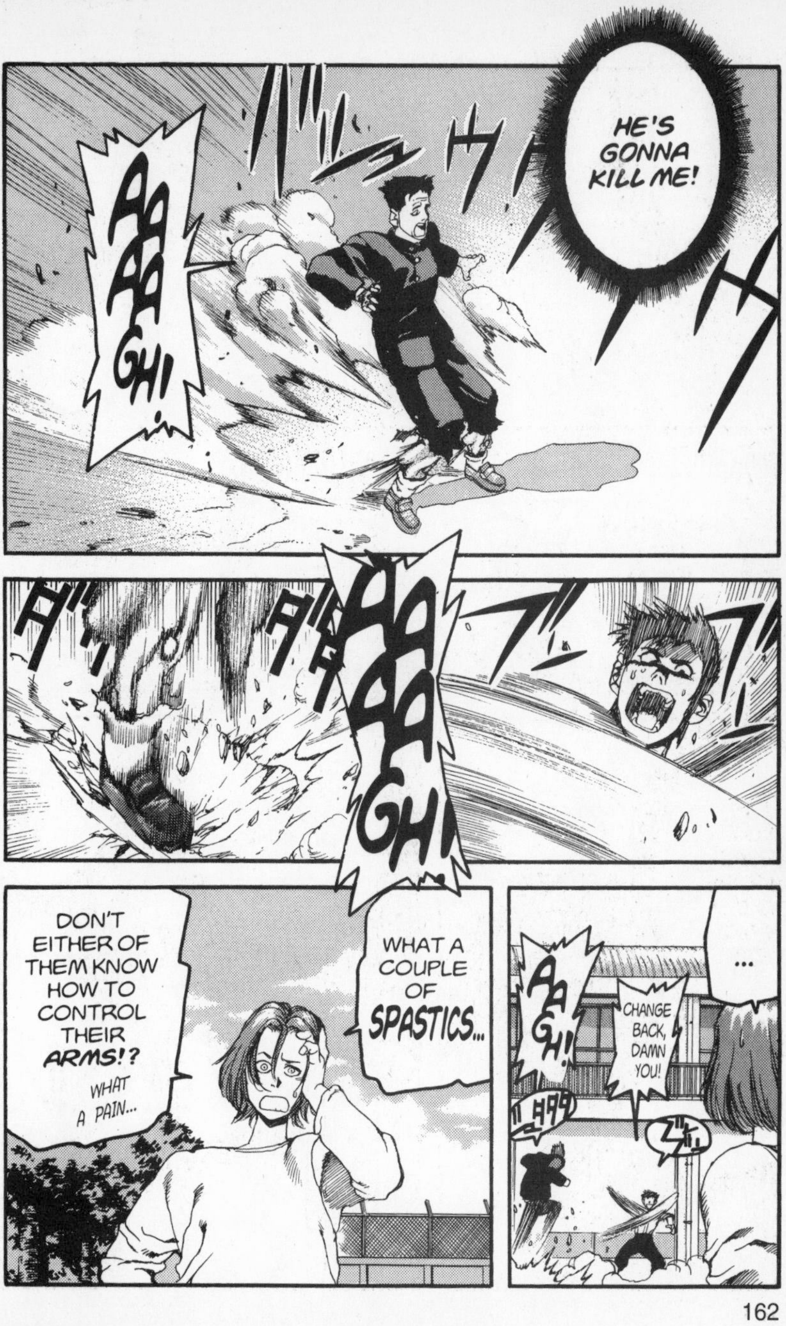
HE'S GONNA KILL ME!
AAAAAAGH!
AAAAAAGH!
...
CHANGE BACK, DAMN YOU!
AAGH!
WHAT A COUPLE OF SPASTICS...
DON'T EITHER OF THEM KNOW HOW TO CONTROL THEIR ARMS!?
WHAT A PAIN...

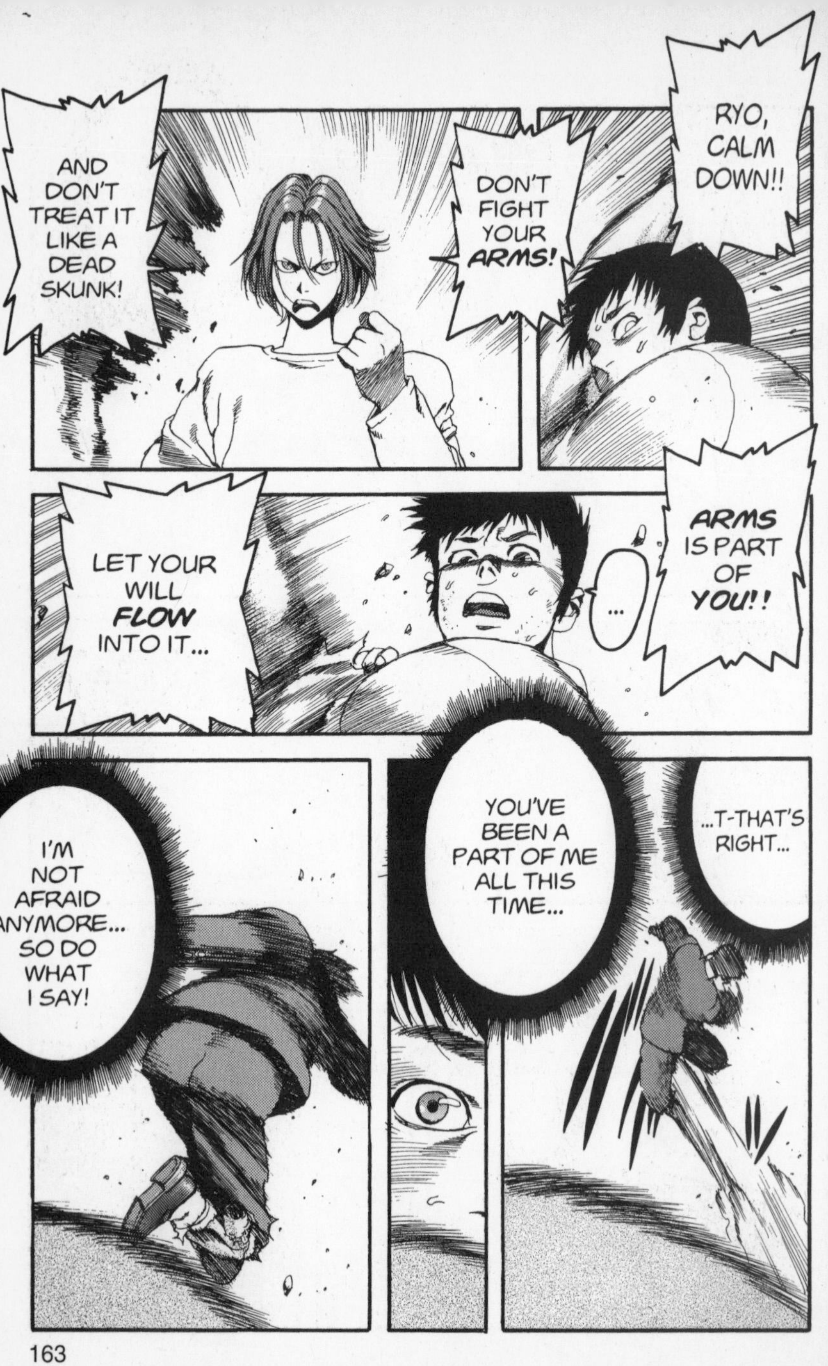
RYO, CALM DOWN!!
DON'T FIGHT YOUR ARMS!
AND DON'T TREAT IT LIKE A DEAD SKUNK!
ARMS IS PART OF YOU!!
...
LET YOUR WILL FLOW INTO IT...
...T-THAT'S RIGHT...
YOU'VE BEEN A PART OF ME ALL THIS TIME...
I'M NOT AFRAID ANYMORE... SO DO WHAT I SAY!

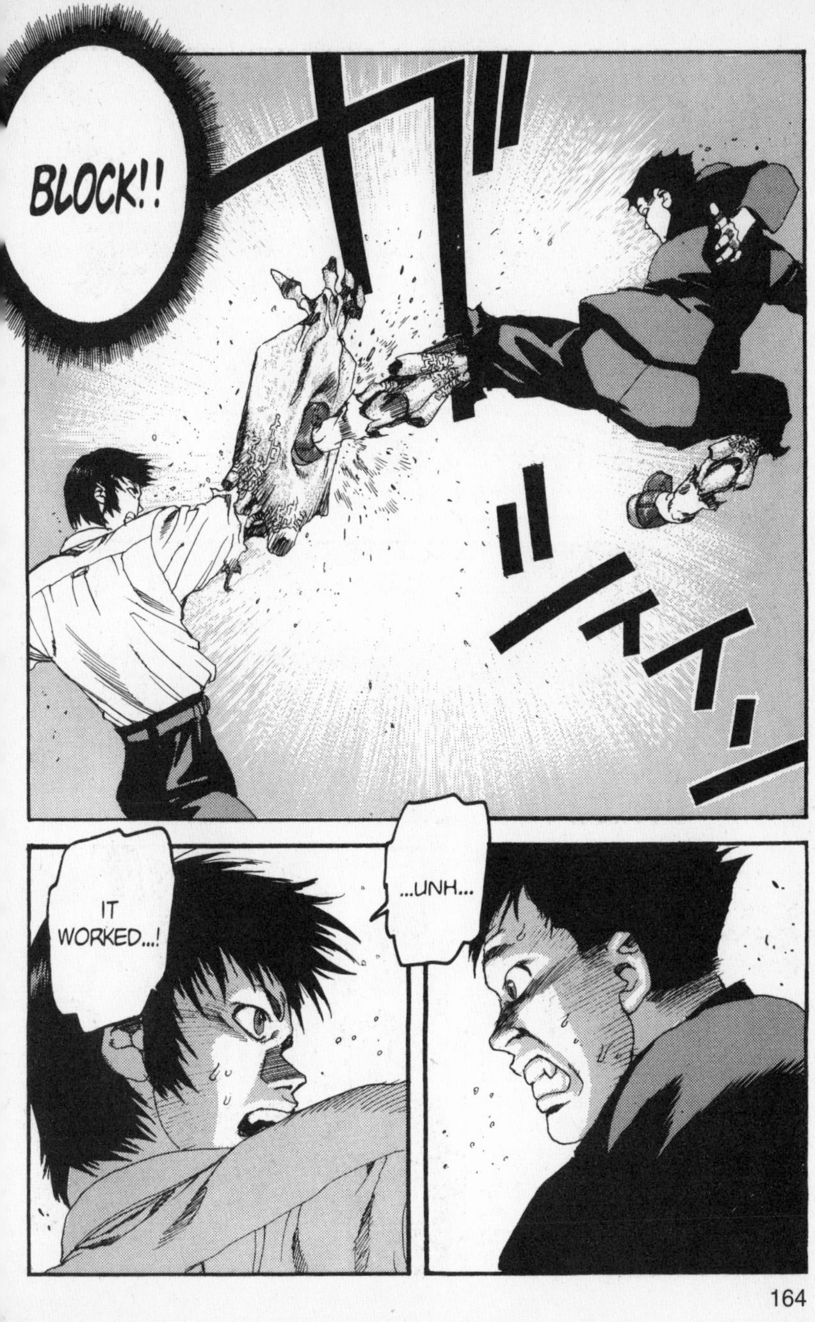
BLOCK!!
...UNH...
IT WORKED...!

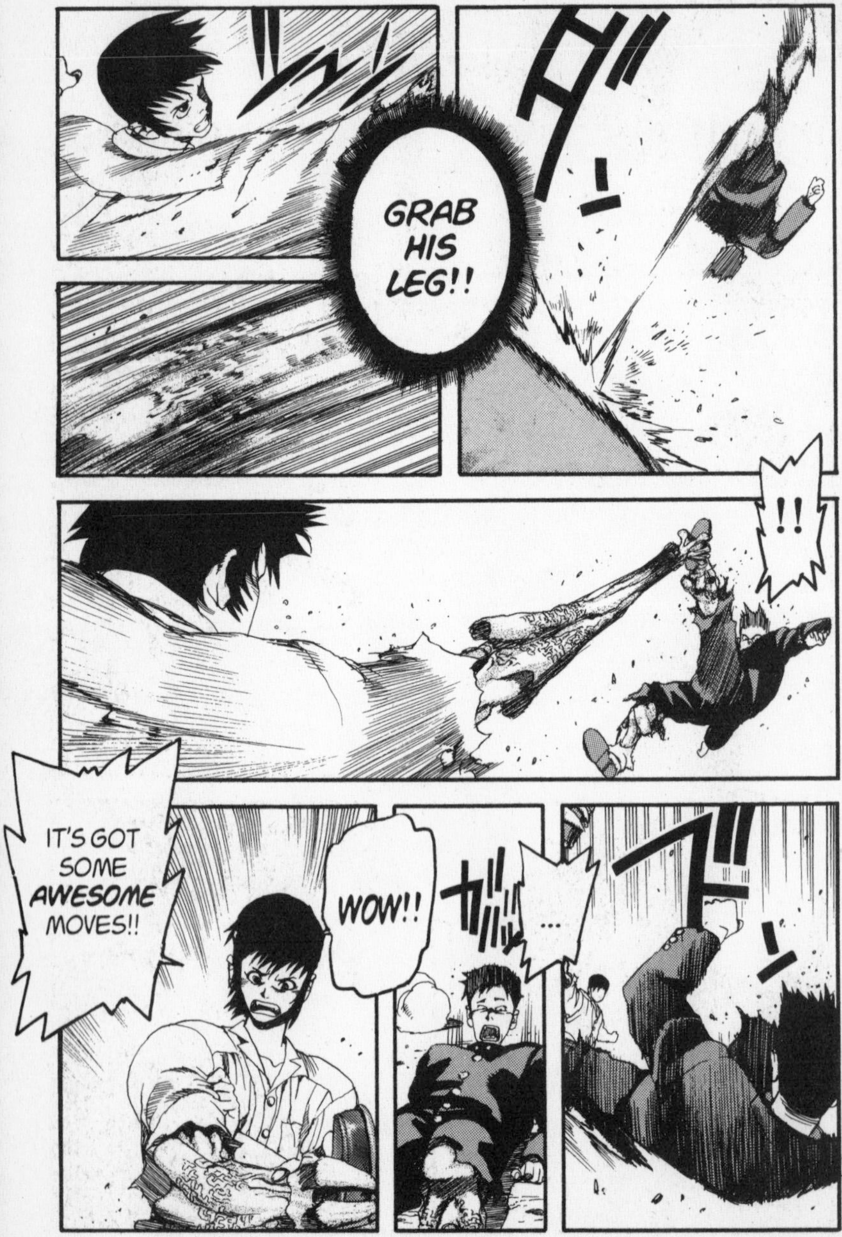
GRAB HIS LEG!!
!!
...
WOW!!
IT'S GOT SOME **AWESOME** MOVES!!

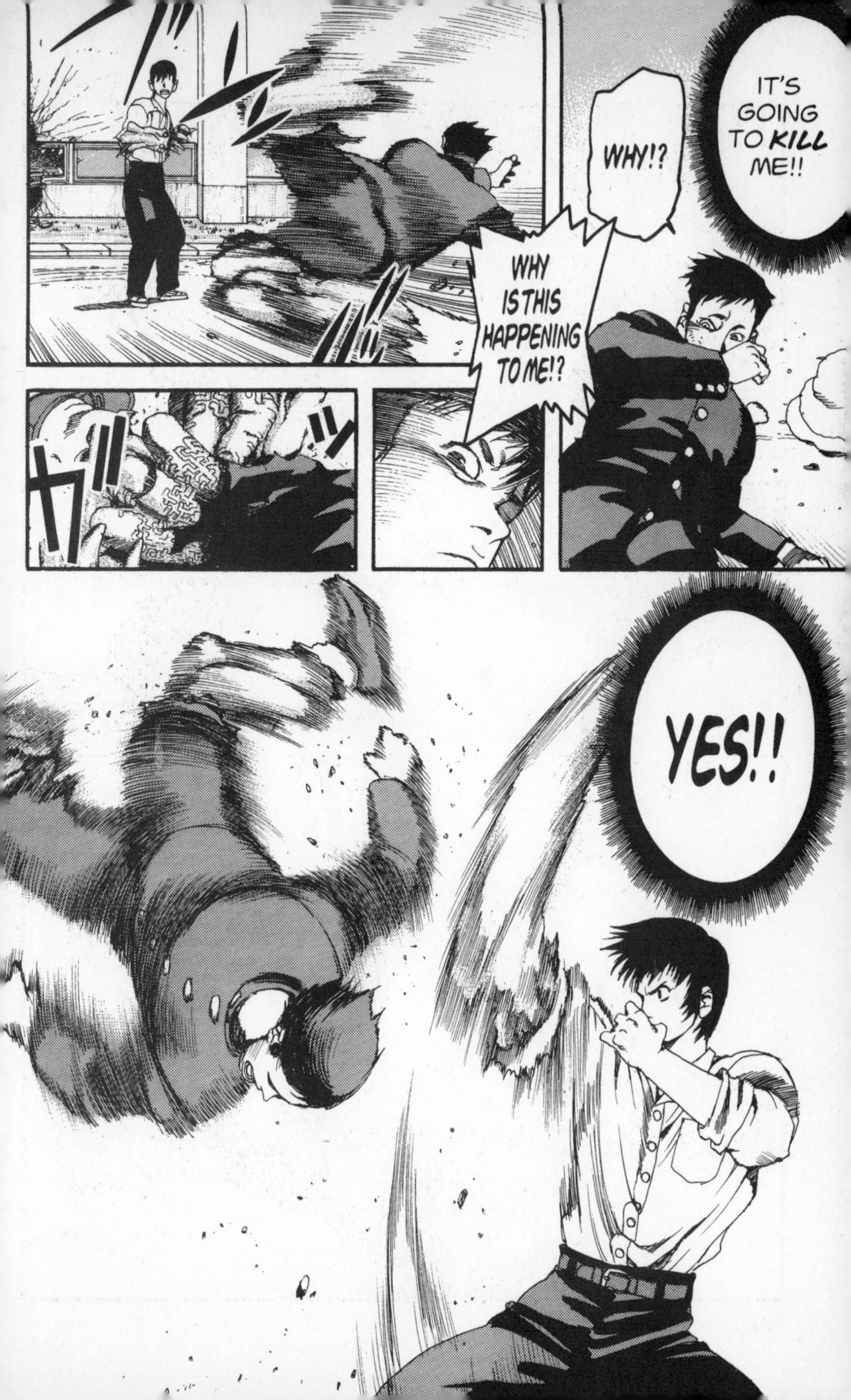
IT'S GOING TO KILL ME!!
WHY!?
WHY IS THIS HAPPENING TO ME!?
YES!!

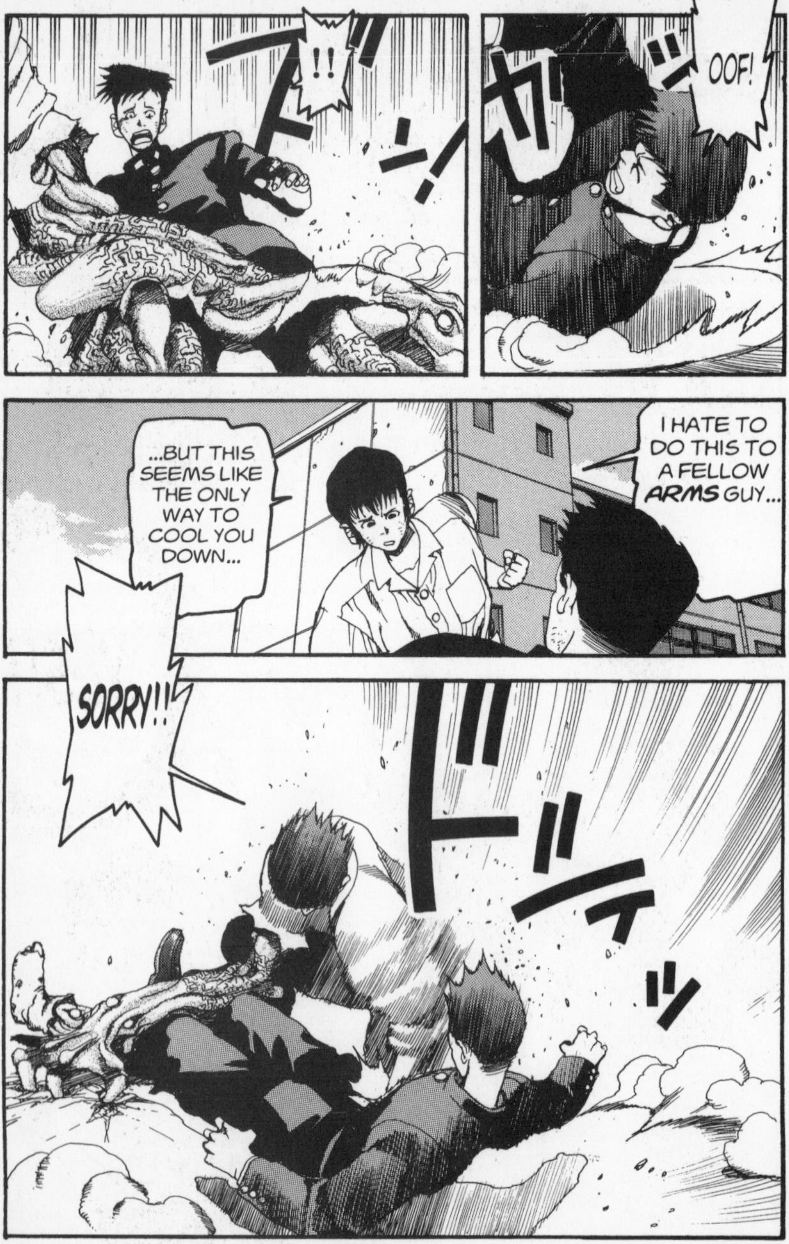
OOF!
!!
I HATE TO DO THIS TO A FELLOW ARMS GUY...
...BUT THIS SEEMS LIKE THE ONLY WAY TO COOL YOU DOWN...
SORRY!!

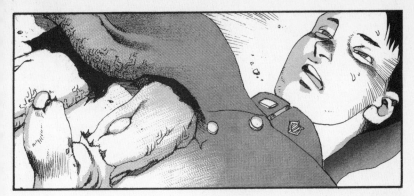

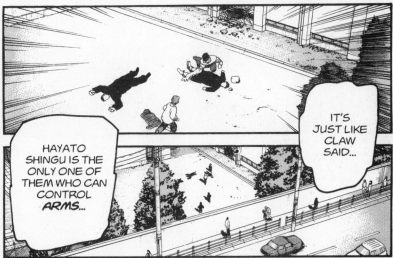

IT'S JUST LIKE CLAW SAID...

HAYATO SHINGU IS THE ONLY ONE OF THEM WHO CAN CONTROL *ARMS*...

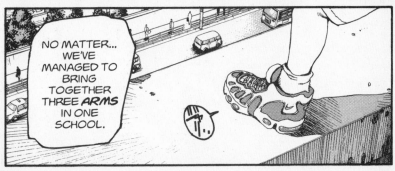

NO MATTER... WE'VE MANAGED TO BRING TOGETHER THREE *ARMS* IN ONE SCHOOL.

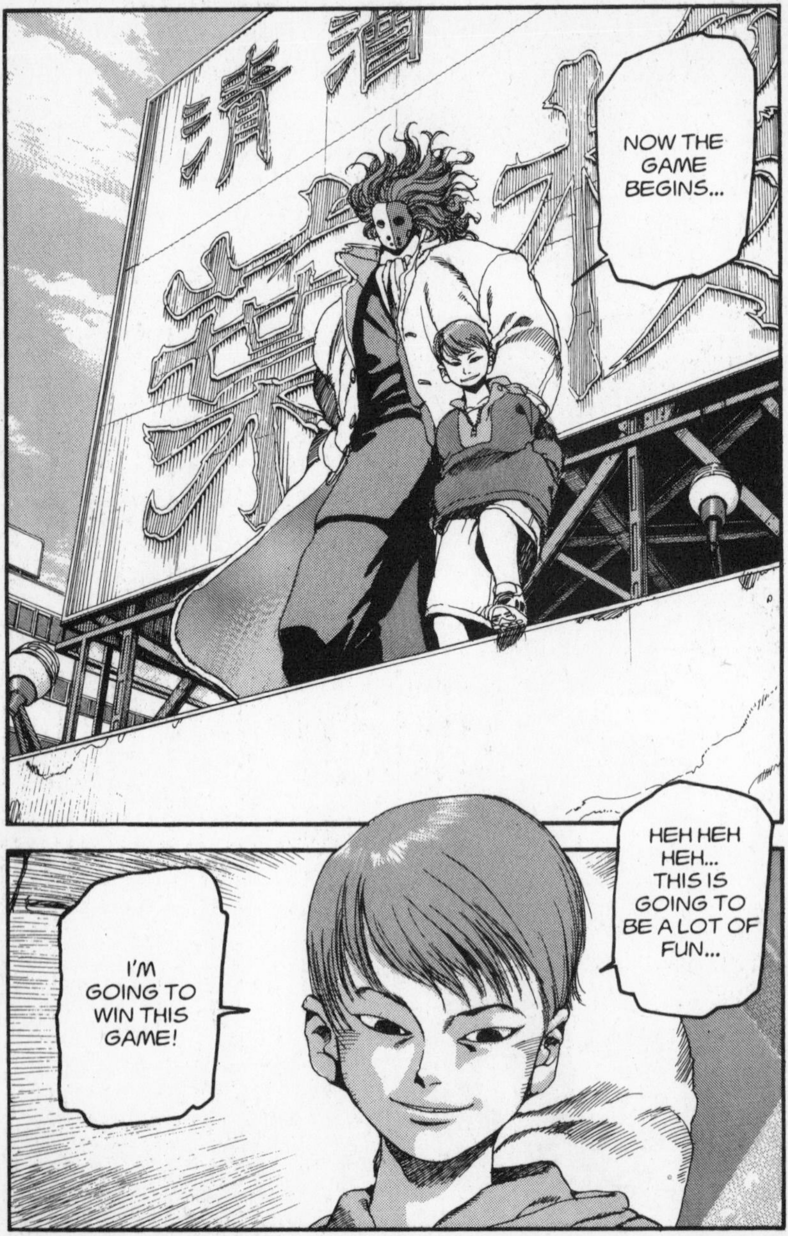
NOW THE GAME BEGINS...
HEH HEH HEH... THIS IS GOING TO BE A LOT OF FUN...
I'M GOING TO WIN THIS GAME!

ARMS

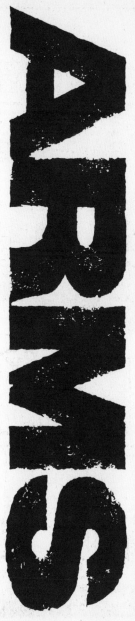

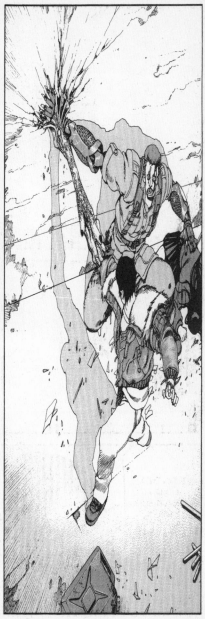

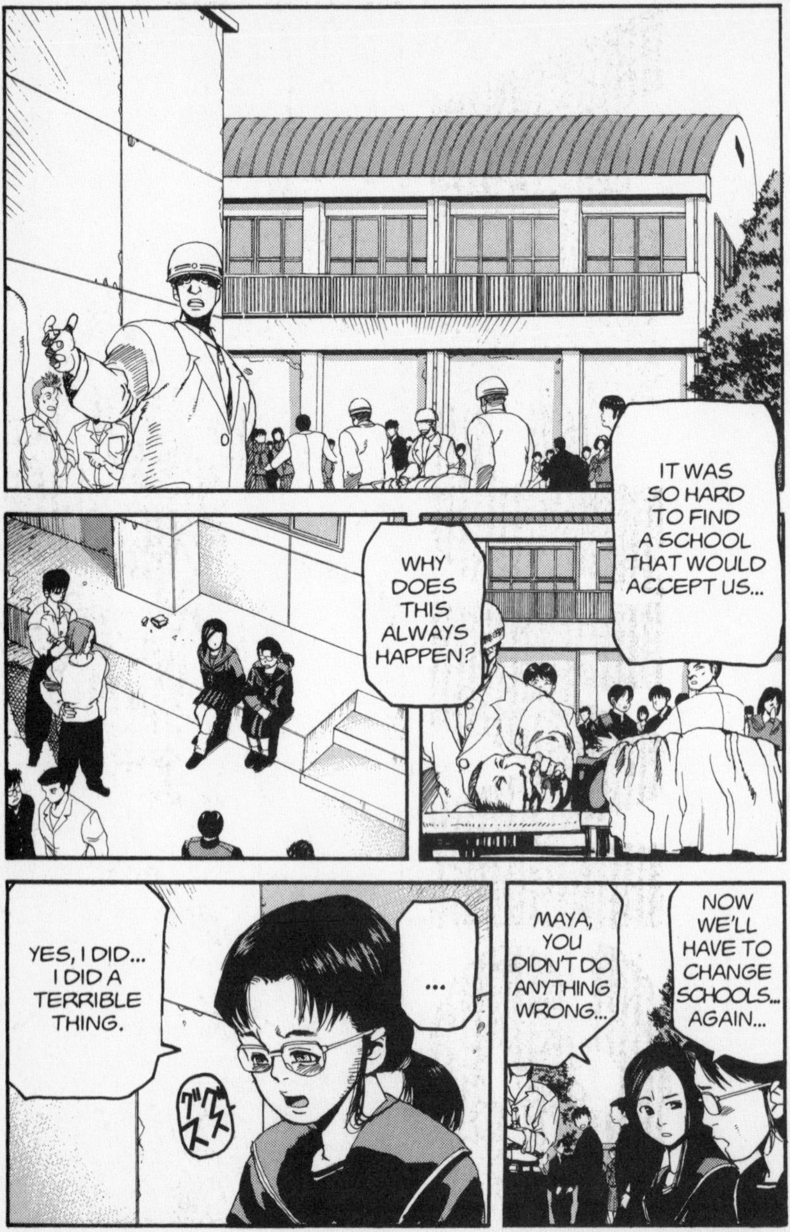
IT WAS SO HARD TO FIND A SCHOOL THAT WOULD ACCEPT US...
WHY DOES THIS ALWAYS HAPPEN?
NOW WE'LL HAVE TO CHANGE SCHOOLS... AGAIN...
MAYA, YOU DIDN'T DO ANYTHING WRONG...
...
YES, I DID... I DID A TERRIBLE THING.
グスグス

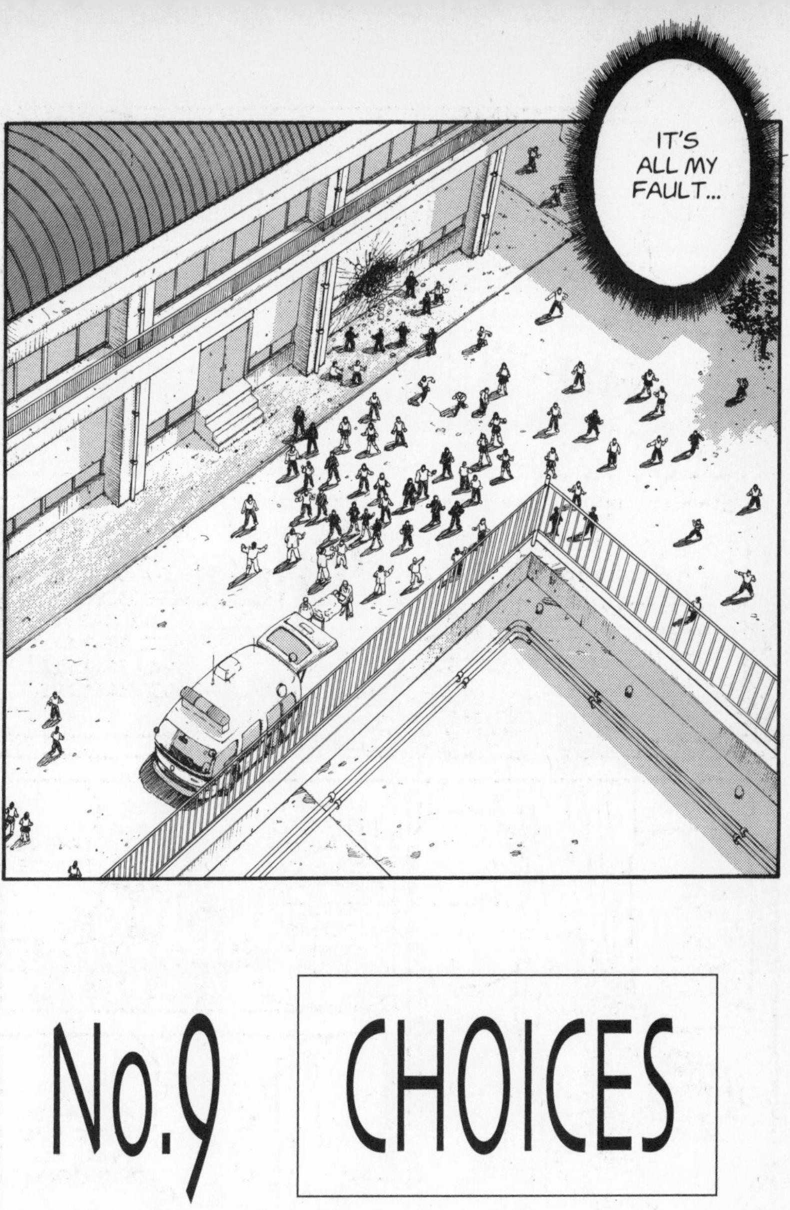
IT'S ALL MY FAULT...

No.9 CHOICES

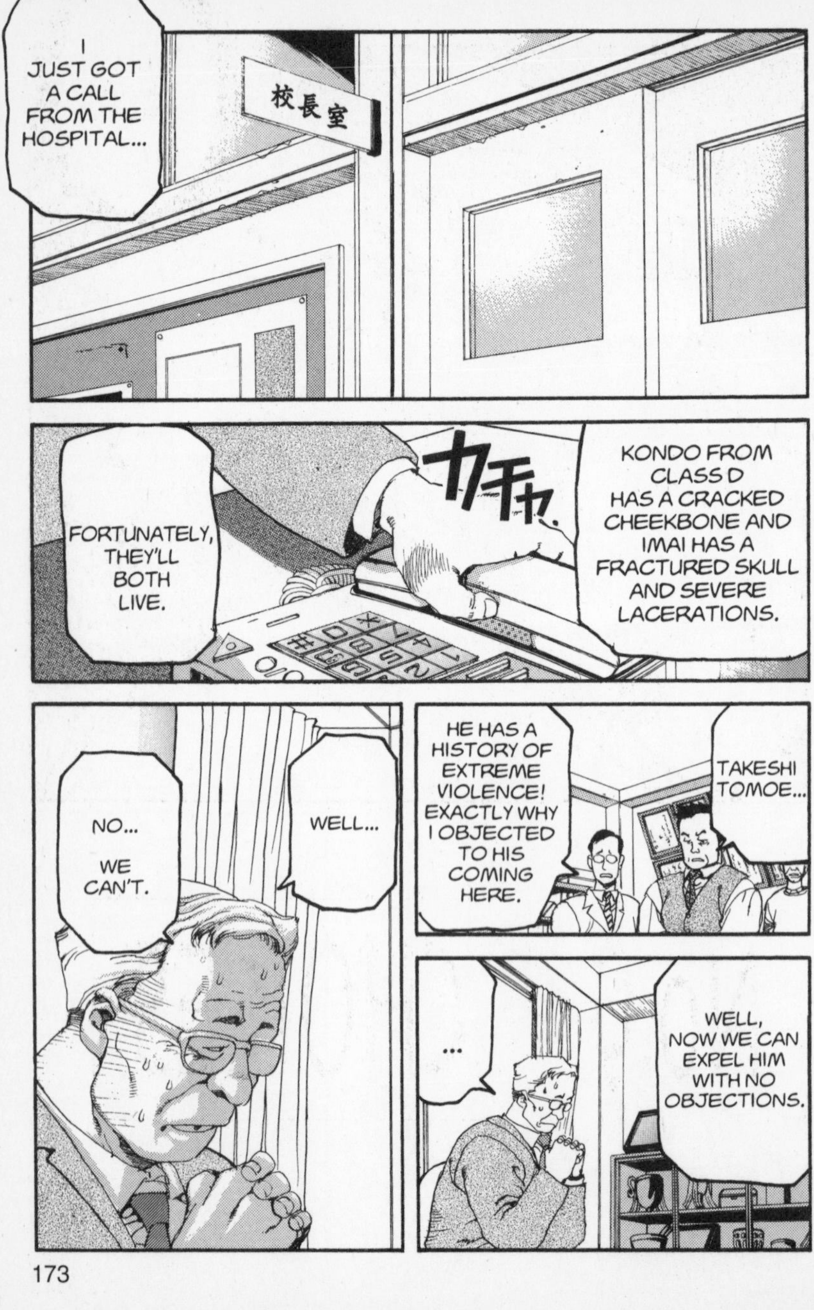
I JUST GOT A CALL FROM THE HOSPITAL...
校長室
KONDO FROM CLASS D HAS A CRACKED CHEEKBONE AND IMAI HAS A FRACTURED SKULL AND SEVERE LACERATIONS.
カチャ
FORTUNATELY, THEY'LL BOTH LIVE.
TAKESHI TOMOE...
HE HAS A HISTORY OF EXTREME VIOLENCE! EXACTLY WHY I OBJECTED TO HIS COMING HERE.
WELL, NOW WE CAN EXPEL HIM WITH NO OBJECTIONS.
...
WELL...
NO... WE CAN'T.

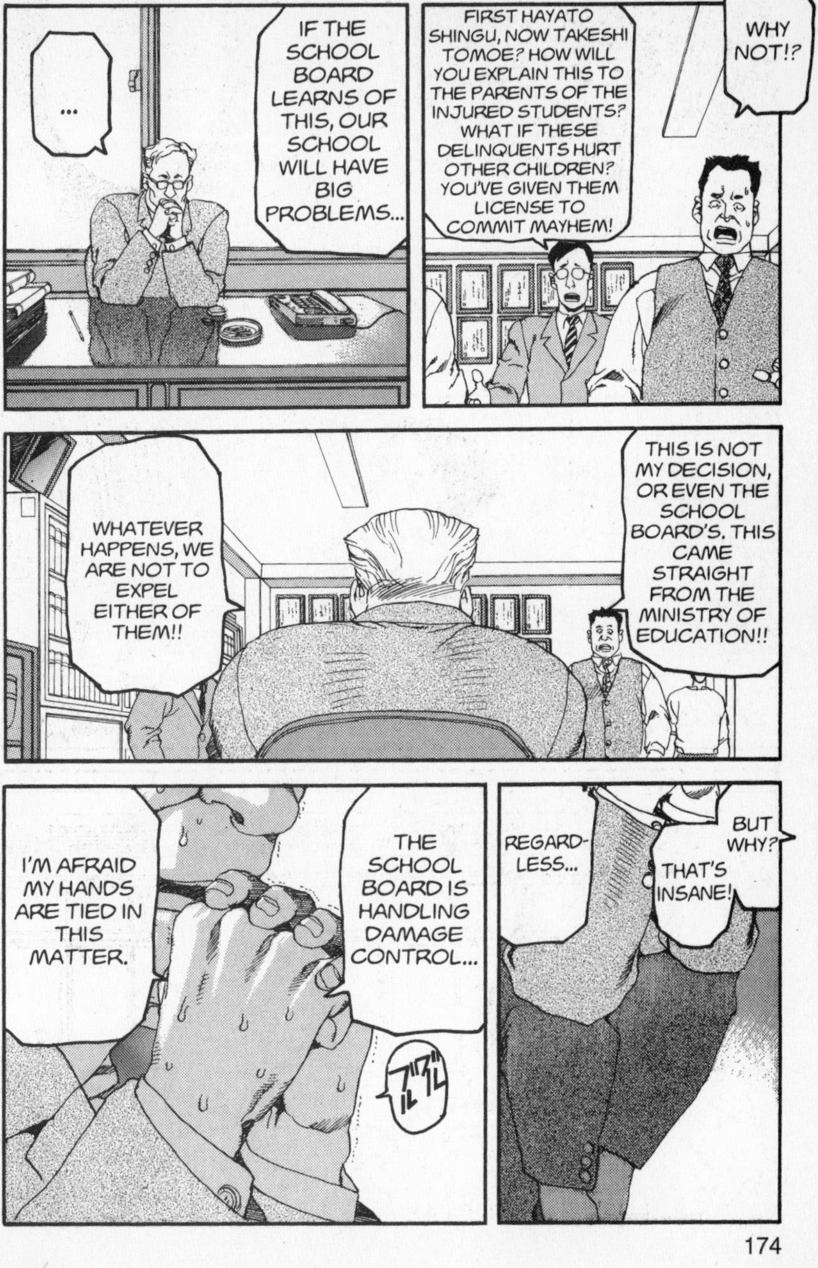
WHY NOT!?
FIRST HAYATO SHINGU, NOW TAKESHI TOMOE? HOW WILL YOU EXPLAIN THIS TO THE PARENTS OF THE INJURED STUDENTS? WHAT IF THESE DELINQUENTS HURT OTHER CHILDREN? YOU'VE GIVEN THEM LICENSE TO COMMIT MAYHEM!
IF THE SCHOOL BOARD LEARNS OF THIS, OUR SCHOOL WILL HAVE BIG PROBLEMS...
...
THIS IS NOT MY DECISION, OR EVEN THE SCHOOL BOARD'S. THIS CAME STRAIGHT FROM THE MINISTRY OF EDUCATION!!
WHATEVER HAPPENS, WE ARE NOT TO EXPEL EITHER OF THEM!!
BUT WHY?
THAT'S INSANE!
REGARD-LESS...
THE SCHOOL BOARD IS HANDLING DAMAGE CONTROL...
I'M AFRAID MY HANDS ARE TIED IN THIS MATTER.

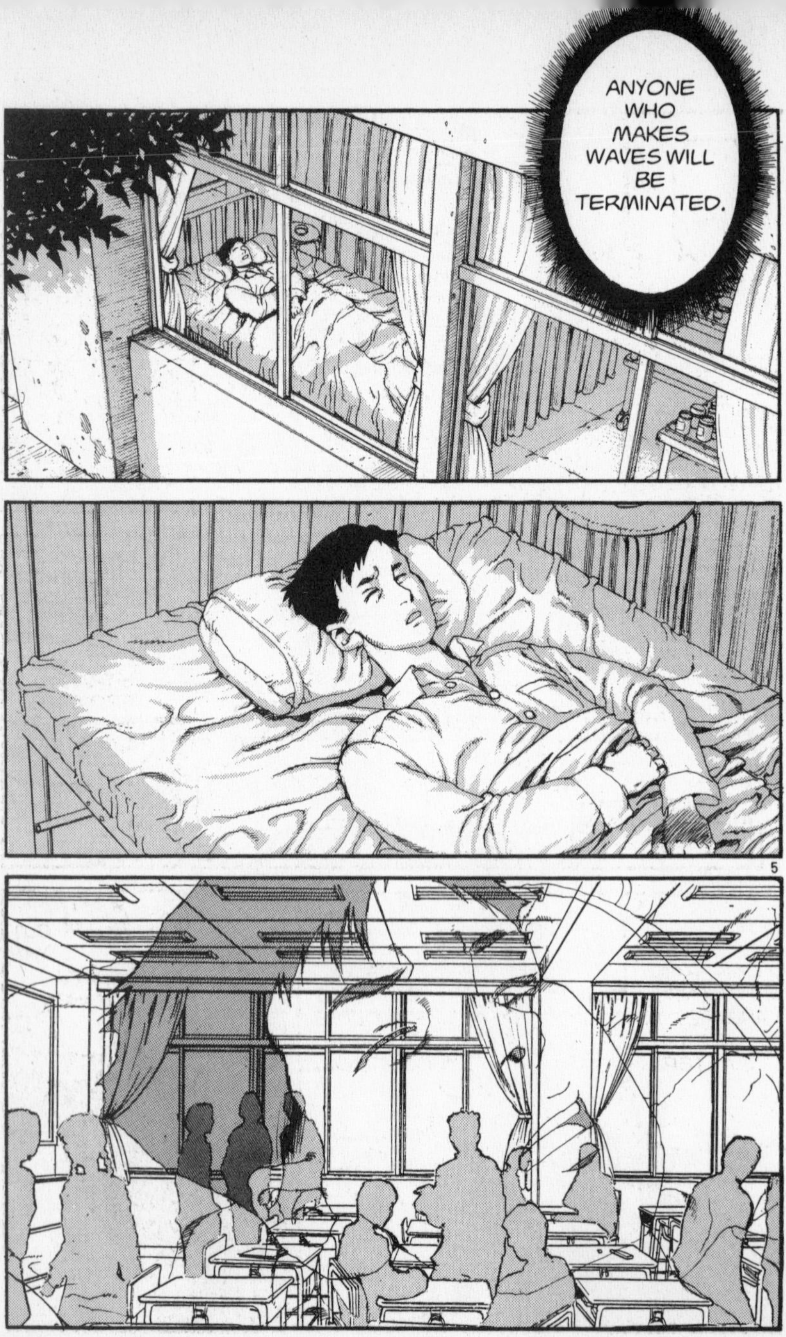
ANYONE WHO MAKES WAVES WILL BE TERMINATED.

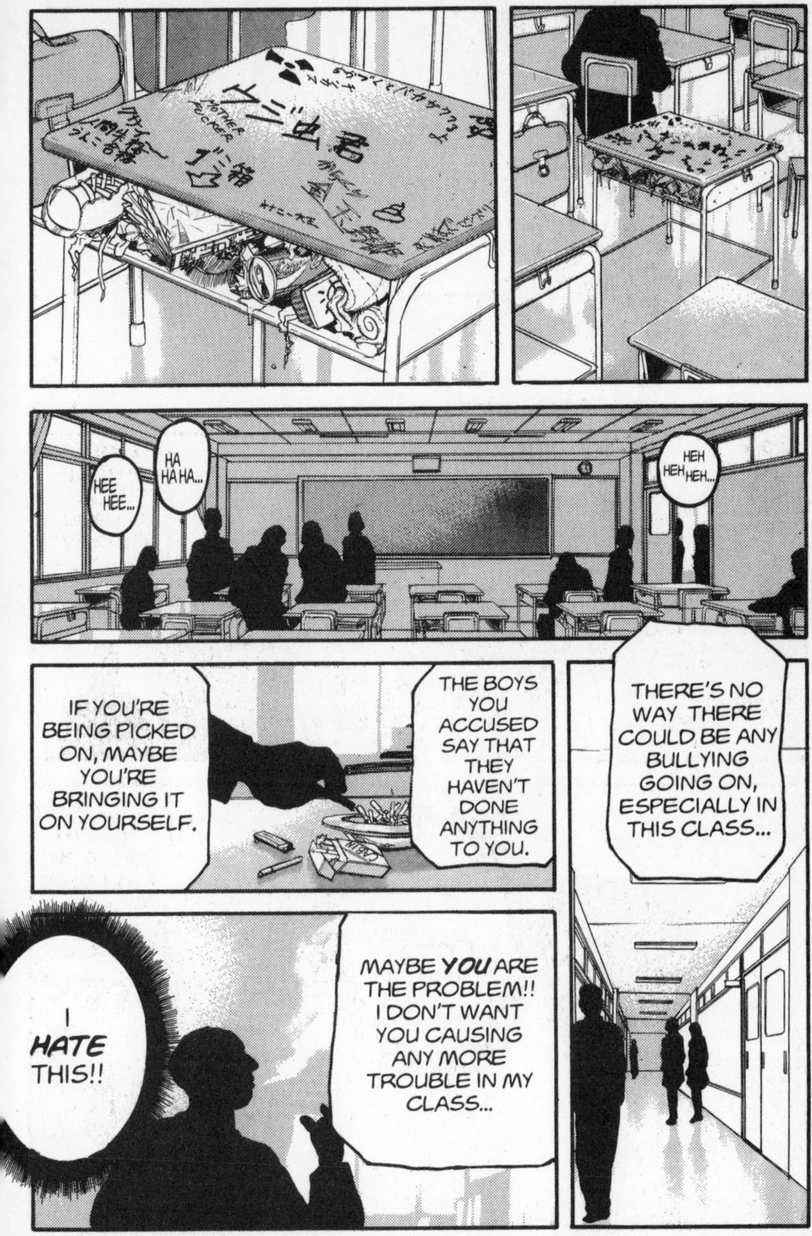
MOTHER FUCKER
HEH HEH HEH...
HA HA HA...
HEE HEE...
THERE'S NO WAY THERE COULD BE ANY BULLYING GOING ON, ESPECIALLY IN THIS CLASS...
THE BOYS YOU ACCUSED SAY THAT THEY HAVEN'T DONE ANYTHING TO YOU.
IF YOU'RE BEING PICKED ON, MAYBE YOU'RE BRINGING IT ON YOURSELF.
MAYBE ***YOU*** ARE THE PROBLEM!! I DON'T WANT YOU CAUSING ANY MORE TROUBLE IN MY CLASS...
I ***HATE*** THIS!!

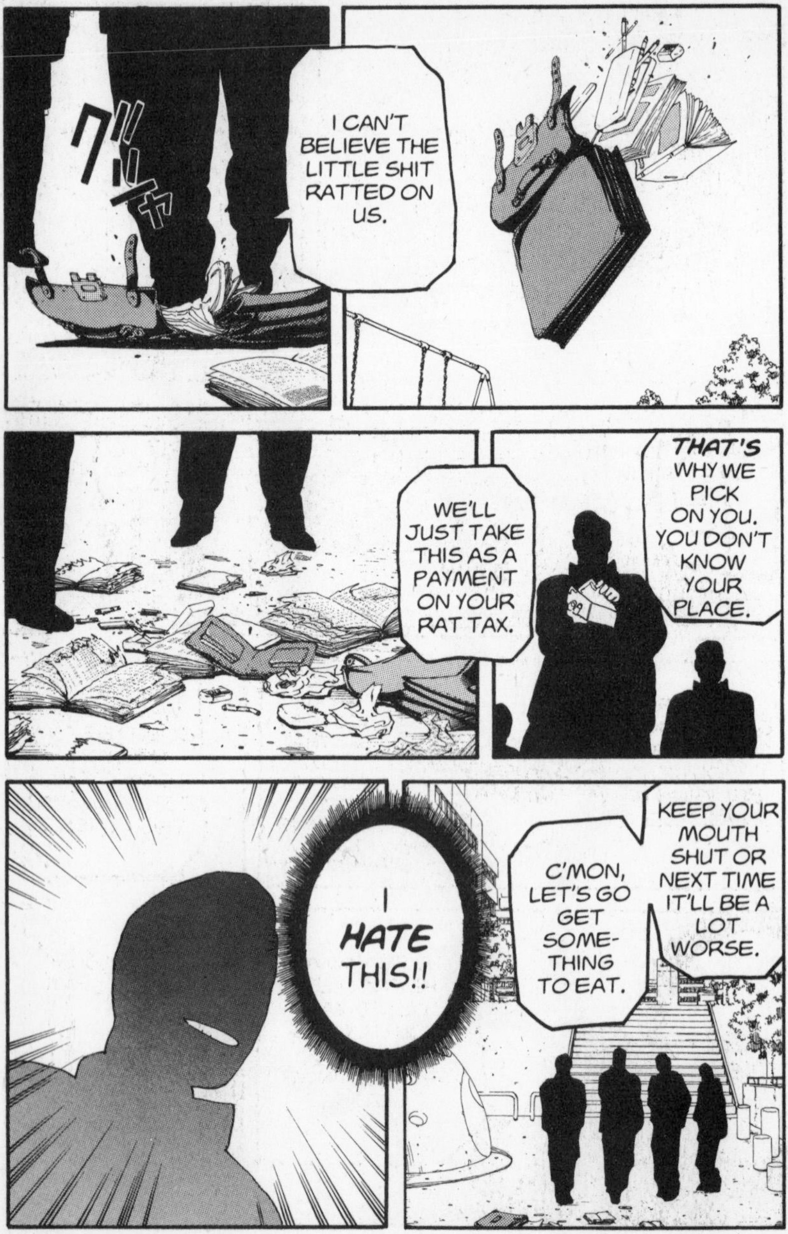

I CAN'T BELIEVE THE LITTLE SHIT RATTED ON US.
グシャ
THAT'S WHY WE PICK ON YOU. YOU DON'T KNOW YOUR PLACE.
WE'LL JUST TAKE THIS AS A PAYMENT ON YOUR RAT TAX.
KEEP YOUR MOUTH SHUT OR NEXT TIME IT'LL BE A LOT WORSE.
C'MON, LET'S GO GET SOME-THING TO EAT.
I HATE THIS!!

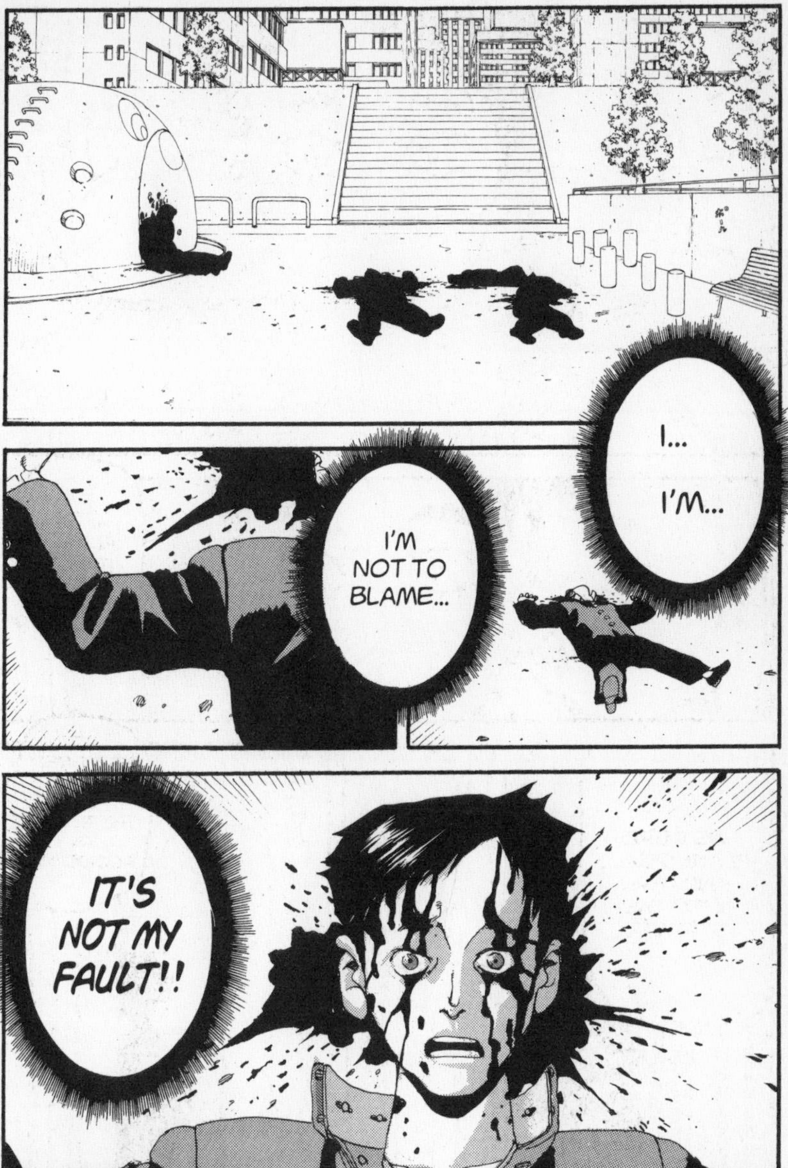
I...
I'M...
I'M NOT TO BLAME...
IT'S NOT MY FAULT!!

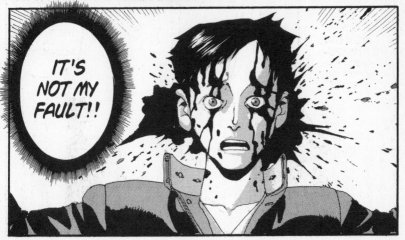

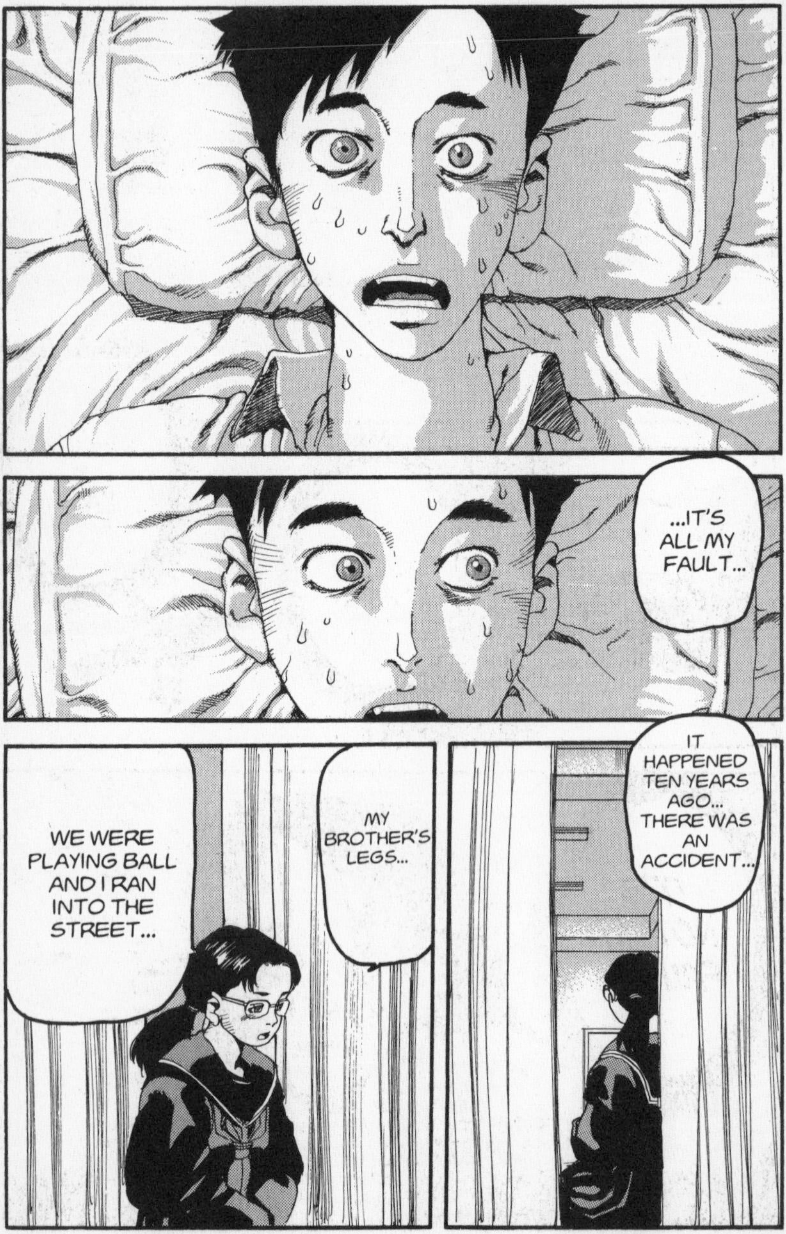
...IT'S ALL MY FAULT...
IT HAPPENED TEN YEARS AGO... THERE WAS AN ACCIDENT...
MY BROTHER'S LEGS...
WE WERE PLAYING BALL AND I RAN INTO THE STREET...

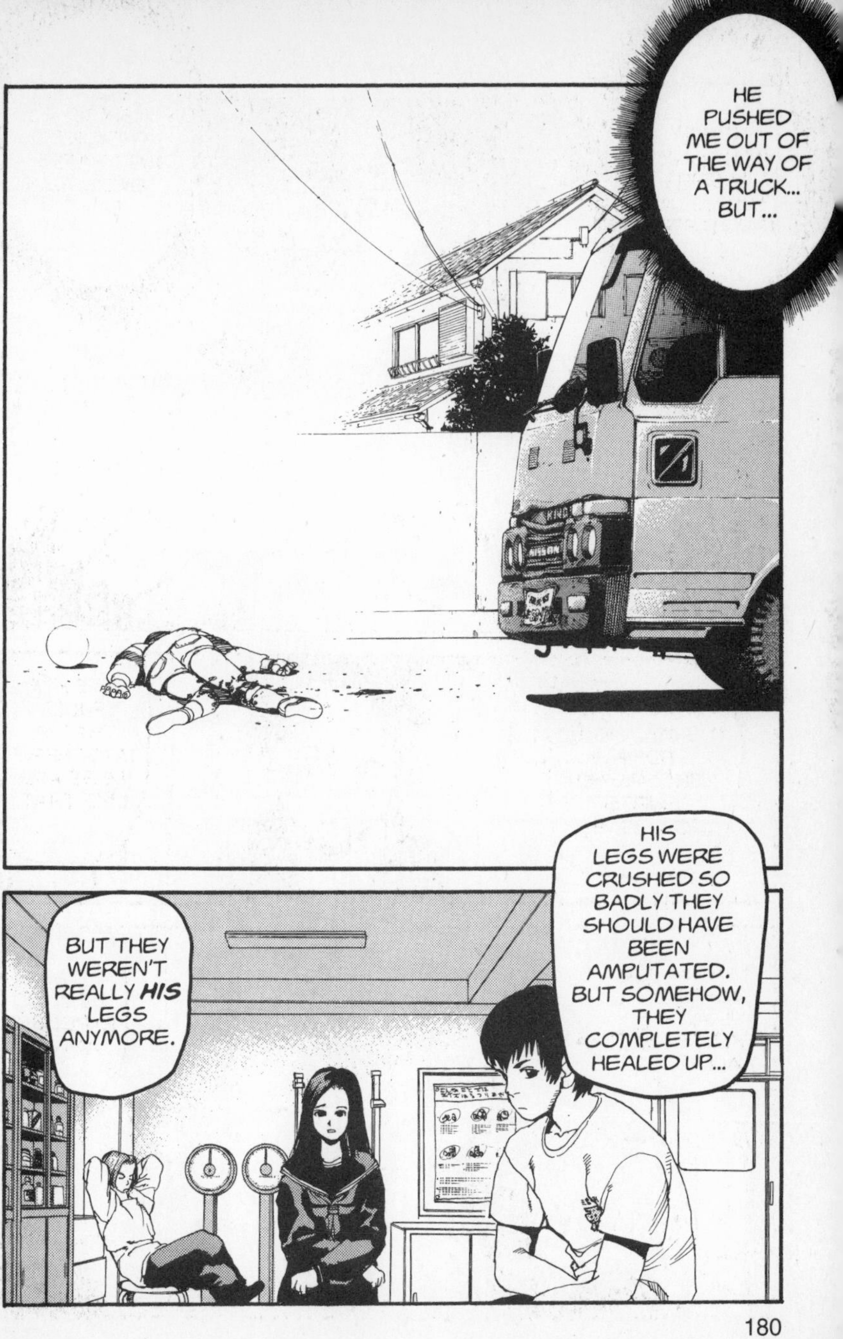
HE PUSHED ME OUT OF THE WAY OF A TRUCK... BUT...
HIS LEGS WERE CRUSHED SO BADLY THEY SHOULD HAVE BEEN AMPUTATED. BUT SOMEHOW, THEY COMPLETELY HEALED UP...
BUT THEY WEREN'T REALLY ***HIS*** LEGS ANYMORE.

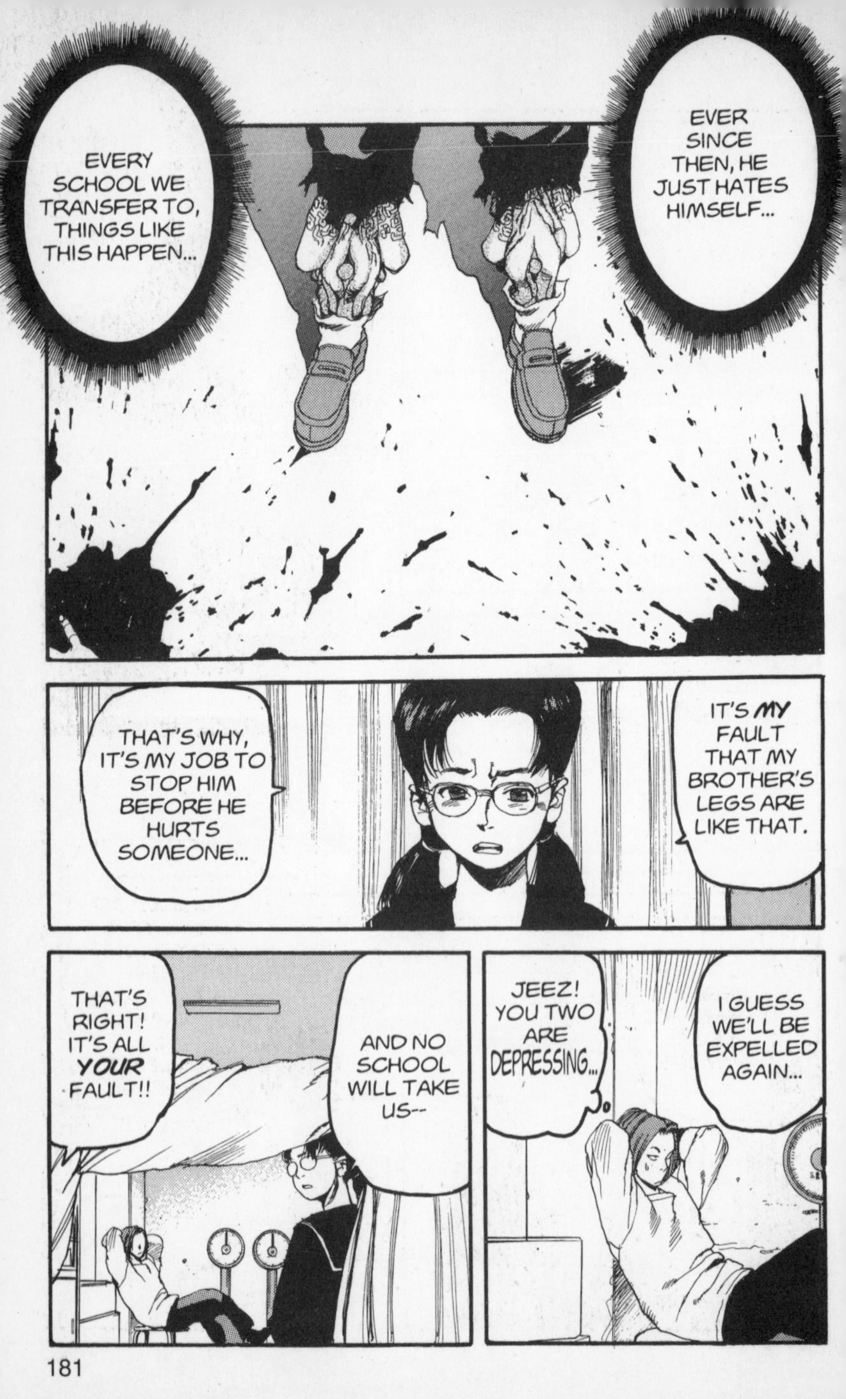
EVER SINCE THEN, HE JUST HATES HIMSELF...
EVERY SCHOOL WE TRANSFER TO, THINGS LIKE THIS HAPPEN...
IT'S *MY* FAULT THAT MY BROTHER'S LEGS ARE LIKE THAT.
THAT'S WHY, IT'S MY JOB TO STOP HIM BEFORE HE HURTS SOMEONE...
I GUESS WE'LL BE EXPELLED AGAIN...
JEEZ! YOU TWO ARE DEPRESSING...
AND NO SCHOOL WILL TAKE US--
THAT'S RIGHT! IT'S ALL *YOUR* FAULT!!

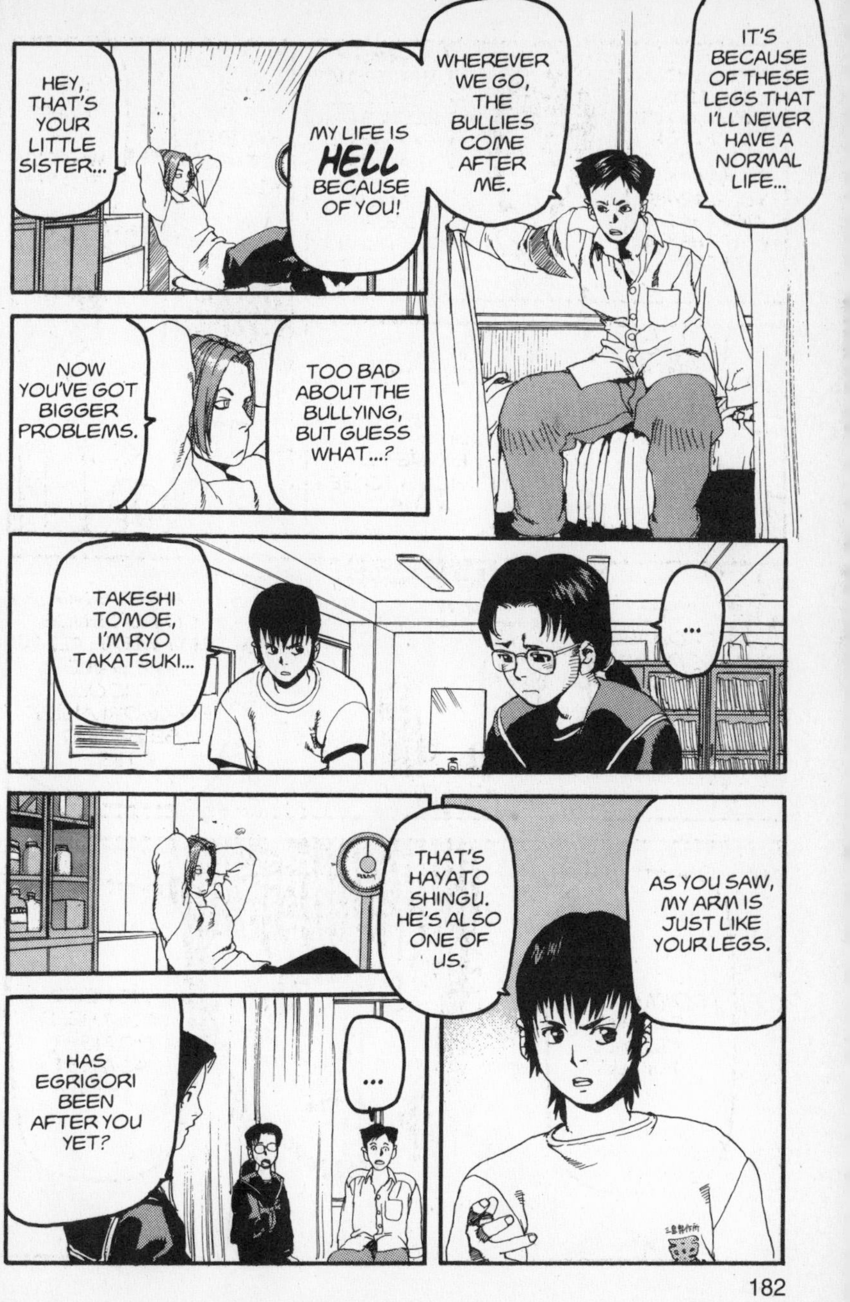
IT'S BECAUSE OF THESE LEGS THAT I'LL NEVER HAVE A NORMAL LIFE...
WHEREVER WE GO, THE BULLIES COME AFTER ME.
MY LIFE IS HELL BECAUSE OF YOU!
HEY, THAT'S YOUR LITTLE SISTER...
TOO BAD ABOUT THE BULLYING, BUT GUESS WHAT...?
NOW YOU'VE GOT BIGGER PROBLEMS.
...
TAKESHI TOMOE, I'M RYO TAKATSUKI...
AS YOU SAW, MY ARM IS JUST LIKE YOUR LEGS.
THAT'S HAYATO SHINGU. HE'S ALSO ONE OF US.
...
HAS EGRIGORI BEEN AFTER YOU YET?

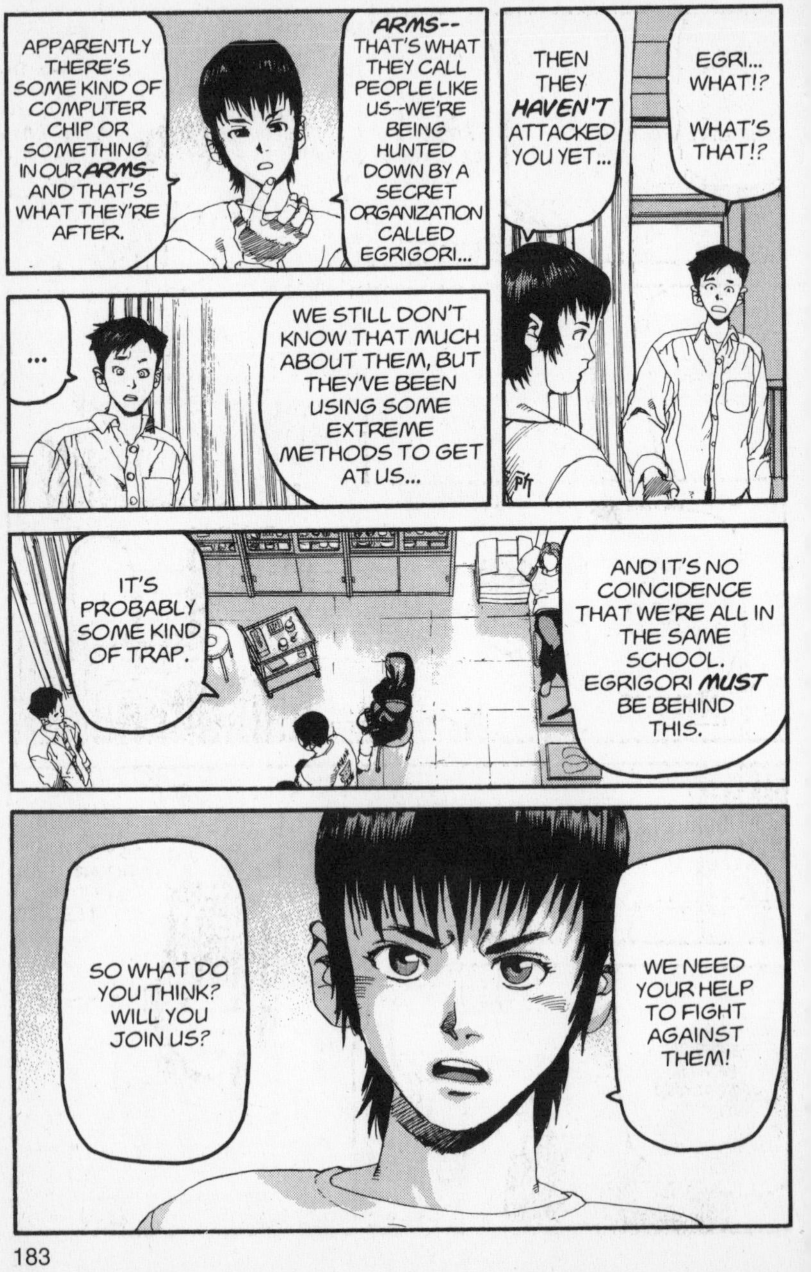
EGRI... WHAT!? WHAT'S THAT!?
THEN THEY HAVEN'T ATTACKED YOU YET...
ARMS-- THAT'S WHAT THEY CALL PEOPLE LIKE US--WE'RE BEING HUNTED DOWN BY A SECRET ORGANIZATION CALLED EGRIGORI...
APPARENTLY THERE'S SOME KIND OF COMPUTER CHIP OR SOMETHING IN OUR ARMS-- AND THAT'S WHAT THEY'RE AFTER.
WE STILL DON'T KNOW THAT MUCH ABOUT THEM, BUT THEY'VE BEEN USING SOME EXTREME METHODS TO GET AT US...
...
AND IT'S NO COINCIDENCE THAT WE'RE ALL IN THE SAME SCHOOL. EGRIGORI MUST BE BEHIND THIS.
IT'S PROBABLY SOME KIND OF TRAP.
WE NEED YOUR HELP TO FIGHT AGAINST THEM!
SO WHAT DO YOU THINK? WILL YOU JOIN US?

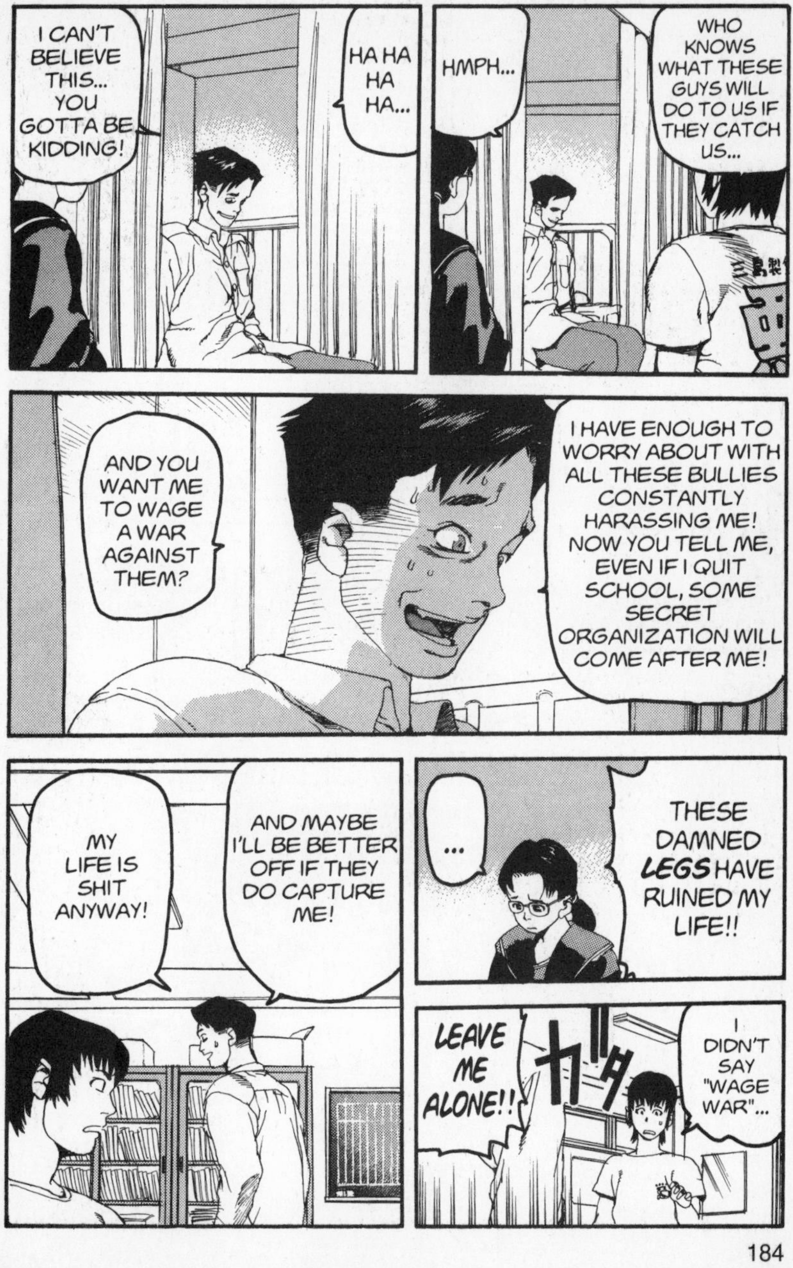
WHO KNOWS WHAT THESE GUYS WILL DO TO US IF THEY CATCH US...
HMPH...
HA HA HA HA...
I CAN'T BELIEVE THIS... YOU GOTTA BE KIDDING!
I HAVE ENOUGH TO WORRY ABOUT WITH ALL THESE BULLIES CONSTANTLY HARASSING ME! NOW YOU TELL ME, EVEN IF I QUIT SCHOOL, SOME SECRET ORGANIZATION WILL COME AFTER ME!
AND YOU WANT ME TO WAGE A WAR AGAINST THEM?
THESE DAMNED LEGS HAVE RUINED MY LIFE!!
...
I DIDN'T SAY "WAGE WAR"...
ガタ
LEAVE ME ALONE!!
AND MAYBE I'LL BE BETTER OFF IF THEY DO CAPTURE ME!
MY LIFE IS SHIT ANYWAY!

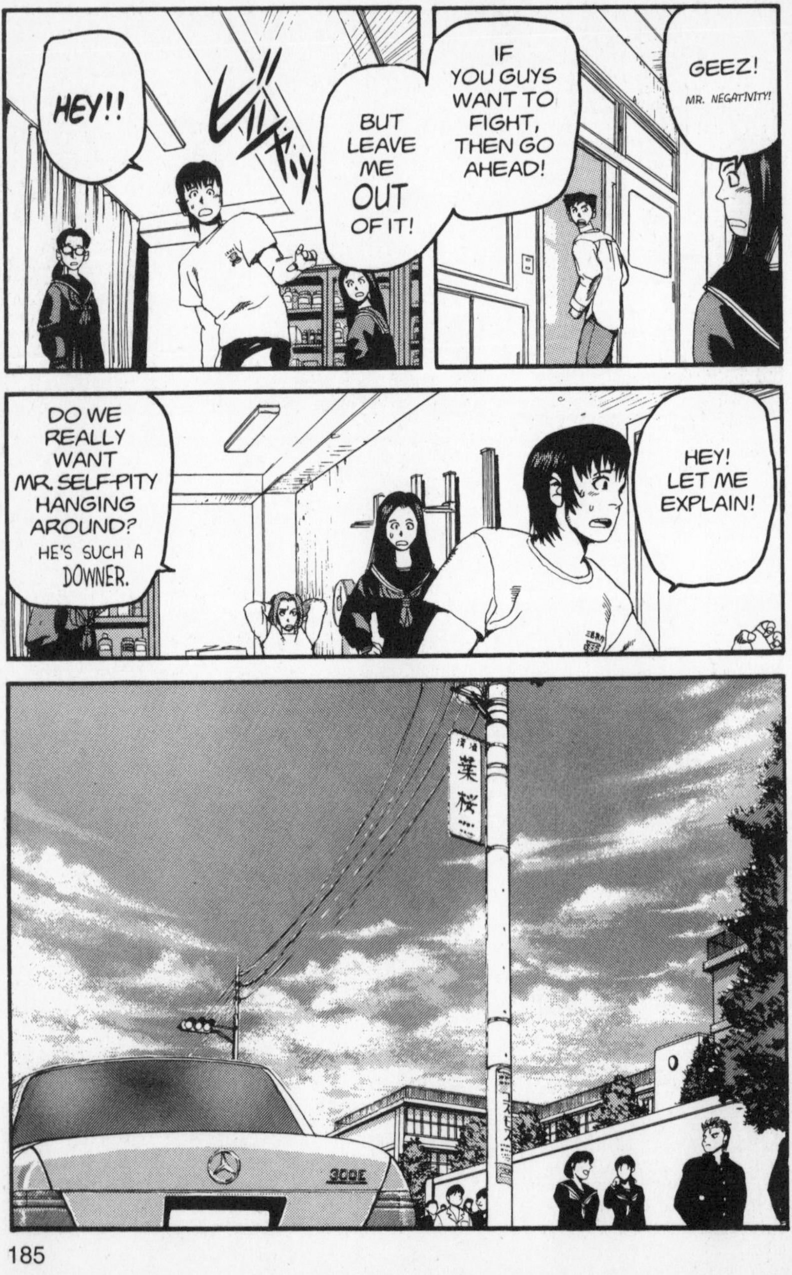
GEEZ! MR. NEGATIVITY!
IF YOU GUYS WANT TO FIGHT, THEN GO AHEAD!
BUT LEAVE ME OUT OF IT!
HEY!!
HEY! LET ME EXPLAIN!
DO WE REALLY WANT MR. SELF-PITY HANGING AROUND? HE'S SUCH A DOWNER.
300E

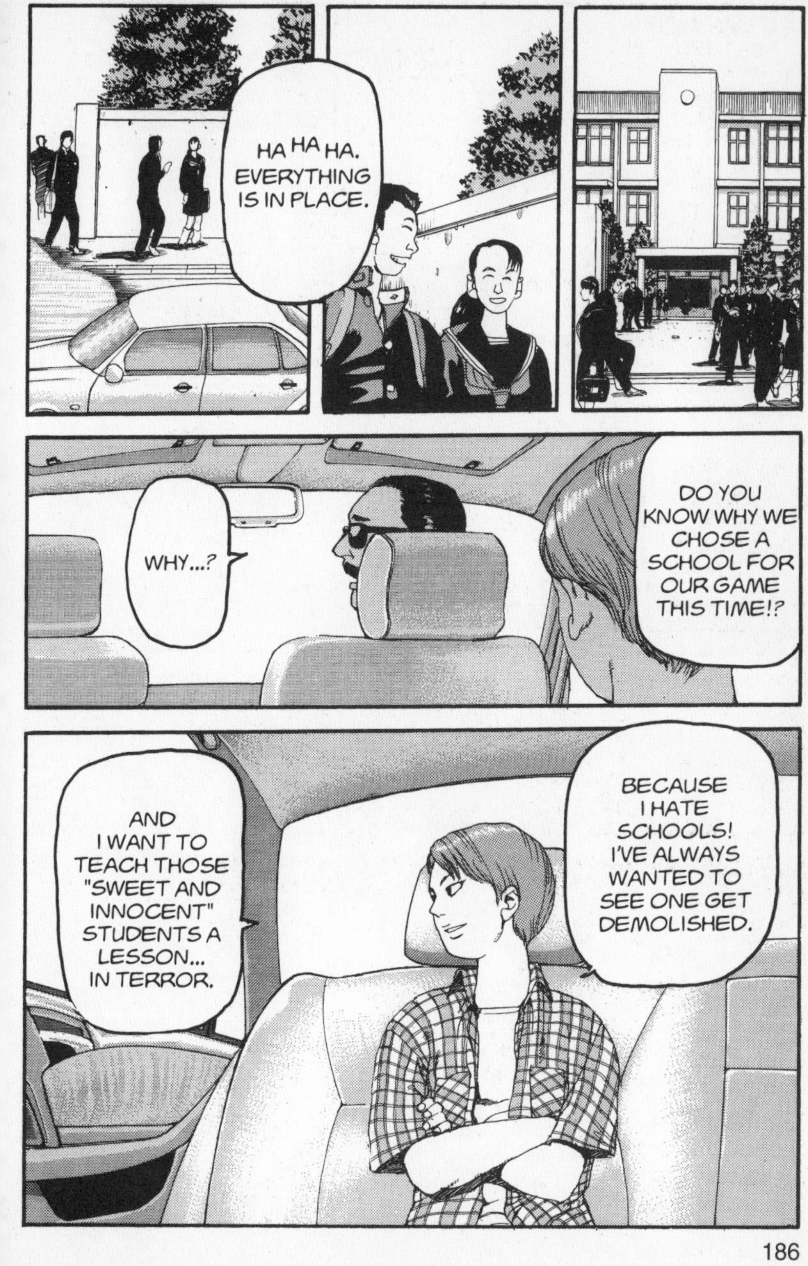
HA HA HA. EVERYTHING IS IN PLACE.
DO YOU KNOW WHY WE CHOSE A SCHOOL FOR OUR GAME THIS TIME!?
WHY...?
BECAUSE I HATE SCHOOLS! I'VE ALWAYS WANTED TO SEE ONE GET DEMOLISHED.
AND I WANT TO TEACH THOSE "SWEET AND INNOCENT" STUDENTS A LESSON... IN TERROR.

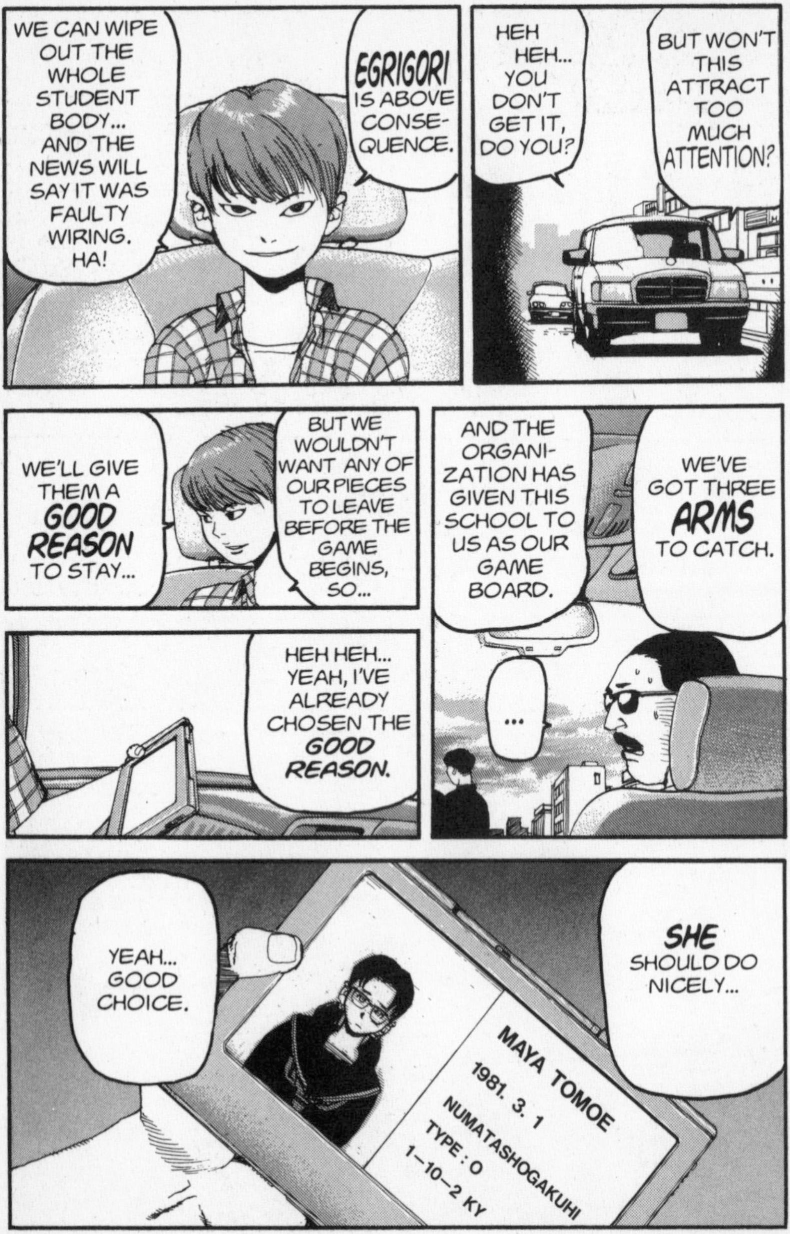
BUT WON'T THIS ATTRACT TOO MUCH ATTENTION?
HEH HEH... YOU DON'T GET IT, DO YOU?
EGRIGORI IS ABOVE CONSE-QUENCE.
WE CAN WIPE OUT THE WHOLE STUDENT BODY... AND THE NEWS WILL SAY IT WAS FAULTY WIRING. HA!
WE'VE GOT THREE ARMS TO CATCH.
AND THE ORGANI-ZATION HAS GIVEN THIS SCHOOL TO US AS OUR GAME BOARD.
...
BUT WE WOULDN'T WANT ANY OF OUR PIECES TO LEAVE BEFORE THE GAME BEGINS, SO...
WE'LL GIVE THEM A GOOD REASON TO STAY...
HEH HEH... YEAH, I'VE ALREADY CHOSEN THE GOOD REASON.
SHE SHOULD DO NICELY...
YEAH... GOOD CHOICE.
MAYA TOMOE
1981. 3. 1
NUMATASHOGAKUHI
TYPE : 0
1—10—2 KY

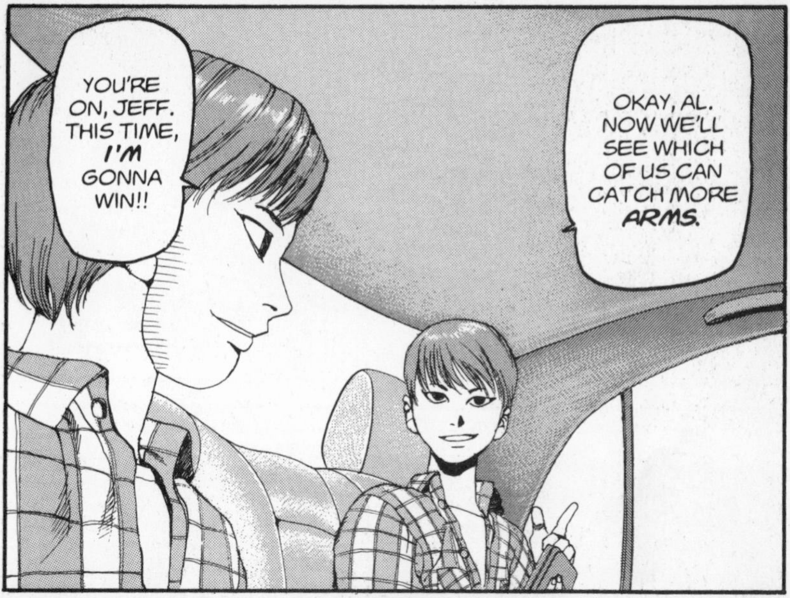
OKAY, AL. NOW WE'LL SEE WHICH OF US CAN CATCH MORE ARMS.
YOU'RE ON, JEFF. THIS TIME, I'M GONNA WIN!!

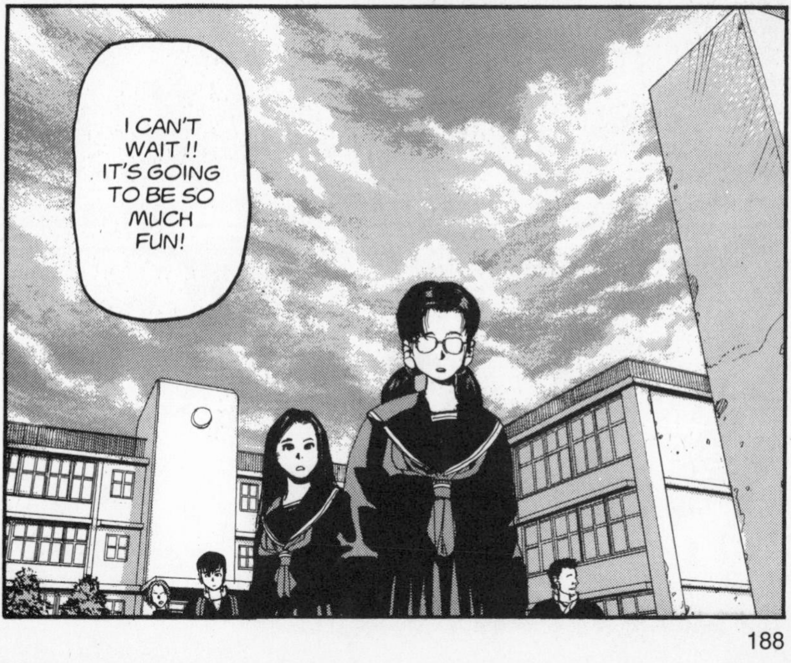
I CAN'T WAIT !! IT'S GOING TO BE SO MUCH FUN!

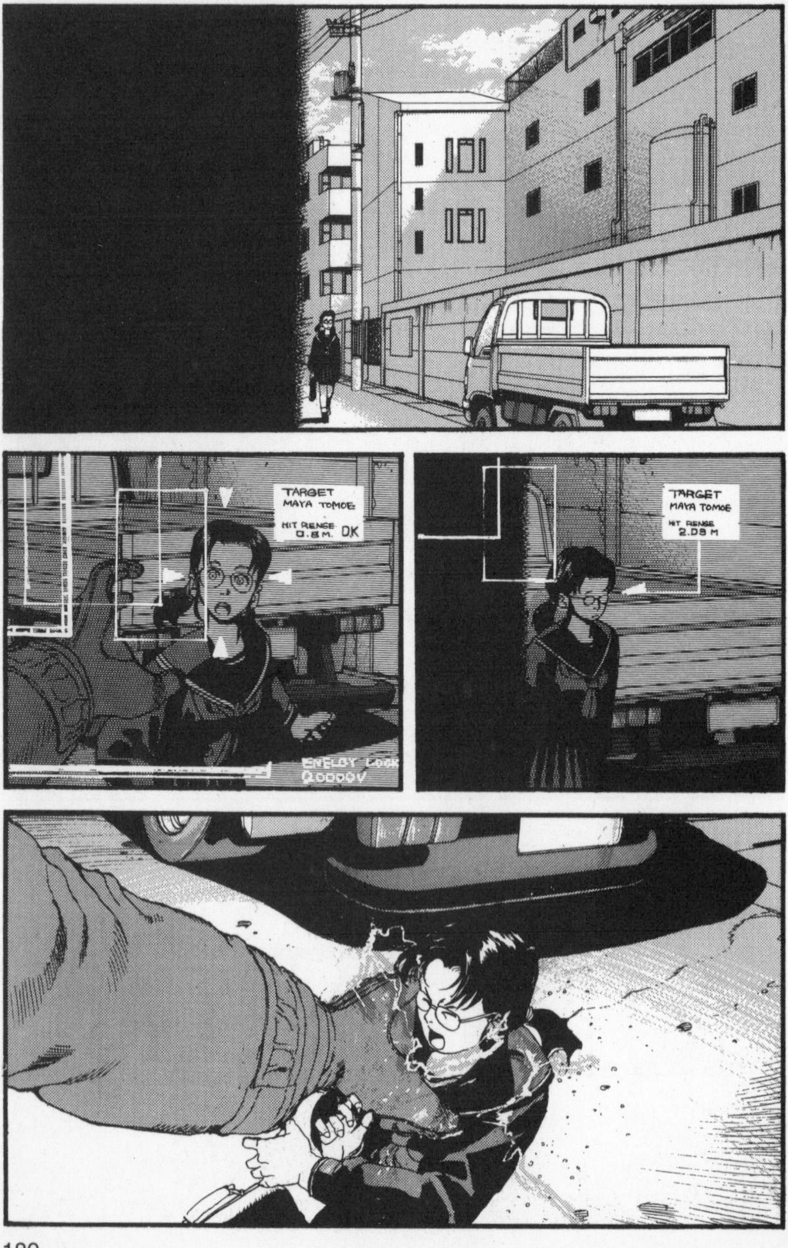

TARGET
MAYA TOMOE
HIT RENSE
2.09 M
TARGET
MAYA TOMOE:
HIT RENSE
0.8M. OK

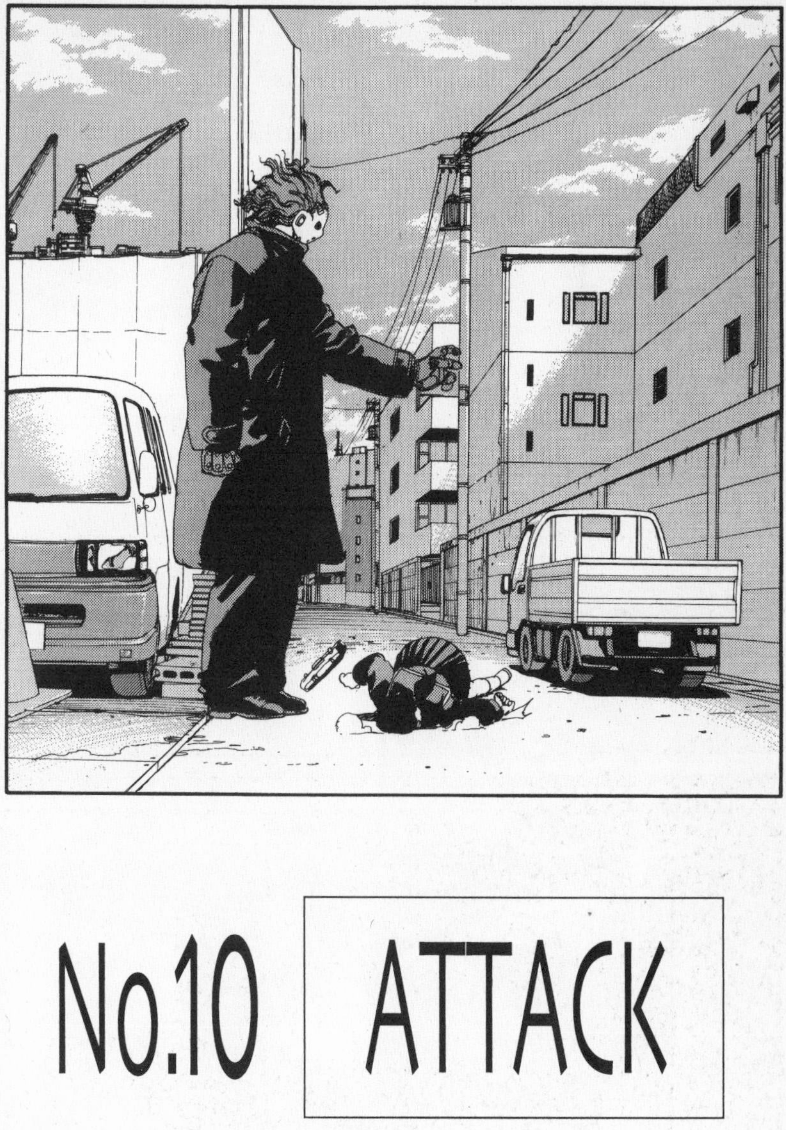

No.10 ATTACK

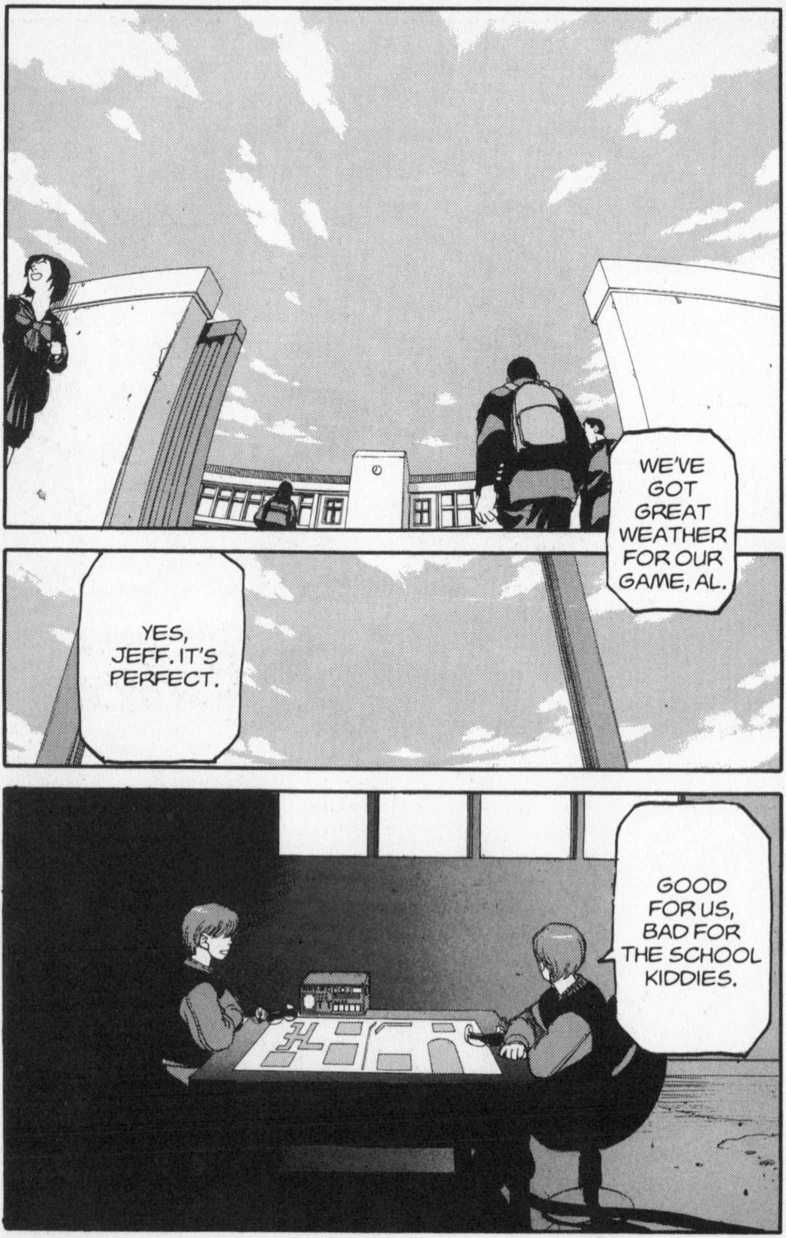
WE'VE GOT GREAT WEATHER FOR OUR GAME, AL.
YES, JEFF. IT'S PERFECT.
GOOD FOR US, BAD FOR THE SCHOOL KIDDIES.

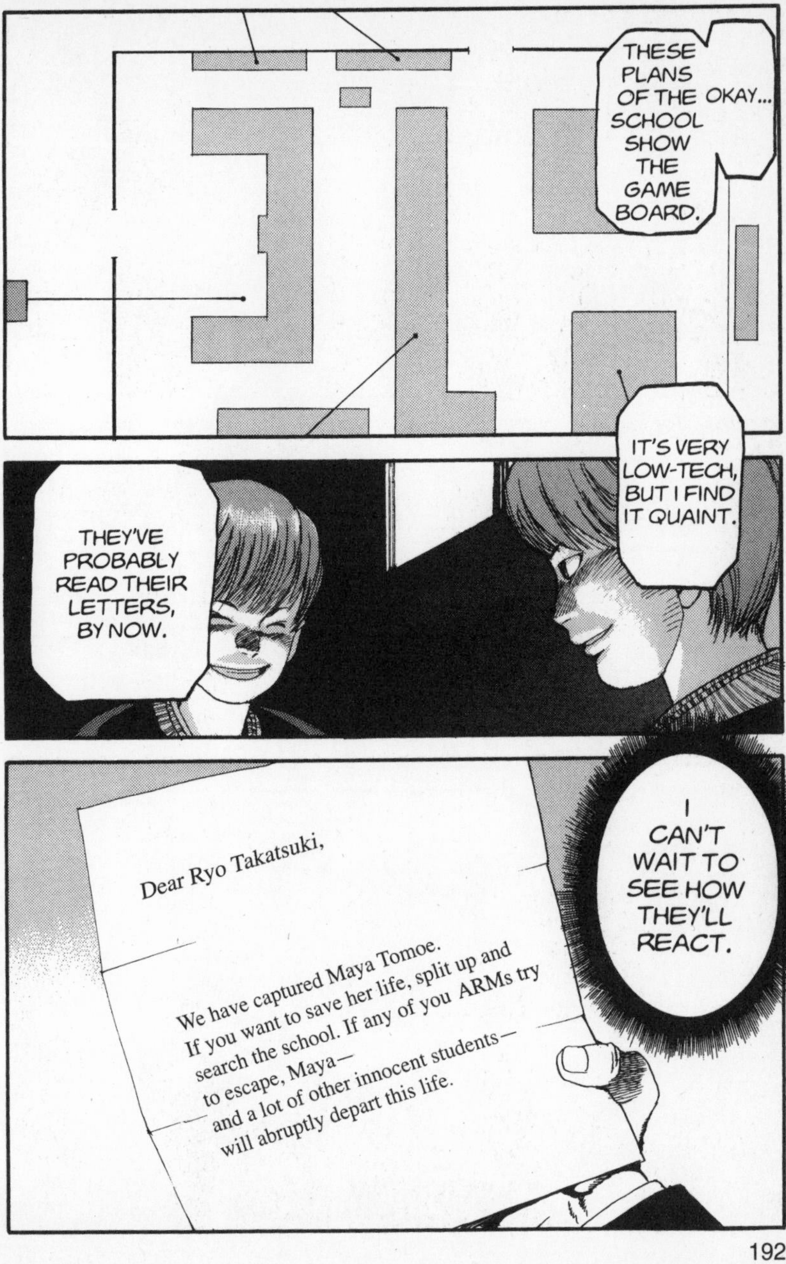
OKAY...
THESE PLANS OF THE SCHOOL SHOW THE GAME BOARD.
IT'S VERY LOW-TECH, BUT I FIND IT QUAINT.
THEY'VE PROBABLY READ THEIR LETTERS, BY NOW.
I CAN'T WAIT TO SEE HOW THEY'LL REACT.
Dear Ryo Takatsuki,
We have captured Maya Tomoe. If you want to save her life, split up and search the school. If any of you ARMs try to escape, Maya— and a lot of other innocent students— will abruptly depart this life.

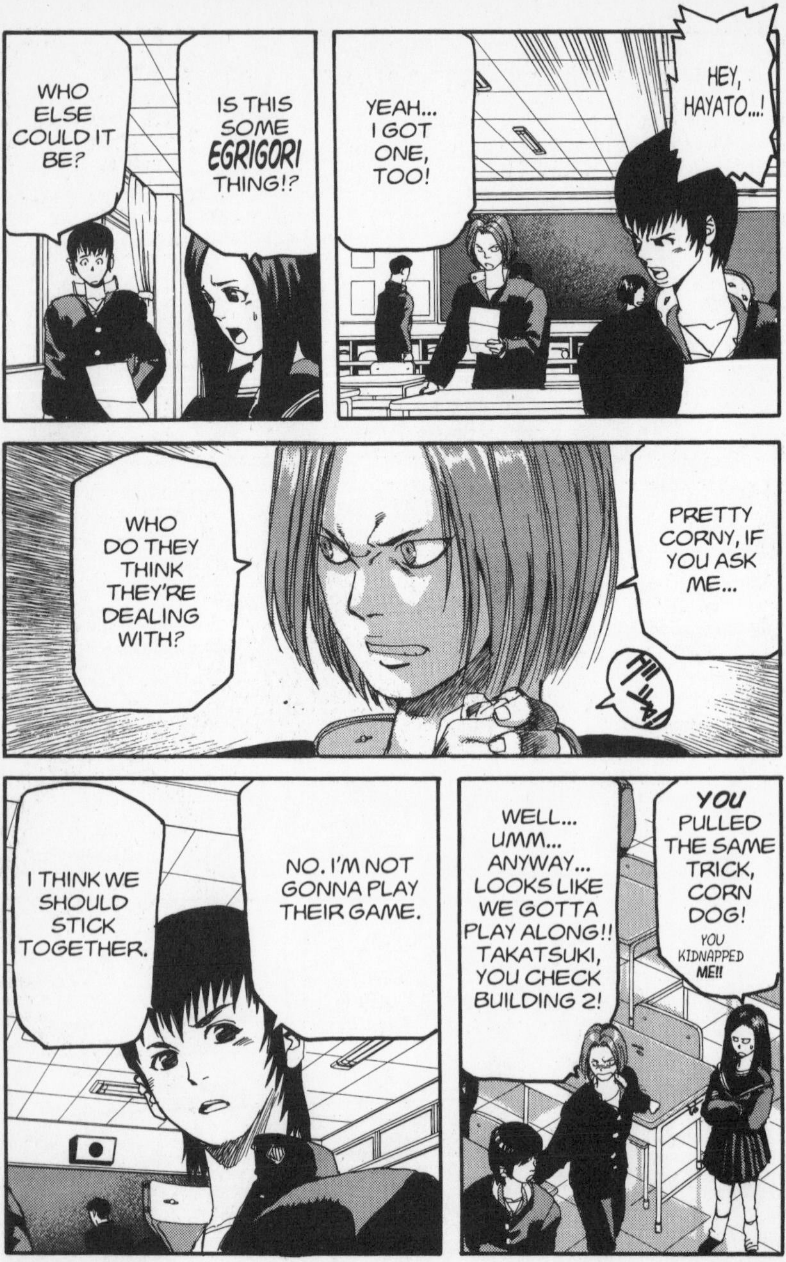
HEY, HAYATO...!
YEAH... I GOT ONE, TOO!
IS THIS SOME EGRIGORI THING!?
WHO ELSE COULD IT BE?
PRETTY CORNY, IF YOU ASK ME...
WHO DO THEY THINK THEY'RE DEALING WITH?
YOU PULLED THE SAME TRICK, CORN DOG!
YOU KIDNAPPED ME!!
WELL... UMM... ANYWAY... LOOKS LIKE WE GOTTA PLAY ALONG!! TAKATSUKI, YOU CHECK BUILDING 2!
NO. I'M NOT GONNA PLAY THEIR GAME.
I THINK WE SHOULD STICK TOGETHER.

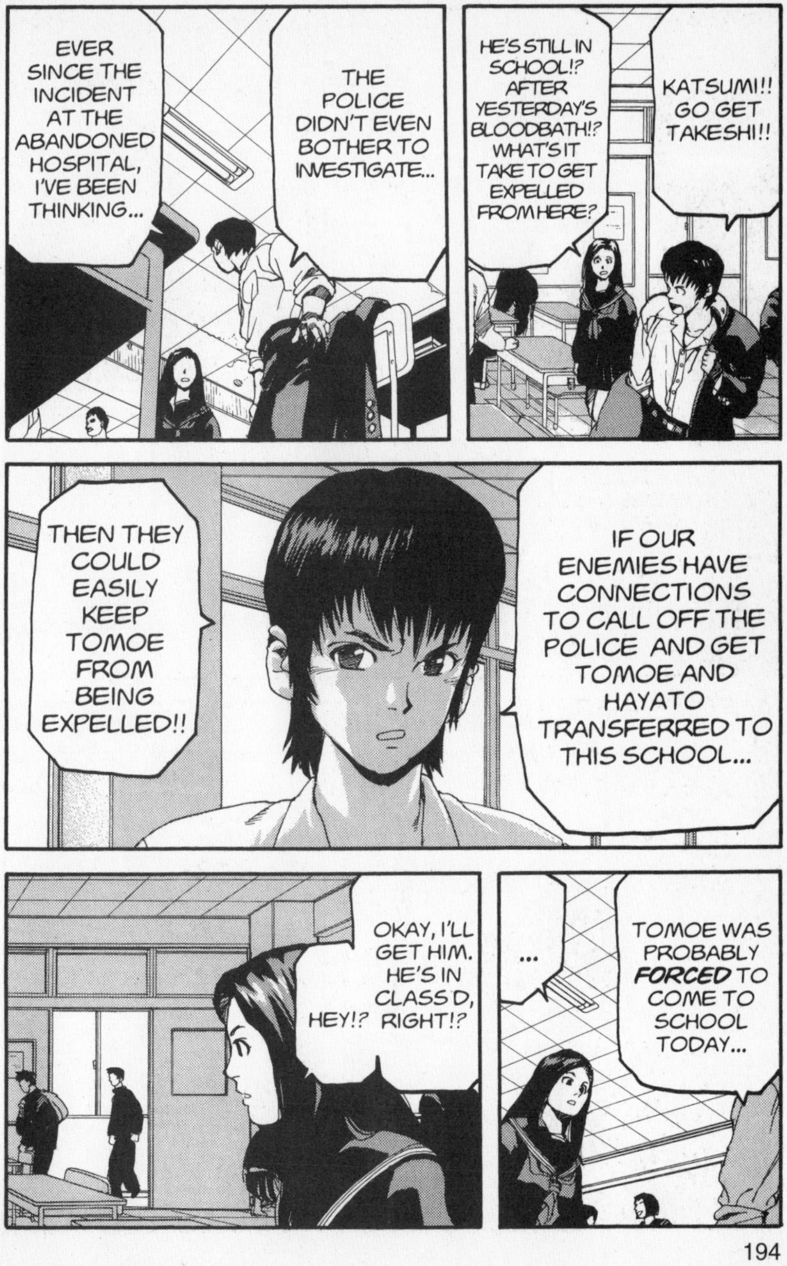
KATSUMI!! GO GET TAKESHI!!
HE'S STILL IN SCHOOL!? AFTER YESTERDAY'S BLOODBATH!? WHAT'S IT TAKE TO GET EXPELLED FROM HERE?
EVER SINCE THE INCIDENT AT THE ABANDONED HOSPITAL, I'VE BEEN THINKING...
THE POLICE DIDN'T EVEN BOTHER TO INVESTIGATE...
IF OUR ENEMIES HAVE CONNECTIONS TO CALL OFF THE POLICE AND GET TOMOE AND HAYATO TRANSFERRED TO THIS SCHOOL...
THEN THEY COULD EASILY KEEP TOMOE FROM BEING EXPELLED!!
TOMOE WAS PROBABLY ***FORCED*** TO COME TO SCHOOL TODAY...
...
OKAY, I'LL GET HIM. HE'S IN CLASS D, RIGHT!?
HEY!?

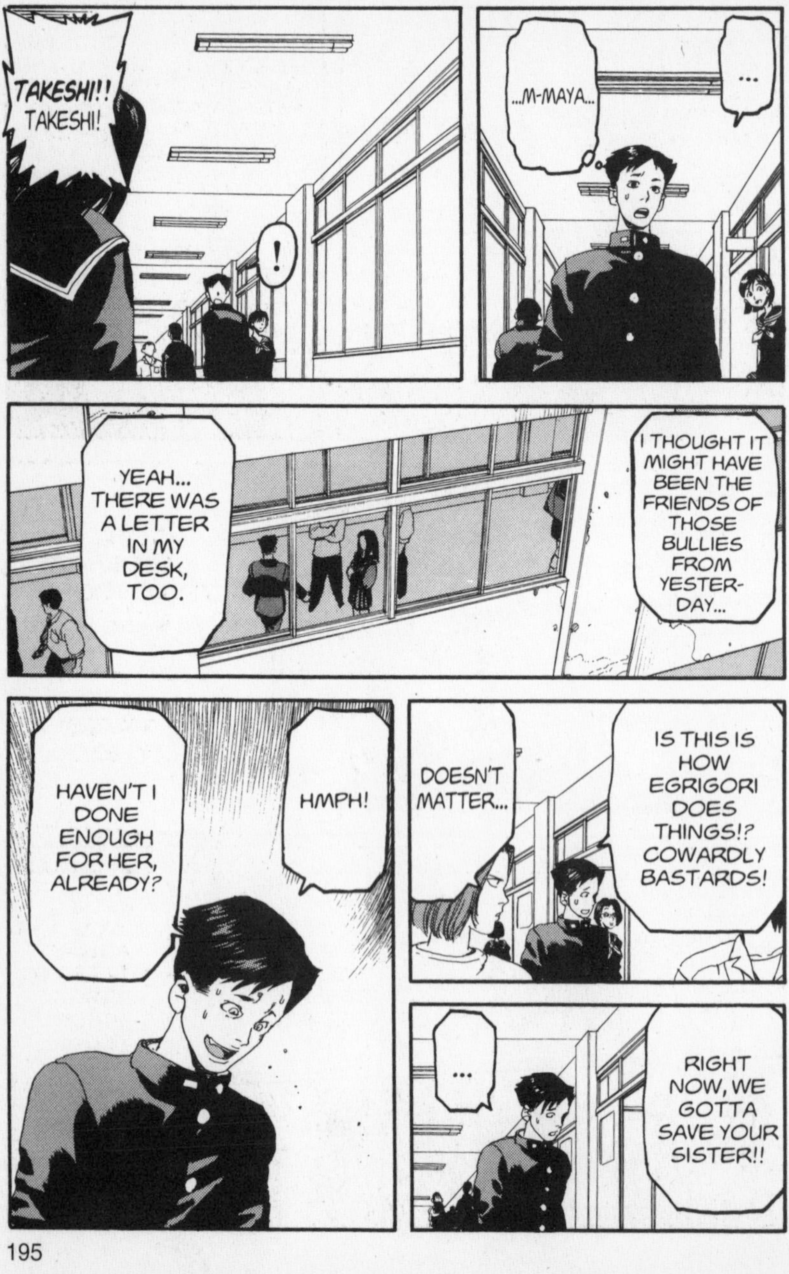
...
...M-MAYA...
TAKESHI!! TAKESHI!
!
I THOUGHT IT MIGHT HAVE BEEN THE FRIENDS OF THOSE BULLIES FROM YESTER-DAY...
YEAH... THERE WAS A LETTER IN MY DESK, TOO.
IS THIS IS HOW EGRIGORI DOES THINGS!? COWARDLY BASTARDS!
DOESN'T MATTER...
RIGHT NOW, WE GOTTA SAVE YOUR SISTER!!
...
HMPH!
HAVEN'T I DONE ENOUGH FOR HER, ALREADY?

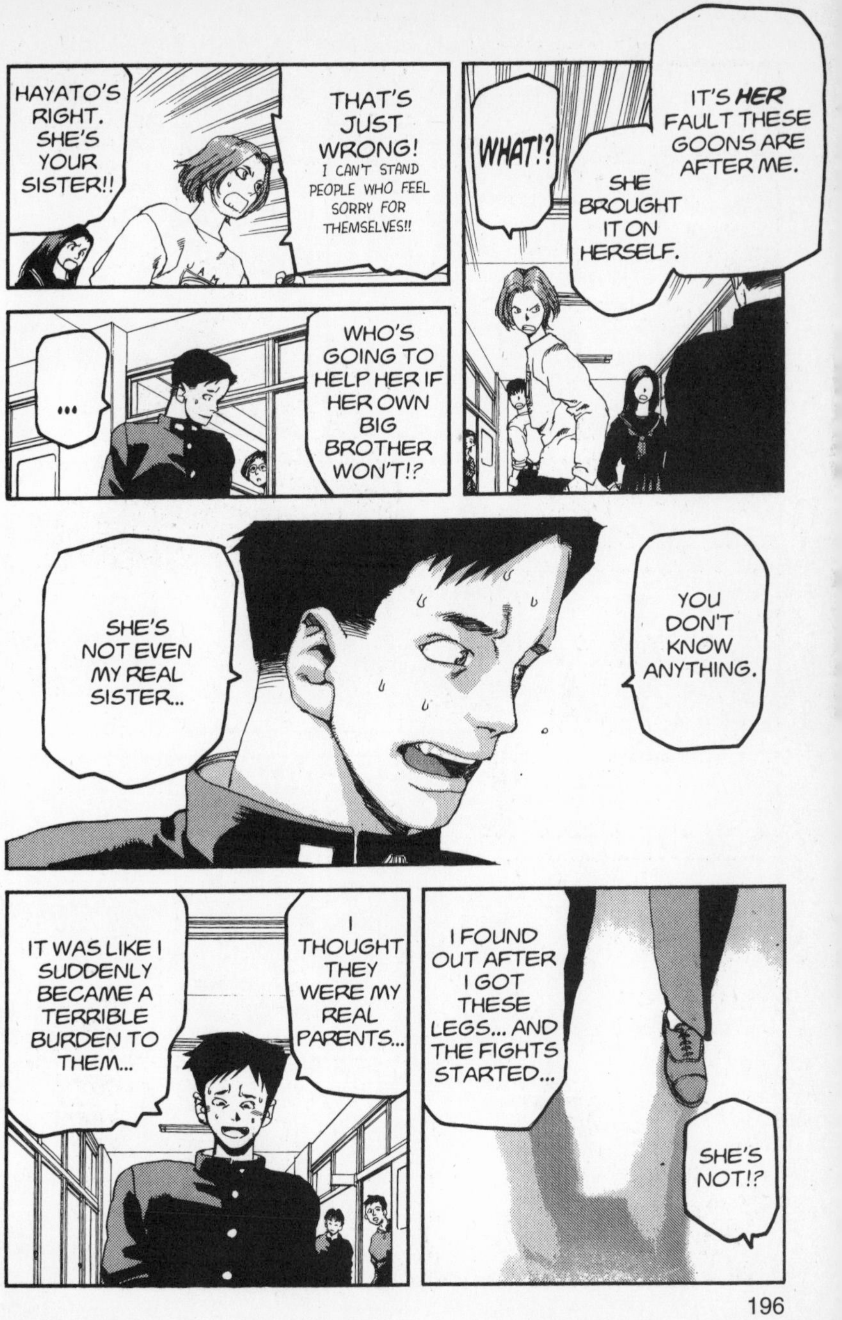
IT'S HER FAULT THESE GOONS ARE AFTER ME.
SHE BROUGHT IT ON HERSELF.
WHAT!?
THAT'S JUST WRONG! I CAN'T STAND PEOPLE WHO FEEL SORRY FOR THEMSELVES!!
HAYATO'S RIGHT. SHE'S YOUR SISTER!!
WHO'S GOING TO HELP HER IF HER OWN BIG BROTHER WON'T!?
...
YOU DON'T KNOW ANYTHING.
SHE'S NOT EVEN MY REAL SISTER...
I FOUND OUT AFTER I GOT THESE LEGS... AND THE FIGHTS STARTED...
SHE'S NOT!?
I THOUGHT THEY WERE MY REAL PARENTS...
IT WAS LIKE I SUDDENLY BECAME A TERRIBLE BURDEN TO THEM...

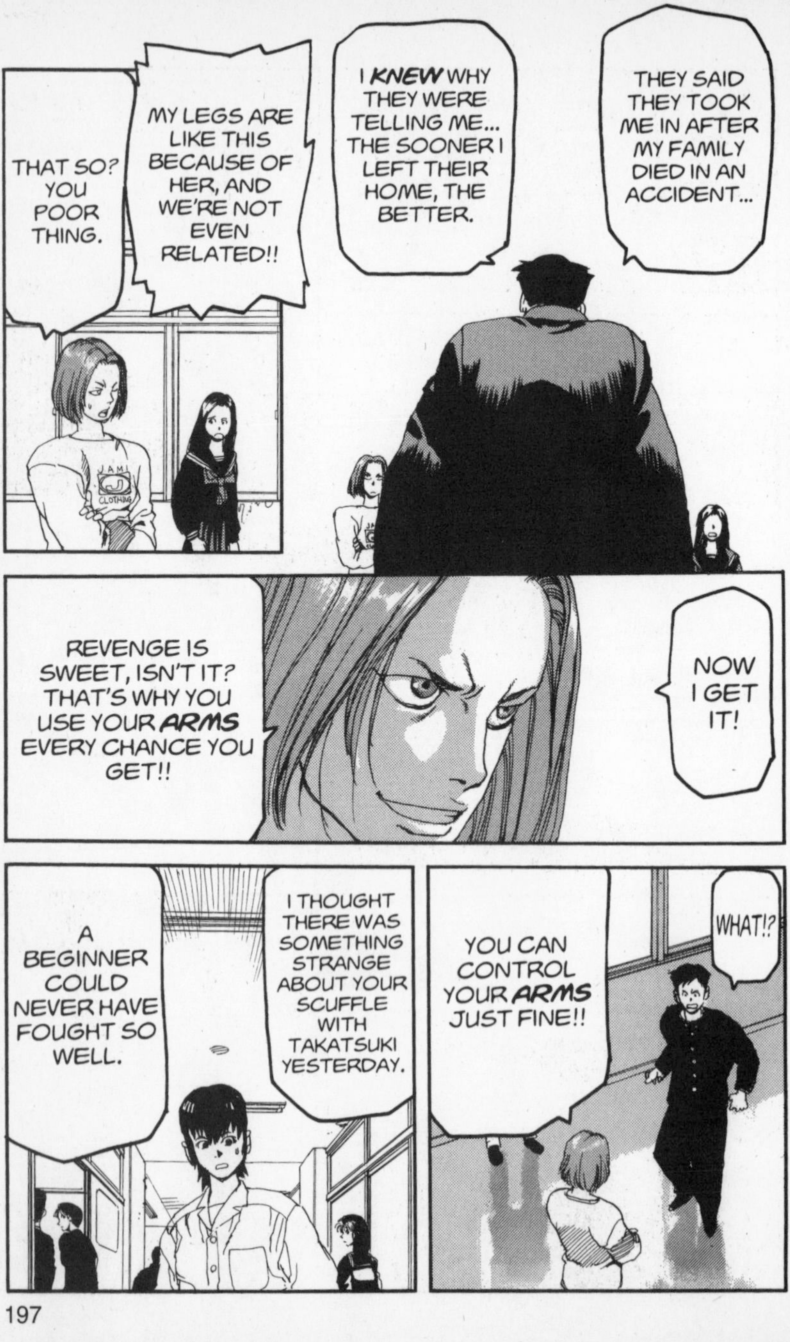
THEY SAID THEY TOOK ME IN AFTER MY FAMILY DIED IN AN ACCIDENT...
I KNEW WHY THEY WERE TELLING ME... THE SOONER I LEFT THEIR HOME, THE BETTER.
MY LEGS ARE LIKE THIS BECAUSE OF HER, AND WE'RE NOT EVEN RELATED!!
THAT SO? YOU POOR THING.
NOW I GET IT!
REVENGE IS SWEET, ISN'T IT? THAT'S WHY YOU USE YOUR ARMS EVERY CHANCE YOU GET!!
WHAT!?
YOU CAN CONTROL YOUR ARMS JUST FINE!!
I THOUGHT THERE WAS SOMETHING STRANGE ABOUT YOUR SCUFFLE WITH TAKATSUKI YESTERDAY.
A BEGINNER COULD NEVER HAVE FOUGHT SO WELL.

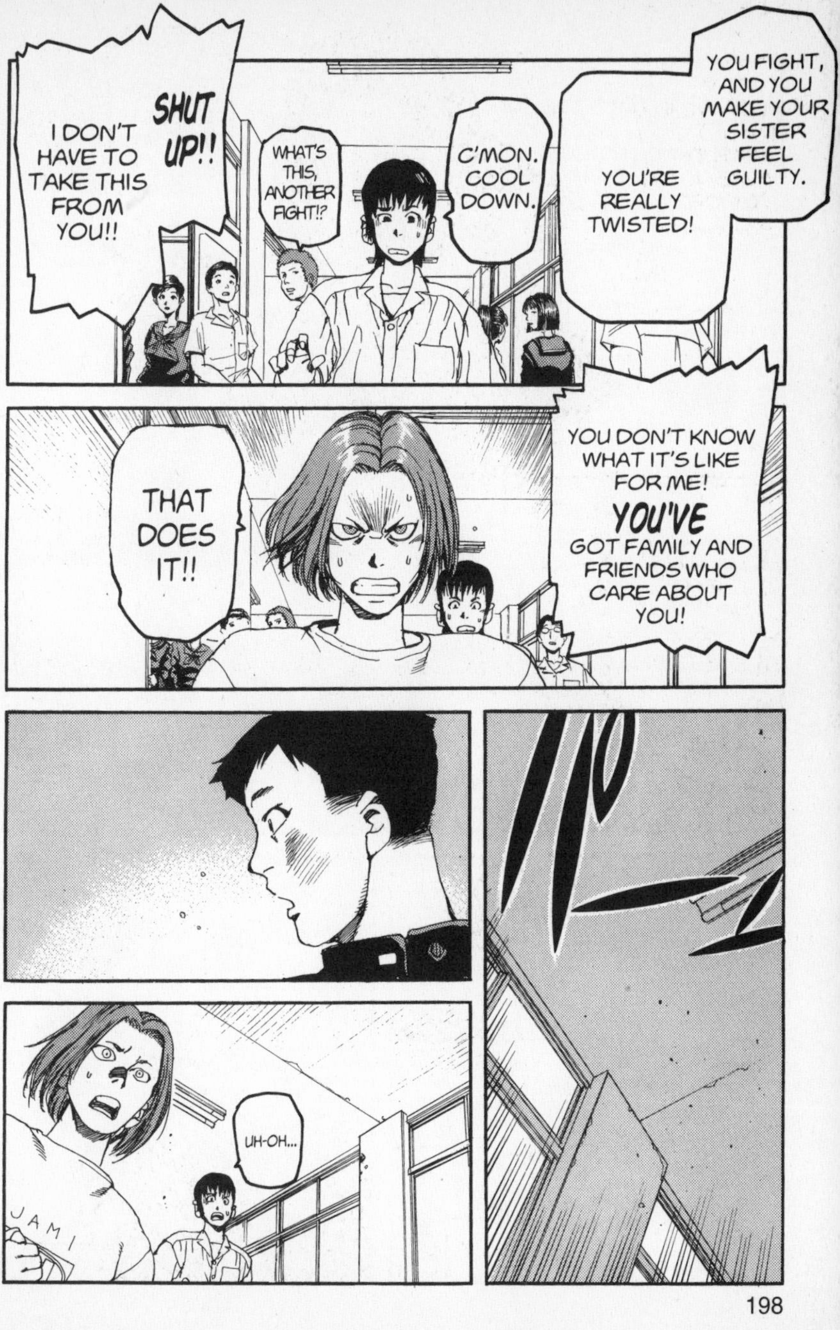
YOU FIGHT, AND YOU MAKE YOUR SISTER FEEL GUILTY.
YOU'RE REALLY TWISTED!
C'MON. COOL DOWN.
WHAT'S THIS, ANOTHER FIGHT!?
SHUT UP!! I DON'T HAVE TO TAKE THIS FROM YOU!!
YOU DON'T KNOW WHAT IT'S LIKE FOR ME! YOU'VE GOT FAMILY AND FRIENDS WHO CARE ABOUT YOU!
THAT DOES IT!!
UH-OH...
JAMI

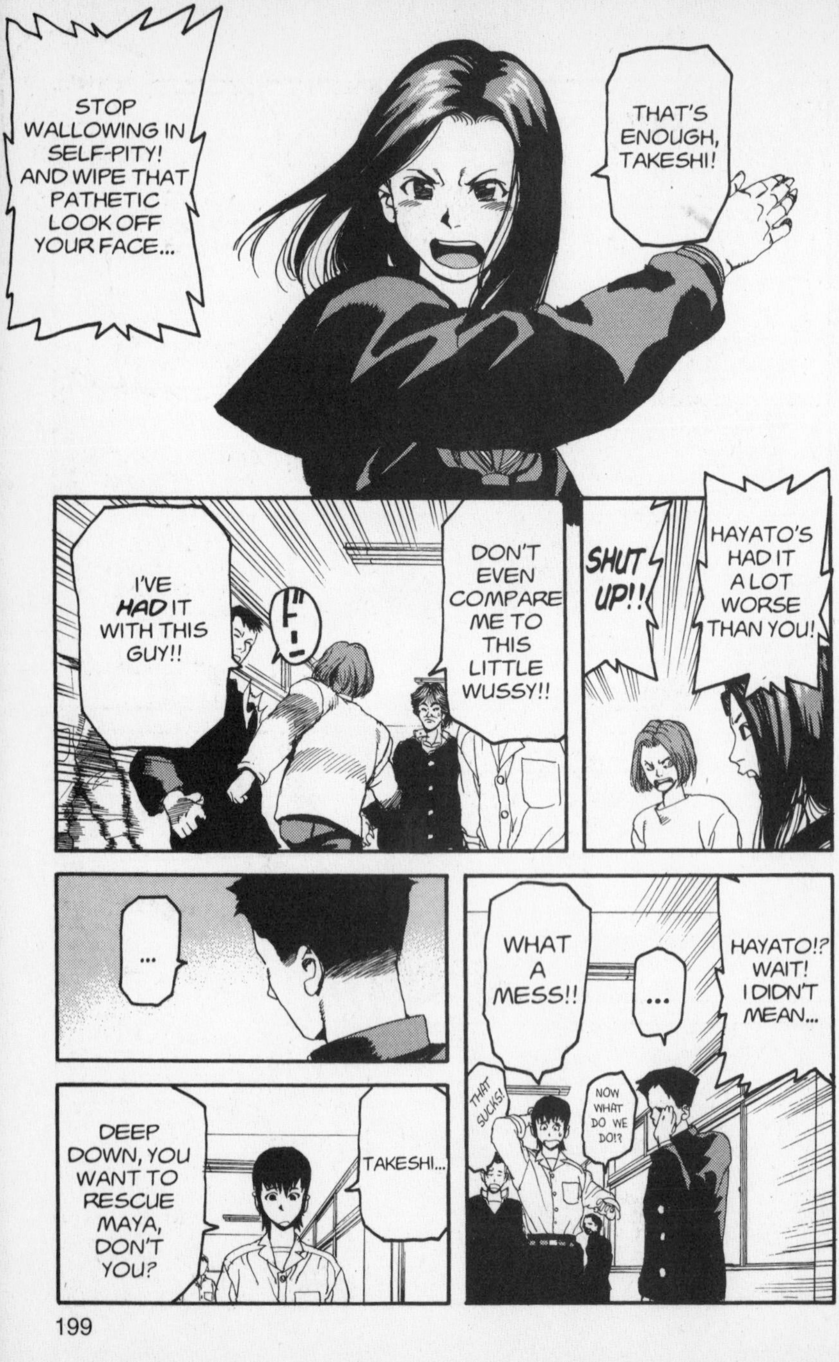
THAT'S ENOUGH, TAKESHI!
STOP WALLOWING IN SELF-PITY! AND WIPE THAT PATHETIC LOOK OFF YOUR FACE...
HAYATO'S HAD IT A LOT WORSE THAN YOU!
SHUT UP!!
DON'T EVEN COMPARE ME TO THIS LITTLE WUSSY!!
I'VE HAD IT WITH THIS GUY!!
HAYATO!? WAIT! I DIDN'T MEAN...
...
WHAT A MESS!!
NOW WHAT DO WE DO!?
THAT SUCKS!
...
TAKESHI...
DEEP DOWN, YOU WANT TO RESCUE MAYA, DON'T YOU?

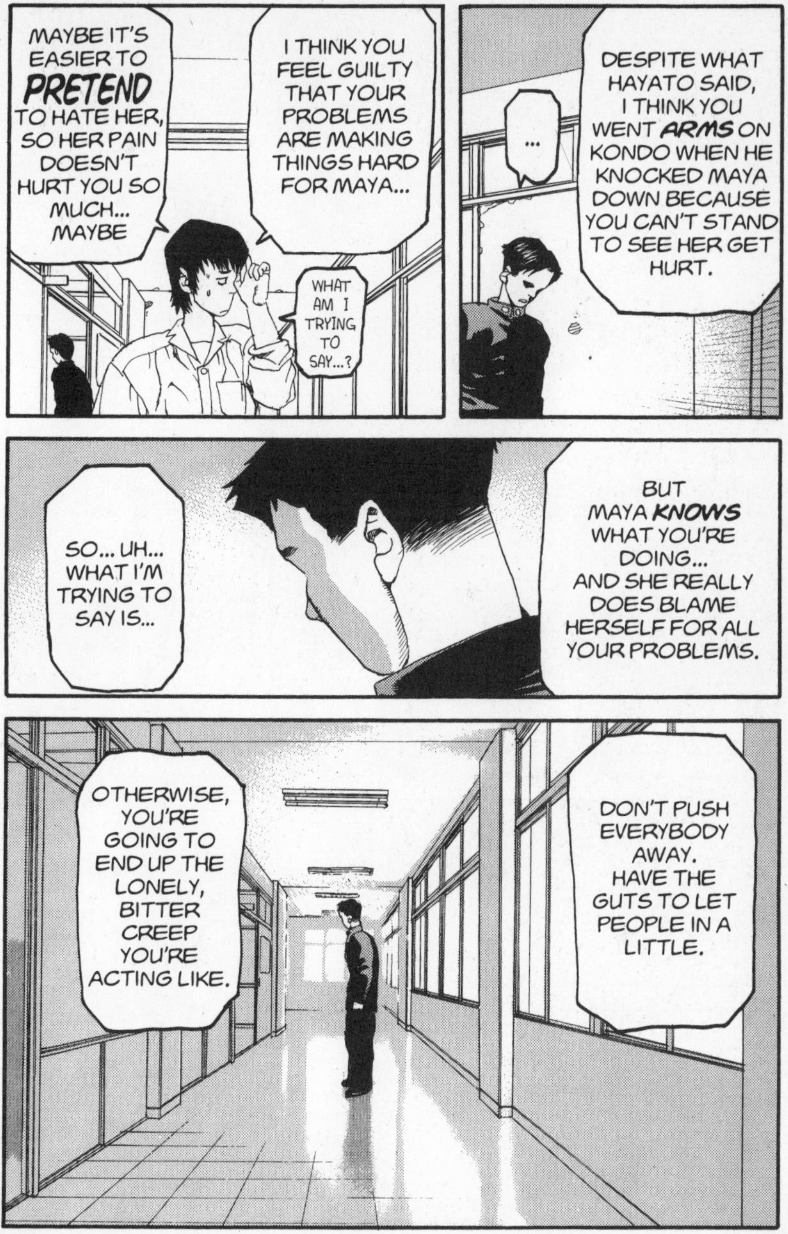
DESPITE WHAT HAYATO SAID, I THINK YOU WENT ARMS ON KONDO WHEN HE KNOCKED MAYA DOWN BECAUSE YOU CAN'T STAND TO SEE HER GET HURT.
...
I THINK YOU FEEL GUILTY THAT YOUR PROBLEMS ARE MAKING THINGS HARD FOR MAYA...
MAYBE IT'S EASIER TO PRETEND TO HATE HER, SO HER PAIN DOESN'T HURT YOU SO MUCH... MAYBE
WHAT AM I TRYING TO SAY...?
BUT MAYA KNOWS WHAT YOU'RE DOING... AND SHE REALLY DOES BLAME HERSELF FOR ALL YOUR PROBLEMS.
SO... UH... WHAT I'M TRYING TO SAY IS...
DON'T PUSH EVERYBODY AWAY. HAVE THE GUTS TO LET PEOPLE IN A LITTLE.
OTHERWISE, YOU'RE GOING TO END UP THE LONELY, BITTER CREEP YOU'RE ACTING LIKE.

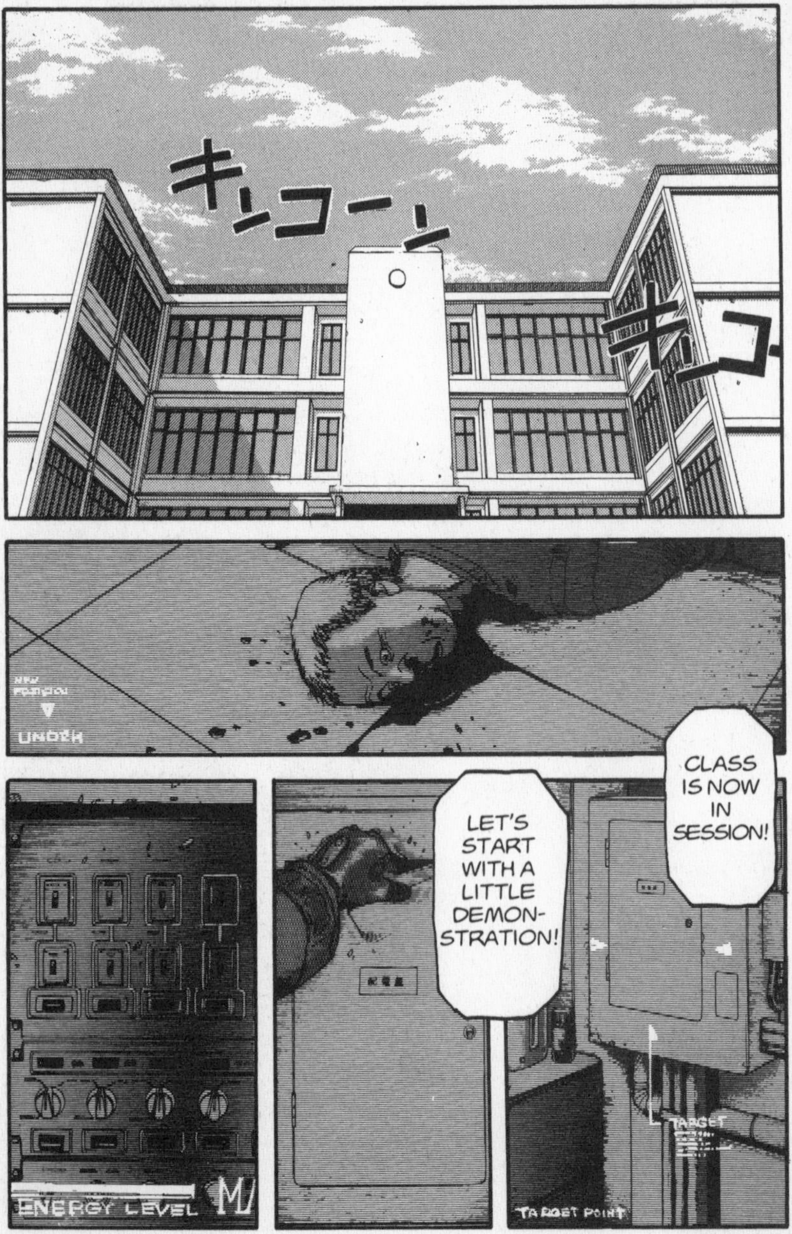
キンコーン
キンコー
CLASS IS NOW IN SESSION!
LET'S START WITH A LITTLE DEMON-STRATION!
TARGET
TARGET POINT
ENERGY LEVEL

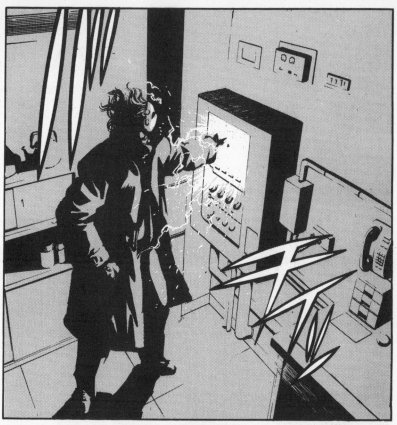

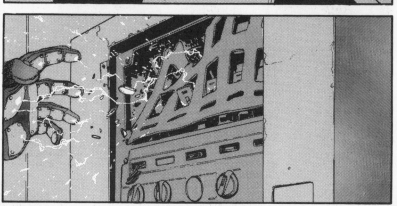

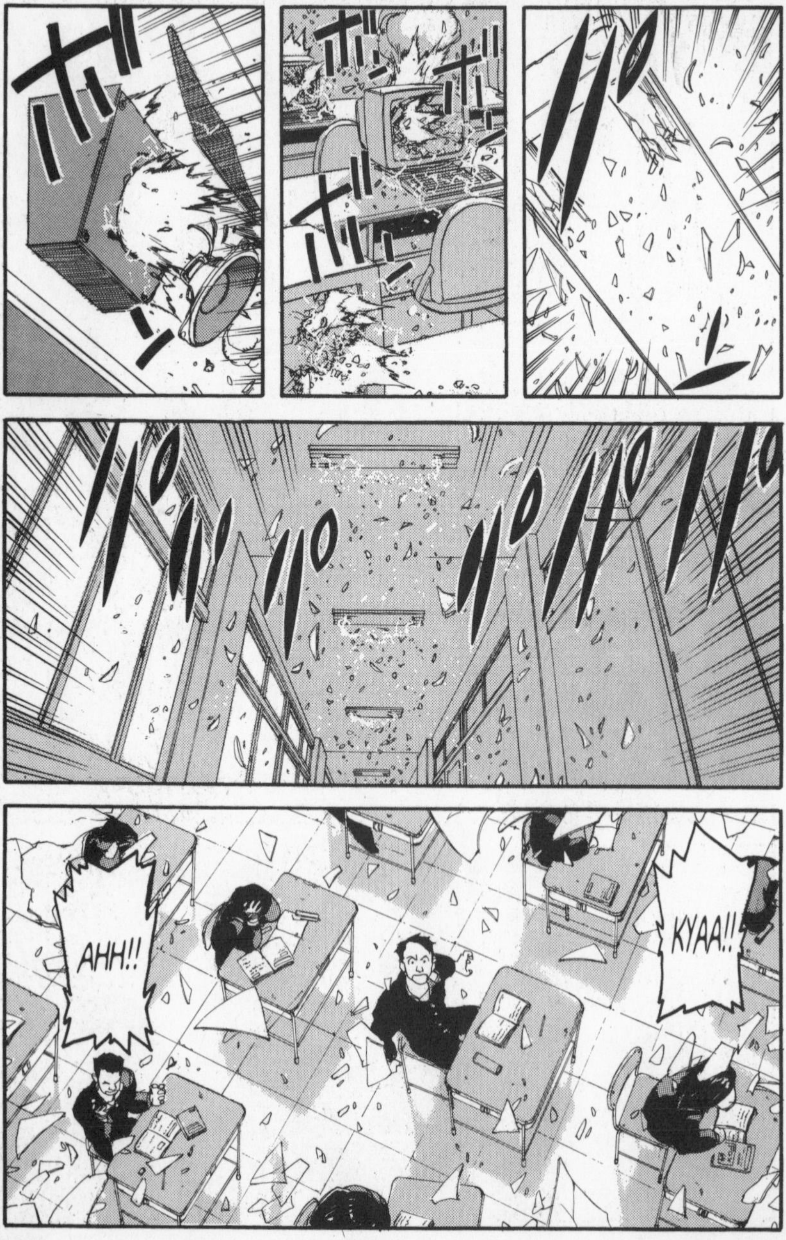
KYAA!!
AHH!!

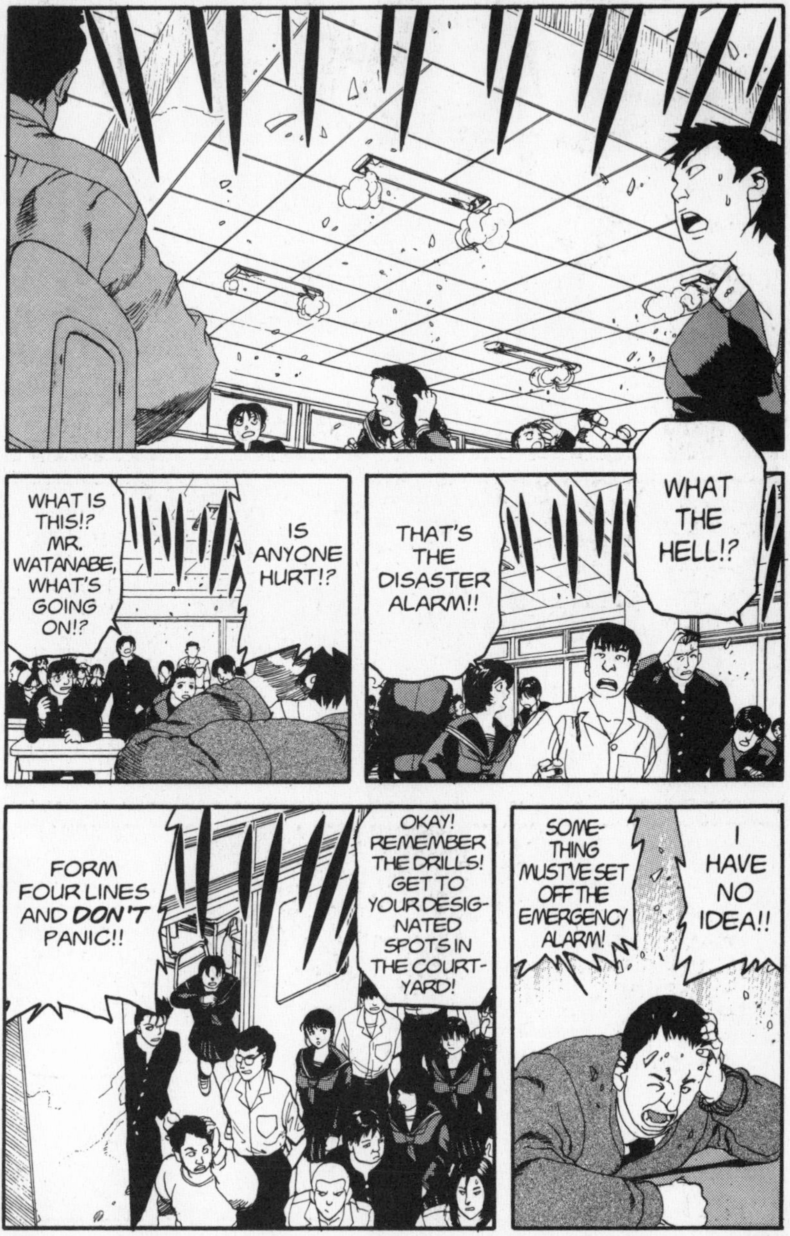
WHAT THE HELL!?
THAT'S THE DISASTER ALARM!!
IS ANYONE HURT!?
WHAT IS THIS!? MR. WATANABE, WHAT'S GOING ON!?
I HAVE NO IDEA!!
SOMETHING MUSTVE SET OFF THE EMERGENCY ALARM!
OKAY! REMEMBER THE DRILLS! GET TO YOUR DESIGNATED SPOTS IN THE COURTYARD!
FORM FOUR LINES AND **DON'T** PANIC!!

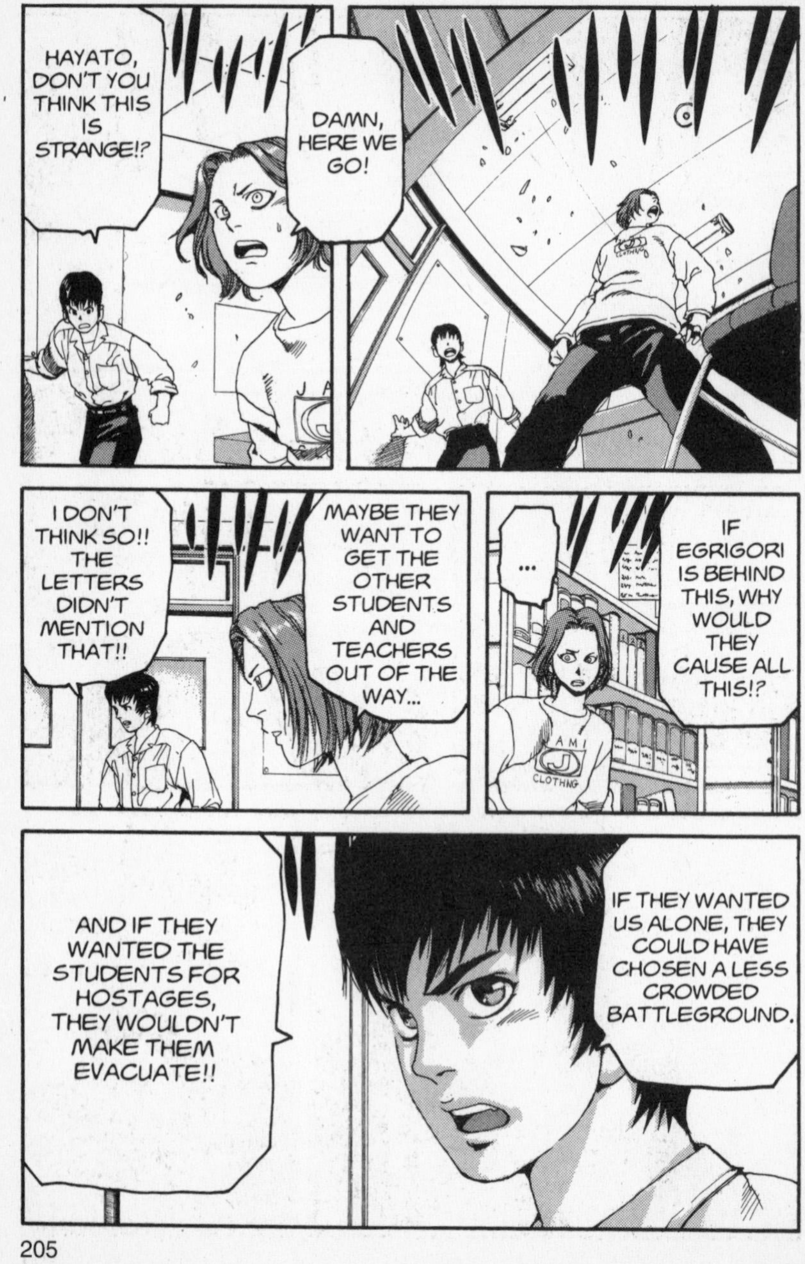
DAMN, HERE WE GO!
HAYATO, DON'T YOU THINK THIS IS STRANGE!?
IF EGRIGORI IS BEHIND THIS, WHY WOULD THEY CAUSE ALL THIS!?
...
MAYBE THEY WANT TO GET THE OTHER STUDENTS AND TEACHERS OUT OF THE WAY...
I DON'T THINK SO!! THE LETTERS DIDN'T MENTION THAT!!
IF THEY WANTED US ALONE, THEY COULD HAVE CHOSEN A LESS CROWDED BATTLEGROUND.
AND IF THEY WANTED THE STUDENTS FOR HOSTAGES, THEY WOULDN'T MAKE THEM EVACUATE!!

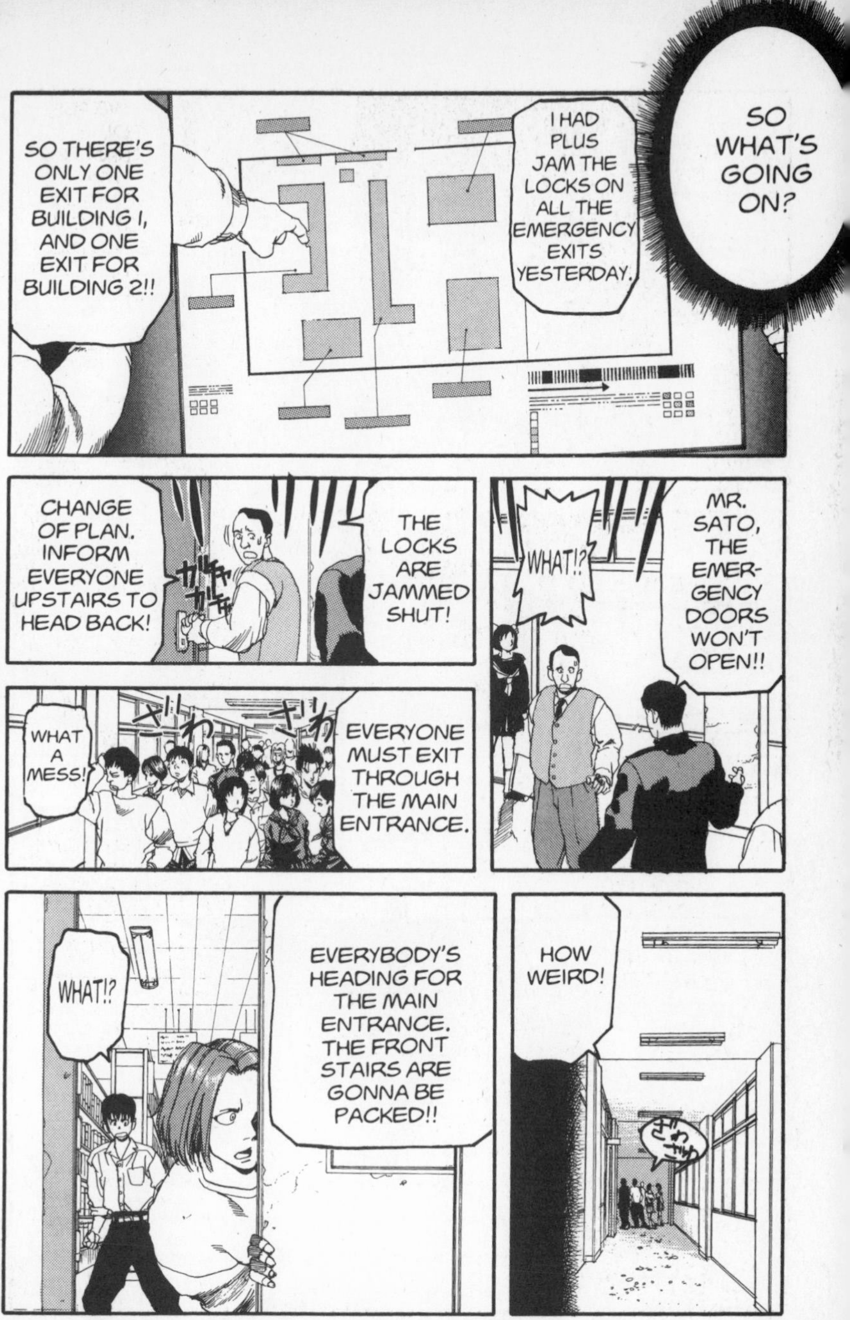
SO WHAT'S GOING ON?
I HAD PLUS JAM THE LOCKS ON ALL THE EMERGENCY EXITS YESTERDAY.
SO THERE'S ONLY ONE EXIT FOR BUILDING 1, AND ONE EXIT FOR BUILDING 2!!
MR. SATO, THE EMERGENCY DOORS WON'T OPEN!!
WHAT!?
THE LOCKS ARE JAMMED SHUT!
CHANGE OF PLAN. INFORM EVERYONE UPSTAIRS TO HEAD BACK!
EVERYONE MUST EXIT THROUGH THE MAIN ENTRANCE.
WHAT A MESS!
HOW WEIRD!
EVERYBODY'S HEADING FOR THE MAIN ENTRANCE. THE FRONT STAIRS ARE GONNA BE PACKED!!
WHAT!?

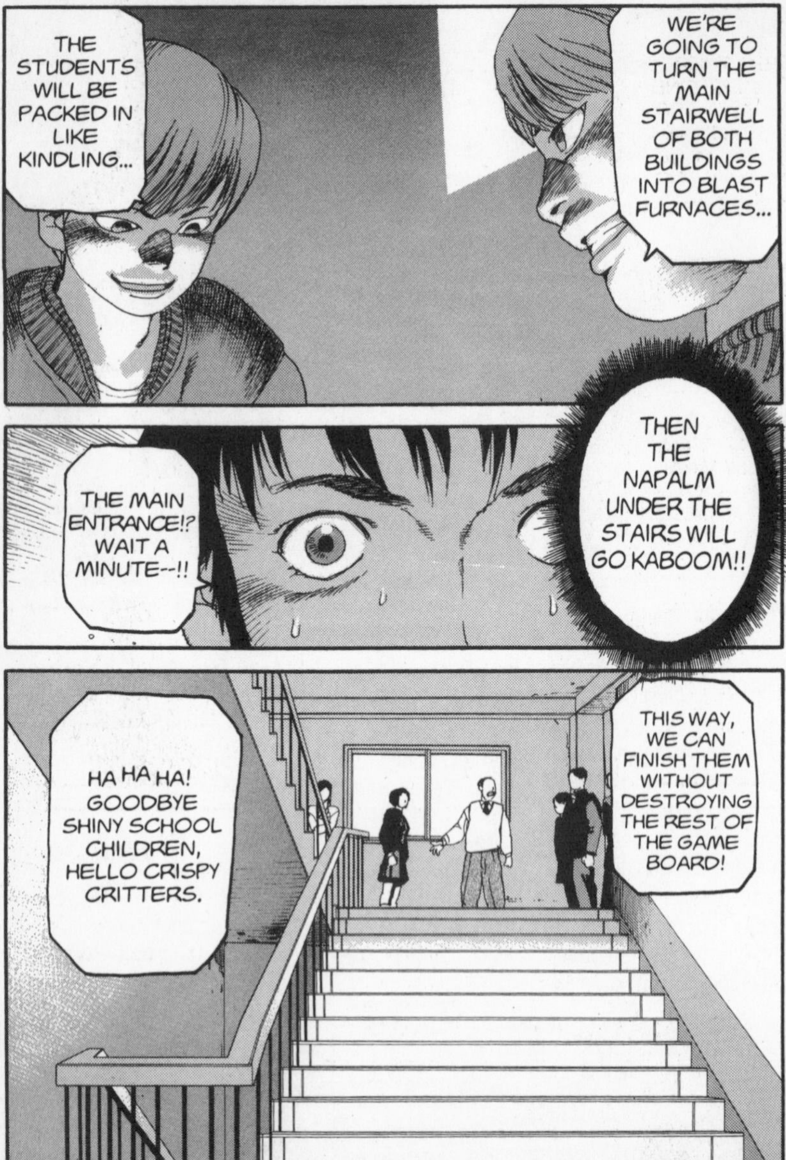
WE'RE GOING TO TURN THE MAIN STAIRWELL OF BOTH BUILDINGS INTO BLAST FURNACES...
THE STUDENTS WILL BE PACKED IN LIKE KINDLING...
THEN THE NAPALM UNDER THE STAIRS WILL GO KABOOM!!
THE MAIN ENTRANCE!? WAIT A MINUTE--!!
THIS WAY, WE CAN FINISH THEM WITHOUT DESTROYING THE REST OF THE GAME BOARD!
HA HA HA! GOODBYE SHINY SCHOOL CHILDREN, HELLO CRISPY CRITTERS.

More Manga!

If you like *Project Arms* here are some other manga you might be interested in:

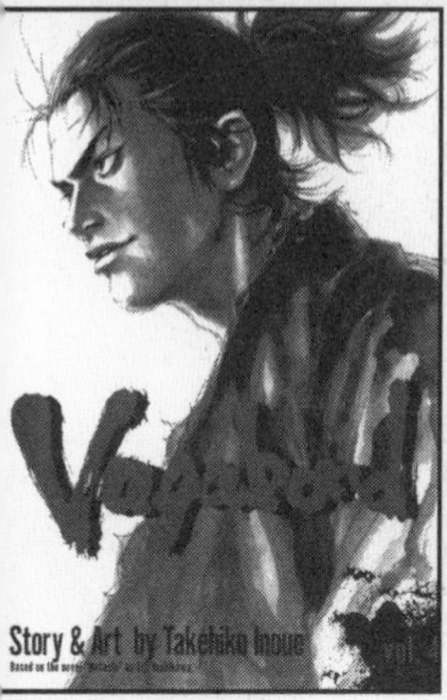
Story & Art by Takehiko Inoue

©1998, 1999, 2001, 2003 I.T. Planning, Inc.

Vagabond

Even if "samurai manga" isn't your thing, Inoue Takehiko's incredibly realistic artwork and his fast-paced, incredibly well-researched story is good enough to satisfy any reader. And if "samurai manga" *does* happen to be your thing, well then, this manga is a must-read!

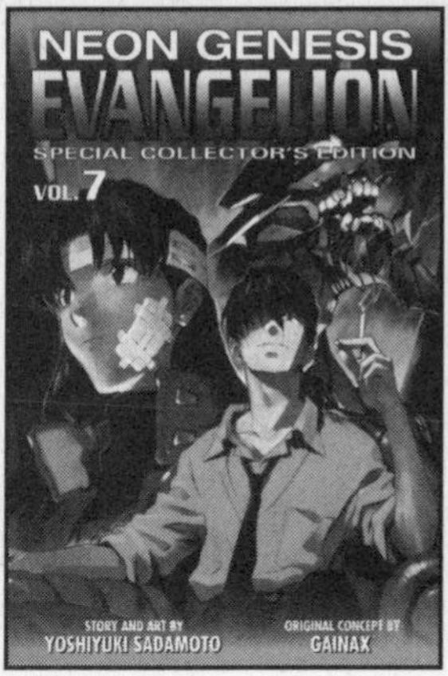
NEON GENESIS
EVANGELION
SPECIAL COLLECTOR'S EDITION
VOL. 7
STORY AND ART BY
YOSHIYUKI SADAMOTO
ORIGINAL CONCEPT BY
GAINAX

©GAINAX 2001

Neon Genesis Evangelion

If secret organizations with dubious agendas, lost technology of mysterious origins, and a story with incredible depth, replete with biblical references is your thing, then check out this seminal epic manga series—*Neon Genesis Evangelion*.

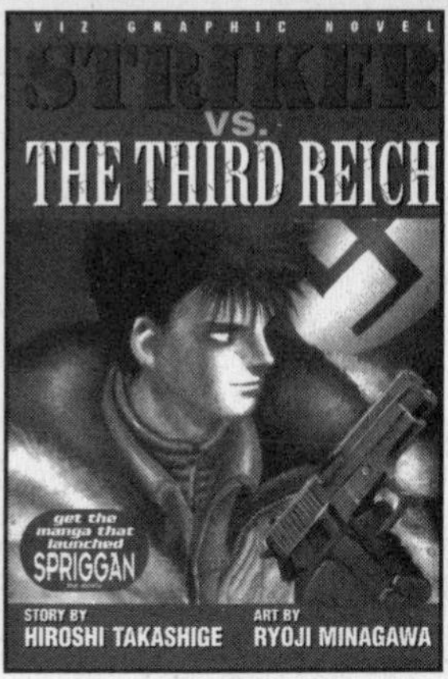
VIZ GRAPHIC NOVEL
STRIKER
VS.
THE THIRD REICH
get the manga that launched
SPRIGGAN
STORY BY
HIROSHI TAKASHIGE
ART BY
RYOJI MINAGAWA

©1991 Hiroshi Takashige/Ryoji Minagawa/Shogakukan

Striker

In the wrong hands, ancient technology and artifacts can have devastating consequences. It's Yu Ominae's mission to stop this from happening. Exciting action a la *Indiana Jones* depicted through Ryoji Minagawa's dynamic artwork!

A word from the editor...

Here it is—unflopped, lower price point, with most of the sound effects left in the original Japanese for your very own manga reading pleasure. Nano-technologically enhanced secret agents, obscure biblical references, an ongoing Lewis Carroll theme—it's all in here! Also, be sure not to miss the *Project Arms* anime available on DVD from Viz Video.

Glossary

5.1	kan kan kan: clatter clatter
8.2	pi pi pi: peep peep peep
8.3	pi pi: peep peep
9.1	pi pi: peep peep ta: tup
9.2	ton ton: tup tup
9.3	tan: tup
10.3	pi pi: peep peep
12.1	gyu gyu: [tightening up string]
12.5	za: sweep
13.2	za za: sweep sweep
14.3	kyu kyu: squeeze squeeze
15.2	za za: sweep sweep
15.4	biki: [sharp pain]
16.1	basa basa: clatter clatter
16.5	kui kui: squeeze squeeze
16.6	gasa: shuf
19.3	pan: smack
22.5	gu: [putting on glove and squeezing]
23.1	gyu gyu: squeeze squeeze
24.1	gata gata: rattle rattle
24.2	gara: rattle
24.3	do: fwump
26.1	pori pori: scratch scratch
26.3	fu: hmph
26.4	bashin: smack
27.2	biri biri: squeezing/struggling
27.4	batan: flip
28.1	tan: tump
28.4	dodon: thwak
29.1	pan: smack
29.2	bashi: thwak
30.1-31.1	go: thwak
33.4	bakin: sharp pain
34.1	bibi: [sharp electricity-like pain]
34.2	suru: slip
34.3	bago: [unsheathing/crash]
36.1	da: dash
37.2	da: dash
37.6	do: bump
42.1	fu: umf!
42.2	piko piko: tap tap
42.4	piririririri pirririri: rrring
43.1	mogu mogu: munch munch
43.5	gi gatan: vurr clatter
44.2	pushi: [sound of soda can opening]
44.4	ga: smak
45.1	bachin: smak
45.2	kan: clatter
46.4	ga: smak
46.5	baiii: vroom
46.5	kyu kyu: screech screech
46.6	biii: vroom
47.1	burorororo: vroom
48.1	ta ta ta ta ta: [footsteps]
48.5	za za: rustle rustle
48.6	za za: rustle rustle
48.7	za za za za za: dash rustle
49.1	za: za: dash
49.4	zaaaa: fwing
49.7	hyun: zoom
50.1	bokon: smash

50.2 za za za za: rustle rustle
50.3 dogagan: crash
51.3 shaka shaka: shake shake
52.3 bachi bachi: bzzt zzt
52.4 gakun: fwump
52.5 busha: splash
54.1 hyoi: fwip
54.6 bachi bachi: zak zak
55.1 bachin: zak
55.1 zugyaaa: arrrghh
55.3 chi chi: tik tik
56.5 basha: slash
57.1 don: fwump
61.2 Maradona sanjo: This graffiti on the wall is a tribute to Argentine soc cer legend Diego Maradona.
61.2 Kono hashira no naka ni hito ga umete—[partially obscured]: More graffiti, "A person is buried inside this pillar."
63.7 bashu: slish
64.4 pan: slap
66.6: meri meki meri: [trans forming noises]
67.1 bashuu: [more steaming oozing bubbling trans forming noises]
67.2 bishii: zzt zzt
67.3 baki beki peki: [trans forming noises—the claws come out]
67.6 bashuuu baki baki baki: [steaming rippling transf ormation]
69.1 ka ka: [heavy footsteps]
69.3 don: bump
70.1 bashi: slish
70.2 da: bump
70.3 giin: zak
71.1 bakin: slash
71.4 za: shuf
73.4 kashun: shik
75.2 ga: smak
75.6 bashu: fwish
79.1 ka ka ka ka: running fx
79.3 ka ka: running fx
84.1 bashu ba: wak whoosh
84.2 da: tmp
84.3 jaki: fwk
84.4 gashu: slish
85.1 zun: thud
85.3 ga: fwump
85.4 guri guri: skrunch skrunch
85.6 do: thunk
87.2 zushu: shunk[pulling out spear]
87.3 ga: thwak
87.6 bafun: [stepping on something]
88.2 dogakan: crash
88.3 bin biin: twang
88.4 gugu: clatter
88.5 zun: [coming out from the dust]
89.1 choki choki: snip snip
89.2 choki choki: snip snip
89.6 gyu gyu: bend bend
90.1 gyu gyu: stretch stretch
91.1 kiri kiri: stretch stretch
91.3 meki: crack
91.4 doga: crash
92.2 hyuu: thwizz
92.3 basu: thunk

92.5 zubu: [pulling out arrow]
92.6 meki: crack
93.3 ga: grab
93.4 jakin: shwik
94.3 pi: slish
95.1 doga: crash
97.4 bashuu: [steaming trans formation]
99.4 baki: shwik
100.2 meri meri: squeeze
100.3 beki: crack
100.5 bashuu: [steaming trans formation]
104.4 pito: drip
104.6 gaba: [emerging from the rubble]
108.6 bishuu: [transformation fx]
109.1 ga: grab
110.4 kachi: click
111.5 ka ka ka: [footsteps]
111.6 byuu: [ARMs noise]
112.4 zaaaa: swoosh
112.5 za: swoosh
112.6 cha: tmp
113.2 tan tan: tmp tmp
113.3 doga: thwak
113.4 dodo: crash
119.2 zuzu: slurp
119.4 kusha: crunch
124.6 chin: chak
128.5 sign: keisatsucho (police station)
132.2 gu gu: clench clench
133.4 ga: thwak
135.5 bun: zzt
136.1 bun: zak
138.5 sign: shokuinshitsu (fac ulty)
139.4 bori bori: munch munch
139.5 bori bori: munch munch
142.2 uuuu: zzzt
142.3 go: smak
144.5 da: dash
146.1 pan: slap
146.5 don: shove
147.3 dokun: ba-bump
147.4 dokun: ba-bump
148.1-149.1 doga: thwak
149.3 shuuu: steaming trans formation
150.1 oooooo: transformation noises
150.3 ooooo: transformation noises
151.5 buoooo: transformation noises
151.5 hiku hiku: sniff sniff
152.1 ooooo: transformation noises
153.3 yusa yusa: grab
153.4 hyun: fwoosh
154.5 hiku hiku: sniff sniff
154.6 zun: fwish
155.2 ga: tup
155.4 zun: fwoosh
156.1 doga: thwak
156.4 bashu: shove
157.2 zuza zuza zuza: drag drag
157.3 pan: fwip
158.2 ga ga ga ga: fwish fwish fwish
158.3 ba ba ba ba: fwoosh fwoosh fwoosh
159.1 bun: fwoosh
159.3 zudoo: crash
161.4 goga: thwak

161.6 gachi gachi: chatter chatter
162.1 bashuu: vwoosh
162.2 bun bun: fwish fwish
162.3 da da da: stomp stomp
162.4 bun bun: fwoosh fwoosh
162.4 shutatata: stomp stomp
163.4 baba: fwish
164.1 gashin: thud
165.1 dan: tup
165.2 shun: fwoosh
165.5 zun: thud
165.6 gaba: fwump
166.2 bun ba: vwoosh
166.4 ga: grab
167.1 ga: fwump
167.2 zun: [ARMs fx]
167.4 doshi: thwak
168.4 jari: shuf
171.5 gusu gusu: sniff sniff
173.1 sign: kochoshitsu (Principal)
173.2 kacha: chak
174.5 buru buru: shake shake
176.2 Takeshi's desk graffiti shows how much he is getting picked on. Highlights include: chinkasu (dick scum); ningen shikkaku, unko gokaku (failure as a human, success as shit); onani daio (king of mas turbation)…
177.2 gusha: scrunch
184.5 gata: clatter
185.2 bisha: (closing of sliding door)
198.3 pan: slap
199.3 don: bump
201.1 kinkon kinkon: school bells
202.1 bachi: zzzak
203.1 pan: shatter
203.2 bon bon bon: boom boom boom
203.3 bon: boom
203.4 pa pa pa pa pa pa: shat ter shatter
204.1-204.5 ri ri ri ri ri ri ri: ring(alarm)
205.1-205.5 ri ri ri ri ri: (alarm)
206.2-206.3 ri ri ri ri: (alarm)
206.3 gacha gacha: rattle rat tle
206.4 zawa zawa: crowd noise
206.5 zawa zawa: crowd noise

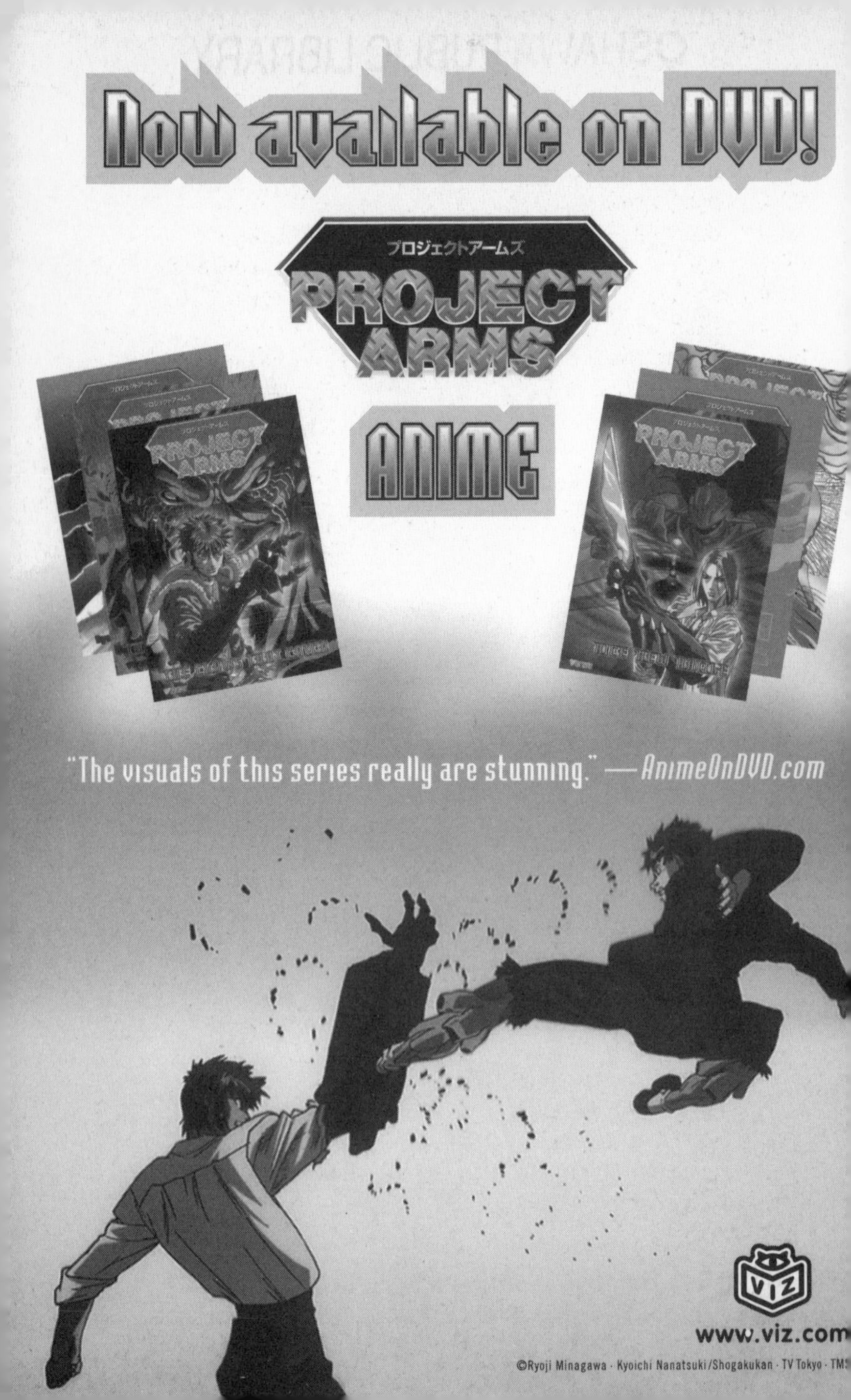

Now available on DVD!
プロジェクトアームズ
PROJECT ARMS
ANIME
"The visuals of this series really are stunning." —AnimeOnDVD.com
VIZ
www.viz.com
©Ryoji Minagawa · Kyoichi Nanatsuki/Shogakukan · TV Tokyo · TM

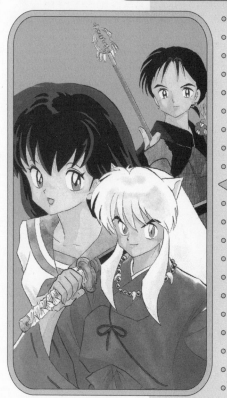

COMPLETE OUR SURVEY AND LET
US KNOW WHAT YOU THINK!

☐ Please check here if you DO NOT wish to receive information or future offers from VIZ

Name: _____
Address: _____
City: _____ State: _____ Zip: _____
E-mail: _____

☐ Male ☐ Female   Date of Birth (mm/dd/yyyy): ___/___/_____ (Under 13? Parental consent required)

What race/ethnicity do you consider yourself? (please check one)

☐ Asian/Pacific Islander   ☐ Black/African American   ☐ Hispanic/Latino
☐ Native American/Alaskan Native ☐ White/Caucasian   ☐ Other: _____

What VIZ product did you purchase? (check all that apply and indicate title purchased)

☐ DVD/VHS _____
☐ Graphic Novel _____
☐ Magazines _____
☐ Merchandise _____

Reason for purchase: (check all that apply)

☐ Special offer   ☐ Favorite title   ☐ Gift
☐ Recommendation   ☐ Other _____

Where did you make your purchase? (please check one)

☐ Comic store   ☐ Bookstore   ☐ Mass/Grocery Store
☐ Newsstand   ☐ Video/Video Game Store ☐ Other: _____
☐ Online (site: _____)

What other VIZ properties have you purchased/own? _____
_____

How many anime and/or manga ti

VIZ titles? **(please check one from each c**

ANIME	MANGA	
☐ None	☐ None	
☐ 1-4	☐ 1-4	☐ 1-4
☐ 5-10	☐ 5-10	☐ 5-10
☐ 11+	☐ 11+	☐ 11+

I find the pricing of VIZ products to be: **(please check one)**

☐ Cheap ☐ Reasonable ☐ Expensive

What genre of manga and anime would you like to see from VIZ? **(please check two)**

☐ Adventure ☐ Comic Strip ☐ Science Fiction ☐ Fighting

☐ Horror ☐ Romance ☐ Fantasy ☐ Sports

What do you think of VIZ's new look?

☐ Love It ☐ It's OK ☐ Hate It ☐ Didn't Notice ☐ No Opinion

Which do you prefer? **(please check one)**

☐ Reading right-to-left

☐ Reading left-to-right

Which do you prefer? **(please check one)**

☐ Sound effects in English

☐ Sound effects in Japanese with English captions

☐ Sound effects in Japanese only with a glossary at the back

THANK YOU! Please send the completed form to:

VIZ

NJW Research
42 Catharine St.
Poughkeepsie, NY 12601

All information provided will be used for internal purposes only. We promise not to sell or otherwise divulge your information.